THE CONSULTANT AND SCRATCH

THE CONSULTANT AND SCRATCH

TWO CRIME NOVELLAS

THOMAS SUNDELL

THE PAPER HOUSE
PUBLISHING

CONTENTS

One Man's Junk Press

One Man's Junk Press
Copyright © 2017, 2024 Thomas Sundell. All rights reserved.

ALSO BY THOMAS SUNDELL

NOVELS

A Bloodline of Kings

Texas Fever

Battle Hymn

At the Faire

The Voyage of the S.S. Penetang

Everyday

Encounters

Tapestry

Lawyers, Guns, and Money

Massachusetts in Rebellion

Axe

Ma'at

Tampa Bay

A Viennese Waltz

Crankright's Millions

Avenge

Casework

City Life

Bastiaen van Kortryk

NOVELLAS

Safe Conduit

Forge

Panther County

Richie's Adventure

FOR YOUTH

A Mother's Ambitions

Crossing Georgian Bay

Experiment of Life

SHORT STORIES, FLASH FICTIONS, AND OTHER WRITINGS

Views of Imagined Lives, Vol. 1 and Vol. 2

and at

sundellwritings.wordpress.com

THE CONSULTANT

A NOVEL

THOMAS SUNDELL

THE PAPER HOUSE
PUBLISHING

1. THE CONSULTANT — RETIRED LIFE

LOOKING OUT THE PICTURE WINDOW OF MY LIVING ROOM, I CAN SEE several crows. I hope they are not gathering. I'd like my retirement to be quiet.

For the first several years after I retired, I kicked around from place to place, mostly overseas. You would have thought I had enough wanderlust in my years as a consultant. I suppose I was under the illusion that I could find quiet in some backwater location in a faraway country. Next, I tried a big metropolis, New York, and then again, Mexico City and Hong Kong. None of that seemed to work out for me for very long.

So now, and for the past four years, I've lived in Winnetka, Illinois, which is roughly 25 kilometers north of Chicago. The heart of what's called the North Shore in Chicago land.

I like that. Chicago-land, as if it were its own country, stretching roughly from the north side of Milwaukee, Wisconsin (not that anyone from Milwaukee would see it that way) to well south of Valparaiso, Indiana, and from Lake Michigan west past Aurora, petering out somewhere in the prairies.

It would have been a reasonably sized fiefdom if this were the Middle Ages.

As for Winnetka, well, it's an innocuous enough suburb. Not that it's without distinction. The community is tabulated as one of the top twenty-five in the country for average household income. Or, the 14th richest zip code in the U.S., which, as you know, is a pretty well-off country on average.

It also has other superlatives, like the highest average level of education of any community in Illinois. Plus, the township high school, New Trier, is one of the finer public high schools in the country, serving not only Winnetka but several adjacent communities: Kenilworth (even richer), Wilmette, Glencoe, and Northfield. The list of community advantages could go on, but why bother?

From my viewpoint, it is more anonymous here than, say the countryside near Thessalonika, Greece, some hamlet in Guangdong province, or a smallish city in Idaho. As a white male over age sixty with some monetary worth that assures no need to keep working, this is a pretty run-of-the-mill spot. Something over 40% above the age of 45. More than 96% white, although the Asian population is climbing.

Oh, females over age 18 outnumber males 100 to 87. Mostly sun wrinkled fake blondes, some overripe but others athletic-club skinny, but that's the North Shore for you. Not that I'm any prize in the looks department anymore myself if I ever was. Still, there are enough older single men to help assure that anonymity.

You get the picture. Here, I blend in.

My condo is part of a medium-sized complex on one of the many tree-named streets. All those species of trees succumbing or already succumbed to invasive species: Elm, Ash, Chestnut. Yes, there are plenty of chestnut trees in the U.S., but they're not the same species as the chestnut trees of 18th-century America. On the other hand, you have to give credit to the ubiquitous Maple, that weed of a tree, unless it's a Sugar Maple, then it's a hardwood and wonderfully useful. So all those tree-named streets: Birch, Locust, Cherry, Oak, Cedar, and so on.

Technically, mine is a three-bedroom condo, although only one is used as a bedroom. The other two serve as an office and a library, respectively. Each bedroom or its equivalent has its own closet. The place has a kitchen with a small pantry, a living room-dining room combo, and yet another coat closet. Finally, there's a laundry room, which also serves as a small shop with a workbench. Out back, there's a shared garage with more storage capacity.

Modest enough for Winnetka but a palace compared to where most of the earth's billions live, especially for one person.

The advantage of a condo over a house is that the condo association arranges maintenance. I have no lawn mowing, nor direct contact with landscaping services or other contractors. All hands off as far as I'm concerned. The advantage of a condo over renting is that there is no landlord, with their own set of keys.

After four years here, I have a nodding acquaintanceship with my neighbors, all friendly waves and hellos. They know me as Randy. So it's 'Hi, Randy—how are you doing today?' — those kinds of pleasantries.

The African-American lady living next door to me tends to scowl rather than smile. African-American is a misnomer in her case, as she's got very little African, and what there is seems to be Ethiopian or Eritrean gracile rather than Bantu robust.

If my neighbors ask what I did for a living, I say human

resource consulting. That's a pretty quick way to shut down a conversation among these lawyers, doctors, financial experts, and business owners.

And, in a way, outplacement is what I did, a form of human resource consulting.

Slowly, I have fitted myself into the community. Not too far, mind you, but enough. I'll give you a couple of examples. The local library often hosts lectures or other events, and I'll attend occasionally. Several of the librarians are used to seeing me. We don't know each other except by sight. They have a name on the library card: Randall Pryor. I borrow books and movies often. If I encounter an acquaintance, we can share an opinion of an event or something we've read or seen. That goes a long way to making one seem open and honest.

Another example is my habit of spending an hour or two at the local coffee shop most days, where I sketch, read, or work on the laptop. All the baristas know me, know my drink, cappuccino. We share mild jokes, anecdotes, and superficial inquiries into each other's well-being. I am always polite and considerate, maybe a little old-fashioned.

They never see my temper, impatience, the tensions I keep bridled, only my apparent affability.

Yet, in my ideal life, I am feeling some disquiet.

Now, I'm not a superstitious man. No black cats, broken mirrors, ladders, or ghosts from the past. Nor do I share in concerns for deities or self-appointed spiritualists who trade on the insecurities of their fellow man, whether they are sincere believers or not.

I could say my subconscious is noticing things that have yet to force their way into my conscious mind. Or maybe there is this, well, not guilt, but awareness that I am doing something unwise.

Or maybe it's just how many crows I'm noticing lately, like outside my window now.

Who knows, perhaps crows are making a comeback after years of being decimated by West Nile Fever. But crows, ravens, and their like, all the scavenger birds, and I have a history together.

So what is this unwise thing that I've been doing?

Remembering, wondering, researching, and writing.

2. NEIGHBOR LADY — CASH FLOW

I CAN SEE MY NEIGHBOR, RANDY, STARING OUT HIS PICTURE WINDOW as I pick up my mail. Most people living here seem to like Mr. Pryor, but the fellow gives me the creeps, though I can't say why.

He's always pleasant enough, smiling. The smile never seems to reach his eyes, though.

Of course, most of the neighbors in the complex don't give me the time of day; the only Black professional living here. Oh, they nod when they see me but rarely exchange a word. Randy always says hello, but it's just a touch too effusive or unreal.

Maybe I'm too sensitive and too concerned about what others think. My shrink seems to think that's the case, although she never says it quite that way.

Randy may be watching the crows. I've seen him before looking concerned, maybe worried, when he sees a crow. I was once walking to my front door after visiting the library. Randy was walking on ahead of me toward his condo. A crow landed on the patch of lawn over by the maple tree across from his front door. I saw Randy jump, literally jump, though whether startled or fearful, I don't know.

Well, there's nothing much in the mail today. The *Winnetka Current* and a lot of advertising are all it is, except for one bill, but no checks. Several clients are overdue, and my cash flow is suffering.

A perpetual problem of mine cash flow. I do the work and send out the invoices; then months drag by. I have been stiffed by one company or another more than once, treating a single self-employed vendor as little better than dirt. I get a collection agency on them if it's enough money to make it worthwhile. Of course, I can write off any further work or recommendation from any company I go after that way, so it's got to be worth it.

I'm a researcher, mostly for marketing purposes, but I've done genealogy, employee attitude surveys, missing persons inquiries, and assorted other searches. Once upon a time, I was a research librarian. And yes, I have a Masters degree.

Well, I've got to do something about the cash flow soon. I hate eating into my assets converting stocks and bonds. Does that make me sound like a big-time investor? Not compared to people here in Winnetka and the neighboring communities. But I can't complain; I have some money and some investments in the city, like part-owner of a nail salon, a café, and a fitness center.

To be truthful, that started with a legacy from my grandfather, that sorry son-of-a-bitch.

I have a twisted family history.

My shrink wants me to be more open, so let's get it out of the way.

My mother, I never knew. She was hired to bear my father's baby. She must have been passing for white. All I know about her is that she was mulatto, maybe three parts African, one part

Native American, probably Seminole, and four parts white, mostly Irish. She may have been a whore, but I'm not sure; maybe she just needed the money.

My father was a real son-of-a-bitch, also Irish, third generation. He abandoned me at birth when it turned out I was a dark-skinned girl. Sometime later, he died of drink. I have a very few hazy memories of him visiting his father and, if unable to avoid it, seeing me. Me a waste of good money, as he would have said. It makes me less than a full glass of Bushmills, which is how he spent a lot of money. He was always called Butch.

Grandfather raised me.

I loved him, and later, I hated him for a time.

He was kind and loving, too loving. I was his sexual object from about age six until I got away at fifteen.

He was never hurtful, always gentle. I never thought of it as abuse. It took me years to realize what we did was not right and was not what other little girls experienced. The problem for me wasn't that he hurt me, shamed me, or disgusted me. The problem was that I liked it, always, even when I finally broke away from him at fifteen.

It was a way of caring for him, showing him that I loved him, making certain he loved me.

Okay, enough confession, that's what my shrink is for.

So I have some money, and I have my bills and unpaid invoices. If I really needed to, I suppose I could go to work for some company. Be a research analyst, corporate librarian, bookkeeper, or something, maybe go a different route, like a sidewalk portrait artist, barista, or masseuse.

Damn, I shouldn't laugh when I've just taken a sip of cold coffee. Now, the *Winnetka Current* is spotted with brown splashes.

The trouble is, I dislike having a boss, any boss.

What's this stuck to the utility bill? A letter to Randall Innes Pryor, hand addressed, but no return address. Well, I guess I should go knock on his door and deliver it.

Weighing it in my hand, I'd say the envelope has a single folded sheet of paper and something else, a coin, button, key? The address is block printing, almost as even as if stenciled. There are no flourishes or misalignments; the lettering just marching along. Curious.

Well, none of my business, though it does make me wonder. I'll just return it to him.

3. THE CONSULTANT — A WRITER

My writing is ostensibly fiction. Not that I'm published or ever likely to be published, so you won't find me on the shelves of political thrillers and action adventures at the bookstore or library.

Not even under the name of Randy Pryor.

You go to a movie theater and see Tom Cruise, Jason Stratham, or Pierce Brosnan in some action flick. Or maybe you prefer someone even more muscle-bound. And maybe you think they echo reality.

Well, there are Navy Seals. So, there are men and some women who fit that category. There are assassins and terrorists and counter-intelligence operatives. So maybe there is some faint resemblance to those movie types.

The overweight, over-tired, heavy-drinking, chain-smoking Gunter played by Philip Seymour Hoffman in *A Most Wanted Man* is closer to reality.

Muscles and beauty attract attention. Operatives don't want attention.

So when I write, I don't write about individuals scaling walls with their fingertips, lethally shooting six opponents in six shots, or making love non-stop all night before going out to save the world.

I write about people like me.

All of us who are ordinary-looking, exercise-abhorring, vice-ridden everyday types who mostly do everyday things like laundry, grocery shopping, and library visiting.

Okay, so I don't have kids or pets to worry about. And I have enough set aside not to be concerned about spending money on a pair of shoes or a night out at the movies (Mondays are senior day, and Tuesdays are the cheap days at the local theater). So, I'm not totally ordinary.

Although to be truthful, you likely wouldn't believe the adventures I write.

You'd find the thread of good luck unbelievable. The serendipitous events and happenstances that occurred repeatedly to save a pretty thick-headed protagonist seem beyond the realm of chance.

I barely believe it myself. How could the hero of my story survive to become an old man?

Certainly, others didn't survive.

Frankly, the hero was befuddled by events at least half the time. That whole 'need-to-know' thing limits any insights. You don't ask why. You rarely ask who. Mostly, it's just what, when, where.

Occasionally, the hero may be part of a team, but there's no bonding, no sharing past or future; there's only the task, the present, and the job to be done.

And you don't see your team members again after the fact. Nor do you want to.

I suppose that's not always the situation. The movie *Munich* portrayed a small team of Israeli agents and a case handler working together for some years, maybe in government agencies that is more the norm. The same movie depicts a family concern in the intelligence business. I can't say my hero ever came across such a thing.

So, how does a hero get started in the game?

Well, in my story, it is happenstance. A man gets hired by a company to do some prosaic work overseas. In London, of all places, in the late 1970s, This is an ordinary man in a relatively ordinary consulting job, which could be accounting or productivity analysis or marketing, just doing work to earn a living and make money for his employer, nothing special.

Now, my hero is flawed, but with ordinary flaws. He has a weakness for young women. Maybe because it always surprises him if a woman finds him attractive, even if she's faking it and expecting money in return.

Now, in this overseas job, the hero comes across some information that would be very useful to the competitors of this client company. It is accidental, mind you. While gathering legitimate information to do his work he has this set of papers and photographs detailing processes and products that are quite innovative for the time.

The hero doesn't realize what he has. Because of a deadline, he is doing work while having supper at a restaurant. Some curry place fairly crowded, and more than one person could notice what he has, and a more knowledgeable person could realize its value.

As our hero leaves the restaurant to return to his hotel room, he is accosted by a reasonably good-looking young woman who would like to spend some brief intimate time with the young fool. After a fair amount of hemming and hawing, our obtuse hero

15

realizes he could experience some unexpected pleasures. And does so.

On the morrow, though, he realizes he no longer has all the papers and photos he had the night before.

You might think that would be the end of it. Our shame-faced hero admits to his client and employer his foibles and errors, the loss of materials that, in retrospect, he realizes must be quite valuable to the right parties.

Not our hero's way. He was way too worried about the repercussions for his livelihood. Instead, he calls in sick.

Then, he starts with the hotel staff. Do they remember the girl who came in with him last night? Do they know who she is?

Yes, he has a name she gave him, but it's a professional name: Jocelyn, Candace, or whatever.

And when she was showering, he could have looked in her purse in case there was anything in it besides condoms and lipstick, but he didn't. The thought never occurred to him at the time.

So he asks, and no one at the hotel admits to seeing the girl, let alone knowing who she is.

Our boy is discreet enough not to come on heavy. It's the opposite, like he's gone soft on the girl. As if he would like to be with her again.

As an aside, when the manager is not looking, and for a small compensation, the bellboy (bellman really) gives our hero the name of a fellow, Lachlan, who should know the girl. For a bit more coin, the bell boy says at what pub Lachlan might be found come sometime after nine o'clock at night.

Our hero doesn't wait for night. He buys a map and finds a phone book, this being long before personal computers and the internet. On the map, he puts an X for his hotel, another for the restaurant where he ate the night before, and a third for Lachlan's watering hole. Then, he identifies other reasonable hotels, bars, and restaurants within or near the triangle of those three Xs, marking the map in dots and appropriate abbreviations.

Then, in the London drizzle, he walks the marked-off streets, umbrella aloft, but discovering his footwear is not waterproof. Squishing and squeaking, he decides where to take station when evening comes. One corner gives him a reasonable view of Lachlan's home pub, the entrances of two hotels, and no less than five restaurants and bars in this entertainment district. Better, there is a covered bus stop, or whatever they call buses in England, with one dry corner.

He would rather find the girl and avoid any contact with Lachlan. Given Lachlan's profession, the man's likely to have more than one unsavory friend he can call on if he dislikes our hero. There may be other young women, Jocelyn's, or was it Candace's, peers who could give a lead to her whereabouts.

Then, our fellow returns to his hotel to find a dry pair of socks.

Evening comes, a bit dryer, fortunately, though our cautious boy has the furled umbrella and a book to help pass the time. To be truthful, our hero is a bit on tenterhooks. He was very uncertain of success in finding the girl, let alone having a productive talk with her. In his mind, he can hear her denials, her call for Lachlan's intervention. Maybe it'd be best to inveigle her back to his hotel room, though he could ill afford a second tryst with her from his meager discretionary funds.

Could he expense this? Probably not.

Despite his lack of experience in these matters, his observation post proves satisfactory for discerning some patterns in activities as the evening progresses. He is pretty certain of at least five women who share Jocelyn's profession, given their coming and going among the hotels and taverns over the course of four hours. Also, he recognizes that at least two men have some connection to one or another of the pretty young women, not counting the doorman at the swankier of the two hotels and a bouncer at the most popular club, who seem well acquainted with the women.

Finally, his vigil is rewarded as a taxi disgorges Jocelyn and a portly older fellow by the entrance of the nicer hotel. Alert now, our boy gathers his umbrella and book to cross the street and walk the half-block to the hotel entrance. In the lobby, he sees the check-in desk, the lobby seating, and beyond, the elevator bank. Overlooking the lobby, on a mezzanine level, is a restaurant and, on the opposite side, a bar. He makes his way to the bar and chooses a table with a view of the lobby and the lifts. He hopes the old fellow with Jocelyn doesn't have the stamina for an all-nighter.

Nursing his oatmeal ale, he tries reading while glancing at the lifts every other minute. An hour passes before the lift doors open to reveal a demurely smiling Jocelyn stepping out. She heads down a back hall rather than going to the hotel exit. Our boy picks up his change and possessions and makes a beeline for the stairs, afraid he'll lose her out a side entrance.

He need not fear. He finds her in a telephone booth. He pastes a smile on his face as he approaches. She sees him as he waves to her. For a fleeting moment, she looks annoyed, and she says something more on the phone before putting on a smile as false as his.

"Jocelyn," he says, "what a coincidence. How are you tonight? Are you free for the evening?" Not that she is ever free, he thinks.

She steps out of the booth, "Why don't you look dapper this evening? Though this isn't your hotel."

"No, just getting out of a company dinner. What a bore. So

glad to see you." He is within touching distance of her now. "You look refreshing."

She reaches and strokes his lapel, "Too bad you didn't let me know. Unfortunately, I have another engagement yet tonight." She smiles, "You are here for weeks yet, I think you said. Let's set another date." She opens her handbag, rummaging in it and pulling free a small notebook with a pencil stub in its wire binding.

"How about next Tuesday?" he asks.

"That will be fine. Shall we say eight o'clock? Where we met last time?" She is smiling, probably without any intention of meeting him.

"Sounds good to me. Thanks."

"Well, until then," she returns the notebook to her handbag, pats his lapel again, and turns to go.

"By the way, I was missing some papers and photographs after you left yesterday. You wouldn't know anything about that?" He keeps his voice light but follows her a step or two.

She looks back, "I'm afraid not. You aren't accusing me of anything, are you?" The look on her face is slightly puzzled and totally guiltless. She continues toward the rear entrance.

He follows. "Accusing? Not really. I understand everyone has to make their way in the world, myself included, so I would appreciate getting those papers and photos back."

She's made it to the rear door and turns the knob, smiling, "I am sorry. There's nothing I can do to help you." She opens the door and steps through.

He follows right behind her.

And immediately regrets it, for a very large man is standing there, who Jocelyn addresses, "Lachlan, this fellow is bothering me."

"We can't have that, can we, Love," says Lachlan, who raises both fists and comes at our boy quickly.

Who, in turn, bats at the right fist with his umbrella as he scrambles sideways along the alley wall. The Irishman laughs, mouth wide, and comes on fast. With the instinct of a Roman rather than a Gaul, our boy thrusts with his umbrella into Lachlan's gaping mouth. Lachlan's rush and weight completes the impalement, only to have it furthered by our boy smashing the handle with his book, driving the point deeper into Lachlan's gullet.

Lachlan stumbles backward, slips, and falls heavily, the umbrella breaking. With a squeak and frantic haste, Jocelyn attempts to flee, only to be clobbered against the opposite wall of the alley by our hero, who, in his sudden rage, slams her head twice more against the bricks.

Choking in blood and some part of the umbrella still lodged in his throat, Lachlan tries rising, fingers scrabbling in his mouth to free his breathing. Our boy is there, bludgeons Lachlan in the face repeatedly, using his thick book, until Lachlan can rise no more.

The girl, Jocelyn, gets unsteadily to her feet when the boy grabs her by the hair and pushes her back down. He says through clenched teeth, "My papers and photos."

So that was the start of a new career.

Oh, not instantly.

There were further entanglements from that event. Jocelyn no longer had the materials. But she did know who she passed them on to, who had paid her to accost the seemingly callow fellow. The follow-up took some negotiating and a bit more violence to secure the materials.

This impressed the employer of the corporate espionage

agents, indicating that the young fellow had potential, though likely not for espionage as such.

As for Lachlan, our boy really did not regret the man's death.

You see, fiction. The kind of thing I write. Not believable, you say? Well, maybe it didn't happen quite like that, and maybe not in London, but it was close enough to the truth for my purposes.

4. THE CONSULTANT — JUST A WORKING STIFF

BY THE TIME OF LONDON, I'D BEEN THAT PROSAIC WORKING MAN FOR better than a dozen years. Earning a modest living, doing legitimate work, hoping to advance further in a large corporation, divorced but dating again, just an average working stiff with average goals and intentions — that was me.

By the way, my advice is not to marry your high school sweetheart.

She or he may be a wonderful person, and it's true that for a small minority, there is mating for life, but largely speaking, those early marriages don't survive.

Anyway, I received an offer after my overseas adventure to do a different kind of work.

Offer is a generous term, what with exposure to a murder charge hanging over my head, with all the evidence and testimony necessary to convict me.

I should add that it's my understanding that Jocelyn did recover over time but not nearly as pretty as she had been when I first met her. I'm glad, as I don't hold anything against her. She was a surprisingly generous lover for her trade, which isn't true of many women in the trade or out of it.

I may have been coerced into my new work, but the compensation offset the conditions of my enslavement to some degree. Though, I was always intent on finding a way to overturn that enslavement, even as I recognized I would need to play the long game to achieve my freedom.

All my training was on the job. In books and movies, the protagonist often comes from some advanced background of athleticism, language skills, lethal training, and operational inculcation. Plus, the hero typically can hold liquor exceptionally well and dandle any beauty in sight. There were times when I wished I had those advantages.

About all I had was desperation and native wit.

Assignments came unevenly. Sometimes, months would go by before I'd be contacted. Other times, there might be a need within weeks of each other. Mostly, I have operated in English-speaking countries, but not always.

To be truthful, I think I was a kind of a throw-away guy. There was a low investment in me, and whether I survived didn't matter except to me. Always in the dark, not knowing much or why, I couldn't have told any authority anything important. I had no clear idea who employed me or what they were about. The only pattern seemed to be no government targets. Everyone else was fair game.

Oh, and they preferred I accomplish accident-like deaths.

A stolen car causing a hit-and-run was okay, which I did on my second murder, my first for them.

So over the next twenty-some years, at six to ten deaths a year, it added up.

All that time, I accumulated every tidbit of knowledge I could about the organization I worked for. Plus, I could squirrel away every odd and end of cover documents, money, weapons, contacts, or other resources that came my way without arousing undue suspicion.

All of which was part of my 'grand plan' of escaping my indenture. Get enough information and where-with-all to get out from under intact.

It never happened that way.

In the late '90, there came a longer-than-normal fallow period. Six months went by with no contact from them and no contract for, in crime parlance, a hit. I never used that term myself. To me, they were always murders. Why shy away from the facts?

I came home to my apartment one night, let's say in Washington, D.C., or maybe Copenhagen, to find a typewritten note. All it said was, "The business has closed. You are on your own."

You would think, given my yearning to be out from under my servitude, that I would have felt relief. In fact, I felt bone-chilling fear.

Who had knowledge of my twenty-six years of mayhem? Were records kept, and if so, who had them? What would happen to them? What did it mean, "…on my own." Should I run for my life?

And, as simple as it seems, what do I do now? How do I earn a living? How do I explain a twenty-six-year gap in my employment record? Who am I now?

Well, if anything, I am a working man. In my early 50s then , I simply didn't have the money to retire. Oh, I had put aside a fair sum. Still, I figured I needed a minimum of another three-quarters of a million to maintain a reasonable, somewhat modest lifestyle into my 70's. I decided my goal was to live to age 80. After that, who cared?

The trouble was I was a guided missile. I didn't know much about finding contracts safely, let alone making any necessary arrangements and getting paid for it. It's not like I was going to do an internet listing.

Sure, I knew a few things. A couple of document people, a technology guy, three weapons people, a plastic surgeon, and an all-purpose doc for scrapes and pains of the profession. However, they were scattered across several continents, and, besides, who knew if one or more of them had been blown?

How do I attract business? A classic small businessman's quandary, at least for any illegitimate small businessman.

At this stage in my life, I figured I had only one skill or attribute: ruthlessness. I was pretty down on myself.

Some months went by. I reached out to some of those contacts and bought four new identities, two from each document guy. And I decided on a complete change in look. I became Eurasian. You know, epicanthic folds for the eyes, dark contact lenses, a shortened nose, some trim to the ears, nothing overtly dramatic, except maybe the eyes, but enough so I was someone else.

I don't like to remember that period. Plastic surgery isn't my thing. Let's face it: it's painful, and I've never been into pain, at least not my own. Still, when all was said and done, I was better looking, and my past self was gone.

Oh, I also developed on my own two additional identities for a total of six. Sure, my two weren't as good as those done by the professionals, but they would do in a pinch, and only I knew about them.

By the end of that year, I figured I was ready—time to find some customers.

I'm embarrassed to say I burned two identities in short order and was nearly entrapped by a federal agency. I was thinking I'd better become a taxi driver, short-order cook, landscaping worker, or take some other job where I could fade from view.

Then Anna K. called me.

Anna was part of my old firm. Not that I knew that immediately.

We met in Toronto and decided to become partners. She knew my work was even a 'fan,' so to speak. As she put it, "All those macho guys have an average lifespan in the trade of six and a quarter years. You've been at it a lifetime. I want ten more years out of you. We split sixty-forty; you're the forty since I take the real risks of setting the deals up."

She'd been an arranger: flights, money flow, bank accounts, identities, covers, weapons, technology, whatever. Though she hadn't set the deals up or collected the money in the old days, she knew the ways and where-for that accomplished it. She was a lifesaver for a sinking man.

I won't describe her. Too many distinguishing marks and such could give her away. Suffice it to say, she was no beauty but had a steel trap mind and, curiously, was true to her word.

She also told me to forget my old contacts. The one doc guy sold me out, which is why those two identities went up in smoke so easily. The plastic surgeon was okay, but I was never to go back. For tech and weapons, she had better people. The old patch-anything doctor was six feet under—apparently. Actually, six fathoms under.

I had confidence in Anna K., even if I didn't believe her Lithuanian, or was it Rumanian, accent. She counseled me to perfect my accents since I'd decided to be Eurasian. What mixes did I want to be: Chinese, Thai, Vietnamese, or Korean with

American, French, German, or, bless them, Canadian genetics as well?

As a basic mix, I thought I'd go for Chinese-Canadian; after all, we were in Toronto, or maybe it was Vancouver.

I liked that I was a working stiff again—putting money aside at a higher rate than my prior employment. I think they say that your top earning years in most careers are in your mid-50s. Mine just kept climbing, all due to Anna K.

The doorbell just rang. A startling sound for someone like me, even if likely innocent: Jehovah's Witness, Girl Scout cookies, whatever. Still, I make sure my Glock is set before answering the door.

"Mr. Pryor?"

The neighbor lady stands there with an envelope in her hand. "Yes?" I try to smile.

"I'm afraid the mail person inadvertently delivered a letter for you to my address." The lady is holding out the envelope.

I take it with some trepidation. I don't receive personal mail, not counting bills and advertising, other than the books I order. The real shock is the handwriting. I could swear it's Anna K's. "Ah, wow, gee, thank you … " I can't think of the lady's name, some bird other than a crow.

"Vivienne — Vivienne Hawk," she supplies.

"I appreciate you walking this over instead of leaving it for the mailman."

"Mail lady."

Puzzled, I ask, "I beg your pardon?"

"We don't have a mailman. It's a woman most days."

"Oh, yes, I see. I guess I have noticed now that you mention it." I feel embarrassed, and I'm not sure why.

"Okay then. Goodbye, Mr. Pryor." She turns and goes down the two steps.

"Randy, just Randy is enough. No need for mister," I call to her, but she's already walking away.

I close the door, weighing the envelope in my left hand, while I set the Glock back on the shelf by the door. Anna K., I think.

But how? Alive? Tracking me? Knows my identity and address? Enough to put the fear of god in you.

5. THE CONSULTANT — MY LAST ASSIGNMENT

THE FIRST TWO YEARS WITH ANNA K. WERE A LITTLE ROUGH. BY that, I mean, not many jobs to do. Oh, Anna K. was her usual superb self as an organizer so the jobs seemed easy for me. But instead of six to ten a year, it was down to four in the first year and only three in the second.

After that, our work picked up and for larger sums each time. I once asked her what the difference was. Her answer: "I raised our prices." People pay for quality work. If you price yourself too low, they assume the worst.

But we didn't make it to ten years together.

In year eight, Anna K. let me know she had cancer of the esophagus. Too much smoking, I guess. Turns out it wasn't just her esophagus. So, our partnership ended in the ninth year with one final assignment, an Australian.

Only it wasn't in Australia, which I would have preferred.

This murder was to take place in China. It seems the Australian went to China twice a year for a few weeks, maybe for business but a lot for pleasure. Pleasure might have been easier in Thailand or Hong Kong, so maybe it was mostly business.

I had done work in China before, but it's not the safest place for my line, though it does seem to be getting a little looser. By the way, it's hard to beat Mexico or some of the other Latin countries for conducting my kind of business. I'm told Africa can be easy, too, at least in many of the bigger cities. I've never tried south of the Sahara, though I almost did a job in South Africa once, but the guy died of natural causes before I arrived. Lost some money on that deal.

So, let me set the stage. Imagine you're in a major Chinese city, it could be Beijing or Shanghai, which most everyone has heard of, or it could be Chengdu, Guangzhou, Shenzhen, Fuzhou, or elsewhere. After all, even their medium-sized cities are larger than most cities anywhere else. There are exceptions — Lagos, Mexico City, Tokyo, and so on— but for the most part, what they call a town is often over half a million people, so cities climb up from there.

I'm in a Western restaurant. Let's say it's in Shenzhen just to fix on somewhere, and let's say it's at Angelo's in the Futian district, which is no longer there. Angelo's, I mean.

Anyway, I'm thinking the stroganoff is interesting, the sauce quite good if a little original, the beef tender, and the mushrooms and onions complementing nicely. The accompanying gnocchi are perhaps a shade overcooked, but their sauce is fresh as well, and the basil is tasty. The red wine, Primitivo, is a tad rough but cuts the creamy tang of the stroganoff.

You're getting the picture, right? Let's shift it to the present tense; let's make it right now.

I'm enjoying the meal. The book I'm reading is adequate for the purpose, if a little macabre at times—*Stiff* by Mary Roach—

and it's holding my interest, yet not distracting me from my purpose and certainly providing verisimilitude.

Angelo's is quite lively tonight, one other single, nine or ten couples at tables, a trio, perhaps a half-dozen larger groups, the largest being an even twelve. Plus, another seven tables, with several of these sporting reserved signs. No one outside, though. It is too hot and too humid, even for the citizens of Shenzhen, with the tropics being, well, tropical, given this year's heat waves.

A slight majority of the customers are foreigners; the rest are Chinese, presumably. I suppose that some of whom I take for Chinese are also foreign. Perhaps Chinese from Taiwan or Singapore, or perhaps from further away, the Philippines or Madagascar say.

Of the obvious foreigners, I estimate most are visitors, though some may be residents. After all, Angelo and a couple of his staff are foreign residents. Visitors but not tourists, no, even on a Saturday night, this restaurant in the Futian district of Shenzhen is not a place for tour groups. The visitors here are part of the community of consultants and dealers doing business in the 30-year-old Shenzhen Economic Zone, the gateway that the wily leader, Deng Xiaoping, used to re-open China to the West.

There is at least one Indian and maybe a few Latin Americans; mostly, though, the foreigners are Americans and Europeans. Perhaps, like me, there are one or two who no longer consider themselves citizens of any country.

Most of the Westerners are middle-aged or older, and some, like myself, are edging into old age.

Of the couples, a quarter or so are Chinese, and another quarter are foreign. The remainder are mixed, inevitably a Western man and a Chinese woman. The Chinese women are young, though most of the Chinese here are young since Shenzhen is the newest city in China, and only a few of its over ten million people are native to the place.

Besides, the Futian district is an entertainment district for foreigners. It is not the only one, not as old or exclusive as Shekou, but still filled with shops, malls, hotels, clubs, restaurants, and many tall office buildings and high-rise condominiums. So, the flocking people are often younger, trendier, and more affluent than in the city's outlying districts.

This brings to mind my stop at the Starbucks in the Coco Park mall, where I enjoyed a cappuccino and reading earlier in the day. While there, I watched two young women playing some game, perhaps a variant of Go, glancing up from my book to take in the skirts hiked above mid-thigh, the flash of cleavage as they leaned forward, intent on the board, jewelry glinting, a peek of red bra under a gold dress, the high-heel slip-ons dangling from bare feet.

To tell you the truth, I was curious about the game even while enjoying the vitality the young women brought to it. And they were conscious of my glances. One pulled her skirt to cover more of her legs while the other, the one of the red bra, looked back at me evenly and made no effort to hide her display.

Yet they were only two of the vast number of attractive and lightly clad women who inhabit the malls, shops, and restaurants of Futian. Less one gets the wrong impression, these are not professional women of the night. Those exist, too, and one can easily be given a card and introduction if that's the route a foreign gentleman prefers. It isn't a route I would choose normally (oh sure, let's not forget Jocelyn, but I'm more sophisticated now).

Still, in the restaurant tonight, I am struck by how easily older fellows find lovely companionship here — some men overweight, balding, well past their prime, who would have struggled back home, wherever home is, to be seen with an attractive woman,

34

unless, of course, they were swollen with readily dispensed wealth. Perhaps so many come here for a second career because their knowledge is still sought after, and the women are less concerned that a man is older.

Though there are younger foreigners, too, at the next table over is a German, perhaps in his mid-thirties, with a young woman who looks to be twenty, though Asian women tend not to age as fast, so she could be as much as ten years older. Partly, it's the quality of skin with tighter pores; partly, it's the slimmer bodies; both are probably an outcome of a better and smaller diet.

I enjoy Chinese food as well. Since my first trip to China fifteen years back or so, I've learned to pick and choose carefully since anything that flies, walks, crawls, or swims that is remotely edible is eaten in China, with the probable exception of mankind. Yet, in the West, it's rare to find delicious Chinese food, even in Chinatown, compared to what can commonly be found in China.

At Angelo's, I'm on the job and I do enjoy a Western meal as a change. Still, in my two weeks in Shenzhen, this is my fourth supper at Angelo's. Of course, I've also eaten Indian, Korean, Japanese, and Chinese meals during this period.

I'm staying close by at the Marco Polo Hotel, ostensibly a five-star establishment—all part of the cover. When I was in Shenzhen a year earlier, I was booked into the Sheraton opposite the Central Walk Mall. That was my first time basing myself in Shenzhen. That job was actually in Hong Kong, but it seemed prudent then to distance myself from the work. But I digress.

This time, I'm practically on top of the work. There's a risk to it. Yet, I kind of like the immediacy.

Maybe tonight, the assignment will be completed From my jacket pocket, I pull out my Moleskine notebook and mechanical pencil to check the dates. Yes, tonight is one of the four dates. The other three have passed by without the opportunity I'm seeking. If there's a miss tonight, it will be time to fold up shop and move on.

Of course, I knew the date—not really needing to look at the little notebook. More an excuse to free up my pencil.

I jot down some of the Chinese characters I'd been learning to while away the days of waiting. *Mí* in eleven strokes, meaning riddle; *wán* in eight strokes, meaning to play or amuse oneself; *hǎo* in six strokes, meaning goodness. I set the mechanical pencil down within easy reach, its yellow plastic barrel reinforced by wire twining about it and, with the lead retracted, the writing tip, a thin steel tube, bringing the pencil to a point.

Then something occurs to me. I glance at the date again. It takes me a moment to calculate, and I realize my mother would be eighty-five if she were alive today. Is that auspicious?

A couple of men enter the restaurant, greeted by Angelo himself. They're escorted to a reserved table not far from where I sit. I watch them calmly while finishing the stroganoff.

Beyond the newcomers sits the one trio, a Chinese couple and an American, bald on top but with a twist of yellow-gray hair in a ponytail. I have been enjoying watching the Chinese woman, who is probably in her forties. A short black skirt and a cream-colored blouse, thin straps, and low cut-over flounces, her face animated in discussion, handsome despite her years, able to hold her own against the many younger women in the restaurant. The beefier of the two newcomers, the Australian, blocks my view of the handsome woman.

The thin Chinese waitress is at my table. She gestures and I nod so that she can take the plate. Soon, she's back with a dessert menu, but I wave it off. It's enough to finish my one glass of red wine.

Across the way, the Australian grabs the arm of a passing

busboy, impatient to order his meal. Angelo is quickly there to take their order personally. The Australian is loud, apparently feeling boisterous.

I fish the passport out of my shirt pocket. Blue with the American eagle on its cover, I leaf past my picture and the name Steven M. Lee underneath it to the photo tucked in the back. Yes, he's my Australian.

Putting the passport back, I finish a last sip of wine. Catching the eye of a passing waiter, I ask, "*Mǎi dān?*"

The waiter returns with the bill. I place the ¥285 of bright-colored cash in the folder. The waiter asks, "*Fā Piào?*"

I decline the government invoice required for expense reimbursement. I won't be needing them. Then, with a "*Xiè xiè*" to express my appreciation, I pick up my mechanical pencil with my right hand, and my book on cadavers with my left, the dry glue on my fingertips makes the touch an odd tap. I make my way toward the door.

As I brush by the table with the Australian I abruptly turn and lunge. The mechanical pencil goes deep into the big man's eye and is slammed home with a swat of the book.

You see it, don't you? The parallel between my first murder and my last? Different yet the same, a kind of poetic symmetry.

That night is fixed in my memory as vividly, maybe more vividly, than my first. I have to say, a lot of those times in between well, they tend to blur.

Anyway, you understand why I am startled by the handwriting on the envelope. If it is Anna K.'s, then this letter has been posted by someone else, or it's sat in a post office a long time before wending its way to me. Anna K. is dead. At least, I'm pretty sure she's dead.

6. NEIGHBOR LADY — MAKING USE OF FACTS

You see what I mean about Mr. Pryor? Just a shade too, I don't know, smarmy? Though I suppose he'd remember my name if he truly were smarmy.

Vivienne Hawk, a name I picked it out myself, had my birth name legally changed. The court had no problem, given my grandfather's conviction.

Before I picked my name, I had a very Irish name, Ide Thea, with a matching surname, not Murphy, Kelley, Ryan, or Sullivan, but still a run-of-the-mill Irish-American family name—no reason to remember it now.

An Irish surname with someone of African features would startle acquaintances sometimes. Sort of like my neighbor, with his bit of maybe Chinese having an English last name. The name Hawk doesn't seem to startle anyone.

I just completed a four-day marketing analysis assignment at $250 an hour, which is my rate for that kind of work. Frankly, it wasn't difficult. A day plus of research, then a day of extrapolation and connecting the dots, coming to conclusions, and the better part of two days writing a convincing report.

Though I am a researcher, it is less the research than the insights from the research that command my prices. It's the accuracy of my projections, predictions, and conclusions. Someone else might have gathered the same facts, observed the same behaviors, and come up with the same data but not see the right patterns, trends, and implications. Data, by itself, does not have a lot of worth.

I am, though, a collector of facts.

Most people amuse themselves in other ways; some read romance novels, some watch television for the quips, some go bowling or bicycle riding, some like going to football games, cooking sewing, or celebrity sightings. I like observing behavior and collecting social, scientific, and historical facts, then using them to try to make sense of my fellow humans and the world we inhabit, both physical and mental.

I am curious — always have been. My shrink says my need to know is my way of anticipating danger and protecting myself. Actually, I think my shrink is pretty insecure herself. She may be projecting herself on my flaws and behaviors.

I need to get off my duff and get going. A couple of times a month, I stop at one or another of the businesses in which I own an interest. Oh, there are more formal meetings with the other owners and their accountants or lawyers, but that's not the same as keeping an eye on the places themselves. What's the quality of their service? Is the place well-maintained, has the customer base changed in any way or in the larger neighborhood around the shops? Besides, I need to have my nails done.

Glancing out my window, I see the crows still cawing away in the maple tree. Their persistence is kind of odd. I wonder what Mr. Pryor makes of that fact.

7. THE CONSULTANT — CROWS

I've said I'm not superstitious, and I really am not. Still there is something about crows.

Let me give you a few examples.

I was born in the dead of winter in a northern climate. There is a photo taken on that day, I guess by my father or some other relative, from the hospital window toward the snow-covered expanse outside that would be the lawn again come spring. In that photo, hundreds of crows are gathered on the snow drifts and among the trees across from that stretch. You know, when crows gather, they're not called a flock. They're called a murder.

You could also ask why a father would photograph crows instead of a newborn son. I don't know. I never had the opportunity to ask him.

Okay, it's my wedding day. We come out of the church after the photo session, with the guests lined up on both sides of the steps, mostly her relatives and friends since my mother and I didn't have a large family, and everyone is tossing rice, showering us with the little hard grains. By the time we reach the car, a rented white Cadillac, crows are flying in among us, not a couple, but a goodly dozen or more, snatching up rice. Crows are carrion eaters but here they are grabbing up tiny grains of uncooked rice.

Do you want another example?

Melody is calling it quits on our marriage. Her name wasn't Melody, and I'm being a little sarcastic because she was not melodious. Still, it's been seven years together, one going steady senior year of high school, two while we were in college until she dropped out after her dad went bankrupt, and four as a married couple.

Melody always thought she was out of my league. She'd been a cheerleader, popular, dated a year older jock stud as a freshman through junior year. And her family had money, at least her dad use to throw it around, a big house, summer house, boat, snowmobile, five family cars, the cheapest a Jaguar. He owned four franchises and seemed to be doing great.

Come the end of her junior year, though and Melody is pregnant. Stud wants nothing to do with her. She suffers an illegal abortion by some hack her father found. Yeah, it's illegal in that time and place. Chalk it up to religious bigots.

So, at the start of senior year, Melody's a much subdued lady. She is still bright and has great looks, but she's no longer so vivacious, generous, and optimistic in her outlook. I guess I became her comfort doll, someone who would never reject her.

I didn't figure this out until after we were married. I can be a little dense, especially when it comes to forlorn women needing my help.

By our fourth year of marriage, though, Melody has bounced back in many ways, confident again, sure of herself and her looks, maybe cynical and stingy in a way she hadn't been eight years previously, certainly more cunning. And she's met a well-off man who is enamored of her at the health club, which, truthfully, I no longer am. Nor can I afford her, despite a good job.

Melody announces the end of our marriage, to my secret relief. Graciously, in her view, she does not insist on more than one year of alimony. Just enough alimony to bridge her financial needs until her next marriage, coming in at a little over half of my income due to the mental cruelty I've inflicted on her with my tirades over our credit card debt.

Oh, and guess what? Her Mr. Generosity and future husband will invest in a new business with Melody's father.

What about the crows, you ask?

I'm on the steps of our apartment building, watching her walk toward the waiting Mercedes; she not wanting help with her handbag, garment bag, and roller case, much to my surprise, until I see the chauffeur hurry up the sidewalk to assist her. Standing there watching her, knowing she's already tagged and boxed the items from the apartment she wants me to send on to her, I notice a crow in the maple tree on the parkway, then a second and a third fly in and land, and then more, until the several maples on the parkway are noisy with cawing, while the big black Mercedes pulls away.

I could go on. At every juncture of my life, even there in London, right in St. James Park, when I acquiesced in my future line of work to a representative of my new employer, although there they may have been ravens rather than crows, they were so huge.

And now, they are out there; from my picture window, I can see several more have landed among the trees while I sip my tea. They haven't gathered in large numbers yet, only a half-dozen, but I have the sense of them circling about, awaiting the moment.

8. THE CONSULTANT — THREAT

If I write what I know, who does it threaten?

Not my former employer or Anna K. because I don't know enough to threaten them.

Okay, over the thirty-five years of my career of violence, I have murdered 269 individuals. An even 270 with Lachlan, though I think that may have been manslaughter.

Of these, 41 were women, and 228 were men, but no children, as I refused each time children were to be the targets. Once, a child was a witness, and the other several times, I believe, due to inheritance. To be truthful, my definition of children might not be the same as yours, as the youngest person I murdered was fifteen. I figure through age fourteen; you're safe from me.

So, who do I threaten? Well, it's pretty obvious. Of my murders, 194 were ruled accidents and 32 as suicides. Do the math. That's 226 uninvestigated crimes, all cleared as far as the authorities are concerned.

If I blew the cover off those events, then a significant number of beneficiaries from my actions would feel the threat.

I'm not perfect. There are 43 unsolved murders out there, as far as the authorities know, across five continents, including that obvious final assignment. Sometimes, the hiring agency wants a statement made, not a murder hidden as an accident. But at least 26 of the known murders are botches on my part where I hoped to hide the truth.

So if I'm remembering right, researching possible beneficiaries, and writing the truth, then you can see that a fair number of people might be pissed off. After all, they paid good or not-so-clean money not to have my actions come back to bite them. Toward the end, I was getting upwards of $50,000 at a clip, although in the early days it was closer to $4,000, but figure in inflation. Of course, my part was only 40%, while Anna K. was getting 60%, so you can see that people were paying a pretty penny.

Accidental-style deaths cost more than some oaf with a sawed-off shotgun walking into a bar and splattering the walls with the upper torso of an owner.

Now, I don't claim to be an artist, more of a technician, truthfully. Actually, I prefer to think of myself as a craftsman. Accidental-style killings require considerable craftsmanship over a safe career of thirty-five years, with not even a parking ticket. Although, I freely confess I've had my share of close calls and more than my share of good luck.

Now, if I'm a threat, then for me to be in danger, the threat needs to be known.

Who knows that I'm writing?

No one.

Yet someone knows my whereabouts to post the note and key.

But as I think about it, there is a way that I have revealed myself. As Edward Snowden has proven with respect to the NSA, we are all being watched pretty much all the time between cell phones, computer links, and the like. And I have been researching online assorted potential beneficiaries of some of my many murders.

Truthfully, it's difficult to remember the details over the years. Some of the events sort of run together in the mind. Fortunately, I've kept a fair set of ciphered notes. I suppose I always thought I might someday want to write a memoir if I made it this far.

So I'm pretty sure I've tipped someone off somehow.

The crows are telling me they sense change, danger, something for me to fear.

Well, it can't be a coincidence that this envelope has a key, so let's start there—a locker key from the looks of it. And the note says Uptown Muscle Farm. There is no address, but I can look it up, probably near Lawrence or somewhere along Broadway, maybe on Sheridan Road.

The question is whether this is a setup.

Since where I live is known, whoever is out there could simply come after me. So that leaves no need for an elaborate setup, just that oaf with a shotgun and there are plenty of oafs.

Unless the setup is meant to snare more than just me.

Despite the handwriting, I don't think this is Anna K. back from the grave. The most messy and most neat handwriting are easiest to fake, but the in-between handwriting can be tough to sustain.

Not that I have any proof that Anna K. actually died. Maybe that whole cancer thing was a story.

Still, if she wanted to start us up again, this isn't her way, this mystery.

I have two choices: go with the key and see what's waiting for me in the locker, or cut and run. I could run; there are other identities, other money, and resources cached, but either I'm getting too old or I'm too curious.

This isn't the first time someone has cropped up from my past with lethal intent. That's why Greece, China, and Idaho didn't work out so well, and Mexico City, I don't know what I was thinking trying to live in Mexico City. New York and Hong Kong were better but not as good as Winnetka.

I don't consider self-defense as murder, so I wasn't counting those several bodies near Thessaloniki and the others by Liantan and Pocatello and the ones in the Coacalco district when I was enumerating my murders. Besides, there was no attempt to make them look like accidents, no craftsmanship, just straight-out shooting, knifing, and garrotting.

Still, as time passes, four years here already, you begin to think I'm safe, begin to relax. And the more that time passes, the more the past seems plain gone, dead to the present. But in my bones, I knew it wasn't really so.

So, I guess the next step is to visit the Uptown Muscle Farm, which as I look at the website, claims to be a family-friendly fitness center.

9. NEIGHBOR LADY — THREE SETS OF PARTNERS

LOOKING AT MY SPARKLING NEW NAILS AS I HOLD MY LATTE, I AM thinking maybe I went a little overboard today. Monique talked me into it and put her best nail tech on it, Banh Ngoc Bich. Ngoc never says much, is always intent on her designs, and is not as pretty or lively as the other three girls, so Monique says she gets fewer customers asking for her.

Nonetheless, Ngoc is a treasure, the most innovative with colors, using decals, glitter, rhinestones, applying acrylic, silk wraps, and the like, and design in general. The other girls often follow her lead.

Now, my hand sports alternating gold and red-tipped fingers, a rhinestone on each ring finger, and glitter for the pinkies. It was a bit much for me, to be truthful, but I think Ngoc was trying to impress a boss lady. I was okay with the red and gold, it was kind of fun, but the rhinestone and glitter isn't really me.

It's not that Ngoc is supposed to know that I'm an investor in

Monique's business, but things like that seldom remain secret among a room full of women.

Monique is Chinese-American. I met her years ago when we were both moonlighting as hostesses at a bar in the city. At the time, I was in grad school. Somehow, the two of us hit it off, maybe because we were the two exotics at the bar, the pretty Asian and African-American chicks. Technically, it was a restaurant, and the food served was fairly good, but the bar business kept the place going.

A place where youngish professionals hooked up after work, and a number of hookers as well.

Monique has her place not far from Argyle and Broadway, so naturally, her techs are all Vietnamese girls, that being the heart of Chicago's Viet community. She married five or six years ago, inherited two kids from her husband's previous marriage, and has one of their own. She's put on weight, which bothers her even if she laughs it off. She's cute, funny, and has a good heart. I'd like to say she's my best friend, though I'm probably not hers.

I always like going to her shop — our shop.

Just like here at the café. It is another good place to stop in, though business isn't as good here. Not bad, just not great, mostly a morning pick-up and a late afternoon stop-by. There's not much of a lunch crowd; there are just two others here, plus me today, so I'm wondering what we could do to make it a more happening place. My guess is it might take investment in upgrading the food, maybe some more equipment and training for making things like hot soup, and a change in advertising — like having some.

Also, if it were only up to me, I'd extend the hours into the evening. Then we might get the students and those who want out of the house but don't like bars.

The trouble is that I can't persuade my two partners and I'm the minority owner. Sadie is happy with the way things are: the slow pace, the long conversations with regulars, a place for her to go, earn a bit, and have some interaction. She's a lovely person, but ambition is not in her make-up.

As for Joel, — Do Duong, half-brother of Do Phuang at Monique's — he is happy as long as Sadie is. Besides, he's got his regular job as an accountant and only works here on the weekends and an occasional late afternoon.

I'm sure he'd be amenable to expanding the lunch menu and experimenting with some soups and a few French items, like adding freshly made crepes and pastries such as éclairs. He just wouldn't go for the expanded hours.

Funny about Sadie Epstein: I was very impressed when I first met her. She's whip-smart and knowledgeable, often amusing, and loves to talk. What I didn't realize until after partnering is how lazy she is. Maybe that's unfair. She is not exactly lazy; just she would rather read than work. Rather be discussing and arguing than working. Rather be painting or sketching than working. Well, you get the idea. And, truthfully, would rather be balling and frolicking than working.

Why Joel puts up with her side adventures is beyond me, but he tolerates it, so it's none of my business. Not that they're married. He's just her regular guy. But like his half-sister, he's so handsome, maybe more so as an Eurasian than his full-blooded sister, that he could readily have his own sequence of conquests.

Phuang, his sister, says he is too straitlaced for that.

Anyway, as I said, it's not my concern. The café, though, is my concern. Neither Sadie nor Joel is here now, which is too typical for lunchtime. Sadie did do the early morning shift, having stayed up all night, and now she is home in bed. Joel will come in today for late afternoon, just before five until closing at six.

For now it's Tran Vinh and Gracie at work. Vinh is a skinny kid from Joel's neighborhood, just 17, a high school dropout loaded with tats. Maybe he's done time, but Joel vouches for him.

Gracie is an ex-prostitute, closing on age fifty, maybe even past it. She epitomizes the eternal slightly overweight, middle-aged waitress, except for her tats, dark purple-dyed hair, and broad goth eyeliner. Surprisingly, Vinh and Gracie get along well and make an efficient team when there's a rush.

One regular eating a lunch brought in from somewhere else, with a pot of our tea. He's having the excellent green tea, which is one of the expensive ones, so I don't mind the outside food too much, especially as he's Vinh's buddy, Van Quan. I'm pretty sure they met in jail, given Quan's matching homemade tats and, more importantly, his guarded manner his arms around the table top protecting his food. I would make Quan to be 22, though he could be older.

Maybe I'm too judgmental. My shrink thinks so.

Anyway, the latte's grown cold. I should go on to the fitness center. I used to like going there. Used to use the facilities, keep my body toned, and all that. But since my first partner was bought out, I don't like the new guy much, nor do I like some of the new staff he's brought in.

I guess Danny, my first partner, didn't sell his share. Instead, I think it was a gambling debt he had to make good on. That was Danny's weakness, gambling. My first partnership was with my less-than-sharp first lawyer drawing up the contract papers, so when push came to shove, I had no say in the change of partners.

The new guy, Todd Bradley Wilkins, is a snake. More precisely, he is an arrogant, heartless, self-centered son-of-a-bitch, who doesn't like being tethered to a woman, especially a Black woman smarter than him. And yes, he has you use all three names, I guess, to distinguish himself from all the other Todd Wilkins out there.

I'd sell out to him in a nanosecond if he offered a fair price. He doesn't see the need, having gotten Danny's share for free. He'd rather force me out for something a good deal less than I put in as my investment. And I have more money tied up in the fitness center than in the nail shop and café combined.

Ah, well. Time to get over there. Face up to Wilkins like a big girl.

Placing my sandwich plate under the saucer and cup, I carry it all to the busing station, then call to Gracie and Vinh, "Thanks, you two. See you next time."

"Okay, Vivienne," calls back Gracie with a wave. Vinh just smiles.

Quan looks up from his booth two in from the front window and nods as well.

10. THE CONSULTANT — THE TARGET

Toweling down after my pseudo-workout, ten laps of walking around the indoor track at a moderate pace, and a shower, I start dressing slowly, waiting for the locker room to clear. Next to my locker is the target, the locker that should fit the key sent to me.

Two old farts, in better shape than me from the look of it, are taking their time getting dressed, debating whether they deserve ice cream as their afternoon treat. I'm guessing they'll go for the ice cream. Of course, in their eyes, I'm just another old fart who needs the exercise.

This place isn't bad, not too crowded on a Tuesday early afternoon. They have the usual array of machinery in one large room, all those treadmills, ellipticals, exercise bikes, and so on, whatever they call that stuff. Separately there's a weight room, plus a swimming pool and the track. All of it is well enough lighted and clean, with music and hotel-style decoration with a sports motif.

A steam room, hot tub, and a trio of massage rooms are off the locker room. I suppose the ladies' side has much the same. None of that's in use right now.

Staff is okay, not too attentive though, busy holding their own conversations as if serving a customer is an afterthought. Still, they greet most of the regulars brightly enough.

Not that I ever expect to come back here.

Okay, those guys are finally heading out. I wasn't sure how much longer I could keep re-buttoning my shirt.

Let's see what we have here.

Ooh, la la. I'd say the pile of cash in hundred dollar bills is about ten grand and the folder of docs is slim. No, make that twelve grand and a note that says 40%. A thirty grand hit, I guess, pretty cheap if it's to be an accident. I suppose retirement and being out of action for a half-dozen years puts a dent in my pricing.

Time to exit. I can look in the folder later. I saw a café on up the street.

At the Muscle Farm entrance, all I can think is, 'Oh, shit,' that's Vivienne Hawk coming through the front door, looking very sharp. Is this a coincidence? Act casual, "Why hello, Ms. Hawk. We're both out of our neighborhood."

Surprised, she says, "Mr. Pryor? Are you a member?"

"No, no, just trying it out. I'm not really much for exercise."

"Pretty long way to come for a workout."

Act embarrassed, I think. "Yes, I didn't want a place on the North Shore. I thought in the city might be cheaper. I'm retired, you know." Now attack, "What about you? Is this your regular fitness place?"

"Used to be. Once upon a time, this was my neighborhood, but I still get down here occasionally to see old friends."

Her smile looks a bit fake which is interesting. There could be some truth to it, though, but something else, too.

The fellow at the counter, with the name tag Bob T., says, "Hi, Miss Hawk. I'll buzz Todd Bradley Wilkins to let him know you're here."

"Thank you," answers Vivienne Hawk, who then turns to me, "Sorry, I have an appointment."

"Right, well, nice to see you." She really is striking; that long neck reminds me of the bust of that Egyptian queen, Nefertiti, except Vivienne's ears aren't so prominent.

Café seems okay. A kid wearing black and an apron talking to a guy in a booth, both Vietnamese from the look of them. A couple at a round top, in their late twenties, both on their computers. An older guy is reading in the far corner booth. And the counter girl, a woman in this case, is not bad looking for her age, though she should lose the eyeliner and maybe try a less attention-getting hair color. "Hi. Cappuccino, please."

"Hi, what size? For here or to go? Whole milk or 2%?"

"Small, here, and 2%," I smile.

A very nice smile back. On impulse, I say, "I'm Randy, and you are?"

"I'm a little randy, too, but this isn't the time or place is it."

That surprises me, but I laugh. "Perhaps another time then, after closing say?"

She does a long sigh, smiling, "I wish. You look my type. But tonight is my yoga class."

"What's your type?"

"The type with money."

Which gets me laughing again, "Okay, I'll settle for the cappuccino."

"Three fifty-one." She makes change, "Go have a seat, I'll bring it to you."

I open my backpack in the booth and glance into the folder, a single sheet of paper with the particulars and a photo. God damn it! Vivienne Hawk's photograph.

Now, it does feel like a setup, and not by Anna K. It's not that I really thought Anna was doing this. Still, I thought it might have something to do with the old firm.

Likely, I should be figuring out and tracking down whoever knows who I am and what I've done for a living. Whoever set this up they should be my target.

Vivienne Hawk is literally too close to home. And I sort of like her.

Not that liking her should matter.

"Here you go," says the counter woman, setting the cappuccino on the table, leaning a bit more than necessary so I can admire her cleavage.

Which I do, even if she's a tad bigger and broader than I prefer. Still, it's been a long time, and she seems pleasing enough. "Thank you. Tell me, is there an evening when you don't do yoga?"

Her turn to laugh, "Perhaps something could be arranged. You would need to come by here more often, though." She turns to go, then turns back, "My name is Grace, though everyone calls me Gracie."

"It's good to meet you, Grace."

"You, too, Randy," she smiles as she retreats to the counter.

I sip the cappuccino and think. It's too much, of course, seeing Vivienne Hawk at the fitness center, her assignment in the locker there, she being my neighbor, someone knowing who I am, where I live, what I do. Did that is. So, I'm going to make an exception here, even if she is over the age of fourteen. I'm not doing

Vivienne Hawk. After all, I'm retired and don't take assignments from totally left field.

So who do I do? This smells like that time in Guangdong province, the fake assignment they tried to sucker me on.

Am I supposed to make a connection between Ms. Hawk and the fitness center? Or was that someone's miscalculation? Her showing up when I was there, our seeing each other.

My gut says a miscalculation. Who knew if and when I'd pick up the folder? Hawk said she had an appointment, so that part could have been planned, but not the instant I was there. So, a miscalculation, pretty sure.

Still, the fact that there is a connection between Hawk and the fitness center isn't a coincidence. So we start with that; it's time to do some research on Ms. Hawk and the question of who wants her dead.

I pull the photo back out to study it. Not so much Vivienne Hawk herself as the background. Where was the photo taken, and how recently? What kind of camera was used? What's the quality of the photo, especially blown up to an 8 x 10?

So it looks to be a camera shot, not a mobile phone, taken with a zoom lens, though anymore that could be on a small camera, a Nikon, Canon, or the like. Fidelity is pretty good, even if it is blown up to this size photograph. Still, I'd say digital, not film, with some graininess on the edges.

The picture itself is a street scene. It's a Chicago neighborhood, so it's probably not far from here. It looks like she's coming out of a shop, a nail salon, or a day spa. I can almost make out the name, maybe Unique Nail or something. She's looking good in this photo. I guess I never realized how attractive she is.

"You know Vivienne Hawk?"

Startled, I look up. The Vietnamese kid bussing the tables is looking at me. I am getting sloppy in my old age. "Oh, you know her, too?" Always attack rather than defend.

"Sure, she's one of the owners."

"Really? I guess I thought she did marketing research and stuff like that."

The kid shrugs, "I don't know what all she does. I know she's got money and is part owner of a couple places. That one in the photo is Monique's shop, for sure. One of our bosses has a younger sister who works there."

That clicks in place, I think. "What about the fitness center? You know, down the street, Uptown Muscle Farm?" I laugh, "Kind of a dorky name, isn't it? Uptown and Farm don't seem to go together."

The kid shrugs again, maybe thinking he's already said too much. To ease him, I say, "Vivienne and I are neighbors. We have condos next to each other in Winnetka." Telling the kid may be too much, but I'm already blown, so I'll be moving on anyway once this mess is cleaned up.

"You're a little old for her, aren't you?" the kid says.

Well, that stings, but I am who I am, and getting older is part of the deal if you survive. I laugh again, "We can let her decide." Then attack, "What's your name? I'm Randy Pryor." I hold out a hand.

He shakes, maybe a tad reluctantly, "Vinh. Some people call me Vinnie."

"Like Grace being called Gracie."

"Oh, I don't think she minds."

"So you prefer simply Vinh?"

He nods.

"Well, it's nice to meet you, Vinh."

"Yeah, you, too. Are you done with that cup? If so, I'll take it."

"Thanks."

After that, I head to my car, start the drive north up Broadway, and swing over to Ridge. Probably, the kid, Vinh, will mention me to Vivienne next time he sees her. Wonder what that will provoke? He'll mention the photo, too. Well, all this is proving interesting. Kind of livens up my day after these years of coasting.

11. NEIGHBOR LADY — WORTH A SHOT

W<small>ALKING BACK TO THE CAFÉ AFTER MEETING</small> T<small>ODD</small> B<small>RADLEY</small> Wilkins, I feel bemused. The guy was pleasant today. Not that I trust him after all our past acrimony. He's up to something, I'm sure. Still, if he goes through with what he said, he buys me out in six weeks at a fair price. It's not a generous price, but just enough to be agreeable.

He said he needs six weeks more to put that kind of cash together. Where does this guy get all his money? Sure, isn't from the fitness center itself.

Well, he doesn't know all my business either, I suppose.

He even apologized for any previous unpleasantries, smarmy bastard.

I've hit my limit for today with one more cup of coffee. At least I can count on good coffee at the café.

"Hi Gracie, hi Vinh."

"Back so soon?" asks Gracie.

I can't help smiling, "Yeah, it wasn't as bad as I expected. Nor did it take as long."

"You want coffee? The Ethiopian or the Panamanian?" Gracie laughs, "I thought you said you were taking your lawyer with you next time you met your new partner?"

"Yeah, the Adame Ethiopian." I shrug, a little annoyed to have Gracie knowing my business, but she got it from me. "The lawyer couldn't make it today, and as it turns out, she wasn't needed this time."

The shop is busier now as it pushes on toward mid-afternoon. Quan has vacated his regular spot, freeing it for others. A couple of businessmen in the front booth, a foursome of neighborhood ladies on the larger round top, three different singles all on their iPads or laptops, a mom and her two kids getting an after-school treat, and a pair of pre-adolescent giggly Chinese girls whose parents probably don't know they're here — okay trade and it will get livelier.

Vinh, back from serving a mocha with whipped cream to the overweight, bespectacled 20-something woman in pink on her iPad, a fairly regular customer, Tammy? Fanny? I should know her name, something odder. Landry, that's it.

"Vivienne," says Vinh, nodding.

"Getting busy here."

"Afternoon, crowd," he shrugs. Then, as if an afterthought, "You know an older guy, tall, maybe 185 centimeters, says he's a neighbor of yours?"

Surprised, I blurt, "Randy Pryor?"

"Yeah, that was the name."

"He was in here?" I think. It's not surprising, given he was at the fitness center, where we're the closest café for a post-workout coffee. "What'd he order?"

66

Gracie says, "A cappuccino. Seemed like a nice fellow. Had a sense of humor."

"Hmmm, I guess." I know Gracie appreciates good-humored men.

Vinh shakes his head slightly, a negative, "He had a photo of you, an 8 x 10, he pulled from a folder. The guy has a file on you."

That sets me back. "A file?"

Vinh nods, "Like he's planning to do business with you." Then, leaning forward and speaking more softly as Gracie turns away to handle a customer, Vinh adds, "Or maybe do business to you."

Now I know Tran Vinh associates with several dubious fellows, some definitely with past prison time, but he's also only seventeen with a teenager's movie-fueled imagination, so I take his whisper with a grain of salt. Yet there is that photo and file, "Was it a good likeness? The picture, I mean."

Now Vinh winks, "Yeah, you looked hot, Vivienne." He laughs at my expression, then says, "You were coming out of Monique's photo of you from the waist up. You were wearing that suit you wear when you're meeting business people, except you had that white blouse with the loose button hole on the second button, so lots of boobage."

I swat at him, and he dances away, laughing. But I know the blouse he means, and I do like leaving two buttons undone and showing some cleavage, not more than an inch, to distract male clients. Not that I'm heavy on top, more like slightly under medium. Still, it works to my advantage.

Hearing that last part as she hands me my coffee, Gracie says, "Your guy likes that too. He gave me a good stare." Then she laughs, "Of course, I was making it obvious."

"My guy?"

"Your Randy."

That's a strange thought. My face must show my distaste because Gracie says, "Hey, the guy's not so bad for his age, though the cosmetic surgery wasn't all that great."

"Cosmetic surgery?'

"Yeah, you see how his face is a little frozen around the eyes?"

Huh, I never realized. Maybe that's why I never trust how he looks; the his eyes don't match the smile. "He had surgery on his eyes?"

"Yeah, and not just for cataracts." Gracie says, "In my former line of work, I've seen a lot of plastic surgery, especially tits and ass, but face jobs too. You know, rhinoplasty, rhytidectomy, that kind of thing."

"Oh, rhytidectomy?" I know rhinoplasty, nose job.

"Facelift." A big grin from Gracie, "I always thought of myself as in the entertainment industry." Then she adds, "Personalized entertainment." And she laughs loudly.

Vinh is there, "So why'd you quit? You could have gone for surgery. Hell, even now, I'd do you."

"Guys your age, I only do it if they have trust funds," snickers Gracie.

"Okay, you two, we have kids in the shop," I say, knowing their banter can be too graphic for the public's taste.

The truth is, there was a time when I was living on the streets and would sometimes do tricks, so I know what Gracie's life really was like. Though I was fifteen, sixteen, or so then, maybe it was both tougher and easier than when Gracie was in her twenties and thirties.

That time for me was long ago now, more than twenty years. I try not to remember those days.

Driving home, I'm thinking about Randy Pryor. We've been neighbors for something like two years. He was there already when I bought the condo from the couple who were retiring to Arizona. He introduced himself after I moved in, but truthfully, I wasn't too friendly. After that, it was just neighborly hellos and how are ya's.

So why would he have a file on me?

Sure there are some checkered things in my past, until I straightened myself out when coming up on eighteen. I did things like shoplifting and some hustling, but I never did jail time; I was arrested once but let off with a warning, an old cop without the humanity squeezed out of him.

Maybe he wants to do business? Buy me out? He was at the fitness center. Could he be a new partner to Todd Bradley Wilkins, buying in? That's not too far-fetched.

What'd he say? Going to a fitness center in Chicago because it's cheaper; this from a guy living in a pricey condo in Winnetka? Doesn't sound likely.

He must not see it as all that confidential, Vinh spotting the photo and file, even having a conversation about me with Vinh. Maybe he's checking out my other partnerships?

So, there is some kind of business deal he's thinking about.

What do I know about him?

He told me once he'd been an HR consultant. I asked if he'd been a recruiter and did executive headhunting for a living. What did he say? Something about outplacement and re-organization; he said he was a strong proponent of performance pay.

The guy's in his sixties, living alone. I don't think he's a widower or gay.

He has weird eyes, like an Asian, what they call an epicanthic fold, but he's no Asian, though I suppose it could be somewhere in his ancestry.

The real question is, should I talk to him? Let him know I know he has a file? He didn't hide it from Vinh, so maybe he wouldn't be surprised if I ask him about it. Worth a shot. Why wait for him to come at me?

12. THE CONSULTANT — VIVIENNE HAWK AT THE DOOR

THE DOORBELL RINGS WHILE I'M WHISKING THE EGG WHITES WITH THE mixer in my left hand and stirring the pot of white sauce with my right hand. I shut off the mixer and the gas flame under the pot, then chamber the Glock 38 just in case. I should also turn down the music, but I like Adele's *21* album.

Glancing at the four security screens, I see that it's Vivienne Hawk at the door, as I half expected. Setting the safety on the Glock, I stow it and shut the closet door to the security screens.

The doorbell rings again. Undoing the deadbolts and keying the lock, I open the door, catching Ms. Hawk with a finger extended for a third bell ring. "Why, this is a pleasant surprise."

"Mr. Pryor," she nods, then says, "Although, I doubt you are too surprised given your discussion of me with my colleague at the café."

"Yes, I thought that might pique your interest, though I wasn't sure if it would cause you to approach me directly." I smile and step back, "Won't you come in." I gesture at my long orange apron, used some years ago in an 'accident' at a restaurant involving a sous chef, "I'm in the midst of preparing a soufflé."

"You cook, Mr. Pryor?" as she steps in.

"Yes, after all I only need to please myself with my cooking." I shut the door firmly, and key the lock.

She watches me throw the deadbolts, saying, "Isn't a soufflé rather complicated? I mean for one person."

"My guess would be that when invented, using hand mixers, they meant a lot of work. Thus, their reputation for being difficult. Now, they are simple enough, though it does mean washing out several bowls and a pot." She follows me into the kitchen, where I reset the gas and re-commence my mixing and stirring.

With the whites peaking well and the white sauce becoming thick enough, I shift to pouring the thickened sauce into the lemon-colored egg yolks using a flexible spatula. Then I add the cheeses, stirring. After that, I softly fold and refold the thick cheese sauce into egg white meringue until it's blended well enough. All of it is now poured into the prepared soufflé dish and placed in the oven. I smile at her as she's been silent throughout these operations. "You don't cook, Ms. Hawk?"

"Some simple things, but I mostly eat out or order in."

Smiling, I nod my understanding. "I find cooking to be a soothing activity, and it can be quite creative." I start washing up the bowls and pot.

"You wash everything by hand? You don't use the dishwasher?" She seems surprised.

"Habit, I guess." I set a clean bowl on the rack. "A lot of single people accumulate dirty dishes then run the dishwasher. I prefer to clean up immediately."

She nods, quite familiar with the routines of single people.

"That will take about another thirty minutes to bake. In about twenty-five, I'll start cooking the broccoli and warming the baguette." I gesture toward the living room, "Shall we talk for a bit."

Vivienne Hawk is quite a striking woman and fairly well-off. Research has turned up a few interesting facts about her, supplementing what was in the file, but there's much I don't know.

Normally, I wouldn't delve too deeply. Just enough to get the job done safely, more about daily routines, patterns of activities and interactions, and the like, not about motivations, reasons, causes, or purposes.

You try to keep things as unemotional as possible. Focus on tactics how to get it accomplished with a minimum of exposure. There is always risk. It goes with the job; really, it goes with life. You cannot control any event entirely, so while there is a plan to follow, improvisation is also needed at times, which often is what the advanced knowledge makes possible.

Anyway, here we are in my living room. It's funny to try and see where you live through the eyes of a newcomer. It probably looks pretty Spartan to her: no family photos, everything clean and in its place. Still, there are a lot of giveaways regarding me: books on the shelves, magazines on the side table, the music playing, and the CDs on the rack, a couple of modest paintings and prints on the walls, I suppose even the type of furniture, a sort of softened Scandinavian style, with touches of Asian — Chinese rather than Korean or Japanese.

She picks the smaller couch, its fabric primarily in tans with strands of blue, green, and darker brown. It works well if you spill a bit of tea, which I have done more than once. I'm surprised she doesn't pick the matching side chair.

"Would you like something to drink? Tea, coffee, water, wine, juice?" I ask.

"Nothing. This is not a social call, Mr. Pryor." She is stiffer than in the kitchen; perhaps we should have stayed there to chat.

"Please, call me Randy."

"All right, Randy," she tries on a smile. "Would you explain to me your conversation with Tran Vinh and the file on me, especially the photo?"

How much to disassemble? Truthfully, I dislike lying although it's inevitable in my former trade. And though my whole present life is pretense, I haven't needed to actively lie in some time, other than those social fibs one does, like 'my goodness, how nice you look today' when you're really thinking 'why would she pick that color for her hair?'

Well, here I am lying to myself, for I've already lied to Vivienne and Vinh earlier today. "I suppose it was incautious of me at the café. Once your fellow noticed the photo, there seemed no reason not to discuss your business with him."

"So you want to do business? Or are you considering buying into the Uptown Muscle Farm, becoming a partner with Todd Bradley Wilkins?"

Before I can reply, she goes on, "If so, then I advise you against it. While it may not be in my best interest to dissuade you, you are a neighbor, and, in good conscience, I could not recommend partnering with him. On the other hand, if you expect to buy him out as well, then I can say the fitness center has brought in an uneven return that averages a modest income over and above the regular costs and the occasional necessary capital expenses."

"You don't like Todd Bradley Wilkins?" This is an interesting tidbit.

She sighs, looks away momentarily, then turns back to me, "No, he bought out my former partner some months back. I feel he has been eager to push me out as well. Now he is saying he will buy my share in six weeks. We have tentatively agreed on a price that is less than I would like but adequate for me to be shut of him."

"You have a pattern of minority ownership in your businesses. Why is that?"

She stares at me a moment, then cautiously asks, "You are interested in more than the fitness center?"

"I am interested in you, Vivienne Hawk." I smile.

"Why?"

I sit back, wishing I had a mug of tea to sip, "We have been neighbors for 27 months, give or take a few days. An agreeable but unassuming neighborliness, an almost kind of relationship I was quite willing to see continue. Recently, though, I have been contacted about you in a manner that compels me to alter our circumstances."

Puzzled, Ms. Hawk responds, "I don't understand."

I sigh, "Ms. Hawk, someone doesn't like you. Or, perhaps, someone finds you extremely inconvenient."

Her frown deepens, but before she speaks, I raise my hand, "I am retired now, but in my former work, I would be contacted to resolve such differences to the satisfaction of the party reaching out for my services."

"Arbitration? Mediation?" she asks.

"As I am retired, I would prefer no longer to take such cases. Due to the sensitive nature of my profession, I find it disturbing to be contacted and asked to take this case." I pause, "What I would like to do is enlist your assistance in determining how and by whom you became a case."

Bewildered, she stares at me, then gathers her wits and says, "Randy, is this some kind of elaborate joke? If so, I must say I don't find the hoax funny."

"If it's a hoax, then someone has paid me $12,000 just to get a laugh." I stand, walk to the secretary, open the desktop, and bring out a box. I turn to her and let her see the stacks of hundred–dollar bills.

Her mouth drops open for a moment, then she asks, "You don't know who paid you? Or why?"

"I know what I've been directed to do, but no more than that."

"Which is what?"

Tiring of my own circumlocutions, probably with the impatience of old age, I say, "Kill you."

13. THE CONSULTANT — SOCIOPATH OR PSYCHOPATH?

I HAVE TO SAY SHE TAKES IT REASONABLY WELL. NO HYSTERICS, A narrowing of her eyes, considering me, considering what I've said, all of it. Maybe she was somewhat paler than she'd been before, maybe already figuring out what objects in the room could be weapons for her defense.

I return to my seat, relaxed, waiting.

Finally, she asks, "That's what you did for a living?"

I nod, "Yes. Not a redeeming occupation, I'm afraid."

A stab of what might be disgust crosses her face, "But you don't intend to do it this time?" She adds, "Why?"

"I'm retired. I don't like being pressured back into doing things I've left behind." I try to look earnest.

"That's it? Not because we're neighbors? We know each other; wave hello. Let alone it not being right!"

I shrug, "I confess, being neighbors does weigh into it; I even like you."

She pauses, considering again, "What happens if you turn down an assignment?"

I admire her strong nerves, "Oh, nothing much as far as I'm concerned, at least so long as I give a good reason. I don't do children, never have, and never will."

"You do women, though?" She eyes me steadily.

"Not as often, of course." Then I feel I must add, "Just because I have my reservations on an assignment and bow out of it doesn't mean it doesn't get done. It just doesn't get done by me."

She reverts to denial. "Randy, I'm not sure I believe you. Is this like some demented reality TV program?" She looks around as if searching for cameras.

"Sometimes, not often, life is like fiction. Yes, you are meeting a retired killer, an assassin. One who has been offered an assignment to kill you, which I am turning down." I sit forward, stretching out my hands to her. "I think it is in both our interests to figure out who is behind this assignment and resolve it so it doesn't threaten either of us."

Skepticism or maybe indecision shows on her face. "If it's true and this isn't some kind of scam, why don't I just go to the police?"

"You can, of course. I won't hinder you. I'll just disappear and move on. I'm good at that. Then you and the authorities can figure out who wants to kill you and try to stop it." I sit back and give her a small smile again.

"Why does this threaten you?" Curiosity in her voice.

"This is my seventh home since retiring. The longest I've stayed anywhere since stepping out of my profession, the longest serving identity. Now I have to go on to an eighth, but I'd like to do so feeling that I won't be found again." And that is the truth.

"You aren't Randy Pryor."

"And you weren't Vivienne Hawk originally." My knowing nettles her.

"Did you work for the government?"

"No, I don't believe so." I shrug, "I never knew for certain who employed me. For all I know, it was some department of a subsidiary of a major corporation. Eventually, I was released from employment and could go freelance."

There is a look of incomprehension on her face.

I explain, "I wasn't given a choice in taking up the work. Or, at least, no more choice if I wanted to live."

That seems to mollify her a tad until I add, "Then I found I was surprisingly good at it, which is probably what my handlers already determined."

"Good at it?"

"Yes, not simply killing but making the kills seem like accidents. That's my talent, I guess." I try to be modest, but the truth is that I take some pride in my craftsmanship.

"For instance?"

"Oh, let's say a certain fellow in Baltimore frequently chooses mushroom omelet for breakfast. One day, after breakfast, he feels nauseous, and is ill, but it passes quickly enough. He's fine, he thinks. Later that evening, he has intense pain and dies quickly. An autopsy shows that he ingested an *Amanita* or destroying angel mushroom in his omelet." I don't add how difficult it was finding a fresh *Amanita ocreata*.

She's looking at me as if I've said something farfetched, but it wasn't really as hard as that time getting a diamondback rattler to strike. They are really quite shy creatures when it comes to humans. I wave a hand, dismissing all that, "Let's get back to you. Who hates, dislikes, or finds you inconvenient?"

"Enough to kill me?"

"Well, it does not take a lot for a sociopath, and on average, there are between one and four among any random collection of a hundred humans," I smile, for I've often wondered if I am a sociopath. I'm pretty sure of it most of the time, but I occasionally feel strongly for others.

"Todd Bradley Wilkins, maybe," she says.

I nod as I already listed him in my mind as a prime suspect. "Yes, and tell me about your other partners."

Vivienne frowns, "I doubt if it's any of them."

"Perhaps you're right, but let's consider it. Could be indirect, a relative or friend who sees some advantage to helping one of your partners."

"Helping?"

Nodding again, I say, "That's how a sociopath might see it."

"What's the difference between a sociopath and a psychopath?" she asks.

"None. A psychologist might say that the social environment induces socio-pathology and genetics triggers psychopathology, but the behaviors are the same. Some theorize that men are more likely to be sociopaths and women psychopaths, but the theoretical argument seems weak to me." I have read some of the articles on the topic. I feel I should add, "That's supposedly why there is more pathology in the West versus Asia because our culture stresses individuality, and Asian cultures stress social cooperation."

"Oh?" She sits up, "You mentioned wine earlier. I think I could use a glass of wine."

I stand, "Good. I should check on my soufflé, too. You will stay for supper, won't you?"

"Only if you're not serving mushrooms."

I laugh.

As she sips her wine and I complete preparations for the meal, I think she should be wary of the wine. There are any number of poisons wine could mask. "About your other partners, tell me what you can?"

She shrugs, "Not a lot to tell. Monique Lee and I have been friends for about fifteen years. She needed money to start her business ten years back. I gave her enough to get it going. She's repurchased most of the business and owns 75% now. She could probably buy me out if she wanted."

"What about her personal life?"

"Married to Roy Peterson, has his two kids, Amanda and Kyle, and they have a girl, Sara, who is three now, almost four. Amanda is thirteen, I think, and Kyle is maybe eleven. No, they're a year older than that." Seeing my inquiring look, Vivienne goes on, "Roy is a bank vice president. They met when she first applied for a loan for her shop. He turned her down."

"Does she have other family?"

"Oh yeah, sure. I think the parents are still in Hong Kong, and she also has a brother there. Another brother lives in Vancouver, Canada, and an older sister in San Francisco. She first came to the U.S. for school in California, but it didn't work out. She followed a fellow to Chicago but that didn't work either, though she stayed here." Then, a little defensively, she says, "Monique is a sweetheart. I'm certain she has nothing to do with this."

Setting the soufflé on a hot pad in the center of the table, I ask, "And your employees there?"

"The girls? They're fine, all four of them. They are good girls on the whole. Ly Tam is a live wire. She's the youngest. Only Nguyn Thuy is married, back last fall. She's the prettiest one. Do Phuang is also very attractive acts very sophisticated. Her older half-brother is one of my partners in the café. Then there's Banh Ngoc Bich. She's my favorite, and she's very smart."

I gesture for her to sit. A simple meal, cheese soufflé — asiago and romano, broccoli with balsamic vinegar, baguette with optional butter — real butter, of course, and red wine, a reasonably priced zinfandel, then an apple for dessert, although there's several ice creams to choose from or biscotti if Vivienne prefers, and tea or coffee. It's one of my favorite meals.

For a time, we eat with little conversation other than a compliment on the food from Vivienne and my acknowledgment.

Setting down her fork, Vivienne says, "Have you considered your enemies? Maybe I'm incidental, and this is just a way of entrapping you."

"Yes, I've considered it." I smile gently, "I doubt I need entrapment. I am compromised already." I stretch, "No, this has to do with you, although it could have to do with both of us."

She is silent, looking at me, so I ask, "Your partners in the café?"

"Sadie Epstein and Joel Do, she's supposedly an artist, and he's an accountant."

"You don't care for Sadie?"

"When we're together, it's fine. She's funny and talks a blue streak, and she has a million ideas. But she has no follow-through, no real push, and she starts any number of projects and activities, but they go nowhere."

"And Joel?"

"He's a rock, solid and stolid, he's Sadie's counterweight. If he promises, it happens."

"You said he's a half-brother to the girl at Monique's, Do Phuang."

"Yeah, I'm not sure of the family history. He's Do Duong, the son of a Vietnamese mom and a Western dad, not married. Phuang's father was Vietnamese and also is no longer around. Joel makes sure his mom and sister are all right."

"You've been partners for how long?"

"Seven years."

"How did it come about?"

"I met Sadie when we were both doing poetry readings. We seemed to hit it off. She had this idea for a café hosting art and literary events. Her new boyfriend then, Joel, was quite smitten with her, so he was intent on turning her dream into a reality, not realizing that six or nine months later, she'd have a different dream. "

I nod, "Still, the café exists."

"Yes, Joel's doing, although Sadie usually works the morning shift before going to bed. She calls it her penance to real life." Then Vivienne adds, "No art gallery or literary salon, though. That would require more energy than Sadie's willing to give it."

"You write poetry?" I ask.

"Used to, still do occasionally." She chuckles, "Usually when I'm feeling down. None of it is very good, I'm afraid. The truth is, though, I stopped doing poetry readings when I realized they were more about performance chops than the quality of the writing."

I wait, thinking there's more she wants to say.

"Sadie's all right if you just accept who she is and don't expect too much of her. It's sort of ironic that Joel would never have gotten into it if Sadie hadn't wanted to, and yet the café wouldn't exist and have continued if Joel hadn't moved it along. I'm unsure whether Joel would keep it if it didn't make a place for Sadie. In a way, the café kind of anchors Sadie."

"Your employees there?"

"You met Gracie and Vinh. Then there are three others: Kal, Nicky, and Macario. Gracie is a manager for all practical purposes; she's there five or six days a week. Grace Freen is her name. Tran Vinh is also full-time. The others are part-time; Kalman Buda is Kal, and he is foreign, from Hungary, if I remember correctly. He works weekends, as does Nicole Harris, a Black girl like me. Then there's Macario Acosta; he does mornings during the week, usually with Sadie. He's a very experienced barista, like Gracie. Hispanic and very handsome, so Sadie likes working with him."

Nodding, I say, "Okay, that takes us to the fitness center. So Todd Bradley Wilkins is new, and you two don't get along. Who were the former partners?"

"Danny Corvino. We were … lovers once upon a time. When I received my legacy, he talked me into becoming a partner with him. He had the business and needed some investment to upgrade equipment and décor. I didn't know then that he had a gambling habit." She sighs, "He was one of my mistakes."

I'm not really listening as the name rings a warning bell. Not Danny Corvino as such. It's the surname that catches my attention Corvino, from Italian, a word for a raven.

I know the words for raven and crow in many languages. Some languages don't distinguish between these bird species, while other languages have more distinctions than English. Take raven as an example; in French, it is *corbeau*. In Swedish *korp*, in Dutch, *raaf*, in Czech, *havran*, in Turkish, *ac olmak*; in Malay *burung*; in Vietnamese *can xe*; in Han or Mandarin *du ya*, and so on.

Pulling my thoughts back to Vivienne, I ask, "How does Danny Corvino feel about you now? Does he still carry a torch?"

Vivienne makes a face, "I doubt it. Even well before he lost the business, we ended the intimate part of our relationship. We were still friendly enough the last four or five years. And he moved on to some other women, mostly customers of the fitness center. There's a big-boned blonde Nordic type he favored the last I noticed."

"What is her name?"

"Gale something, A-L-E, not A-I-L. Maybe Cederholm, something like that." She shrugs, "Unless Danny told her, she probably doesn't know he and I had been lovers. I doubt Danny would have said. He is discreet when it comes to women; I'll say that much for him."

I am pretty sure she knows exactly Gale Cederholm's name. Maybe Vivienne still feels something for Danny. "Who else is in your current life or in the past of whom I should be aware?"

Vivienne looks at me oddly. Then says, "Say that again?"

"Anyone else of whom I should be aware?"

"English isn't your first language, is it? You speak too formally."

Wincing, I curse myself inwardly, caught. "Just the scholarly side of me coming out," I smile brazenly.

She nods as if accepting my words at face value, though I can tell she doesn't believe me. But I am distracted as she begins describing her grandfather. She goes on for some time, her voice becoming a monotone as she goes into more detail.

Finally, I hold up a hand, "Your grandfather died in prison. He's in the past, right?"

"Yes. He and my father both." She looks away a moment, then back at me, "Grandfather had a friend. They had been buddies during the war, both veterans. Toward the end, Grandfather sometimes shared me with Mac. That's really why I ran."

"The Vietnam War?"

"Yes." The word a whisper.

"Mac's name in full?"

"Robbie McQuillan. I suppose Robert or Robin, but I only knew him as Mac."

I nod, "He was never charged over your abuse?"

She looks away again, "It only happened twice. The second time, he hurt me, and Grandfather was extremely angry and upset."

I wait.

"I think that ended their friendship. Anyway, Grandfather said he banned Mac from the house." She is quiet a moment, then adds, "But I ran anyway. I didn't believe Grandfather." Then, more pensively, "Mac may have been the one who anonymously reported Grandfather."

"How old would Mac be now?"

"He was a couple of years younger than Grandfather. Probably 65 or 66."

So, Grandfather and I were likely born a few years apart, I think. The abuse of Vivienne went on from 1983 to 1992. Mac would have been in his early forties in 1992, maybe 42. A thought strikes me, "How old is Danny Corvino?"

"Danny? Oh, he's at least fifty now."

"And Todd Bradley Wilkins?"

She has a grimace on her face, but she says, "Mid-thirties, younger than me."

"You'll be 38 this year."

She nods.

"Okay," I get up to start clearing dishes. "Dessert? I can slice up an apple. Or there's ice cream."

"You have some if you want. I'm fine. You could pour a second glass of wine."

Which I do, thinking how impolite I've been in not offering

when her glass was empty; I'm usually a single glass of wine at a time person, so I become neglectful. As I pour, I wonder if sex with his granddaughter had become too routine, so her grandfather intended to spice it up by adding his friend in the mix. Sexual pleasure is an odd thing, the turns and twists it can take.

"Okay, so our immediate suspects are Todd Bradley Wilkins, Danny Corvino, Sadie Epstein, Joel Do, Monique Lee, and possibly Robbie McQuillan. There are the employees and relations, too, but they have less obvious gain from your death." I sit opposite her again, "Now, the next step is to think how any one of these individuals might make the connection between you and me."

She swallows and nods, her eyes on mine. "I may have mentioned you once or twice to Monique or Danny, maybe Sadie or Joel, or to Gracie."

"Why?"

Vivienne waves a hand, "Oh, I don't know. Sometimes, you talk just to fill space. Like Monique mentions a neighbor, so I mention mine. Or Danny talks about the elderly guys who work out at the gym, and I mention my elderly neighbor. You know, just idle talk."

Elderly neighbor? I understand her view, but I'm still slightly offended.

My turn to cogitate out loud, "Who is likeliest to have questionable friends? Friends of friends, maybe, who could have knowledge of my past life? My work is known by reputation to a circle, but I never had direct contact with a client."

"Someone tracked you, right?" she points out.

I nod, saddened by the thought. I thought I was clear of it this time. Maybe I've been tracked as far back as my first feeble attempts at enterprise before Anna K. My boast isn't true; I did have direct contact with a client then.

And the Feds nearly got me. Maybe someone in the government did get me, though which government or which agency? And they decided to observe but not act until needed, though why there's a need in the person of Vivienne Hawk seems strange.

Alternatively, I suppose Anna K. could have shopped me. Probably, medical cancer treatment is pretty pricey. Or, maybe Anna K. had colleagues. What did I ever really know about Anna K.?

Who knows, we could have been part of some huge global corporation, with me being a kind of subcontractor.

All right, let's reverse, I think. Why should Vivienne Hawk die? "We were concentrating on your partnerships, but they're a sideline, right? Tell me about your real work and the research you do."

14. NEIGHBOR LADY — CONNECTION

HOW DO I GET MYSELF INTO THESE SITUATIONS? BORN INTO MY Grandfather's household, so that wasn't my fault, surely? Unless it's karma and rebirth.

My whole life is a kind of soap opera, except less believable.

Randy is washing dishes, and I'm sitting in his living room, waiting, thinking how unreal this all seems, yet he has convinced me. What is the difference between a serial killer and a hitman? Maybe a serial killer does it for personal pleasure, while a hitman does it simply for money? So, what is a hitman who enjoys killing? Perhaps a serial killer picks his own targets, and a hitman gets told who are his targets?

And why does our society glorify serial killers and hitmen while pretending to be horrified by them? Count the number of magazine articles, books, TV programs, and movies that feature one or the other? More than the total number of books about Jesus, Hitler, and Napoleon?

Maybe I should do some research on the topic and publish a paper.

He comes into the room, "All set. Now we can talk about your work assignments."

Something I've realized as Randy takes a seat, he makes no notes. Maybe he's smarter than he looks, though Gracie is right; he's not bad-looking for his age — at least if you discount the weird, fixed eyes. "There's not a lot to say about them; they're pretty common kinds of assignments, mostly marketing trends for retailers, service firms, and manufacturers. Anymore, I tend to get international or foreign companies hiring me, wanting to understand the market for a service or product outside their home country." I think back, "I could describe the last half-dozen jobs if you think that helps."

He nods, and I launch into a recitation. I don't know what Randy makes of them. They sound repetitious to me as I outline the most recent assignment and then the next several, going further back. Cosmetic medical treatment, telecom technology product, high-end toys, fitness equipment for the disabled, weekly soft porn subscription, specialty vinegars and edible oils, luxury massage centers (Asian, of course), all different, but the process is pretty similar, and none of the corporations are all that exciting. Oh, brand names, sure, names Randy recognizes. I suppose the most common thread is that they are all niche products and services, not mass markets. I suppose the corporations' marketing departments handle the large-scale stuff.

I give him the names of my primary contacts and project leaders describe various team members, project results, all of that. I can tell, though, that none of it sparks his interest. Oh, he is attentive and asks cogent questions, but there's no 'aha' moment.

He does get a bit intrigued by the massage centers. I

acknowledge that the client's thought was an early market entry in preparation for the legalization of prostitution given the current trend of legalizing marijuana in the U.S. And, I suppose, with major corporations eyeing that market and putting their money behind the politicians, it will come about, coupled with safeguards to criminalize the freelance talent still and assure legal offerings of only corporate product. Health will be the lever for that purpose.

Still, nothing there was so secret or endangering to require my death, and that's what he's looking for, I'm sure. I have seen some of the other research done by the company with the massage center concept, mostly on turnover of staff, considering an average max of three years, four years, five years, or six years in the service, coupled with severance packages linked to years of service. Mostly, that was a lot of numbers, projections of costs and revenue, and the like, based on various assumptions. Believe it or not, the main impediment was immigration laws.

Even that didn't seem dangerous enough. Oh, the public might be horrified if a well-recognized brand name was linked too early to the commercialization of prostitution, so the study was ostensibly restricted to massage and to the luxury audience, not the neighborhood places or the mall shops. Who cares about an overpriced back rub?

Not Randy, anyway. "That's it?" he asks.

"That's all the most recent corporate work," I answer.

"You do non-corporate stuff?"

"Sure. Not a lot, non-profits don't pay all that well, and government work is a labyrinth of rules and forms, or it goes to the well-connected, often both. But I do some individual requests on a variety of topics, not necessarily marketing." I notice he's staring for a moment at my hands. I knew this manicure was too fancy for me.

"Give me some recent examples, please." His eyes are off my hands again.

I describe the research for classmate contact information in advance of a high school 30th reunion that I did for a reunion committee. That was during a slow point in corporate assignments and didn't take all that long, mainly as the committee supplied about one-third of the contacts at the outset. Heavily discounted work, too, but they paid promptly, and I needed the money.

Then, more recently, the genealogical research I did for an older couple. The fellow's interest was twofold: first, the sheer identities and interrelations of family members as far back and as broad as possible and then, secondly and more pointedly, personal facts and contact information for all living relatives within two degrees — the grandparents and others of that generation, parents and all their siblings, all the cousins and second cousins, nieces and nephews, their own children, grandchildren, and grand nieces and nephews. Surprisingly, that was a lot more work than the high school reunion, despite all the basic information the couple provided me.

It took several months, and the first segment isn't complete for all branches. That could take years if they want me to pursue it further. But I'm an expensive researcher for that purpose.

This assignment seems to intrigue Randy. "They're paying you $250 an hour to do that kind of research?"

"They're wealthy enough, so they've lost touch with real-world costs."

He shakes his head no, "In my experience, the wealthy know exactly how much to spend on things and how to get the best possible deal, even if it means cheating." He cocks his head to one side, "You didn't find any blood tie to you?"

I laugh at the absurdity, "No Irish branch to the family except a few distant in-laws."

Still staring at me, he asks, "How about your mother's side?"

"Sorry, I can't help you there. I don't know who my mother was." I shrug as if it doesn't matter to me.

He seems puzzled, "You've never tried to research your mother? Hospital records, birth records, all of that?"

I am dismayed. Perhaps it's denial or fear, but it has never occurred to me to try to identify my mother. Perhaps I simply accepted that she was a whore or druggie and not worth pursuing. Though, come to think of it, Butch would want a healthy girl, so no druggie.

Unbidden, the thought surfaces that the Rochefort family, the one I have been researching, does have one African connection, not as you might guess from some 19th-century Southern plantation but from a great-uncle, a French adventurer who fought on the side of the Ethiopians in the mid-1930's against the Italian invasion. He is known to have had a lover there, a young woman of the Amhara, sister to one of the intellectuals killed on Yekatit 12, the day of Italian reprisals for the assassination attempt against Marshal Graziani. The French adventurer and his Amhara mistress had a child, but I did not trace the child.

Still, I shake my head no in answer to Randy, "No, I've never tried to find my mother."

15. NEIGHBOR LADY — MOTHER

LATER THAT EVENING, AT HOME IN MY OWN APARTMENT, FEELING I'M not sure what … trepidation, doubt, pity, scorn… I begin the search for my mother.

Next to my laptop, beside the mug of tea on its small hot plate, the lamp, the stacks of books and papers, pens, and other paraphernalia, sits a new object, courtesy of Randy Pryor, a pistol. Giving the gun to me, he had smiled, saying it was really a lady's weapon but more powerful than most.

I've looked it up, too: Para-Ordnance Slim Hawg from Canada, a six-shot automatic firing a .45 caliber bullet. It's small, only six and a half inches, and reasonably light. The gun is loaded, and he gave me an additional magazine, so I have a total of twelve bullets. He asked me to keep it with me at all times.

Truthfully, I took it more as a matter of trust between Randy and me. How likely is he to kill me if he gives me a pistol?

Not that it's legal for me to have a gun like this.

As for my mother, my birth certificate says she is Maryam Davis. Davis is an extremely common name. And there is Butch's name as the father. Mother was born in 1959, making her eighteen at the time. Butch was twenty years her senior. Her birth state is noted as Maryland. Butch's from Virginia, of course.

So I'm guessing Butch found her in Baltimore.

I should be able to trace her if the certificate is accurate. My mother is only fifty-five. She could be alive, have a whole life, not just be a shadow in mine. Does she ever think of the child she gave up?

Two in the morning, Wednesday, and I should go to bed. My standing appointment with Dr. Farness-Dayan on Thursday, shrink day, is at 3 pm. So how much do I tell her?

No Maryam Davis born in Baltimore in 1959 during the month of May. There is a Maryam Dawes. Could she be the same person? Maybe used a false name with Butch and on my certificate? But if it is a false name, perhaps the Maryam is false too.

Daughter of Sidney Dawes and Celeste DuPont. According to Maryam's birth certificate, Celeste DuPont was born in Delaware in 1940, and Sidney Dawes was born in Egypt in 1936. So, given my skin color, is Sidney Dawes an Englishman or an Anglo-Egyptian? It says white on the certificate, as it does for Celeste DuPont.

Is this the right Maryam? Where's the African-American bloodline?

I also looked at the Rochefort material and what I have on the great-uncle. I was mistaken in my memory; he was not French but Belgian. There was a French branch and a Belgian branch of the family. He's from the Belgian side, Bernard Guy Camillo del Rochefort. Apparently, in his adventuring days, he just went by Bernard Roche, perhaps to spare the family embarrassment.

There is only one reference to the girl's name from Ethiopia, though back then it was known as Abyssinia. It is hard to make out the handwriting on the photostat, but it appears to be Dawit Meseret. The child was a son, Dawit Sisay. I don't have dates of birth for either the mother or son. Bernard, though, was born in 1895.

So much for any family connection, not that I expected any. However, I wonder if my mother used a friend's name. Maybe there is Maryam Davis, who was not born in 1959 in Baltimore, Maryland.

Yawning, I shut down the computer, turn out the light, and pick up the pistol.

Just after nine Wednesday morning, while brushing my teeth, it strikes me that I researched my mother but paid no attention to who might want to kill me. Are my priorities screwed up, or do I just not believe, deep down, that someone hired a hitman to take me out?

But there is Randy's pistol to remind me. And the twelve thousand dollars in a shoe box that he gave me. What did he say, "You might as well take the money. I don't need it and won't be earning it."

I guess it solves my cash flow problem, although it's kind of macabre to use the money someone gave to have me killed. Curious ethic on Randy's part that he doesn't consider the money his because he didn't earn it.

Honestly, I can only think of Todd Bradley Wilkins as an enemy. It's just too convenient for him to finally tell me he'll pay a fair price for my share of the fitness center in six weeks with a coincidental contract to kill me. I wanted a hundred and twenty thousand for my thirty percent. He's offering a hundred and five. Paying twelve is a whole lot less.

Randy wants to know who found him and how they know about his past. If it's Wilkins, then the bastard has to have some connection to Randy. At least he knows someone who knows about Randy.

I agree with Randy that it's too pat that we're neighbors. Using the drop at the fitness center is also too suspicious. It's my one hesitation about Wilkins. Even he isn't stupid enough to foul his own nest. So I do have to ask myself, who would want to kill me and cast blame on Wilkins. The only name I can come up with, reluctantly, is Danny Corvino — or, just maybe, his current babe, Gale.

Randy's concern about my research seems like a red herring. He assures me that corporate espionage can be deadly, and I guess he should know. Still, all I do is routine, even if the companies are all in a twitter over their particular concept.

Or is there a sociopath out there playing games with Randy and me? A sociopath other than Randy that is. I still think there's a strong possibility that I'm incidental, a target because I'm Randy's neighbor, and it's Randy who is the real target.

So, do I tell my shrink any of this?

In the afternoon, driving to the office tower at the mall, I keep asking myself why I see Dr. Farness-Dayan. This is ritual: asking myself why I'm throwing good money away to see a shrink. Basically, I blab on and on about what's on my mind, what's worrying me, about my social insecurities, or, in answer to the good doctor's occasional question, about some aspect of my past history, usually related to my early upbringing and Grandfather. For three years, no almost four years, I've been doing this nonsense.

Yet if I don't go, I miss it. Maybe it's cathartic. Or I'm addicted to talking out loud to someone, however noncommittal, about what's bothering me.

Maybe I don't have anyone else in my life.

Once in a great while, the doctor sets me a task to think about or act on — maybe once in every four or five months.

I won't think about how much this is costing me. It borders on the obscene, but that's what's required for help from a healthcare or legal parasite in the U.S. Makes me consider emigrating at times, that and taxes, the erosion of our liberties, and the futile venality of our governing class: the politicians, financial institutions, and corporate leadership.

All right, I'm ranting to avoid thinking about my problems.

Damn, I hate going, yet I know I'll feel better afterwards, like going to a dentist for the annual teeth cleaning.

Well, I'm here; I might as well go in.

"Hi, Vivienne. You're a little early, but I think Dr. Farness-Dayan can see you promptly. Let me just check with her." The receptionist, Glenda, is always very chirpy, with a big smile and capped teeth, as if it's her job to make the lives of the drabs who seek the doctor's wisdom buoyant. And she's pretty, too, which always strikes me as odd that the trio of psychiatrists who share the receptionist would hire a cheerful young woman rather than a stolid middle-aged matronly type who wouldn't alarm the patients with bright, aggressive vibes.

"Thank you, Glenda. You know I come early just to see the latest issue of *National Geographic*," I laugh. Yeah, I know it's not that funny, even though I do like glancing through the magazine.

But not today, as Glenda says, "You can go on in, Vivienne."

Walking into Dr. F-D's always makes me wonder how staged her office is. I do my usual inventory, maybe to avoid starting.

There's a wall of filled bookcases to the right, her large desk off to that side with two armchairs before it and her assorted diplomas on the wall. A small couch against the front wall next to the door, which I've always avoided. I'm not about to get comfortable. I know there's a washroom behind the far door, where I once spent fifteen minutes vomiting. The other door in the room must go to a closet or maybe an exit. I do like that she always has a vase of fresh flowers on a stand by the bookcases. Staring at the flowers has saved me more than once, letting me become calm again.

Glenda once told me that Dr. F-D has the largest office, although Dr. Morris' and Dr. Manny's offices are nearly as large. I told Glenda that I thought her office, the reception room, might be the largest, and she'd laughed.

Dr. Morris and Dr. Manny are first cousins and have the same surname, so they are called Morris and Manny rather than Gelderscheidt. I was first referred to Dr. Manny, but I preferred a woman shrink. Dr. F-D for Farness-Dayan because it's too much effort to keep repeating the hyphenated name.

As for Dr. F-D, I'd say she's in her late 50s, petite, with hair once dark now silver, and having large, inquiring dark eyes behind wide circular glasses. Her eyes might be her best feature, given her long nose and prim mouth. Well dressed in an understated way, usually in a skirt, jacket, and blouse, sometimes with a colorful scarf and black modestly high heels. Her manner is not unfriendly or aloof but also not familiar. She does not try to be your buddy; she is always professional. There is a sense of strength, of character, despite her slight size.

She stands to greet me, gesturing at a chair, "Good afternoon, Ms. Hawk. How are you today?"

"Well, to be truthful, I've been better." I smile to make light of my statement and sit myself in the nearest armchair.

"You want to tell me about your concerns?" Dr. F-D smiles, as she re-seats herself and takes up her listening posture.

So I relate to her the events of yesterday, editing a bit to shield the identity of my putative assassin and the fact that he's my neighbor. I'm unsure if I've mentioned my neighbor by name in past sessions.

Dr. F-D asks some clarifying questions along the way but otherwise doesn't comment; simply hears me out. When I come to the end, she nods and says, "You believe the retired assassin?"

I open my handbag and stack three rubber-banded small bundles of cash on her desk, each bundle having 40 hundred dollar bills. Beside them, I place the Slim Hawg automatic. "Yes," I say.

"And you believe Maryam Dawes of Baltimore may be your mother?"

"Perhaps, hard to say without more research."

"Well, your yesterday was certainly eventful." She smiles, "Now, tell me how you feel about it? You've said what happened but very little of how it strikes you."

"It angers me." I think about it, "It saddens me, too."

"What about fear?"

"I won't let myself be intimidated," I declare with maybe more bravado than I feel.

"So whatever apprehension you feel, you channel into anger?" She smiles her cryptic smile.

I nod. "I suppose so, though truthfully, it seems unreal despite this," I gesture at the money and pistol.

"What do you think of your retired assassin? You do believe him." Her head cocks to one side, a habit I've noticed many times.

"Yes. I've have always felt there was something odd about him. He is, in his way, scrupulous. Fortunately, he's retired and willing to work together to solve this." Then I must add, "I do feel some trepidation around him. Like if you owned a pet cheetah or boa constrictor." I laugh.

"So you've known him for some time?"

"We are acquainted. So I see him around, have for some years now. Just it never seemed important before." I am dissembling a bit, which Dr. F-D could easily pick up on as she knows me quite well.

"You have not mentioned going to the police. I take it you do not intend to involve the authorities?"

Shaking my head no, I say, "You remember three years ago when I was troubled by that stalker? I went to the police, and all they said they could do was patrol more often unless I could identify the fellow." I shrug, "Seems like there's even less to go on in this case."

"That was the teenage boy, right?"

"Yes, it was really nothing. A friend of another boy in the apartment complex who saw me at the swimming pool one summer day and tried to catch more glimpses of me." I might have felt flattered if the boy hadn't been so immature and awkward. "Both of them are away at colleges now. The geeky boy from the complex is at MIT, and the stalking one is out in Washington, maybe at Evergreen."

Dr. F-D reaches across her desk and taps the stack of hundreds, "Then I have a suggestion. Why not use some of this money to put a security system in your home, just as a precaution? And, if you like, I can put you in touch with a reliable private investigator. His team can help you identify your threat."

Turning it over in my mind, the only downside I see is whether Randy would go along with a private investigator. "Please give me the contact information. I'll consider it."

Flipping through her old-fashioned Rolodex, Dr. F-D takes a slip of paper, jots down a name, address, and phone number, and then passes it to me. "In the course of my work, there have been a few occasions where this fellow has helped. I can vouch for the work he's done on behalf of my clients. Thomas Cromwell has a small office, three or four people. He is discreet."

I read what she's written on the slip of paper, an address in Highland Park, further north of Winnetka. The company name is Investigative Research Associates.

"Is it all right if I call him to let him know I referred you? You can still decide yes or no about employing him."

Uncertain, I nod okay.

Picking up her phone, she touches a speed dial button. "Hello, this is Dr. Judith Farness-Dayan. Is Mr. Cromwell available to talk. I see; yes, if you could put me through. Thank you." She holds a hand over the mouthpiece, "He's out of the office, but the administrator can connect me."

I nod, feeling like I inhabit another piece of fantasy land. A private detective, really? They exist outside of television and movies?

"Hi, Thomas. Judith here. Yes, fine, thank you. I am with a client, a Ms. Vivienne Hawk. She has received a credible death threat. She may be in touch with your agency, but she first needs to speak to another party who is involved before making a decision. I wanted to let you know that I've given her your contact information. Yes, thank you. I hope your day goes well. Goodbye for now."

Placing the phone in its cradle, she says, "There, now you can feel free to contact him. He only works on referrals from known individuals." She smiles, "I have a request of you. I would like you to ask your retired assassin if he would be willing to meet with me."

"You don't believe me?" I blurt.

"I do believe you. That is why I want to meet your ... associate." Dr. F-D waves a hand, "Now, more importantly, let's talk about your mother."

16. THE CONSULTANT — THE DEVIL MAKES THREE

THERE ARE 42 EXTANT SPECIES OF CROWS, COUNTING ROOKS, jackdaws, ravens, and the like. While they originated in Australia and evolved in Asia, they are everywhere except South America probably because the other most intelligent bird family is there, the parrots.

The intelligence of crows is equivalent to that of the major primates, like the great apes, but not humans, at least, not yet like humans. They are communal, can make and use tools, enjoy play, and are omnivorous, all human traits. They are long-lived, 20 to 30 years in the wild. The oldest known crow, a captive, lived to 59.

In myth, they can predict the future, warn of ambushes, and, for that matter, know the coming of rain.

I'm not sure it's a myth.

Outside is a gathering — too few to be called a murder — of *Corvus brachyrhynchos*, the most common crow of North America; only six or so of the birds right now, all in the maples and the one larger oak tree.

They're taking flight. Oh, I see; it's Vivienne Hawk on the sidewalk coming this way.

I open the door for her before she rings the bell.

No greeting, she just says, "I've thought about it. I think we start with Danny Corvino. My guess is he's trying to implicate Todd Bradley Wilkins."

"Why don't you step in so we can talk," I open the door wider.

She enters, and I firmly shut the door, gesturing toward the kitchen, "Tea? Coffee? Wine or beer?"

She precedes me, and as I follow her, I unsling my backpack, setting it on the counter. Unzipping the pack, I haul out my laptop, "Just need to shut it down. I was about to go to the café."

"You go to Peet's?"

"No, when it was Caribou Coffee, I went there, but when they closed to make the changeover to Peet's, I got used to going to the Glencoe Roast. It's farther away and more expensive, but it's quieter, not a chain. When the site here re-opened as Peet's, I tried it a couple of times, but it's louder now, more industrial, and like a Starbucks."

"I saw my shrink today, Dr. Farness-Dayan." She leans against the further counter, arms folded across her chest, as I complete shutting down the computer.

"Yes?"

"Well, I told her about the situation." Hastening, she adds, "I didn't identify you or that you're my neighbor."

"And how did she respond?" Cursing inwardly that I never asked Vivienne to keep all this confidential, I just assumed she had the good sense to do so.

"She believed me. Wants to meet you. Oh, and she offered me a referral to a private investigator, a Thomas Cromwell, and she suggested I have a security firm wire my place."

The doctor wants to meet me? I think, does the doctor have a death wish? "Wiring the place and setting up cameras is okay. Keyth is a good outfit for that."

"Did you use them?"

"No, I did my own." I smile as if I'd let someone else do my security.

"So, do you think hiring an investigator's a good idea? I was thinking he could do the open inquiries while you and I do the covert work. Whatever he learns, he turns over to me, and I share it with you." She stands there expectantly, almost holding her breath, and I realize she's afraid of me, which she should be, but it still pains me.

Thinking out loud, I say, "That would telegraph that you are suspicious, that you know of the threat. Right now, you're safe because someone thinks I've accepted the gig and am working out the way to best kill you."

"Only if they figure out I hired Cromwell. What's to say I'm his client?"

"Coincidence," I respond. "Coincidences may happen, but they're suspicious." I leave unsaid that I would likely bow out and leave her to work this out if she calls in the detective, though I'd hate to run, leaving open who and how I'm being tracked. If I did so, this situation could arise again in another context. The truth is, Vivienne Hawk is about as stable a partner as I'm likely to find.

Seeing doubt on her face, I add, "How about we check out Danny Corvino? If that's not fruitful, then we call in the detective."

"If you're willing to consider it, then why not get the help immediately?" she counters.

Frowning, I say, "Vivienne, think about my viewpoint. I'm a murderer. How many people do you think I want to know that?"

Staring at me, chewing her lip, obviously troubled but not freaking out. Finally, she says, "I don't know who is standing there. You've given me a name, which you've already told me is your seventh or eighth name. You have a face modified by plastic surgery, which likely you'll get reworked again when you move on. I know there's a person underneath that, but who could identify that person? I suppose there are fingerprints and DNA, but only if they match someone known. If they're unmatched, then they're anonymous too."

Smart girl, I think. I might as well be one of those malleable erasers we use in drawing sketches. Today, the curving line is here; tomorrow, it's erased and gone. "I won't meet or talk with the detective. You are not to give him my current identity or how we know each other. If you want to engage him, that's up to you, but I hope he doesn't get in my way for his sake. I am a violent man."

"Will you meet with Dr. Farness-Dayan?"

I shake my head, feeling exasperated that she is pushing me to consider it.

Vivienne smiles at me. "Silly idea, maybe dangerous, you're thinking, but you do wonder why the doctor wants to talk with you, don't you? I wondered why, too, but then we got talking about my mother."

I hadn't wondered, but now I do. Would I be a psychological specimen for her, a case study? Or does she want to hire an assassin? Or, maybe the doctor wants my insight into her client, Vivienne Hawk? I snort at the thought. "Not going to happen, Vivienne."

She shrugs, "Think about it. If you change your mind, I can put you in touch. I find her easy to talk to."

Talking to a psychiatrist is hardly what a hired killer wants to do. I dismiss the notion.

"So what's next?" she asks.

"Danny Corvino," I answer.

After much discussion, a division of labor is agreed upon. Vivienne will do deeper research on both Danny Corvino and Todd Bradley Wilkins, engaging a set of shadowy hacker friends from the Vietnamese community to help her. Apparently, they are more like sub-contractors than friends, and that's okay so long as they leave a clean trail and know nothing of me.

She will also reach out to Thomas Cromwell to have him check out her other partners from the café and nail salon. If that turns up nothing as she expects, then she may re-direct him to take a look at two of her research project clients, the elderly Rochefort couple and the corporation anticipating the legalization of prostitution.

I will focus solely on Danny Corvino and his girlfriend. Though I don't say it to Vivienne, I intend to be prepared to cause their deaths if necessary after extracting any information I can about their connections back to me. I buy her theory that Corvino is the likeliest candidate to want to set up Wilkins over her elimination. Two birds with one stone, as they say. And speaking of birds, there is Danny's name, the raven.

"You won't do anything yet, right? I mean to Danny. We aren't sure it's him," she asks, seeking reassurance.

"You're not partners or friends any longer? Still feel affection for him?" I smile.

"No, but he's a human being, sort of," she responds defensively. "We should know if he's guilty first."

I nod, "Okay. But don't worry, he's sure to be guilty of something." I smile again. Like too large a carbon footprint, taking up space, something he's sure to be guilty of, I think to myself.

Somehow, she's not reassured. "If it is him, you'd arrange an accident?"

"If there's time enough and opportunity." I shrug, "If not, then so be it."

"You'd shoot him?"

I shrug again, "If need be, or use whatever's at hand, an umbrella, mechanical pencil, steak knife." Then I ask, "Why do you care?"

She looks down at the floor, then up to my eyes, "I'd want it to be quick. We were lovers once."

I sigh; I doubt it will be quick if I need answers. Still, I say, "I understand your feelings," which isn't the same thing as agreeing, even if Vivienne takes it as agreement.

She shakes her head slowly.

"What?" I ask.

"I can't believe I'm talking about someone being killed, let alone someone I know well."

"It's a shock," I agree. "But you didn't start it."

"Do you get used to it?" she asks, perhaps trying to understand me or fearful of becoming callous herself.

Am I used to it? With close to three hundred dead; well, 282, if you count Liantan – 2, Thessaloniki – 3, Pocatello – 1, and Coacalco – 6, you'd think I'd be used to it.

I miss the adrenaline rush; it's true. Never at the time, I'm too busy, but what's the line by The Devil Makes Three in their song *Black Irish*? Something like, '*I want to feel that blood rushing in my veins ... If I could only do all the things I want to do while fear is rushing down in my veins*'.

No, I'm not used to it as such, but it's a job. Who really likes their job? Only the lucky few. If I had to do it over again, maybe I'd be an illustrator or, like Vivienne, write poetry.

"Not really, if I pause to think about it. But I rarely think about it."

"So you'll shoot Danny if it's him?"

Well, I have my Glock 38, the Markov Type 549 (thank you, my assailants in Guangdong province), my Para-Ordnance Nite Hawg, the Taurus-Rossi R461, and, if need be, the Skorpion M61 (a Czech item scavenged by way of Mexico). "Yes, if I must."

Later, after Vivienne leaves, I make a list of who else I need to check out. Ms. Hawk is so focused on herself that she hasn't truly considered that the threat may be from my end. She once said she might be incidental to my entrapment, and though I dismissed the idea for her sake, there is the possibility.

There is the Anna K. connection, so try to retrace it—my brief foray as a freelancer and that one flaky client situation. There was my original employer in the trade; probably the contacts I had are gone, but is the organization? Then there is my writing, and let's face it: foolish internet searches I did. I know which beneficiaries of my murders I was researching. There were twelve instances, but I think I can safely dismiss seven, so that leaves five.

The danger is that none of these connections are involved, but by poking around, I arouse one or more of them to take an active interest in me. Yet someone is involved beyond Vivienne's candidates, or how would they know about me?

My instincts say it's through Anna K. Think of the envelope with the locker key. But that, too, may be misleading. Whoever is involved likes sleight of hand and misdirection. That was never Anna K. herself.

The old man, my original handler, loved anonymity and misdirection and never liked the few direct homicides I was requested to do, let alone my botches that shouted murder. Accidents and suicides, he would insist.

So, let's assume the organization was also like that; it preferred operating as secretively as possible.

As for the post-retirement run-ins, I think I have a proper understanding of them.

The Liantan attack was due to the last assassination of the Australian in China. It was probably fairly stupid of me to think I could retire in Guangdong province. The follow-up in Thessaloniki was the same thread. So, I think those killings ended any Australian interest in me. Or was it Chinese interest?

The guy in Pocatello was a surprise. It nearly got me, too, and I have several scars to prove it. Backtracking on him, I ended up with that foul-up when I went solo. So I'm pretty sure that closes that deal. Though if there's enough of a drought, they'll find his car with him in it and the trauma to the skeleton that no accident caused.

New York was just a feeling of not being safe. Nothing overt happened there. Maybe it was my conscience if I have one. Or maybe I was being shadowed and picked up on it subconsciously.

What to say about Mexico City? It was such a fucking slaughter. If ever I've been lucky, it was that time. The question is, did I step into something that was purely local, or did it have anything to do with my past? At the time, I chalked it up to a local gangster mess. Yet, I don't truly know.

I picked up some scars that time, too, so I went on to be patched and recuperate in Hong Kong, then moving on since someone could know of my health care need.

Now, four years in Winnetka, this one smells, and I'm supposed to know it smells. So, was I being tracked all this time, or did the tracking start somewhere along the way in retirement, like in New York? Or is it something recent? Did someone stumble across me, or did I signal them with my internet searches?

Well, let's give it a rest. I need my Z's. Put some music on, maybe play The Devil Makes Three. Keep the Glock in hand and relax.

17. THE CONSULTANT — CORVINO'S MATERIAL LIFE

Corvino's condo is on Stratford between North Broadway and Lake Shore Drive. It's a fairly upscale building with a doorman, which is good because it promises the anonymity of a large structure with many apartments. I'd estimate close to 50 condos, lots of security cameras, and, no doubt, alarms in place. I don't mind.

Gaining entry as a delivery man, repairman, inspector, or police doesn't work in this instance. So it's best simply to be invited in.

Between public records of condo owners, Facebook, some genealogy sites, and the like, I know to be Maxwell, a grand-nephew of an elderly lady living in number 7F. She is delighted to see me in answer to my call, as her niece, Marjorie, purportedly suggested. So, I will stop by early this afternoon with flowers for the old gal.

Corvino lives at 6C. Unbeknownst to him and ancient Mrs. Kozlowski of 7F, I will also visit his home.

Having lunch at a diner on Broadway, not too far from Stratford, I am thinking about a question Vivienne Hawk asked me. She wanted to know how I justified to myself the life I've lived, the murders I've committed. I suppose my response was both dismissive and facetious, yet possessing an underlying truth. I told her I don't bother to justify.

Which does make me a sociopath.

It's true I don't weigh the deaths I've caused against my own life. Nor do I measure my worth in that way, save for some pride in the ingenuity of my craftsmanship. I do not take pleasure in the killing itself or in causing pain and anguish. By and large, I am glad to be alive to be able to enjoy what there is to enjoy.

Do I feel remorse?

No, not truly. Oh, there were some I would have preferred not to kill.

I recall a movie I saw once, maybe a Hong Kong flick or, perhaps a mainland film about a hitman. It was a comedy film, and in the end, the hitman always gave his victims a warning to run and hide, only appearing to have killed them. It was preposterous, but then it was a comedy.

Life is not a comedy.

Everything is transient. We all die. Does it matter so much when? Does it even matter how, other than the duration of pain?

Oh, some of us will do marvelous things or dastardly things that will outlive our brief lives, and all of us cause consequences and creates waves of influence, but even all that is a candle flicker in the life of the universe. Not even the ash of the candlewick will remain.

So to whom or to what does it matter what we do in this instant of life?

Oh, I know about the rigmarole of religion, that crutch for the weak-minded. All the many thousands of words called god that billions have prayed to, sacrificed for, maimed, and killed for. And to be honest, here, have acted in goodness for.

I think I know Vivienne Hawk well enough now to hear what her response would be. We do good for our own well-being our own sense of healthy self, we do good because it is better than doing evil. Being ethical feels right. Caring for others, having empathy, is part of goodness.

And I think that's true for 96 to 99 out of every random 100 people. But it is irrelevant to the psychopath.

And I think I know whether I'm part of the 4% or the 96%.

Searching Corvino's condo, I can't help being amused in the delight Mrs. Kozlowski took in the flowers I gave her. A very nice spring bouquet, if I do say so myself. I didn't stint. I think she took even greater pleasure in being remembered by a distant member of the family, even if I did have to pass myself off as a good half-dozen years younger than I am. At 90 herself, her perceptions weren't keen enough to tell the difference, and her nurse has Thursday afternoons off.

My amusement doesn't hinder the efficiency of my search at Corvino's. I am thorough yet quick, after years of practice. There are patterns to hiding places, and fewer such places in a building of newer construction than one of fifty or more years ago. I have a few tools to help in the search, in a sense to peer behind walls and under flooring, though there's not much flooring here on top of the concrete.

That Corvino uses a cleaning service is obvious. His taste is actually good in terms of décor, not extreme like an interior decorator would do, so I take it as his haphazard choices of an actual life lived, whatever has caught his eye or been given to him one time or another, from ash trays to wall hangings to furniture and other furnishings.

He has big screen TVs in the living room and bedroom, as well as a Bang & Olufsen sound system, and he likes tech toys and gadgets. Brookstone or similar stores must love him. Same thing in the kitchen, his espresso machine could almost serve for a Starbucks. Maybe he hosts lavish parties?

A Smith & Wesson 351PD revolver in the nightstand, which fires a .22 magnum cartridge. It is loaded with seven cartridges. The closet reveals a cleaning kit, an empty storage box, and boxes of 9mm shells for a Ruger P95. It's not here in the condo, so that one may be on him or at an office. It's a pretty good choice, a very reliable automatic.

Likes magazines but isn't a book reader, especially likes *Casino Player* and *Volo*, the 'art' nude magazine. He is not really a collector of much except for photos and videos of various women he's known, in that biblical sense, stored on a closet shelf. I do find Vivienne in their number, some years younger than now and looking quite fine. She does have a lovely body.

Clothes are about what you'd expect. It tends toward designer knock-offs that are too flashy for my taste, mixed with the odder stuff, like leather pants. It's funny how we make costumes for ourselves with our clothing choices. He's defined himself as a sophisticated, edgy, cool guy, yet the truth is it's kind of a tired, trashy symbolism.

Gale or someone was with him overnight. They were in a hurry to get out this morning.

He's a protein kind of guy, as is Gale or whomever, eggs and sausage for breakfast rather than cereal. Maybe he's on a paleo diet.

I'd say Gale is a frequent overnight guest but doesn't live here. They do like sex toys and maybe a tad kinky with scarves used for tying down limbs. That may be a Gale influence since I see little evidence of it for the dozen or so others in Corvino's collection, including Vivienne.

Lots of marijuana but no other drugs save some prescriptions and over-the-counter stuff; it seems like he suffers from hemorrhoids and bad cholesterol. Oh, and there is a lot of liquor, wine, and beer in the oversized fridge. His wines are overpriced, but some of them are good. The liquor is similarly high-end, with a large array of liqueurs, though whether for himself or his guests is hard to say.

He's a smoker, Marlboros. So is Gale, except she likes Kools.

As for any connection to me, I don't find anything. There is no iPad or laptop here. I'm pretty certain he's an iPad user. So likely I need to return when the man of the house is in.

As I drive home, I muse on how creepy it is, peering at someone's belongings and making judgments of them. I wouldn't particularly want someone to do it to me, but it's part of my job. Of course, my purpose in the past was to discover vulnerabilities I could exploit.

From time to time, someone would rouse my curiosity beyond my purpose, and a very few I found quite fascinating in their material selves. I particularly remember a quite brilliant graduate student with what for me were interesting charts, models, maps, projections, and the like of what society will be like in the future, going one through ten generations out, with alternatives set out based on a variety of assumptions. There were really quite logical inferences based on existing knowledge, with results ranging from extremely bleak to surprisingly, though unlikely, multi-cultural fluorescence.

Not that he will see that future.

From my viewpoint, the Corvino exploration was a bust, neither confirming nor denying his involvement. Maybe Vivienne and her hackers will have more luck.

18. NEIGHBOR LADY — GETTING HELP

"Quan, come here. You got to hear this," calls Vinh to his buddy at the café, which is embarrassing as several patrons look up to see what Vinh is exclaiming about, especially the pudgy girl in pink. Vinh and I are sitting at the small back table, which staff use as our table unless it's especially crowded. Quan, of course, is at the second booth in from the windows, basically across the room, while Gracie is handling the counter. We have eight other customers right now, a trio, a pair, and three singles at their computers or iPads, all regulars except the trio, including Miss Pink, whose real name is Landry Nemeth and who, I think, has a crush on Kal, the weekend barista.

Van Quan is looking up, his face inscrutable as usual. But he rises at Vinh's beckoning and comes over.

I could be annoyed with Vinh, but I don't mind his youthful eagerness, and the possibility occurs to me that maybe Van Quan could be useful in my dilemma. I have seen him possess a quality of menace at times that I might enlist. I know he is a kung fu expert or whatever is the Vietnamese equivalent; I guess vo vinam or maybe vo binhdinh, or maybe he does both schools. Neighborhood knowledge of the schools of fighting gained from a fellow I dated before Corvino.

"What is it, Vinh?" asks Quan.

"Sit, sit. Look, Vivienne asked me to get in touch with the Loi twins and Yin Cuong to help her run down some guys. See what they could come up with, bank statements, criminal records, whatever."

Quan nods and looks at me, "So?"

"Tell him why, Vivienne," commands Vinh.

Curious to see Quan's reaction, I say, "Someone hired a hitman to kill me. I'm trying to figure out who."

Quan just asks, "For real, right?"

"For real."

Interrupting, Vinh says, "Tell him how you know."

"The hitman and I are acquainted. He won't do the job. We're working together to solve this. He wants to know how someone knew to get in touch with him."

"Way cool, huh?" says Vinh. Then, suddenly putting it together, Vinh says, "He's that old dude that was in here, right? The one with your photo."

I nod, "Yeah, that's him."

Contemptuously, Vinh says, "He didn't seem dangerous."

"Do you remember what he looks like?" I challenge Vinh.

"Sure, old guy. White, well, maybe. Not tall, not short. Wasn't ugly or handsome, just sort of average." Vinh shrugs.

I press, "You'd know him if you saw him again?"

"Sure, I mean, yeah, I think so."

"If I lined up six old guys, you could pick him out?"

Now Vinh looks uncertain, "Maybe."

"He's been killing since his early twenties, and he's now in his sixties—a half-dozen to ten a year. And you think he's not dangerous. Yet you can't really remember him." I shake my head, "He's beyond your league, Vinh."

"You know all this?" says Quan.

"Yes, now I do."

Quan says, "Dangerous knowledge."

"Yes, it is. I think I'm okay with him."

"Why?" asks Quan.

I have to think about that. "He's offended, angry, that someone has disturbed his retirement. He could have walked away, shed it like rain bouncing off an umbrella. Instead, he warned me, armed me, and is partnering with me to get both the person who did the hiring and the go-between."

"Why not off you, too, when he's done? Leave no trail, no witness. Vinh here, too, and whoever else."

I think Quan put that last in there to twist Vinh's tail, but who knows, maybe in Quan's world, you do a clean sweep. "He can disappear without having to do so much killing it attracts attention."

Now Quan nods, "Yeah, it could be." A tight smile at Vinh, "You're probably safe, too minor to kill. Be best if you don't remember him."

Vinh wants to feel indignant. I've seen his upset before, but this time, there's just enough possibility to give him disquiet. And Quan's deadpan delivery makes it difficult to say how serious he is. I say, "The hitman's angry at some level, but he's also amused. I think he was becoming bored with retirement."

"What's he do? Hands, knife, gun, explosives?" asks Quan.

"He can, but mostly accidents. You know, weird things: piano falls three floors onto a guy leaving his apartment, a grad student at a university. That kind of thing."

"Whoa, that's cool," exclaims Vinh.

"Useful guy to know if he's willing to work with you," says Quan.

"So, Quan, I'm thinking I could use some insurance," I say.

"Yeah?"

"You ever do bodyguard work?"

"No. But for you, I'd be willing." He shrugs, "How long and how much?" His eyes twinkle. Is it predatory or amusement?

"Earliest of the problem being solved or ten days, at $250 a day." That should cover it for ten days.

"A bodyguard's life is on the line. Make it $500."

"$300."

"Vivienne, no offense, but you want to toy with your life? $500."

Shit, I think. As it is, I've hired the detective, too, and he's paid $750 a day, plus expenses. Maybe I don't need a bodyguard. "$500, but nothing for expenses," I counter.

"Done," he holds out a hand, and we shake.

Then we work out the details, how he'll stay in my spare bedroom. He says he needs to make a few calls to put some plans off and pack clothes. He'll meet me back here in an hour. In the meantime, I'm to stay put. I like how he's taking the assignment seriously.

"You're safe here, right? For now? No pianos above the front door." Then, his tight smile, "And you got Vinh here to protect you."

I slip the pistol Randy gave me onto the table, blocked from the view of other customers by Quan and Vinh, "Yeah, I'm safe here for now."

"Whoa, Vivienne, you get foxier every day," says Vinh.

But I can see that for Quan, this confirms that this is for real.

Waiting for Quan, a pot of Pu-erh tea in front of me, I try to read the book I brought, *Code Name Verity*. It's a good novel and normally holds my interest readily, but not this afternoon, with thoughts whirling about what to do next. Vinh will set the meeting with the hackers. I'll catch up with Randy this evening. I doubt he'll like the idea of Van Quan, but it's my life we're talking about. I've engaged Thomas Cromwell and his associate, Simone Partridge.

I feel like the sands are streaming through a timer.

Surely, whoever wants me dead is expecting it to be done soon. How much patience would he or she have waiting for Randy to act?

Cromwell was a surprise. I guess I was expecting another chameleon-like Randy, someone who takes on the color of wherever he is, instead of a great ugly bear of a man.

How many truly physically ugly people do you meet? I mean, ugly enough, that you want to avert your eyes?

In Thomas Cromwell's case, it isn't his size, going on seven feet tall and broad, an impression of being overweight until you realize it's all solid. No neck to speak of, freckled all over, wisps of blonde and gray hair, an upturned nose so you're peering at his nostrils, bloodshot eyes of pale blue, almost translucent blue, and scars: missing one ear and seams of scar tissue running across the left side of his face, almost like claws took him, losing most of one eyebrow and a chunk of his cheek.

Soft-spoken, though some gravel in his voice. Talks slowly, deliberately, long pauses but no hems or haws or 'you-knows'. The impression at first is of him being slow witted until you realize he is carefully considering what he says, and he prefers listening to speaking. His associate, Simone Partridge, is more what I was expecting. Smallish, dark-hair, plain enough, white yet with something else in her so you could see her among Hispanics, blacks, or Native Americans as well without finding it remarkable. Hard to place her age, one of those timeless people who could be in her late 20's or early 40's.

Cromwell is definitely in his mid-40's, I'd say.

If a mountain lion or alligator didn't chew his face, then I'd guess it was shrapnel from an IED or some other explosive.

Still, I felt confidence in him. His questions were dead-on. He respected my holding off the hitman's identity, and understood the parallel purpose of Randy and I while assuring me it was my purpose that would be his focus. Both he and Simone would work my case, though the primary investigator would be Simone as she attracts less attention. If need be, other associates could join the case.

That the referral to him came from Dr. Farness-Dayan seemed to give me considerable credibility in his eyes. He always referred to her as Judith, rather than Dr. Farness-Dayan, and when I asked, he chuckled and said Farness-Dayan is too long a name. I'd admitted I call her Dr. F-D.

Simone said that sounded Middle Eastern, Effdee.

She didn't say a lot, and that was her only witticism. She, too, asked good questions, but only twice in the hour and a half, simply to clarify my answers to Cromwell.

Vinh returns from serving a new customer, "Okay, you're set to meet the Loi twins at 4 pm. Here's the address. It's their home. They'll be there after school, and the dad and mom don't get home until after six, so you'll have time."

"How old are they?" I blurt.

"Fifteen," says Vinh with a shrug.

Why should I be surprised? Vinh is only 17. "How about the other fellow, Yin Cuong?"

"Cuong's old, past 30." Vinh says, "Don't worry about him. He doesn't come out during the day and hates meeting people. The Loi twins will get him up to speed."

"What are the twins' names?"

"Oh, Chau and Truc. Chau is the girl, Truc the boy."

I nod, wondering if using this group makes sense. When I reached out to my regular hacker buddy, he couldn't take the job. He's in court, not for hacking but for shoplifting. "Okay, 4 pm. Will having Quan along bother them?"

"Shouldn't, they know him, too?" Vinh smiles. "You've seen the twins, too; they've been in here, usually Chau, with her friends. She'd be the quiet one in any pack of girls."

"Maybe I'll recognize them."

From the front, Gracie calls, "Vinh, handle the register."

With a start, I realize it's Simone Partridge at the counter, only now looking young, late teens or early twenties, dressed casually and sexily, make-up bringing out her lips and eyes, making her look surprisingly good. I could easily have missed the connection to the woman I met this morning if she hadn't looked my way for a moment, and I could have sworn winked.

19. NEIGHBOR LADY — EL-EPHANT

"This is preliminary, you understand. Just what my ... colleagues located after an hour or so this afternoon," I tell Randy while I pull up bank account statements on Danny and Todd Bradley Wilkins. "Of course, they both could have other accounts and hidden assets."

We are in Randy's kitchen, and Quan is with us. I've already brought Randy up to speed on Quan and my meeting with Cromwell and Simone Partridge; now we're going through the first few deliverables from the Loi twins.

I'm not sure what Randy is thinking. He showed little reaction to Van Quan other than a terse acknowledgment. I continue, "You're looking at Wilkins' personal account. Separately, I've got the statements for the Uptown Muscle Farm."

"Well, he's not coming up with $105,000 from this account. On the other hand, there's no $12,000 withdrawal either," comments Randy.

"The colleagues will keep digging. Their associate will come online later tonight and work through to morning," I say, feeling a little defensive and unsure why.

Randy nods absently. Closing that file, he opens Danny's statement, "Well, this is more interesting."

I know what he's seeing: debits, debits, debits, then a big deposit, smaller deposits, too, but eroded with so many debits, some really good sized, then another big deposit, and so on. If you were charting it, the spikes would be wild and irregular, with the general trend being downward. At least Wilkins' account was modestly trending up.

"Your Danny is going under," says Randy.

It is surprising how irritating it is to hear Danny referred to as mine.

Randy adds, "Still, a couple of these withdrawals are more than enough to cover $12,000." Looking up at me, Randy says, "Since Danny-boy lost the fitness center, he's heading down the toilet."

I nod, "Yeah, that's what it looks like. Nothing else gives him a regular flow other than that annuity."

Randy looks at Quan, "What do you think, as a more objective view?"

"If it's only these two, then Danny's your man," answers Quan.

"Yeah, if it's only these two," I agree a little bitterly, emphasizing the 'if.'

Randy smiles, "I think you keep all your hackers digging, your Cromwell people too, on your other partners. In the meantime, I'll have a talk with Danny. His apartment turned up nothing, so a talk might be more productive."

"You went through his condo?" I ask. "I thought that was a pretty secure building."

"Sure," he shrugs. "Pretty average place for a guy like him, maybe more tasteful than you might expect. Not that he can afford to stay there a lot longer at the rate he's draining his funds. By the way, has he always carried a gun?"

"Not five years ago, but I couldn't say since then."

"He has a collection of photos and videos. Some were of someone we know that we probably don't want to leave on the premises. When I go back, I'll retrieve them." He smiles brightly at me.

I can feel myself flush, remembering now some of the antics Danny and I got into, his love of taking photos. "Videos?"

"Yes, cameras are hidden in the bedroom and living room."

I feel a touch sick at that thought.

Randy shrugs, "At least you weren't into bondage."

Even Quan smiles at that.

I turn back to the screen and look at the numbers: "The only regular things are debits for car payments, utilities, and mortgage. Oh, and every few months, over three grand each time."

Randy looks again, then hits Previous, returning on the statement. "You're right, every three months, $3,333 to EL-ephant LLC." Scrolling, he adds, "Looks like it started while you two were still partners, goes back ... let's see, 27 months." He glances at me, eyebrow cocked.

I shrug.

"Check the fitness center a couple of years back," suggests Quan. "Just to see if anything like that went from that account."

"Nothing there," I say.

Randy returns to Danny's statement, "That annuity, it's not small. Most people would love $555 coming in every other week. It's as regular as a paycheck. Most annuities are paid monthly, you know. It only looks small compared to his payouts."

Quan nods, and I say, "True. I'd love it." I try to remember if Danny ever said anything about it. I called it an annuity. Was that because of something he said a couple of years back? "You know, $555 every two weeks more than covers a payout of $3,333 every three months."

"So it comes in biweekly and gets paid out in three-month increments. Strange, huh? What happened 27 months ago?" says Randy.

I shrug, "In the wider world, I'm not sure I remember Arab Spring, wasn't it? For me, I moved here."

"Yes, you became my neighbor," agrees Randy. He looks thoughtful, remembering. "A Russian jet disappeared in Indonesia, then they found its debris and black box," he muses. "And Putin was sworn in for a third term. What else?"

Quan says, "Messi set a new European football goal record."

"Didn't that Burmese politician, the Nobel prize lady, you know, the famous lady, get to leave the country?" I ask.

"Aung San Suu Kyu?" says Randy. "Yes, that was then. And Zhou Yongkang in China had to give up his post as head of Security due to the Bo Xilai scandal. But I doubt either event ties to us." He laughs.

Quan says, "Los Zetas was fighting it out with the Gulf Cartel."

We look at him, and he says, "There were Mexican guys in prison following all that then."

Randy shrugs, "Yes, and down there, Los Zetas was killing any journalist brave enough to report on the gang wars." He sighs dramatically, "A very violent country for being our neighbor. I guess we are lucky to have Canada to the north."

"Well, I don't see any direct connections in any of this," I say.

"No, probably not, although I remember wondering if my old

firm was still in business when I read about the Russian jet going down." Randy grimaces and says, "Maybe that Mexican stuff. I lived down there for a time."

Quan says, "The gangs have links here, you know."

"Yes," says Randy pensively, then he smiles, "I doubt it's them; they're known for brutality. This is too subtle." He looks at me, "The only real connection is you moving next door."

Quan says, "The nine payments of $3,333 over 27 months, that's $30,000. The $12,000 is only 40%."

Randy looks at Quan with some respect, "So from where is the biweekly payment coming? And why use Danny as a conduit? He still had the fitness center when this started."

I say, "The annuity deposits are from Ramco, whatever that is." I'm feeling perplexed. Maybe we're putting too much weight on this. Has got anything to do with Randy or me.

Randy asks me, "When did the Rochefort assignment start?"

"That was a year back, in July 2013."

"And the other one, the massage spa research?"

"Almost three years ago now. Well, that's when I first bid on the work. There was a delay, and it didn't kick off until later, maybe a couple of months before I moved here." I can see he's still trying to line up connections.

"You closed on your place in May 2012 and moved in the second week of June, right?" he asks.

"Yes," I nod. Thinking about it and remembering the timing a little clearer, I say, "The bidding and negotiations for the Sybaris Ventures assignment took place from September through November 2011. Then, the company that owns Sybaris put the project on hold. I didn't actually start the work until March 2012."

"Completing it when?"

"The first full report was released at the beginning of May

2012, and then there were additional requests and some follow-ups. It was all wrapped up by the first week of June. That's why I delayed moving in until the second week."

"I seem to recall you being at your place earlier?" he smiles at me.

It's all coming back to me now, "Well, I was over there painting, having some refurbishing completed, that kind of thing for several weeks before the move. I closed on Saturday, May 12. The Emersons were out by May 19. I had the contractor in there the week of May 20, May 21 to May 24, then that Friday morning, the 25th, I inspected it with the contractor and signed off so he could get away early for Memorial Day weekend. I painted three rooms that weekend."

"And you've heard nothing further from Sybaris Ventures?'

I shrug, "No, though that's not too unusual. You complete a project and unless they have something else; you're done. You stay in touch, of course, so next time they think of you."

"With whom did you stay in touch?"

I think about it, "The project director there, Paul Kinkley, and his assistant, Jen Sadler. Though I haven't been in touch in probably four or five months now."

"Sybaris is owned by a cruise line, which is owned by a shipping company, which a financial services company owns, and so on, right?"

"Yes, last time I looked them up, they totaled more than 200 corporate entities from the series of holding companies, down through the operational and sales companies, and on into joint ventures and the like. Something like 250,000 employees worldwide."

"None of them, Ramco or EL-ephant LLC?" asks Quan.

"We could double-check, but not that I remember." By keying,

I enter the name Ramco on the internet, and item after item pops up — Ramco Aviation, Ramco Systems, Ramco Equipment, Ramco Supply, Ramco Reliable, Ramco Engineering- and so on and on.

"A popular name for a company," comments Quan.

I try EL-ephant LLC. There's a design firm in San Francisco using a small-e for elephant, plus a Blu Elephant LLC, a Crystal Elephant LLC, and a Radiant Elephant LLC, also various other colors Ruby, White, Red, Blue Elephants, Elephants that do Racing, Entertainment, Capital Management, etc., but no EL-ephant LLC. I search deeper, and the closest I find is a single web page for EL-ephant with a logo of a small-eared Asian elephant and a phone number.

Randy has an odd look on his face.

"What is it?" I ask.

"I worked for an older fellow long ago. He used the name Edward Fantasia, which I thought was strange. I once saw him sign a document like this," he types L. Edward Fantasia on the computer screen.

"L.E.Fantasia," I say, catching on. "L.E.Fant Asia — Asian elephant."

20. THE CONSULTANT — IMPROVISATION

As the night comes on, Corvino's apartment darkens. I have wiled away the time collecting Vivienne memorabilia from Corvino's closet. I am not an especially lascivious man, but I confess that the temptation is strong to hold onto some of these photos for myself rather than return all of them to Ms. Hawk.

Photos of naked or near-naked ladies in magazines, like Corvino's *Volo* or the traditional *Playboy*, don't interest me much. While the eye may be caught momentarily, it soon glides on past the airbrushed fantasies. I might linger longer on a found photo, maybe on the internet, of someone real, an amateur, natural, perhaps even attempting a provocative pose but awkwardly. But really, what is an image compared to the reality of a person.

Yet a photo of Vivienne, of someone I know, for whom I can readily recall our own interactions, is different. And these photos of Vivienne are beautiful. I suspect there were more, but Corvino only kept the best ones. I especially like one where she sits up in bed, uncovered from the waist and laughing. I have never seen her truly laugh in person.

They are in the knapsack at my feet as I sit in Corvino's chair, watching the entryway and waiting for his return home. I am curious to know whether he will be alone or if Gale or someone else will be with him.

It is just past 20:00, and I can hear a code being entered into the door keypad. There are voices, and both are male. Quietly I step to the wall by the hallway, hidden from immediate sight, pull the face mask down, and screw the silencer on my Markov, the throwaway gun.

You might ask about the mask. It's for their benefit. If they see my face, they'll assume they won't get out alive and would be much harder to control.

They come in, and I can understand what they're saying.

"I tell you, Todd, the money will be there. You will buy out her share, no problem."

Corvino's voice is a low rumble, raspy with the effects of tobacco and alcohol. The higher-pitched voice answering must be Todd Bradley Wilkins, "I just want the bitch out of my hair."

"Believe me, you won't have to worry about her soon."

They enter the room, and I raise the gun, "Excuse me, gentlemen, for interrupting."

They whirl, and Corvino's reflexes are good as he starts for me, but I say, "No, that would be foolish."

Corvino, I recognize from the many photos in the closet. Good looking for a man in his fifties, even with a life of dissipation, normally with a too-ready smile and that reassuring baritone. Wilkins is the bigger man, in very good shape, a face that just misses being handsome, jaw long, nose and ears dainty, the head really looking small for the size of his body-builder torso.

"What do you want? You're the guy that was hired?" asks Corvino.

"What I want is for you both to sit down in the living room. We can chat briefly."

Corvino shrugs, "This better be good."

Wilkins finally finds his voice, "Whatever shit Danny's in got nothing to do with me. He pays his own debts."

"Mr. Wilkins, you may be unwittingly involved. Let's find out. Please do as I ask and take a seat." I smile, though they can't see it through the mask. The fact that I know his name seems to be persuasive for Willkins walks into the living room with Corvino following.

Two kitchen chairs are in the middle of the room. I point with the pistol barrel. A roll of duct tape and blunted children's scissors are on one chair.

"Danny, why don't you sit down." I turn to the big fellow, "Todd Bradley Wilkins, you see the duct tape. If you would be so kind, please tape Danny's feet together, then extend his hands behind the chair and tape them. Tight but not too tight; we don't want to cut the circulation."

Corvino looks like he would balk, but the lift of the gun barrel with its silencer ends any protest. A silencer makes a pistol far more intimidating, I've found.

When Wilkins completes the task, I say, "Now, it's your turn to sit, hands behind the chair. Understand that this is purely precautionary on my part. I wouldn't want to shoot anyone just because you have a sudden itch to scratch."

I tape Wilkins' hands and then his feet. Then, before anything more can be said, I tape his mouth, making sure not to cover his nostrils, though it's going to hurt when that duct tape is pulled free, given his Bandido-style mustache.

Finally, I tape Corvino's mouth. "There, now we're all tidy." I put the tape roll and scissors in the knapsack. To be truthful, they're not as secure as they might think. I was once in a similar situation in Mexico City and still managed to kill the fellow guarding me, though not without taking some wounds of my own. People underestimate what human teeth can do.

"You know the game twenty questions, right Danny? Well, we're going to play a questioning game, too. If all the answers are correct, then tonight can end quietly." I turn to Wilkins, "Todd Bradley Wilkins, I may have a couple of questions for you, too, but if not, then I am sorry for inconveniencing you."

I extract a folding knife from my left pocket. Extracting the blade with my teeth allows me to keep the gun on target. "See if you can open your mouth a tad, Danny. I don't want to cut your lips." I give him a moment, then cut a small slit in the duct tape over his mouth. It will sound odd, but he'll be able to answer questions with more than a nod or a shake of his head.

"Okay, let's start. Danny, you receive biweekly checks from Ramco, correct?" I kick his shin hard enough to wake him to the idea that he must answer.

He nods and croaks, "Yes."

"Every two weeks for the past 27 months, ever since Vivienne Hawk moved to Winnetka, correct?"

An affirmative nod.

"Who or what is Ramco?"

No answer, so a clout to his ear. He manages, "I don't know."

I wait, tapping his knee lightly with the flat of the knife. He twists in the chair, so I tap a little harder at the point of the blade.

Hoarsely, in his raspy voice, he says, "A guy from way back, when I was in juvie, contacted me. Said I could make three grand if I was willing to transfer money. One grand upfront, one grand after a year, and one grand at the end, which could be anywhere from a year to a year and a half more, so I figured what's the harm. It ain't much, but every little bit helps."

"When were you in juvenile detention?"

"Back in '75 and '76."

"You stay in touch with this guy for thirty some years. What's his name?"

"Pouch we call him. Maurice something, but we just call him Pouch."

Conversationally, I say to him, "You know if you cut a guy's Achilles tendon right there behind the ankle, he can't walk on that leg ever again without a crutch?"

I turn to Wilkins, "Being into good health for the body, you likely know that that there's an amazing number of places in the body where you can cause real damage, and, I'm told, cause excruciating pain, without coming close to killing a guy." I wait for his nod, then say, "I knew a guy who was really into using needles, not the little acupuncture needles but good-sized horse doctor kind of needles that he sharpened. Whoa, the kind of damage he could cause, you just wouldn't believe. I always wanted to try it but never thought I'd have the nerve. I have a delicate stomach. Still, I like to carry one with me just in case I get the opportunity and feel up for it."

Stepping back, I set the knife down, and take a long, relatively broad needle from the knapsack, and remove the cork protecting the sharpened end point. "This guy would use it in the person's mouth or eye socket, for example, or in the ear or nostril; he also had this thing about using it on people's private parts."

I set the needle down by the knife and turn back to Corvino, "Danny, we can make this evening easy or a night that will be etched in your memory forever. Now, let me ask about Pouch, I want everything you know about him. And, please, for your sake, don't lie. I hate lying and just can't help punishing a liar."

It takes an hour to get as much as Danny Corvino and Todd Bradley Wilkins know. Of course, Danny is a shit and has to be persuaded to follow the ground rules of telling everything and not lying about it. I try to keep the bloodletting to a minimum while crossing his pain threshold.

The first story is that Maurice Brown or Pouch has an uncle, Horace, who is under an obligation to a guy you don't cross. That guy is Ramco, among other things. Horace has Maurice come up with someone, Danny in this case, to be a cut-out for transferring the money to EL-ephant LLC every three months. Pouch chooses Danny because Danny's got a business that can hide cash flow.

Well, that story doesn't wash. So, after a little to and fro, Danny admits he was conspiring to kill Vivienne Hawk. He went to Pouch to get the job done, but that level of violence wasn't Pouch's thing, so Pouch turned to Horace. Like me, though, Horace is trying to retire.

Ramco gets wind of this through Horace and learns who Vivienne Hawk is. He says he'll buy out Danny's interest if Danny can come up with a plausible fall guy for the job.

Danny is delighted not to pay. There's a guy he owes money to that he'd like to snare, Todd Bradley Wilkins. If he can get rid of his partner and remove his chief creditor, life could be roses. It takes a while to set the trap, and Ramco can't come up with the money quickly, so they agree to put up with the current situation for two years.

Not what Danny wanted, but he was going to pay Pouch $10,000 to take care of the problem. Ramco wants this killing they plan to be done at arm's length. Ramco arranges for EL-ephant LLC to be the clearing house. The killing will go down once the full amount is paid, only it's thirty thousand, not ten, but it's not Danny's money so why should he care and he still gets three grand for his trouble as well.

So Danny temporarily loses the fitness center to Wilkins, and Wilkins is set to be the fall guy.

Hearing all this, Wilkins is frothing on learning he was to be the patsy for the murder of Vivienne Hawk. He claims Danny came to him with a plan to buy out Vivienne's share. Danny didn't want Vivienne knowing he was buying back in. Then Wilkins and Danny would be partners with the idea that Danny has a backer who would be willing to finance expansion as franchisers. The backer is Ramco, who is already paying Danny over a grand a month as a retainer to consult on entering the fitness industry.

Wilkins is innocent of any plan to murder Vivienne Hawk, although he'd be happy, in his words, "To see the interfering bitch gone from the center."

With some prodding, Wilkins does confess that he's doing a fair business, over and above club fees, in selling health and virility supplements, recreational drugs, and harder drugs through the club. Hawk is suspicious of all the supplements being sold, but is, so far, unaware of the drug trade.

According to Wilkins, Danny and Ramco do know about the drug sales and view that as good value in assuring franchise profits.

That's it.

Corvino has never met Ramco, Horace being the link. Corvino has had three phone conversations with Ramco on landlines. Ramco always called, and Corvino had always to be at specified public phone on time. No call lasted longer than five minutes.

So the obvious question is where do I find Horace and Maurice Brown?

With that answered, I shoot Corvino in the eye. Well, technically, I have Wilkins shoot Danny, overcoming his reluctance with the threat of the needle in his own eye.

After that, I untape Wilkins. Have him clean-up in the bathroom. Return his chair to the kitchen, and have him take a drink of water and swallow a small pill, assuring him that it's only to calm him down. I have him take a breathing exercise called 4-7-8, showing him how and saying that it's meant to calm him before we leave the apartment.

Then we exit. I go out the front door after seeing Wilkins over the balcony rail with the Markov pistol in his hand, its firing pin now disabled. A fall or leap, in this case, from six floors up could be survived depending on what's below. I make certain it's a hard concrete surface.

It's tidy enough for improv.

21. THE CONSULTANT — WHAT A GODDAMN WASTE

VIVIENNE, TO HER CREDIT, I SUPPOSE, IS APPALLED. I'M NOT SURE what she expected. I feel confident that I have explained thoroughly that I am a killer. Van Quan, on the other hand, seems unaffected by the deaths of Danny and Todd, though he likely didn't know them.

"Think of me as a magician. Now you see them, now you don't," I say to her. More reasonably, I add, "Vivienne, Danny ordered your death."

"And Wilkins, what did he do?"

"Used the fitness center as a front for dealing drugs," I answer.

She goes silent.

Thinking she's calming down, I say, "So that was the good news, they're out of the picture. Now the bad news is that Ramco also wants you dead, and we don't know who or what Ramco is or why Ramco is fixed in the purpose of your demise."

"EL-ephant?" asks Quan.

"Oh, yes, them too, but only as a contractor. We may be able to rescind that order. I think they're my problem to solve." I smile, I hope, genuinely.

I try to understand the effect of my words on Vivienne. She's been a trooper so far, but killing seems to unsettle her.

It's difficult for someone like myself to really get into the head of someone like Vivienne; well, really, like most people. I mean, intellectually, I understand she's feeling a turmoil of emotions. But I just don't feel the same intensity for others.

Really, from the look on her face, I'm guessing revulsion directed at me.

This morning, walking over to Vivienne's condo to give her the good news, I couldn't help but be pleased that no crows were in the trees or on the lawn. Oh, I saw one flying east toward the lake, but he could have been anyone's crow, not one of mine.

"Randy, I just … I know you think you're helping … I mean, you killed two people," says Vivienne, her voice going a little shrill again.

"Well, yes. Try to think of me as a force of nature, like a tidal wave or avalanche. Normally, it's really not personal, just bad luck." I admit it's a feeble analogy. "People die unexpectedly every day. You know, a pile up on the Interstate, a sinkhole opening in the back yard, wind blowing down a tree limb … "

"An encounter with a rabid dog," offers Quan, which is closer to the mark.

I nod, "And that's not taking into account the suicide bomber in the marketplace, the pedophile with a youngster, the drunk husband beating his wife. It's a fucking tough world out there, and I'm simply part of it."

Vivienne closes her eyes; I think she's counting to ten or maybe to a hundred.

"Look, if you're worried about this coming back to bite us, I really made it easy for the police. Todd Bradley Wilkins killed Danny. Then Todd jumped off the balcony. Case closed. Police like it simple, not some convoluted hard-to-prove conspiracy-driven scenario." Her eyes are still closed, and maybe she's praying, not counting. "I wore surgical gloves and booties, a face mask, you know, really careful. Very little trace of me there, especially compared to Gale, and who knows who else Danny had over, which reminds me, I have those photos and videos to give you."

That last point brings her back to the surface. She opens her eyes and stares at me for a moment. She shakes her head slowly, "All right, Randy, enough. What's done is done."

"Right," I say brightly. "So I think our next problem is Ramco." She stares at me, so I go on, "Corvino did give me a lead. Two fellows were go-betweens, Maurice and Horace Brown. While I follow up with them, you can have your people — you know, Cromwell and the hackers — see what they can find about Ramco. My guess is it's one guy without a lot of money, or else why string this out over fifty-some biweekly payments. And the guy is dirty, a criminal or cop or some government functionary. How else would the Browns know him and he know about EL-ephant?"

She nods, understanding my logic.

Quan says, "I betcha they met in prison."

"Ramco and Horace?" I ask.

"Yeah."

"Probably you're right." Quan is a useful kind of guy. I wonder how he makes his living. "Though you never know, it could be a cop who busted Horace, a parole officer, or whatever."

I open my knapsack and pull out the three video cartridges and the stack of photos, mostly 4 x 6, but a couple of 5 x 7s that must be the ones Danny liked best. The one of Vivienne just coming out of the shower, the light through the translucent window hitting her with a golden color, is on top. She is lovely in that shot. It's not really a sexy photo; it's more artistic, more basic like she's the epitome of woman.

It's obvious that Quan likes the photo, too, so maybe his taste and Danny's are similar.

Vivienne glances at the top photo, then, with one finger, flicks through the next several. "Five years ago, six in some of these. Surprising how besotted I was over that man." She seems disdainful of the photos, oblivious to her own beauty in her dislike of the photos' context.

Then there are tears running down her cheeks, "What a goddamn waste."

I don't know if she's referring to her time with Danny or to Danny himself.

Without much empathy for others, it's easy for someone like me to imagine indifference to causing pain and sorrow. Yet that's not the case for most criminals and other small-minded people like Danny. They're like most folks. They require elaborate self-justifications for the evil that they do, and the believers in one faith or another require even greater ability to excuse their guilt before their gods, usually by attributing evil to others, especially lack of the right faith. "Yes, well, as you say, what's done is done." I try my smile on her.

Later, back alone at my place, I am thinking about my mother. Why? Not like I often do. Maybe it's the influence of Vivienne.

Anyway, I came to the U.S. when I was eleven after a couple of years in Canada. My mother was Finnish. My father was Canadian but originally from Corsica, coming to Canada as a child. Of course, I could be lying. Maybe she was Lithuanian, Latvian, or Estonian; maybe he was from Sardinia, Malta, or Majorca. Does it really matter?

We lived in Buffalo or Cleveland or Detroit, one of those rust-belt cities, back when it was the rust-belt. Detroit remains, so I guess while Buffalo and Cleveland seem to be re-inventing themselves.

Father was long gone by the time we came to the U.S.

Mother was a painter. You didn't need a green card to paint art. She also let various men support us. No green card for that, either.

She wasn't much of a painter, but enough to get by at summer art fairs. Every year, her watercolors had a theme or two. One year floral still life. Next year, bubbling brooks in scenic settings. The year after, children at play.

From May through September, we traveled in a beat-up van from one art fair to another, all over the country's eastern half. For the rest of the year, we'd be in Buffalo or another city. October through April, she painted. Painted and home-schooled me until high school. Passing exams and writing essays got me into high school. Then I boarded out the months she was on the road.

By October of my third year of college, she didn't return. I never discovered what happened to her. Her truck was found, by then the van had been in the junkyard a few years and she had a pick-up with a cabin top. Her art was packed neatly in the truck. That was down in Virginia.

My inheritance, an old pick-up truck with more than 100,000 miles on the odometer, thirty-seven framed watercolors, another dozen unframed, and about eighty prints, her business cards, some art supplies, the stuff in the apartment where she lived after I got my own place when Melody and I married.

Most people would have grieved, demanded answers, and searched. I might have, except college was a challenge, and there was Melody to worry about, so I never got around to seeking answers. Now, forty-some years later, I find myself wondering what happened to her.

Today, seeing Vivienne upset over a pair of shits like Danny and Todd Bradley Wilkins makes you kind of wonder. Who or what kind of shit ended my mother's life? Because I think she would have come back for me if she could. I'm not positive, but I think she loved me or, at least cared about me. She had always been there, maybe not a demonstrative mother, maybe finding me irritating a lot, especially when she tried to paint. Summers were usually better for us.

I liked Mom or, at least, relied on her. We rarely argued. Hell, we rarely talked. We didn't need to. She was my mother and I was her son.

Nothing is left of her except my memories, everything else gone what with too many moves and too much desperation in my life. I can't hold onto things. When I die, doubtless, that's her end too.

She was, I think, a pretty good mother.

22. NEIGHBOR LADY — UNLIKE WHAT I FEEL NOW

I AM WAITING AT THE GLENCOE ROAST, A CAFÉ IN THE COMMUNITY north of Winnetka. It is not as large as our place in the city, but it is still adequate. I like the owner, the Polish lady. She's here most of the time, with normally one other per shift. Her grown son works here some days, and there are four other part-timers.

A different clientele than our café, of course, many north shore ladies, tutors, or college-entry advisors with their charges, small committees who like meeting here from churches or schools or the village government, members of the Polish community, and the usual flotsam and jetsam of business people, students, retirees, and couples. Oh, plus the moms just before school lets out and then the after-school kids, with more than enough money for their afternoon treats.

I'm in the back, beyond the sideboard with its napkins, stir sticks, assorted additives like cinnamon, cocoa, or honey, and the jugs of milk, cream and ice water. Like we have at our café in the city. There is a nook here with comfortable chairs. My latte sits untouched on the low coffee table. I wait.

Thomas Cromwell and Simone Partridge enter together. I raise my hand, though I believe Cromwell already noted where I am sitting. He proceeds here while Ms. Partridge stops at the counter to place their orders.

"Ms. Hawk, how are you doing?" says Cromwell.

There is a stir among the closer tables of North Shore ladies, the ugly scars on the man causing a couple of gasps, but Cromwell ignores the disruption. I am sure he has long concluded that the reactions his looks create are the onlookers' problem, not his.

"I'm not certain, Mr. Cromwell. Given the deaths of Danny Corvino and Todd Bradley Wilkins, I'm not sure I am still under threat." I had decided to act the innocent and see what the private investigators make of the killings.

Cromwell takes a seat before responding. What may be a smile or a grimace flits across his face, "From what we've learned, the authorities are undecided whether the deaths are a murder-suicide or a double murder. The crime scene evidence points to the first conclusion, yet it doesn't jibe well with the instincts of the homicide detectives, two very experienced fellows. No one sees Wilkins as suicidal."

I try to act surprised and likely fail, "Oh. It's not as obvious then as I was led to believe?"

Again the grimace on his face, "Obvious? Yes, I think so; your man has been at work. Provable? Probably not."

Simone Partridge joins us, carrying ice water for Cromwell and a mocha for herself, "Hello, Vivienne."

Today, she looks quite plain again. It's amazing how she can alter her appearance with changes in clothing and make-up. "Hi, Simone. What have you learned?"

She glances at Cromwell, who nods. She proceeds, ticking my partners and employees off on her fingers, "Your partnerships for the nail salon and café seem to be as straightforward as you described. Sadie Epstein is having an affair with the barista, Macario Acosta, which doesn't seem to be an issue for Do Duong. She is also an occasional lover with two other men. Do Duong— Joel — in turn, has a long-term lover as well, Miss McCandless, who is another accountant at his firm. I think the only tension that could be disruptive is with Macario Acosta's wife, Maria. They have two children." She shrugs, "Maybe Maria will put up with it, as this is the longest Macario has ever held a job."

I nod.

Simone says, "As for the other cafe employees, Grace Freen has an extensive rap sheet from her early twenties through her mid-thirties but nothing for the past sixteen years. She is a reformed dove. She sends money monthly to an aunt who is in assisted living in downstate Illinois. Her passions do seem to be yoga, reading, and her two cats."

"As for the other baristas, Nicole Harris and Kalman Buda, I have not had time to pursue either deeply, but they appear to be as claimed. Nicole is a full-time student at Oakton Community College, working on an associate degree as a medical technician. She has no romantic attachment currently. Kalman Buda's full-time job is at a Jiffy Lube, a job he dislikes. He's searching for something cleaner. He lives with an older brother and the brother's family. He is an amateur photographer."

Nothing new in what Simone is telling me except the details of Sadie and Joel's relationships. Still, I suppose it's confirmation that what I know of these folks is true. She's not said anything of Vinh.

"Turning to the nail salon," continues Simone, "is altogether more interesting."

By interesting, I take it to mean in terms of a threat to me.

"Roy Peterson, Monique's husband, lost his job three months ago. Though it's not confirmed, I believe it was due to embezzlement for which Mr. Peterson has made restitution. That restitution has depleted their savings."

I am surprised that Monique hasn't confided in me.

Simone continues, "According to the nail technicians, Peterson has been urging Monique to sell the business. Apparently, Monique discussed this only with Do Phuang but asked her to sound out the other girls about jointly buying Monique's share of the business."

Why not come to me? I wonder. Maybe it's because I hinted some months back about Monique buying me out. "If there was embezzlement, why?"

"Roy Peterson has a mistress."

"Oh," that's a shock. I thought they were a very happy couple.

"If you were to die, according to your partnership contract, insurance would pay out a significant sum more than sufficient to buy your share of the business from your estate," says Cromwell.

I nod. I knew this, of course. There was the same condition in the event of Monique's death.

"So, there is a motive in a sudden need for money and a convenient means for obtaining it, your death," says Simone.

She shrugs, "As for the nail technicians, the only possibility of buying the business is if Do Phuang's brother, Joel, lends his sister the cash. From what I've learned thus far, there is nothing out of the ordinary with the four girls."

I'm still stuck on why Monique hasn't talked with me. It hurts. No doubt she is hurting, too. Maybe it's pride or shame getting in the way. "So you're not pursuing anything more from the partnerships?"

Simone shakes her head no, and then Cromwell says, "Have the police contacted you yet about the deaths of Corvino and Wilkins?"

"Yes, I spoke with Detective Thompson by phone. He said they may have follow-up questions."

"There was no contract provision about insurance in the partnership papers for the fitness center, right?" asks Simone.

"You mean like for Monique's and the café? No, that was my first partnership, and the attorney I used then wasn't too sharp."

Cromwell says, "Well, at least you have no motive for gain the police can latch onto."

It hits me then that I will probably have to manage the fitness center for a time while Wilkins' estate is settled. Or would the executor want to close the center? I need to call my lawyer to get on top of this. I sigh, surprised to be wishing Todd Bradley Wilkins was alive. "So what's next?"

"Based on what you told us in your call, we go after Ramco and EL-ephant LLC next," says Cromwell. "You'll share whatever your tech search people come up with on that score, correct?"

"Yes, of course."

There is a pause as Cromwell and Simone exchange looks, then Cromwell adds, "You need to leash your associate. If we do come up with anything, it must be handled through legal recourse."

I nod, "Yes." Truthfully, I have no idea how one leashes Randy Pryor.

After an awkward silence, as if they could hear my thoughts, Simone says, "Our first line of inquiry will begin with determining if there is any link between Ramco or EL-ephant with your Sybaris Ventures and Rochefort assignments."

There is little more to discuss, and the meeting soon ends. Accompanying Cromwell and Simone out, I overhear conversations going on around us — a woman and garden designer planning landscaping changes, a trio discussing a new hairdresser — all seeming so normal, so safe, so unlike what I feel now.

23. THE CONSULTANT — DAMN IT, I FEEL SOMETHING

According to the information Vivienne provided from her hacker friends, Pouch should be living at 319 Howard Street, except that's the Howard station's address on the Red Line of the EL. His uncle, Horace Brown, is supposed to be on the 7200 block of North Damen Avenue, above Rogers and near Chase. Driving there, I'm thinking it may turn out to be a fake address like Pouch's place.

Again courtesy of the hackers, I have a photo of Horace taken some years ago when he drove a taxi. It's better than the blurry photo they came up with for Pouch, which looks like it was downloaded from a surveillance camera. I glance at them while at a stoplight. These are not the best pictures, but should be adequate to recognize these guys.

Both appear to be big men, though there's something odd about Pouch, like too much tilt to one side. Could it be from a stroke? Or something congenital?

No matter, really. They won't be the first big men I've handled.

I pull to the curb up the block from Horace's address. Cruising by, it looked like a decent enough place, a condo building given the gates, probably sixteen units, with eight in each wing, at a quick glance, although there could also be basement apartments. Early morning, so if he lives here, he should be in. An hour before most people get up to go to work. If he's a party guy or has a late-night job, all the better, he should be asleep.

The gate is no problem. Now, it's time to find 3B from the back side of the building. That should be it. Up we go. Okay, there is no obvious alarm system, but several extra locks are on the rear door. There are two accessible windows, except as I'm about to use the glass cutter on the larger one, I hear a small dog yapping on the other side of the wall. Then the dog starts going batshit with its barking, the yips having become bellows, so I'm guessing a beagle.

I step back and find a deck chair. I move it out of view from the windows and wait. While waiting, I screw the silencer onto the Nite Hawg. I think my eyes suffer from mild presbyopia because the threading on the Nite Hawg is hard for me to discern here in the shadows. It takes a moment for the silencer to be fitted.

By now, the dog's bays have roused the household. I can hear cursing and what sounds like a man yelling, "Maybelle, shut your damn dog up." If the neighbors get roused, too, I will likely need to exit the scene.

Bolts are being thrown and locks turning before a runty dog that is, in fact, at least part beagle comes hurtling out the door, and there in the open door must be Maybelle, a behemoth though the skimpy pink lingerie may accentuate her size. The dog is a smallish mutt, but it seems to be all teeth, and in the moment it takes me to deal with the animal, Maybelle is already retreating at the sight of a masked man.

I wish I could say, like in a movie's credits, no animal was hurt, but I don't have time for niceties. I boot the creature off the deck to the ground below and charge for the door. Except Maybelle wasn't retreating; she just stepped back to gather up steam and is now coming at me at full speed with an iron skillet in her hand. I'm like the hunter who realizes the rhinoceros is charging him.

Fortunately, I am sufficiently adroit to step aside, duck the swinging fry pan, and trip the lady as she goes by. Her momentum carries her to a painful crunch against the deck rail. I attempt to hoist her over, which is my undoing as I can't budge her, and she turns to throttle me. The thrust of the silencer-weighted barrel to the bridge of her nose causes her to pause.

We stare at each other for an eternity that's only a few seconds long. Then her ham-like fist comes crashing into my gun hand. The resulting shot takes much of her ear, though it does little to stop her. She is on top of me like a dump truck unloading many yards of sand. I could drown between her enormous breasts.

My gun hand is pinned. So I bite her nose, as if I'm a ravenous boy chewing a hot dog. The effect is all that I hoped. She heaves herself back, breaking free. I manage to sweep the pistol barrel into her right eye, causing a screech that could wake the dead, but I am free of her. Clubbing her viciously dazes her, and I think I'm getting the best of the woman when a voice behind me says, "You hit Maybelle one more time, and I blow you in half."

I fire three rounds in that instant of turning, taking in Horace in his pajama bottoms, holding an old-fashioned double-barrel shotgun. His gun should have fired if he'd just taken a second to slip off the safety. As it is, only one of my slugs hit him, but it is enough to throw him back onto the threshold of the rear door.

Maybelle is up and at me but goes crashing down with a bullet through her knee.

This is not happening as planned.

That's when, ungainly, Pouch barrels out the back door only to slip on his uncle's blood and fall hard onto the softball bat he's carrying. Despite breaking his arm, he makes a desperate lunge for Horace's shotgun. Unlike Maybelle, he goes still when a pistol barrel hits the bridge of his nose.

Running out of time, I rasp, "Who is Ramco?"

No answer, so I thrust the pistol harder, "Maurice, last chance. Who is Ramco?"

"Mac," his voice surprisingly shrill for such a big body. He seems older than his uncle.

"Mac?"

"McQuillan. Robbie McQuillan."

"Where do I find him?"

"Indianapolis, maybe." Then, at the push of the silencer, "He moves around a lot. He thinks he's going to be the next senator from Indiana. Crazier than a hoot."

This is perplexing but I'll think about it later, "What's his connection to EL-ephant LLC?"

"None. That's my uncle's doing." Then, "Did you kill Horace?"

"I don't think so." With that, I withdraw, rushing down the stairs and to the fence line.

All three still alive, though all damaged. As for me, I am winded from the run. The likelihood of being caught on camera is high, but I doubt I'll be in town much longer, and it won't be easy to identify the fleeing figure on any video footage.

At least, that's what I tell myself.

Waiting through the day is difficult. I'm antsy about going after Ramco, but first, there's more to learn about El-ephant LLC. I avoid Vivienne Hawk. If there is blowback from my early morning adventure, I don't want it to smear her.

Am I feeling something for her?

No, I don't think so; I'm just being practical.

As always, the news report on TV blurts out more than it should while getting the basic story down wrong, fortunately.

Horace is out of danger at St. Francis Hospital in Evanston, resting nicely. Maybelle is at St. Francis, too, while Maurice has been released. The three are being talked up as heroes for thwarting an armed intruder.

So I will be testing the security at St. Francis later. Horace and I still need to talk.

You know of all the saints, I think Francis of Assisi is one of the more attractive. It's not that I'm into saints. Of the originals, the apostles, I like Thomas the Doubter best. I think he was right to doubt.

Well, with that, I'm going to bed. I'll set the alarm for 1:30 and see if I can visit Horace between 2:30 and 3:00 in the morning.

Timing may not be everything, but it helps. Wearing a white lab coat with a fake St. Francis ID and carrying what appears to be a medical folder certainly made entry possible, but the distraction of a noisy family with a bloody teenager at Emergency made it easy, and that was the luck of timing.

Some things are easier too because I'm old. The old get deemed as either authoritative or harmless, as if they were never wild or even evil when younger.

Finding Horace's room is not difficult. Unfortunately, he is sharing it with a restless neighbor. Still, I pull the curtain around Horace's bed in the time-honored hospital method of assuring a minimum of privacy.

The man is drugged. The bullet took him in his right shoulder, just where the clavicle meets it. Not a serious wound, really, unless he gets a staphylococcus infection from staying at a hospital.

He's sufficiently alert after I prod him a few times with the needle point of my horse-sized hypodermic. His eyes grow wide at the sight of me; even with the surgeon's mask on my face, he knows me from our earlier encounter, though the Nite Hawg with its silencer probably gives it away, too.

Truthfully, I thought about tossing the gun in Lake Michigan after its use in our fray. Then, I decided it was still okay for this venture despite the likelihood of police ballistics trying to match slugs to their database. There were five shots in that first encounter, and I guess that at least three were recovered.

Still, in this case, familiarity does not bring contempt but rather respect or, better, abject fear at the sight of the pistol and its silencer. I say softly, "Horace, we weren't properly introduced before. You can call me Killer, and I can call you Victim if that's how you want it."

His eyes bulge.

I continue, "Alternatively, you can tell me all you know about EL-ephant LLC and Ramco."

He nods. Maybe it's not the pistol in my right hand but the long needle in my left that makes him suddenly cooperative. The words spill out of him, "Don't know much. Just that there's a number you can call. People get sent out to solve problems and you know take care of business. Somebody disappears or gets into a fatal accident or offs himself, those kinds of things happen. Expensive, though. But clean neat. That's all."

"How is payment made?"

"Money gets wired. Account changes each time. Even the phone number changes pretty often."

"How do you get the new account and phone numbers?"

"If'n they knows you, shows up on your cell phone."

Maybe we're getting to the heart of it. "How do they know you, Horace?"

He shrugs, "Not sure. They contact me the first time. Make me a broker."

"When was this?"

"Oh, it must be six years ago now after I had my court case. Was up for manslaughter, but the case was dismissed." He smiles bleakly. "My lawyer brought in a consultant, Mr. Kalvaitis. After that, the case sort of went away."

Kalvaitis? Mr. Smith in Lithuanian. Anna K. connection, I'm pretty certain. "Did you meet Mr. Kalvaitis?"

"No, but I did see him once with my lawyer, Terence Dikjas."

"Can you describe him?"

Slyly, Horace says, "Long time ago."

I rest the tip of the needle on Horace's cheek, just below his right eye. Hurriedly, Horace says, "Very thin and tall, maybe in his mid-thirties. There was some silver in his dark hair. That's all I remember."

"And Terence Dikjas?"

"Oh, he died. He went in his sleep very peaceful, a couple of years later. He was an old fart." Horace actually chuckles, "I liked Dikjas for a lawyer. Always fair and upfront with me, though pricey."

I nod, "Now, tell me about Ramco."

A sigh from Horace, "Oh, that's Corvino's guy, someone Pouch knows. Crazy guy, maybe from syphilis, you know. He says he's going to be a U.S. senator from Indiana, but he needs to clear up a few things from his past."

I nod encouragingly, so Horace continues, "One is this

Vivienne Hawk. We laughed at him, but he kept paying Corvino money. I mean for years, like clockwork. Finally, there was enough for me to make the call. Corvino got some, I get some, and Pouch got some, and the rest got wired to the elephant." His eyes narrow, "Corvino, that was you? Not that other guy, Wilkins?"

"Pouch is older than you?" I ask.

"Yeah, ten years. It probably seems weird, me being his uncle. Mama had twenty-one children. I'm the youngest. Pouch is the son of my eldest brother."

"So Pouch knew Corvino in Juvie, right?"

"Yeah, they were tight ever since."

"Mac, that is Ramco, knows Pouch from where?"

"Not sure, you could ask ..." stops and gives me a bleak look.

Behind the surgeon's mask, I smile, "I could ask Pouch?"

Horace waves an arm, "The guy used to work in Chicagoland. I think a Sheriff's deputy or something, maybe in Forest Preserve security. Something, anyway. Comes up to Chicago still about every other week. He gets his rocks off, you know. Won't do it in Indiana."

"Where?"

"One hotel or another. Deaver gets him a girl; he likes young, skinny black or Asian girls."

"Deaver?"

"You'd be a fool to mess with Deaver. Don't nobody mess with Deaver."

Amused, I ask, "Why's that?"

"Deaver be bad enough, but he gots Kilgore, too. And Kilgore is terrifying."

I wonder how bad a man can be to terrify Horace. Horace is a big man, not soft either, though; having seen Maybelle, I'd say he's not as big as he might be.

"Is there a hotel Mac favors?"

Horace shrugs, "I don't keep track of the man."

"So, how do you know about his habits?"

"Pouch, he knows. Years ago, this Mac liked staying at the purple Hyatt in Lincolnwood. Nowadays, maybe the Orrington in Evanston or Holiday Inn there, which is cheaper."

"When's he due in town?"

"Don't know. Soon. Pouch said there's a bonus if this Hawk thing is wrapped up by the weekend. Pouch wants me to call the elephant and get them to hurry it along."

"You have a current number for EL-ephant?"

"In my cell phone," he nods at the nightstand.

I secure his cell phone, "Okay, I guess that's it for now," I say pleasantly, taking the needle off his cheek.

"I'm cooperative, right? No need to do me. You can bet mums the word from me. You a ghost, and I never saw you." There is sweat on Horace's brow.

It's stupid of me not to kill him. But I'm doing many stupid things now. "Horace, I'm going to give you a pass. But it's conditional. If you do give into temptation and talk to anyone, Maybelle and Pouch included, then I will know, and your pass will be rescinded."

I'm partway down the stairs and thinking, what a fool I am. I turn to go back to shoot Horace but stop short with the image of Vivienne Hawk in my mind, her reaction to the killings of Corvino and Wilkins.

Continuing down the stairs, I tell myself that it's only because Vivienne would likely come apart with more killing. It may be true. Yet I don't really need Vivienne any longer. I could pursue EL-ephant LLC on my own, and Ramco, too, for that matter.

What danger is Vivienne in now, anyway?

Sure, this Mac wants her dead for his own insane reasons, but if I take out EL-ephant, what means does he have?

Why should I feel any attachment to Vivienne Hawk? That's what I ask myself. And I don't really have an answer. Yet, damn it, I feel something, maybe a simple curiosity to see how it all turns out.

24. THE CONSULTANT — PROCOPIUS

HORACE'S PHONE IS THE KEY. I FIND THE CURRENT PHONE NUMBER for EL-ephant and, thanks to the phone's history, a whole series of older phone numbers. I'm thinking Vivienne's hacker friends could probably make faster progress with this than I can.

But first, I think I'll deal with Ramco, which means finding Pouch. With Horace's phone, I text Pouch, asking where he is now.

In a few moments, he replies, no doubt he's thinking I'm Horace. 'At the Oasis.' It takes me a moment to place the bar out on Sheridan Road. I think they close by 4 am. I text back, 'You need to meet a guy at Starbucks. Corner of Sheridan and Columbia at 7. Guy from the elephant, to close out the deal.'

Pouch texts back, 'WTF, why?'

I respond with, 'You wanted me to hurry elephant, before the weekend. Just do it.'

Pouch's response is, 'OK.'

It's good. Now, Pouch will come to me.

After I forward the EL-ephant phone numbers to Vivienne for the hackers, I go home to catch a few hours of sleep.

Though I prefer supporting independent coffee shops, I use Starbucks as a backup. They are reliable, and I like the company's environmental philosophy. The most beautiful Starbucks I've been to was in Seoul, Korea. I used to collect Starbucks experiences from different locales. In general, I prefer their overseas stores, maybe because it's a touch of home when in a foreign land, but more likely because they tend to be less cookie cutter than in the U.S.

This Starbucks on Sheridan Road is a typical shop. The early morning line, though some of the tables are already occupied.

I'm there ten minutes early and sit in the back, sipping a cappuccino. I've already ratcheted the Glock before leaving the car.

Here's a complaint: in Starbucks, they serve you in a paper cup, a take-out cup, unless you specifically ask for a mug, even if you're sitting in the shop. Most independents will serve you in a China mug or cup if you are staying on site.

Given Starbucks's commitment to the environment, I find that habit of theirs both annoying and contradictory.

But I digress as Pouch enters the store, he looking all about to find the contact. His arm is in a sling, and he looks like he could use a shower and a good night's sleep. Of course, some of that bleariness could be from drink even if the Oasis closed three hours ago.

Most customers are standing in line then leaving with their coffees this time of morning. The baristas are busy. Even the few customers who stay are buried in newspapers, their laptops, or mobile phones. I ease the Glock free under the table so it's out of sight. I wave to Pouch.

He shambles over in his lop-sided way. Customers step aside, looking at him oddly, though he doesn't seem to notice.

No mask today to hide my features, so I half expect him to recognize me from our encounter yesterday morning. As he approaches, there's no hint that he's made me for the intruder.

Coming closer, he says, "Horace said to meet you. You're from the elephant?"

He is really asking why he needs to meet an EL-ephant agent. With my left hand I gesture for him to take the seat opposite me, as if the answer comes once he's seated.

Taking the chair, he flops down awkwardly, still listing slightly to one side and favoring his broken arm.

I reveal the Glock, safety off and cocked, his body shielding it from the sight of others. "I have a few questions of my own, Maurice. If you answer honestly, we can both be gone from here quickly."

Now, I think he may realize who I am. He starts to shift the chair back as if to rise. A slight lifting of the Glock makes him go still.

Smiling, I say, "Ramco is Robbie McQuillan. He wants Vivienne Hawk dead, presumably in his crazed mind; his link to her could embarrass him in the effort to become a U.S. senator. Mac knows you and knows you might be able to help him solve his problem with Ms. Hawk. You go to Horace, who has the connection to get it done. The cost is high, but Mac pays it over 27 months, and you persuade Corvino for a piece of the action to be a cut-out. For his own reasons, Corvino agrees, seeing it as a means of trapping Wilkins. Are we all in agreement on this sequence?"

Pouch blinks. Has he absorbed what I've said, this cockamamie conspiracy screwed up in the way most convoluted criminal enterprises are by the greedy, short-sighted, and foolish perpetrators?

"You really from the elephant?" he asks.

I smile at that single-minded question, "You could say so."

In a harsh whisper, he asks, "Why isn't she dead yet?"

"Because you and your colleagues fucked it up," I answer.

"What?" Even befuddled, he's getting angry. "What'd we do? It's your job."

"Mac is in Chicago this weekend?"

Startled, he says, "Yeah. He wants it done, and he paid the money to get it done."

"When does he arrive, and where is he staying?"

"Sometime in the afternoon. He'll probably go to the motel around seven; nowadays, he stays at the Heart O'Chicago on Ridge, off of Peterson."

I nod, knowing where the motel is, "Okay. Mac is in his mid to late 60's. Anything distinctive about his appearance?"

Eyes narrowing, Pouch says, "You don't want to mess with Mac. Crazy as he is, he's the baddest guy you'll ever meet."

"Big guy, right?"

"Yeah, big and mean." Repeating himself as if remembering, Pouch says, "You don't want to mess with Mac."

"I understand. I think that about concludes our meeting. I appreciate you taking the time to join me here. You want a coffee or anything before we go?"

Surprised, he blurts, "That's it? When do you kill the girl?"

"The end is nigh," I say, liking the old-fashioned phrase and deciding to be an oaf. I fire twice, the loud noise cutting through the chattering and clattering of the café.

Pouch is knocked backwards; he goes down with the chair, his head hits the floor with a solid thud. I turn and walk briskly to the back door, my empty cappuccino cup stuffed into a pocket and the Glock held down at my side, past the people who've flung themselves to the floor.

Crows are settling on the dumpster further down the alley. Not wanting to face them, I turn abruptly and go in the opposite direction. Killing Pouch, that way was likely a mistake. In my mind, I can hear Vivienne berating me. I originally had the idea of putting a slow poison in his drink. The vial is in my pocket. But Pouch didn't get a drink.

He was dead the moment he saw my face. I knew that was the case despite really holding nothing against Pouch. I understand we all have to earn a living while going through life. He was doing the same. Still, I can't say I regret his passing. Instead, it's having to act with open violence that causes me concern. It's just not something the authorities can write off.

Plus, it undoubtedly caused some customers to lose their coffee and hot chocolates. Maybe their breakfasts, too. However, I count on their confusion in attempting to describe me even with whatever quality video the shop will possess.

Of course, Pouch might not be dead. One to the head and another to his throat should do it, but I didn't stop to check. If you've read your Procopius, the historian of Justinian's reign, back early in Byzantine history, then you may recall the arrow that struck Arzes between his nose and his right eye. Remember, Arzes was one of the officers of General Belisarius' bodyguard when they were besieged in Rome. Anyway, the arrow was stuck in the man's head, so the doctor, Theocristus, had the arrow shaft cut off at the face and then cut into the rear of the skull to pull the arrow point and the rest of the shaft out. Arzes recovered nicely.

My point is, Pouch — Maurice, if you prefer — could survive for all I know.

At least, I consider that idea, which might mean I need another round of cosmetic surgery, and I heartily dislike surgery. There's the sheer overpriced bloody expense of it, the possibility of catching something else as a result of any medical procedure or treatment, and the pain or, as doctors call it, the discomfort.

I reassure myself with the thought that an arrow isn't the same as two .45 slugs.

Do I go home or find something else to do to wile away the hours until evening when I can visit the Heart O'Chicago? Too much adrenaline rush to just go home, I decide. Maybe I'll go to the Uptown Muscle Farm and try a workout for a change of pace. Get my Zen calm back.

25. NEIGHBOR LADY — NIGHTMARES

MONIQUE IS CRYING SILENTLY, TEARS RUNNING DOWN HER CHEEKS. I sit on the other side of the table at the back of the Café. She whispers, "I don't know what to do. He says he doesn't love her that it's got nothing to do with love. I think it's because I got fat, and there's always the kids and the store, so we don't see much of each other. I mean time when it's just him and me."

"If you want, I'll buy out your share of the shop. Then you won't have that in the way," I offer.

"No, I won't do it. If he leaves me, what will I have if I sell the business? As it is, he's put a double mortgage on the house. All our savings are gone. Amanda expects to attend college in a few years, but there's no money. It's all gone." She wipes at her eyes, "Oh, god, I probably look a mess."

"You're beautiful, Monique." I can't reassure her about the money. She is beautiful, too. I mean it, as much about who she is as a person as her looks.

"I know I should have told you. I feel so ashamed. I come into the shop, and the girls are all so cheerful, and I have to be cheerful, too, and it's so hard."

"How much money?"

"We paid over $300,000 to the bank to make up for his stealing. The rest is gone, all to that … Dalal."

"Dalal?"

"The girl — other woman — you know, Dalal Muammar, his exotic kept woman." Monique laughs bitterly, "I thought I was his exotic woman."

I nod, wondering about the girl's origin, "Can you get anything back from her?"

"Roy says no."

"What is he doing? Is he finding work?" He'd always seemed like a decent enough guy.

"Oh, he's finally stopped moping. He's trying. Hard if you don't have a job and a good reference."

"He probably needs to lower his expectations. Rebuild trust." I briefly consider his problem, "Is he willing to work at anything? Or is it just a senior white-collar job he wants?"

"I told him that if he wants to stay married, then there are three conditions." Monique ticks down her fingers, "One, no more Dalal or anyone like her; two, start earning a living; three, pay attention to his kids and to me."

"And what did he say?"

"Oh, he agreed, very contrite, tears and all." She sighs, "I don't believe him. He'd give it to Dalal if he had any more money, and she'd still be opening her legs for him."

"She's just a gold digger?"

Monique waves a hand, "To be truthful, I don't know. She could love him for all I know, maybe taken in by him, maybe didn't even know he was married. She could be a victim, too."

Then, more emphatically, "Or not. Just some bitch after the money."

"How'd they meet?"

Monique chuckles, "A loan request, of course — a cousin, a brother, and she wanting to open a Middle-Eastern grocery." She falls silent momentarily, then says, "I wonder if there were other women over the years who wanted loans."

I'm curious, "They open the grocery?"

"I guess so. A lot of money poured into it."

"So, is Roy a partner?"

"No, all just given away." She looks away for a moment, then back to me, "He wouldn't be with me now except for the embezzlement being found out. And she miscarried his baby."

Ah, shit, I think, always sad to hear that.

"The brother threatened to kill Roy. That much, I know. Maybe that's why he stayed home, hiding for three months."

"What do you want, Monique?" My hand is taking hers.

"I can't decide. There are days I want to throw his ass out. And there are days I just want him to realize how good his life is with me and the kids." She shakes her head slowly, "For now, it's just one day at a time."

I nod, understanding. Thinking it over, I say, "Nicky Harris will graduate soon. She'll be finding a job as a medical technician. We'll need a new part-time barista. Would Roy be up for trying something like that?"

Monique looks about her, "Here? Maybe. I can ask him. He's pretty frustrated with the job search."

"Kal could introduce him at Jiffy Lube."

"Oh, he'd go for barista before that. He's pretty outgoing, you know." Monique's hand tightens on mine, "Thank you, Vivienne. Thank you for just listening and being here for me."

"We have each other's back, Monique, always." I have to be careful, or I might cry too, realizing I haven't told her about any of my troubles. I hesitate, then decide no, murder is too much to confide.

Though, god knows, I'd like confide in someone. Wait for the next session with Dr. F-D?

Anyway, if Roy does take a job here, he might not be safe from Sadie, then what would Monique say to me.

Hunting in her purse, Monique finds tissues, wipes her eyes and blows her nose. "I need to get back to the nail salon."

I smile, glad to see her in charge of herself again, "Okay, we'll talk more."

At the fitness center, I check in with Bob T. at the front counter, while Quan, my now omnipresent bodyguard, finds a magazine to read while waiting in the lobby. Bob's pleasantries don't reach is eyes. I distrust him and several others who Wilkins installed. Two have quit already; they'd been handling the in-house store. According to Mandy, one of the long-time employees who is reliable, the two took stock with them but nothing that was on the books. She says good riddance and I'm best off not knowing what all they'd been selling.

Mandy's not the brightest girl, but she is a firm believer in exercise and nutrition as the keys to good health and is relentlessly good-natured, not just cheerful, but kind and generous. So now she's the temporary day manager. I wish she'd had the confidence to come to me sooner, back when Wilkins was alive.

I am resolved to stay on top of this place, giving it at least three hours a day, until I can find a capable professional set of managers for days and evenings. Mandy knows this, and that I will make her the women's locker and bath manager when the new people are in place. She is taking lessons to become an accredited masseuse as well.

As for Bob Tippit, his days are numbered unless his attitude and actions improve to my satisfaction. He knows this as well after the talk we had yesterday.

Today, I have the accountant coming over. We need to go through the books. How much is fabricated by Wilkins? Are we profitable? I know we've lost many of our old clientele, and if Mandy is right about the drug sales, we'll soon lose a number of the new customers. Though that will hurt us financially, as Mandy says, 'good riddance'. We can build up the kind of customers we truly want to serve. That's what I tell myself as I enter the office.

Just past 2:00 and I'm starving. Downstairs, Quan must be hungry too.

Quan sat in during the meeting with George, our Greek accountant. Having a bodyguard did not seem to fluster George. I wonder how common it is among the accountant's clients.

At least the accountant was reassuring. The books are honest, per George. Whatever else Wilkins was doing, he kept it off the books and did not use this business to launder his money. I have no idea what else he was into or what other companies he had. Maybe Wilkins laundered the drug money through his gambling income.

I decide to go back to the café for lunch after first checking in with Mandy. She knows she can call me anytime with any questions or problems. She's already done it twice in the morning but she's new to her expanded duties.

Going down to the gymnasium, I pass by the pool. Through the windows, I see several people in the water doing laps. One fellow is toweling himself off, apparently done for now. It's a shock to realize I'm seeing Randy Pryor with the towel. It's also a shock to see the amount of scar tissue across his side, chest, and as he turns, his upper back — the external oblique, pectoralis major, rhomboid, and latissimus dorsi muscles, plus, as I stop and stare, his right tibialis anterior, his lower right leg. Good lord, he's paid for his profession in flesh and blood.

I hurry on before he notices me, though knowing him, it's probably too late.

In the lobby, Quan stands as I appear. "Hungry?" I ask.

As we walk back to the café, my growling stomach embarrassing me beside Quan, I spot a very tall, thin man dressed in a gray suit standing between a parked green Fiat and a black GMC Yukon with tinted windows. I suppose I might have just passed by in earlier days. Now I'm more alert, I nudge Quan, who nods. Already, I am gripping the SlimHawg in my handbag, just in case.

The fellow glances at us, eyes narrowing as if he knows who we are.

I stare back, outwardly cool, and continue on with Quan. The café front door is on ahead, a customer, Landry, just arriving. The café seems a haven to me.

Still, I puzzle over the man I've seen, not looking back at him. If I were to guess, he was armed, given the bulge of his suit coat. Wearing a shoulder holster with some good-sized weapon? He certainly recognized me or, I suppose, Quan. Is he someone else from Ramco, EL-ephant LLC, or something to do with Wilkins? Could he be DEA, watching the fitness center? Or maybe Detective Thompson, the cop on the Corvino-Wilkins case?

Quan mutters, "You know him?"

"No, but he's in the picture somehow."

"Yes," agrees Quan.

As we step into the café, I stop and fish out my mobile phone. I call Randy Pryor. When he answers, I say, "A tall, thin gunman is watching the fitness center. We saw him when we walked to the café."

"Hi, Vivienne. How are you today?" Randy's voice is chipper. He adds, "So you're at the café now? I may come by in a little while. You looked surprised to see me at the pool." He chuckles.

"You heard me, Randy, a gunman?"

"I appreciate the tip. I'll look out for him. Don't worry. I'll see you later." And he hangs up.

I can't help shaking my head at Randy's nonchalance.

Gracie calls from the counter, "You two here for lunch? Vivienne, you have some people waiting."

Following Gracie's gesture, Simone Partridge sits at the back table with the Loi twins, the hackers Truc and Chau. Simone waves. Waving back, I say to Gracie, "Thanks." Then add, "I'd like the tomato pesto sandwich and a green tea." Turning, I ask, "What do you want, Quan?" I am trying to avoid worrying about Randy and the man in the gray suit.

Quan does a shooing gesture, sending me to the back as Vinh comes over to greet him.

Going to the back table, I say. "This is a surprise seeing the three of you together. I take it you have some news?"

"Come sit with us," answers Simone with a bright smile.

I join them.

Simone turns to the twins, and the boy, Truc, says, "We were able to trace your family."

"Your mother's side," interjects Chau.

Truc slides a color photocopy of a photograph across the table to me, "This is your Mom when she was twenty-nine, with her husband and your two half-siblings."

I can't help but gulp; the woman is light-skinned, looks almost white, and her husband and children are white. She is good-looking and has dyed her hair red. There is a trace of me in her features but not much. "My father must have been shocked when I was born."

"Yes," says Simone. "Daniel Patrick Connolly, Junior, died when you were eight years old. Raised by your grandfather until you ran away at fifteen, after nine years of his sexual abuse."

I look at her, not really wanting all this said.

"Your grandfather, Connolly senior, died in prison in 1996." Simone looks at her hands, lays them flat on the table, then looks up at me, "You've come a long way, Vivienne, since you were Ide Thea Connolly or Ita, as your grandfather called you."

"He didn't like me using the Connolly name." Thinking about Grandfather, how he would have hidden his dark-skinned granddaughter, his negress, away if he could. He would have kept me for himself if it weren't for laws requiring me to attend school if it weren't for neighbors, given a few of them who were friendly to me. Had I been as light-skinned as my mother, would my life have been wholly different?

Chau interrupts, "Your mother's maiden name was Maryam Dawes, not Davis. Her father was Sidney Dawes, or Dawit Sissay, his birth name. He was raised in Egypt under British rule. Your maternal grandmother was Celeste DuPont, who was also of mixed blood. Your great-grandmother was Dawit Meseret from Ethiopia, and your great-grandfather was the Belgian Bernard Guy Camillo del Rochefort."

Somehow, it is not a surprise. I say, "Rochefort?"

Simone picks up the thread, "Ambrose and Larissa Rochefort already knew you were related when they asked you to trace the family. They wanted you to discover the connection for yourself. They've not said why."

"You talked with them?"

"Thomas Cromwell talked with them."

"By phone?"

"Oh, no, in person."

In my mind, I picture the great bear, Cromwell, in the Rochefort house, with all its delicate Louis XIV style furnishings, the Rochefort couple, as thin and fine-featured as their furnishings. It makes me smile. They were so assured of their sophistication, elegance, and wealth, and he so certain, shrewd, and practical. "That must have been interesting."

Simone smiles at my understatement.

It is then that it happens.

The door of the café is thrust open with a crash. The big man, masked, bellowing, "Vivienne Hawk, Ita!" His shotgun is already raised.

Even with the mask, I know him for Mac, a man of my nightmares for over twenty years.

26. THE CONSULTANT — BLACK IRISH

I WAS WATCHFUL, DID SOME SCOUTING, HAD THE SKORPION MACHINE pistol out of my gym bag, and held it at my side under the light jacket draping from my right should , No Mr. Kalvaitis, though, for that's whom I assume Vivienne saw. Perhaps EL-ephant sent a different assassin but the description sounded like a match.

The Skorpion has a 20-round round magazine, and I have two more loaded magazines with me, one in the gym bag and the other in a buttoned jacket pocket. I feel ready for Kalvaitis but — poof — he seems to be gone for now.

So I walk to the café.

On ahead, I see a big man exit a beat-up Saturn, rear taillight duct-taped on. He pops the trunk and hauls out what, from this distance, looks like a Mossberg 590 shotgun, the one with the compact stock. He hefts it under his arm as he ties a bandanna over the lower half of his face like some outlaw of the Old West.

I start sprinting, certain it's Robbie McQuillan with the shotgun. I'd fire, but between me and him is a woman pushing a perambulator with her right hand and holding a child, maybe three years old, with her left.

The man chambers a round in the 12-gauge and stalks to the café door, thrusting it open with one hand. The lady between us stopped at the sight and swiftly turning away, says to the child, "Quick, Jamie, this way," as I run by her.

Standing in the doorway, McQuillan calls out something. He starts forward, and I hear the boom of the shotgun going off. Then I'm at the door, finger on the trigger of the Skorpion, but I stop from firing in time.

McQuillan is down, blood pumping furiously from a severed carotid artery.

Quan stands over Mac, a long, slim knife in his hand.

Beyond them, there is a big woman sprawled and screeching, apparently having taken some part of the shotgun blast.

Vivienne is standing at a back table, my Slim Hawg in her hand, and across from her, another woman is also holding a pistol while two teenagers are crouched under their table. The rest of the customers seem frozen in the instant, but Grace is moving from behind the counter to help the lady on the floor.

I'm not needed here. I walk away quickly.

With their client dead, will EL-ephant continue in the effort to kill Vivienne? I doubt it so far as Mac goes. By now, they know I have no intention of harming Vivienne, and that she and I are allied.

So, if they wanted to force me back into the business through this scheme, they now know it's not happening. The cleanest thing from their view at this stage is to eliminate me. And, depending on how much I've shared with Vivienne, kill her.

So we are both still in danger.

Damn.

I need to find a route to them, find out who they are, and what level of resources they possess. Given the attempt to force me back into the game, I don't think they can be all that strong. Why do they want or need me?

I'm thinking this as I retreat to my car, all the while scanning rooftops, doorways, alley entrances, parked cars, hell, everything for a hint of them. I have not been this alert, this scared, this filled with adrenaline rush, in a long time.

It feels great. I find myself humming *Black Irish,* the Devil Makes Three song.

27. NEIGHBOR LADY — YUKON

DRIVING HOME SLOWLY, STILL FEELING SHAKIER THAN SEEMS RIGHT, I can't help but think, my god, what a day. It took hours with the police. Poor Landry Nemeth, buckshot peppering her shoulder, so lucky that the primary blast hit her laptop and the table. There could be a lawsuit, though she calmed down after the paramedics got a shot into her.

Maybe I should ask Kal to bring her flowers at the hospital.

Grace was a pillar of strength with the wounded girl, then with all the customers once the paramedics took over with Landry.

Thank god the police chose to overlook Quan's knife, a boning knife, so they ruled it a utensil and not illegal.

It all might have gone faster if Sadie Epstein hadn't shown up, such a drama queen. Vinh helped settle her down until Joel arrived.

It all keeps buzzing in my head as I drive. The images: Simone ushering the Loi kids out even before the police reached the scene;

Quan waiting quietly in the booth; Gracie getting Landry to lie still; me trying to placate the elderly couple, the Semples — Mac lying in that dark pool of blood.

And where was Randy Pryor?

I think I saw him once. I have this faint picture in my mind. He's at the door, the sun behind him, just beyond Quan and Mac; he's got a gun in his hand, the kind you see criminals, secret agents, and SWAT teams carry in the movies.

Did I hallucinate that? I can't be sure.

The police — Detective Thompson — had me go over the events repeatedly. And his partner, Detective Fussell, an older guy, is trying to tie Mac in with Danny Corvino and Todd Bradley Wilkins. Well, that is better than with Randy Pryor.

Is it all over now with Mac dead? Can life get back to normal?

Will I stop having nightmares of Mac?

I stop at The Grand to buy orange juice. What's breakfast without orange juice? I should have stopped at the Wilmette Jewel when I went by, but I didn't think of it then. My head still abuzz with today.

Then I drive south on Chestnut to get to my street. I spot a black GMC Yukon with tinted windows near the corner where I turn. The plates are Indiana plates, like the vehicle near the fitness center. Rather than turning, I drive on. After several more blocks, I pull over and try calling Randy. No answer.

My impulse is to keep driving, go back into the city, maybe stay the night with Monique or at the fitness center.

Dusk now, in another half hour it will be full dark. What to do?

I can't abandon Randy. Dammit. I can't call the police either.

Maybe the guy's not after Randy. Maybe the guy's waiting for me.

Letting Quan off body guarding me was premature. I try

several deep, calming breaths. I start up the car, turn left at the next intersection, and at the next block, turn again, going north. I park a block away from my street. Sit for a moment more in the car, which feels safe, then retrieve Randy's pistol from my handbag. Carefully, I let off the safety. Out of the car now, pistol in my hand, I walk to the apartment complex.

No light on at Randy's or my place.

There is a rustle in the tree above, and I'm surprised to see a pair of crows. I suppose they must sleep somewhere at night.

With considerable trepidation, I ring the bell at Randy's, stepping well back after doing so, gun ready.

Nothing. I lose my nerve at the thought of ringing again.

I cross to my place, moving slowly, very alert. Decide against the front door and go around to the rear gate, entering my little garden. Then, standing still and listening.

Most condos have lights on, blue of televisions playing, and people in the kitchen or living area. The neighbors on the other side, the Fremonts, are home. Faintly, I can hear the game John Fremont is watching in their den, always on loud with his poor hearing.

Maybe I should have a dog, something to bark at intruders.

I go to the back door, and as quietly as possible, I unlock it. Carefully, I ease it open and slip inside. More calming breaths.

Search downstairs in the dark, room by room, including the closets, then go up to the second floor and through each room. Nothing, what a relief; I feel light-headed for a moment. Then it occurs to me to look in the basement.

There is nothing in either the finished half or the unfinished half of the basement. I sit on the couch in the finished half for a while, just letting myself drift and recover from the tension.

Going back upstairs, I close the curtains and then turn on a lamp.

I nearly shriek at the sight of the envelope on the kitchen table. Someone has been in my place.

My name in block letters is on the outside. Block letters like the lettering on the envelope I took to Randy Pryor not so many days ago.

I set the gun down on the table and pick up the envelope, hefting it to be certain it's not a letter bomb of some kind. I'm a little paranoid, given that the letter is flat and can't hold more than a sheet of paper.

All it says is, 'Contract canceled. You are free to live.' No signature, of course, but a rubber-stamped image of an Asian elephant.

My first thought is to show it to Randy.

Then, it occurs to me that Randy could be gone. He will move on to his next identity if it's all over here.

Curiously, that thought is a mixture of relief and sadness. What a sorry life he has.

After making certain everything is locked up tight, including doors and windows, I remember the orange juice is in the car, and I can't leave the car parked on the street. So it's out again to walk back to the car.

After putting the car in the garage, I walk around to my place, carrying the orange juice jug. Going by Randy's, I notice a flicker of light, maybe candlelight. I almost drop the orange juice as I fumble for the gun in my handbag. There is an audible whoosh, and the glass blows out of his windows. The explosion knocks me off my feet. I scramble on all fours away from the heat and flames. Birds, maybe crows, fly up from the maple tree.

Retrieving my handbag, I find the phone to call 911.

Neighbors are spilling out of their homes. I find I am crying.

Though it seems to take forever, I'm sure the fire trucks are here quickly as we live close to the fire and police stations. I feel in a daze.

Shards of glass have cut open the orange juice jug and my left hand. Pain from my sliced hand is arcing up my arm to my heart.

Once the fire is out, they pull a body out of the debris of Randy's home. I hear the fire marshal speculating to a police lieutenant about a gas leak. I know better.

A paramedic binds up my hand after checking to see what else might be wrong with me. There are abrasions and bruises on my right side from being blown down. Shaky, but okay, alive. It might have been worse if I'd been opposite the picture window.

Sandy Fremont helps me to my house, and John picks up my handbag. Sandy is saying, "We have orange juice. I'll bring some over." I must have explained about getting the orange juice from my car, but I don't remember.

John says, "You were on the News. You and your café in Uptown."

About four in the morning, I wake. My left hand is throbbing. I lie in bed feeling low. I know I'd been dreaming. I'm not sure, except it featured a black Yukon.

Suddenly wide awake, I sit up. A black Yukon, is it still there?

Quickly, I get up, throw on clothes. Grab the pistol from my handbag and hurry out the door, my right leg hurting a little.

Sure enough, a fast walk brings me to the Yukon, a ticket on its window for parking overnight on the street.

I feel such lightness and relief at seeing it.

The body they carried out can't be Randy. It must have been the man in the gray suit.

28. NEIGHBOR LADY — R.I.P

I<small>T'S BEEN A MONTH NOW SINCE</small> M<small>AC WAS KILLED AT THE CAFÉ, AND</small> Randy's place exploded. Life seems to be back in its even tenor. The surge in business at the café, with all the curious coming to see a crime scene, has leveled off.

The legal issues surrounding the fitness center or Wilkins' estate are ongoing. Still, I hired a manager for days and made Mandy the night manager, given how good she was as a temporary manager. I confess she surprises me. She seems to grow in ability with each new responsibility I give her.

Monique is doing okay. Roy works weekends at the café and works part-time at a shoe store. Monique said they're going to counseling of some kind after Amanda and Kyle told their dad that if he and Monique split up, they were staying with Monique. Three cheers for Monique as a good step-mother.

I even have a new freelance assignment doing market research for a firm proposing an innovative home security system. The company is a subsidiary of one of the giant international companies that's main business is in the defense industry.

So why am I feeling blue? Maybe blue or unhappy is too strong; it's not like I'm down at the mouth all day. I get along, have my cheerful moments, and enjoy my friends. Yet, I feel like I'm missing something, like life is flat.

Lifting my cup, I take a sip of the latte. Glance around the room at our customers, all very typical, half bent over their laptops, mobile phones, or books and half in conversations. Gracie is leafing through the mail. Vinh is chatting with Quan while holding a stack of dirty dishes he's collected.

Quan looks handsome this morning, the light slanting in and touching him. It's too bad he is ten years my junior. I enjoyed his companionship when he acted as my bodyguard.

Gracie gives a little exclamation, holding up what looks like a postcard. She comes hurrying over. "Vivienne, take a look at this." She holds out the postcard.

It's addressed to Grace. The front shows a building on a leafy street. The back identifies it as the University Library on the campus at Ann Arbor. I read the message: 'Hi, Grace. I hope you are well after the recent excitement. I wanted you and Vivienne to know I'm doing well. R.I.P'

"R.I.P.?" asks Grace.

"Randy Pryor," I say, thinking of the man's sense of humor; Randall Innes Pryor, rest in peace.

Grace stares at me, troubled. "So he didn't die in the fire. Someone did, though." Then, more slowly, "And you knew. Someday, Vivienne, you must tell me everything that happened last month."

"I'm thinking, Grace, that Randy liked you."

"So now he lives in Ann Arbor?"

I shake my head no, "I doubt it. My guess would be some college town, though. I think he's saying that much."

Shrewdly, Grace says softly, "Not by the name Randy either, right?" She sits down opposite me as Vinh is now manning the counter. She asks, "It was more complicated than some crazy old man fixated on you, wasn't it?"

I shrug, "That was the heart of it, but others thought they could take advantage of the situation but it didn't work out like they expected."

"Because of Randy?"

"Pretty much."

She nods goes silent, thinking. She looks up, "Life goes on, right?"

"For the survivors."

"Yeah," moodily, then she smiles, "Well, we're survivors."

I laugh and take her hand, "Yes, we are."

Squeezing my hand, she changes the subject by asking, "You're not going to contact your mother, are you?"

"No," I shrug. "She must not have wanted a Black child if she was passing as white. No reason to think that's changed."

"If I were her, I'd be proud to be your mother."

"Thank you, though you would have been quite young for motherhood." I laugh, "You and I know some things are best left in the past."

Grace nods in agreement, then smiles softly, "You know, back twenty years ago and more, there was a man I knew. An elderly gent, what I would call a regular. He was quite fond of me, I think. He would have taken me in, maybe married me if I had wanted. He was a sweet man. I was too full of myself back then despite everything. If I had to go back in time, I would let him have me. I think it would have been good for both of us."

"We all make choices, take paths, and other paths go unheeded." It sounds pretentious to me, a platitude, yet true.

"You don't think your mother regrets abandoning her first child. Regrets the choice she made when she was eighteen?" Grace is serious.

"Maybe. But she has two other kids. I doubt she wants her life upset 38 years after the fact."

"You know, I regret not having children. I might have. I had two abortions in my twenties, not that I would have been a good mother back then. Now, though, I would be, you can just ask my cats," Grace laughs. "I made a lot of bad choices."

I find myself patting her hand, "Maybe we all do. I nearly went down your path, but it scared me too much."

"I didn't think anything scares you, Vivienne."

I confess, "Men scare me. Not all, maybe, but many. Legacy of Mac and Grandfather, I guess." Then I add, "But none of them scare me as much as I scare myself."

She looks at me quizzically, an eyebrow arched.

I try to explain, "There is a wildness in me, a wanton self, which I must keep tamed." I pause, then say, "Before you came over with Randy's card, I was thinking how much I liked the dangers of last month, how alive it made me feel, how at any point life could change instantly. Even the fear was worth it. I understand why Randy is addicted to it."

"Quan is pretty dangerous," says Grace knowingly.

I nod, "He was amazing, acting so quickly. If it weren't for him, how many might have died?"

"You saw Randy there, too, didn't you? Your Mac wouldn't have gotten far."

"So Randy was there. You saw him?"

"Oh, yes, then in an instant, he was gone." Grace gestures at Quan in the second booth, "You two get along pretty well."

"He's so young."

"I was, too, when the old gentleman wanted me years ago. I shouldn't have let age difference stand in the way."

"It's different for a man than a woman. Easier for an old guy to take up with a girl." I laugh.

Grace shrugs, "I'm just saying what matters is who you are." She gets up as a trio comes in the café door, "It's up to you, but I wouldn't waste time. He's interested in you."

I watch Van Quan as Gracie walks away. As if he knows, he looks up and we stare at each other across the room. I smile.

29. THE CONSULTANT — PIPE SMOKER

AFTER PICKING OUT A BOOK AT COMMON GROUND BOOKS, I WALK south on Snelling to the Caribou Coffee for a late-morning mocha. Across the road is Macalester College, where I enjoy seeing the bustle of the students between classes.

I try to blend in, though I'm not really used to my beard and thick glasses yet. I like the brown corduroy sports coat I wear, with leather patches on each elbow. I also have a pipe in my jacket pocket, wooden matches, and pouches for both McClelland's Beacon Extra (Virginia & perique tobaccos) and Orient 996 (Turkish tobacco).

Being a novice pipe smoker, trying to imitate a practiced smoker is not easy. Still, it seems a necessary camouflage, and I find it kind of fun puffing up a storm until I grow dizzy.

Not that I smoke when at Common Ground or Caribou Coffee.

I'm not sure how I'll take to Minnesota winters, but living in this area is quite pleasant for now. My new place is 10 or 12 blocks from the Mississippi River, with colleges both east and west of me.

Not much in the place yet, after losing my belongings in Winnetka. It's a shame, really, but in my profession, one has to be ready to leave all possessions behind. Well, not quite all. I still have my Skorpion sub-machine gun.

At the same time, it's been enjoyable picking out things to stock in my new home. I've acquired a lot of books from Common Ground and from the used bookstore, Midway, on Snelling and University.

I find Caribou Coffee quiet after the early morning rush. You don't want to be here too early, at lunchtime or late afternoon. An hour mid to late morning is good and an hour between lunchtime and late afternoon, those are the times to be here. I read or get on my new iPad.

Around here, they have begun to know me. I try to give the impression of a retired academic in a slightly eccentric, maybe even quaint manner, though if anyone asks, I mention publishing technical journals and obscure monographs. They'll say, "Hi, Dana. The usual? Mocha with no whipped cream?"

I think this persona will fit well enough, Dana Thomas Haverly, DTH.

No more writing my memoirs. That was a foolish idea. It really got me in trouble.

The only truly foolish thing I've done lately is sending a postcard to Grace Freen that I'm sure she shared with Vivienne. Stupid, really, to do that rather than leaving myself dead. Yet, I'm confident Vivienne saw through that charade with the fire. Poor Mr. Kalvaitis, may he be in a better place now. He was forthcoming about EL-ephant LLC with a bit of persuasion.

To be truthful, I miss Vivienne. It was surprisingly refreshing to be honest with someone. I guess I just wanted to be sure she knows. I trust her.

The quick trip I took to Montreal, Canada, took care of my erstwhile employer. No more EL-ephant LLC to contend with as it also burned with all its servers, databases, physical records, and its three remaining employees. I think I am truly free and clear now.

Unless its joint venture partner, a very large international defense contractor — one of those ABC or FGH or XYZ initialed organizations — maintained its own data set.

Just in case, I intend to keep a very low profile.

I shall live out my twilight years, which I hope last a good 20 or so more, in quiet ease.

Provided, of course, I don't become too bored.

Or, the crows gather in a murder.

SCRATCH

A NOVEL

THOMAS SUNDELL

THE PAPER HOUSE
PUBLISHING

One Man's Junk Press

CHAPTER
ONE

HE LAST SAW CHEVY MACGAVAN IN TORONTO. HE LEFT MACGAVAN lying dead on York Street, then he disappeared.

That was in '72 when he was twenty-six. Now he's sixty-two and has left those days far behind. At least, he'd thought so.

Who gives a damn anymore about Chevy MacGavan? That's the question.

Maybe Chevy's little hunchbacked sister, Fionnuala, if she's still alive. What would she be? Fifty-one or fifty-two now.

Or, maybe, a more important question is, who gives a damn about Chevy's buddy anymore? Who gives a damn about Scratch? Who from that past life anyway?

He hasn't been Scratch for a long time. He hasn't lived the life that Scratch lived.

He sighs. Nuala was a good kid. He'd always liked her and knew she'd had a soft spot for him, even after he married Gloria.

She was a funny kid. For a moment, he smiles in memory.

In August 1972, he'd disappeared. He left his wife and little ones behind, left the rest of his family—his brother, Keith, and all the others; and left Mackey's Donegal gang.

Now he's here, back in Buffalo. Here, sitting in a Toyota Camry just off the exit ramp from I190. It's cold, with snow all around and twilight.

In the back seat, under a blanket, is a Tikka M-68. It's a Finnish sniper rifle with good optics in the scope and a capital suppresser to keep down the noise. Bolt action, with five rounds, is meant for carefully measured shots. He's not sure he'll need to use it.

Beside him is a real bulldog on the floor in front of the passenger seat. Some cop in Europe must have sold it or had it lifted from him. He doesn't know how it made its way to Cleveland, where he picked it up. It's a Belgian FN-P90, more than a pistol and less than a rifle, but semi-automatic with a fifty-round magazine, of which he possesses three. Most body armor won't deflect the bullets it fires.

In his hands, where he's loading cartridges, is a Beretta Storm, with a four-inch barrel and a fourteen-shot capacity at .40 caliber Smith & Wesson. Fifteen shots if one round is added in the chamber. He decides to go with the fifteen.

Strapped to his ankle is the little Taurus 905 that he picked up in Arkansas sixteen days earlier when all this started happening again.

This is a lot of firepower when he doesn't know if any of it is needed. He's guessing he feels a bit paranoid.

Where does a thing like this start?

CHAPTER
TWO

GOING THROUGH SECURITY AT O'HARE, HE'D HANDED HIS ID AND boarding pass to the TSA guy. He'd be the first to admit that he's not at his best in those long, dragging security lines. First, he resents the necessity of it, the whole tax-wasting charade. Second, he doesn't much like authority to begin with and likes it less when it slows him down or can paw through his belongings at the least excuse. Third, getting up at four in the morning is not his idea of joy. Listening to the audiobook about Queen Nefertiti of ancient Egypt on the drive down from Racine to O'Hare hadn't helped.

Anyway, the TSA guy took a long time on his ID, squinting at it, squinting at him, before grunting, "Have a nice flight," without a smile.

So, it's nagging at him on the plane ride down to Arkansas. He can't concentrate on the history of the Anglo-Saxons that he's trying to read. He keeps picturing the TSA guy squinting at him as if this businessman isn't what he appears to be.

In truth, something about the TSA guy is bothering him,

something familiar. The puckered, rough scars on the guy's face and neck didn't help, looking like the guy was caught in a fire many years ago. There are the heavy jowls, not to mention the good-sized gut. Yet underneath all that, there is someone who teases at his memory.

Finally, high over Missouri, he places the guy as the plane heads toward XNA. At that moment, three decades and more, with all its wrought, had fallen away. The guy is Chevy MacGavan's second cousin, Boyo Farry. Boyo, who was an obnoxious kid back in the day, always wanting to be part of something he was too young for and too what smarmy, nervy something you just didn't trust. And now he's TSA, a junior official, a minor annoying form of authority.

Well, he placed Boyo, but did Boyo place him? How does he look now? He has short iron-gray hair that is thinning. Glasses and wrinkles, the flush of high blood pressure, and the attendant drugs that control it. Still, his height is the same if he is a good ten pounds heavier. Likely, it will be his jawline, the set of his ears and mouth, the scar on his forehead, and especially his eyes, deep sunk and light in color below the dark brows. Yes, even with the glasses, Boyo will know him.

Well, maybe. He's been dead for a long time. People's features run in patterns. No two exactly alike, maybe, but they are often quite close in appearance.

So, he went about his business in Bentonville, Arkansas. He met up with his two colleagues, Alex and Reah, who'd flown down two days earlier to set things up. They called on Wal-Mart to try to sell their wares. Once again tried to persuade the behemoth of retailing to add a more upscale toy line, although it was late in the season.

Promised to deliver within one to two days of receipt of the purchase order. They pledged to cut prices by seven percent, not the twelve, which was the Wal-Mart buyers' first requested. Promised an increase in the advertising budget and that the new advertising would be on television in the selected markets within five days after the buy.

All this is for a line of specialty toys plastic models of horse, dog, and cat breeds that can be assembled by seven to ten-year-olds without the need for gluing.

Manufacturing, they job out to factories in China. However, a Korean firm has given them an interesting bid that's being considered. And they have inquiries from the Philippines and Viet Nam.

Design is done in their shop in Racine, Wisconsin. They have three distribution centers, their own in Racine, and services leased in Seattle and in New York. Seattle is their port of call from China.

There are only thirteen in the company. They have a half-dozen lines of toys and a number of specialty items. They're contrarians in that they don't try to compete for the hook-ups to movie and cartoon character rights. They go for high quality and enough realism to satisfy but not so much as to be uncomfortable for their young audiences.

Cracking Wal-Mart means going big time for the company. He's not sure they're ready for it, though the boss says that the money's there to push production. The gambles already been made, which is how they can promise shipment one day from the purchase order. The boss says that's what it takes.

He's glad it's not his money they're gambling. Although, when you think of it, it is probably his bonus and everyone else's, and maybe even his job.

He's a jack-of-all-trades at the firm coordinating production, assuring quality, managing the manufacturing costs, taking the product designs into full-scale production, whatever the boss, Frances, wants him to do.

Quality assurance is what got him down to Bentonville to assist the sales team. Wal-Mart is focused on quality, particularly given the lead-paint scare for Chinese-made toys.

So, with all that going on, he let Boyo slip from the front of his mind.

Not until supper that night did he think of Boyo Farry again. The three of them were out celebrating the likelihood of the company's biggest contract to date.

Something Reah said about adding farm animals and zoo animals to next year's line triggered a memory of Chevy and him at the zoo with a nine-year-old Boyo. Boyo's sister was there, too. Though he was only sixteen himself at the time, even then, he knew Chevy was screwing the sister, who might have been fourteen. What was her name? Melinda? Melanie? Melody? Something, doesn't really matter.

Boyo, though, knew it, too, 'cause he laughed at a zebra trying to mount another, comparing it to Chevy and his sister. Chevy knocked Boyo to the ground and probably would have stomped the kid if Scratch hadn't wrapped his arms around Chevy, saying, "Easy, easy," repeatedly until Chevy's temper cooled. Laughing, Chevy had pulled Boyo to his feet.

Millicent — that was her name. Millie, they called her.

Well, if Boyo made him, maybe it wouldn't mean anything anymore. That's what he thought. Or, perhaps it'd mean something, except Boyo was far enough out of that life that there's nothing he'd do about it. After all, Boyo's working for the TSA, and it's a sure thing they'd have checked his background. He must have come up clean.

Not that being a cop or any other tinker-toy kind of security didn't mean a guy wasn't bent. Look at those FBI screw-ups in Boston who ran with Whitey Bulger for twenty years or more.

He pretty much convinced himself not to worry about it. This shows how sloppy he'd become after running straight for thirty years.

The following day, he got a wake-up call in his room at the Homewood Suites. The call wasn't something he ordered, and it rang three times before he answered it.

Instead of a recording, it was a man's voice, sounding not over thirty, with just a hint of amusement. Not an Arkansas voice either, with that peculiar twang that combines the south and southwest.

Fortunately, it's not hard to pick up a handgun in Arkansas. He had to make excuses to his colleagues, letting them think that the food at the prior night's meal had given him a twinge of something.

He changed his car reservation on his own credit and drove it home, the handgun on the seat beside him. He wasn't sure if he was overreacting.

Arkansas to Wisconsin is a long drive, but it's not so easy flying these days with a pistol on your person. Still, with a couple of audiobooks he'd picked up at the Barnes & Noble, it wasn't bad.

The gun is the same Taurus 905 that's strapped to his ankle as he sits in the cold Camry near the old neighborhood. A two-inch barrel—9 mm, five-shot—not what he would have liked if he'd had more time and choice in Arkansas. Serviceable, though. The kind of gun a cop would use for backup, just like he's doing here in the Camry.

Let's be clear. He believes he's had a better life than he

deserves. And that he's not the punk kid he was all those years ago. Not at all.

He knows right from wrong. More than that, he's come to believe that being ethical is important for the self and those around you. He's not so sure about God and certainly doesn't think much of organized religion, despite his wife's beliefs. It isn't because he doesn't think about how to live right, raise his kids to be good people, or live with yourself.

Anyway, there's plenty to regret from his early years.

Even back then, he doesn't believe he was a sociopath.

He was married. Gloria was his wife then. They had three children: Teddy, Ronnie, and Jack, six, four and two. Teddy and Jack are boys. Ronnie, properly Veronica, is a girl.

He doubts those three remember anything of him. Maybe Teddy would, but not the others. Just as well.

All of them are adults now, out in the world, living their own lives. Bless them.

Leaving them behind that was pain. Maybe it was mental, but it felt physical, tight, searing pain like you're having a heart attack or like a plague, maybe cholera, ripping through your insides and killing you in a few hours.

He doesn't like to think about it. Doesn't, can't, talk about it. Not that he wants sympathy. As far as he's concerned, it was his fault that he left them behind. It's his fault that life became a train wreck for them. Yet, it's nothing that he can undo. So he lives with it, just as they lived with it.

He guesses that Gloria gave him up for dead long ago.

He's wondered down through the years what all has happened to them. He expects that Gloria re-married and imagines that the kids think of that fellow as their dad.

It doesn't bear thinking about for too long.

Of course, he was no prize back then. Sure, Gloria knew the life he was in. Was in it herself, so to speak. Knew the Big Guy, knew her husband worked for him. Knew the risks that were run. She was as much a part of the Donegals as he was.

The Big Guy, Big MackeyPatrick Francis MacGavan. Don't call him Pat. Big Mackey, all of six foot four, broad, with hands like vise grips.

The Donegals were Mackey's boys. Like any gang, some of them were a tight crew, center stage, and core. Others were more fringe, and some few just came and went. Big Mackey was the puppet master.

The Old First Ward in Buffalo is Irish. It has been since the Irish built the Erie Canal back in the 1820s. And he'd guess no, he knows, that someone or two Irish bosses ran the Ward or even well beyond the Ward ever since.

Hell, there was a time when the Irish had the police, the judges, the mayor's office, most of the city council, plus a lot of the taverns and bars and much of the crime. That time is long gone; was gone before he was born in 1946.

In his day, his Donegal day, the rackets were held by the Mafia out of Niagara Falls, the Magaddino family. His Irish mob had to acknowledge them and pay tribute and taxes. The Donegals occasionally rubbed shoulders with the wops, and Mackey paid them a piece of everything.

Nonetheless, the Donegals owned the First Ward, the neighborhood.

The Mafia were into narcotics, labor racketeering, high-level gambling, prostitutes, pornography, money lending, bust-outs of businesses they took over, and sweet swindles with the help of the politicos they owned—all the big money stuff.

They figured the Irish mob for penny ante. Which was okay

with Big Mackey as that made it all the less money he had to pay those sons-of-bitches.

Remembering, Scratch thinks how nickel and dime they must have seemed. Still and all, good honest thieving adds up, especially hijacking, which was one of their specialties. Running protection, moving contraband back and forth to Canada depending on which items made an extra buck where, even simple prosaic burglaries, all of it contributed to the pot.

Ah, he sighs, shaking his head. Who is he kidding?

They were no better and not much worse than the Meatballs. They'd take the wops' contracts if someone needed to be whacked and the Meatballs didn't want it on their hands. Blame the Irish has a long tradition.

It's a truism that there is no honor among thieves. You can believe him that there's nothing good or romantic about a life of stealing and killing—just betrayal and pain.

Once, though, he thought it was romantic.

At least, when he was fifteen, he thought Big Mackey's nephew, Chevy, was about as cool as it gets.

CHAPTER
THREE

HIS FIRST PISTOL WAS GIVEN TO HIM BY CHEVY.

How it happened was this. Chevy was seventeen when his uncle asked him to pick up the dry cleaning downtown. Scratch, or Kiddo as his brother Keith called him back then, was two years younger and always tagging along with Chevy. Except not that day, as Angie, his sister-in-law, had him watching the little kids.

So late on Saturday afternoon, Chevy goes to the dry cleaners. Just a small storefront place situated in an office building near a swanky hotel, with city hall across the circle.

There are other dry cleaners around, certainly in the First Ward. Only Big Mackey favored the one downtown, maybe because the Jewish lady who worked there was attractive and a touch exotic to Big Mackey or maybe because he ran some scam regularly nearby.

However it was, Chevy came away with the dry cleaning and an idea. He's seen how much cash is in the register on a late Saturday afternoon.

CHAPTER THREE

He's got a problem, though. It's the place his uncle favors, and as wild as Chevy is, he knows you tread softly before you step on the Big Guy's shadow.

So Chevy brings his problem to Kiddo.

Now Chevy knows that Kiddo admires his Walther P-38. A World War II gun, a bit antique in 1961, yet it's got a good action, feels like a force in your fist, with an elegance a .45 doesn't quite match.

So Chevy lays it out. Kiddo is to go there the following Saturday at about four p.m. Kiddo is to make a withdrawal without hurting anyone because that would piss off Big Mackey. For that, Kiddo gets half. Chevy gets the other half for fingering the place and keeping watch while Kiddo is in there, and because Big Mackey is his uncle and not Kiddo's—Fair's fair.

Well, Kiddo does it.

His first score outside of shoplifting.

Despite all the nervousness beforehand, when it's happening Kiddo is cool. Not just cool but clicking, like a machine, concentrated on the task at hand.

Though he felt like vomiting afterwards.

And because they didn't get permission and because they do piss off Big Mackey, Kiddo gets his first true beating, like when making it back to all right seems touch and go.

Chevy also gets a dressing down and is slapped around a bit. Still, he's not carrying the gun; he didn't scare the Jewish lady so that she doesn't want to be alone in the store ever again, and he is Big Mackey's nephew, so fair is fair.

As for Kiddo, from then on, he's part of Big Mackey's people, the Donegals. Though he doesn't have a rep for smarts, he does for balls, standing up, taking a beating, and keeping his mouth shut.

So Kiddo doesn't make any scratch from the robbery but gets the name Scratch from Big Mackey himself.

Speaking of names, Chevy's was Tristan—Tristan Michael MacGavan. Who wants to be known as Tristan in Buffalo, New York, especially in the 1960s?

Tristan, Kiddo and a lot of other guys admired the 1957 Chevrolet. Sure, some guys swore by Caddies, Imperials, or Lincoln Continentals. Younger fellows enamored of Corvettes and T-Birds. Yet no one didn't admire a 1957 Chevrolet. Sitting in his Camry, Scratch shakes his head. It is no wonder Chevrolet is in the dumpster today. They hit their peak over fifty years ago.

So naturally, Tristan stole '57 Chevys every chance he got. What followed, like an immutable law, is that he became Chevy MacGavan. In Scratch's opinion, that's better than being known as Tris or even Little Mackey.

From the day that Chevy handed Kiddo his Walther, it was Chevy and Scratch, the crime duo for the next eleven years.

Fucking wasteful.

CHAPTER
FOUR

The windows are fogging, and his feet are freezing. He starts the engine, thinking he ought not to idle given the gas price. Then, he laughs at himself for how much he's accepted his wife's ethic of frugality. Not like back then, with Gloria.

There are two choices.

He can go down to Mackey's Place, which is still in the phone book and even has a website that looks like a trendy restaurant. Or he can run by the old house on O'Connell and see if Nuala MacGavan still lives there.

Maybe there's a third choice. The limousine service they used to run is gone, but there's still a garage at the address. Maybe someone is running hot cars through it or keeping a particular set of wheels as if they were murder special, like in the old days.

He feels stupid for going at this thing cold. But whom does he have to reach out to anymore, thirty-six years after he's supposed to be dead?

So why is he here?

Driving home from Arkansas, he thought he was returning to his life as he lives it now. Back to Helena and the girls, his family now. Back to Thanksgiving at friends, to plans for the next Girl Scout event, enjoying music recitals, watching the girls do their homework or read or make up their play of horse toys, lists and maps and stories shared, their ice skating at the rink or swimming lessons, all of it so normal and wonderful.

He has come to think of himself as a fortunate man.

They played the game of *Life* on Thanksgiving at their friends' home. His eleven-year-old, Penelope, had brought it with her. A lot of laughter over that game as the adults and kids play. It is a fun game because there is no criminal track in the game of *Life*.

After turkey and game playing, he felt good as he drove his family home, the girls already retelling the day's events. As they pulled into the garage, he sees that the back door is unlocked and open. He tells the girls to stay in the car, tells Helena to move over and take the wheel, and leaves the car running.

He steps to the back door, wishing he hadn't left the little Taurus pistol on the nightstand. No forced entry. He goes in cautiously. Checks the house over; no intruders, no vandalism, no disturbance. Just like at the Homewood Suites in Rogers, Arkansas, roughly a week earlier, someone is giving him a wake-up call.

Now, he doesn't scare easily. No, that's not quite right. He scares, but in a detached way. It hits him on delay, so he can think clearly, probably clearer when things are going down than when the world is running smooth.

That night, though, he was scared. Not for himself, since he believes he's already running on gravy time. He should have hit the pavement back in '72. No, he scares for his girls, for his

Helena. Someone is playing with him here—they're in his home, where his girls sleep and dream good dreams.

So he scares for that instant, and then he becomes enraged. Anger like he hasn't felt since he was a hot-blooded fool in Buffalo, New York, making his way up with Chevy MacGavan.

So here he is. The Camry's heater is already pumping life into his feet.

The Beretta Storm is loaded. Maybe it's time to rock n' roll.

Shit, that's what they used to say. Crank up WKBW on the AM radio to let the tunes pulse through them and go for a ride.

Scratch puts the car in gear and eases onto the street. The way is open enough, though it's about time for a snowplow to come through again.

He flicks the lights of the Camry up, the snow flakes glittering back in the night. Not much traffic for a Friday. The car seems to glide along, not fast, but with purpose.

He's decided where he'll start. Come in softly. He'll start at Keith's, see if his brother still lives there. If not, then it will be on to Nuala's.

He's been online and searched back issues off the *Buffalo News*, but he didn't find much to tell him who was running things today. Sure, there is plenty about the Magaddino family from back when of their crimes, killings, feuds, and prison stretches.

Back in 1972, he thinks he and Chevy got caught in a war between the Mafia factions. The old man, Stefano Magaddino, lost power in '69, so the family split.

The son, Peter Magaddino, couldn't hold it together, not after an FBI raid found a stash of $521,000 in cash that in a year when Peter Magaddino was crying poor and not paying out bonuses to his underbosses. Salvatore Pieri—known on the street as Samuel Johns—went for the top job with the help of his brothers and a *capo* on the West Side, Johnny DiCarlo, who was Pieri's brother-in-law. That lasted maybe 'til September of '70 when Pieri got taken down for stolen goods and got five years in prison.

Then Joe Fino took over. Several *capos* were with him—Dan Sansanese, John Cammilleri, and others.

Pieri got early parole after having paid off someone. He and his brothers came back with guns blazing, literally.

Somewhere in all that, the Donegals got fucked.

What's up nowadays, though, Scratch isn't sure. Salvatore Pieri's brother, Joe, was on top until 1982. Then lost out to Joe Todaro, who brought in help from Pittsburgh, the boss there being Russ Buffalino.

Does the Mafia matter as much anymore? What with Central American gangs, the Asians and the Russians, or even some of the black mobs and other Hispanic gangs, who controls what? It's not as if plenty of non-ethnics aren't into crime; just look at the unions and construction industry. Maybe they should start calling it a disorganized crime. And in Western New York, you even have to deal with the Senecas since they got the casinos.

So, there are more players, but still the old game. Scratch guesses a lot is still based on neighborhoods, even if the organizations reach across the nation or are even international.

What does all that matter to him?

Someone learned that he's alive and how to find him. Someone reached out, ignoring thirty years. That's what matters to him.

CHAPTER
FIVE

THE TOYOTA CAMRY IS MAYBE FIVE OR SIX YEARS OLD, GOLD-COLORED, and a family-type car. It is as common as weeds and just not that noticeable. Perfect, what with its six cylinders that can put out plenty of juice for city streets if need be. Probably, it's better than most tricked-up cars were in '72.

When Scratch acquired it in South Bend, Indiana, he was assured that it was from a family away on vacation to a warm climate for three weeks, and so, while stolen, it is not hot.

Maybe so. To be safe, he changed the plates out down the road in Elkhart.

Strange to shed thirty honest years so quickly, still knowing how to make contact even after all this time, acquiring a getaway car, guns, and a new ID.

Makes him want to puke. Didn't those thirty years mean anything? What of his family—Helena, Chloe, and Penelope innocent of all he is doing now, thinking he is on yet another business trip? Where will this lead? Can he ever make it safe for his wife and girls again?

This time, he vows he won't disappear. Not without them, which would require a lot of explaining and persuading. Knowing Helena's temper, knowing how betrayed she'll feel after so many years not knowing his secret, he may not be persuasive enough.

This trail he's created the car, guns, and ID comes with high risk. Someone could be picking up the vibration that he's on his way.

On his way, he thinks. That's the worst of this. The thirty-plus years of being straight, gone, no more than a threshold between rooms, because he knows he's still capable of doing the kinds of things he did back then.

He killed his first guy when he was eighteen.

It happened in a sort of roundabout way.

Back then, Scratch led a dual life. That was because of the Big Guy—well, truthfully, because of Big Mackey and Scratch's brother, Keith.

Mackey's crew was all right; some were smart enough but they were all street guys. Mackey was looking ahead; he wanted someone clean on the inside. He had a guy or two straddling the sides, his lawyer for one, but he also wanted a dark horse.

Scratch's brother knew his Kiddo was running wild, and he didn't want Kiddo to be any part of that life. So Keith, being Keith, braces Mackey in his own restaurant. He tells Mackey in no uncertain terms that he's to keep out of their lives.

Mackey could have set Keith straight right then, let the brother know where he stood in the neighborhood pecking order, but that wasn't Mackey's way. Mackey never acted too quickly, always looked at all the angles, the directions things might take.

Mackey tells Keith that he will make certain that Scratch stays in school, keeps his grades up, and that Scratch doesn't do stupid things. What Mackey won't do, though, and what Keith won't do, is keep Chevy away from Scratch, that they're friends, and anyway, maybe Scratch is a good influence on Chevy.

So Keith agrees, reluctant to let Big Mackey set the rules but smart enough to know it's the best he's going to get unless he wants to move his whole family several states or provinces away. Certainly, New York, Pennsylvania, Ohio, and Ontario would be ought of bounds, and if Mackey got hot under the collar, it would be a good deal further away than that.

That's how it was for three years until Scratch was eighteen.

Sure, the kid still got pulled into things with Chevy, mostly as a driver or on watch, occasionally as a temporary receiver, only never into doing the action itself. And Scratch stayed in school, never less than a B, except for German and Physics, where he just scraped by, and those were offset by As in advanced placement English and American History.

In senior year, 1964, only a few weeks from high school graduation, life for Scratch changed again on a Saturday night after the school dance.

Chevy was impatient at the dance, him not wanting to be bothered by young girls who thought they invented the sexual tease. Chevy shouldn't have been there, not being in school himself, twenty years old, and a known tear-away. That was it, though. He was known to be Big Mackey's nephew, and even the teachers at South Park High knew to step lightly unless Chevy acted up.

Scratch remembers that night. Roy Orbison was singing, spun by the high school DJ, and Scratch was dancing. He was laughing as his girl, Gloria Wyeth, did her walk-away steps on *Oh, Pretty Woman*. Gloria was smiling over her shoulder and beckoning to Scratch. My, she looked good that night. Only Chevy was scowling at him from over by the gym door and waving for Scratch to come; it was time.

They were hitting a warehouse that night. Scratch's job was to watch over the north and east side approaches from a corner spot. So with a few dance moves of his own and a light brush of his hand to Gloria's ass, he whispered, "I gotta go."

She whispered back, "Come to the side door after your Chevy thing, make it two a.m."

"You got it, my lady." His phrase for her is always, 'My lady.'

With Chevy was Shout Body, about twenty back then, who would watch the south and west approaches. Shout was a Hunkie, but the Donegals were equal-opportunity employers outside the core. The three got into the car Chevy had picked up, a nice two-tone Chevrolet, cream over light blue, though a '58 with its curled-in fins so it looked bashful compared to the bold '57.

Shout wasn't as steady as his younger brother, Miklos, so that's why he'd stand guard. Miklos, they called 56, which had to do with the short-lived Hungarian rebellion against the Soviets. That's the year the Body's got out of Hungary.

Miklos was picking up the others in a van taken from the lot of a sausage-making company. The others were Red Frankie, properly Francis MacGee, and Tierney, who was Francis Tierney MacLoughlin. The exception was Twist Rafferty, who would come on his own in a big empty eighteen-wheeler he'd acquired.

The crew all reached the warehouse within five minutes of each other. Soon, Chevy took down the security guard and put everyone to work. Twist backed the semi into the bay and kept the engine running; Red Frankie cracked the pull-down door, then Chevy began tagging the crates he wanted while Red and Tierney fired up the forklifts and began hauling out the crates. Fifty-six directed the loading and secured the crates. Shout and Scratch were on watch.

So it was all going good. In less than twenty minutes, they should be away with a load of cosmetics worth enough to give everyone two to three grand plus the extra cuts for Chevy, his source, Big Mackey, and the Meatballs.

Somewhere in the chain of things, word leaked. Someone was hungry enough to set another crew on them. They came in fast in three cars from two directions.

At first, Scratch thought it was cops. He came running and yelling to warn the guys when the first car was already past him. With the second car came shots pinging all about him, but he still kept running, dodging, pulling free his Walther as he ran.

A shoot-out was not on Big Mackey's list of desirable things. His word was to get out of the way and let him deal with the aftermath. When he went to war, it was on his terms and done tight, not some sprawling firefight. Firefight being a word they'd all learned from television as it showed what was happening in Viet Nam.

Except that Scratch was concerned that his guys would get trapped in the warehouse. So he kept on running. By the time he was on top of the situation, his guys were scattering, and the three cars were unloading a bunch of crazy fuckers waving a medley of pistols and sawed-off shotguns. Several were still firing at the fleeing Donegals.

Only Scratch wasn't fleeing.

That's what he should have been doing once he warned the

others. So that's why it was kind of accidental, killing the first crazy that noticed him. Bullets whipping at Scratch while he's fumbling with the Walther, having forgotten to release the safety. Finally, he got off his first shot without much effect. That helped, though, easing the fear.

A deep breath and a spreading calm allowed Scratch to squeeze off his second shot with more purpose, punching in the nose of an assailant and blowing out the back of his head.

The sight was unnerving, that spray of blood, bone, and tissue. There wasn't time to think about it.

The kill sent the other crazies diving for cover.

Scratch's third shot took one of them high up in the thigh. The fellow's screaming didn't help settle any nerves.

Another of them, young-looking, peaking from behind a forty-gallon drum to get a clean shot at Scratch, lost his jaw and left cheek.

Scratch's fifth bullet sent the crazies running for their cars. That fifth bullet creased the skull of their lead man, a huge fellow, putting him out of what was becoming a one-way fight.

The sixth shot took another scrambling man low in the back. By then, one of their cars was backing and careening away into the night.

Sirens could be heard, coming on strong. Another car of thugs was pulling away. With the mayhem caused by Scratch, the third car wasn't needed.

Scratch stepped forward, watchful. With care, he reloaded his Walther as he walked toward the warehouse. At the bay, he stepped up into the semi's cab, its motor still running. Pulling shut the cab door, keeping the Walther in hand, he released the brake, shifted the gear, and inched the big truck forward.

The back doors were still open, but Scratch didn't let it worry him. Shifting again and avoiding the enemies' Ford and the several downed men, he pulled out of the yard and onto the street. Shifting a third time, he had the truck well in motion and on its way to a profitable night's work.

That was his first killing, that fucker with the blown-out head. Accidental.

CHAPTER
SIX

PULLING UP ACROSS FROM KEITH'S HOUSE, SCRATCH IS FEELING qualms. Six years Scratch's senior, is Keith even alive? If so, does he still live here? How will he react to his ghost brother? How could he forgive thirty-six years of silence?

Putting a hand on the car door latch, Scratch hesitates. Slowly, he withdraws his hand. Angie, Keith's wife, will be the angry one.

Angela Quaile was known for her temper from childhood on. Famously, at the age of eight, she'd hit her neighbor, the then ten-year-old Keith, over the head with a rock for calling her pig-headed. Concussed and bleeding, Keith still managed to give her a black eye, for which, once he was well, he'd gotten a tanning from their father. You don't hit a girl.

Scratch sits back in the seat—the memories this street brings back. Even with the snow, he knows that the sidewalk lifts over by the large oak tree. Not paying enough attention, he'd once hit the angle of the sidewalk hard enough to send him over the handlebars of his bicycle. Still has the slight scar on his forehead, where his hairline used to be.

Sitting in this car across from the house gives Scratch another memory. Big Mackey, in his dark blue Buick, waving him over. Scratch gets in the front seat next to Rory Lawless, who was behind the wheel. Mackey leaning over from the back as Scratch turned to face him.

Mackey was smiling, "Look at you, freshman in college. How does it feel, fella?"

Wary but grinning back, Scratch said, "Good, you know. Different from high school."

"So what's your favorite class?"

Scratch considers, "Probably 'Man and His Culture,' it's an Anthro class. You know I'm an anthropology major."

"Listen to him, Lawless. Already sounds like a professor."

Lawless just gave a grunt of agreement.

"Well, I'm pleased as punch for ya. That I am." Big Mackey, smiling his broad smile at him, slapped a hand against his arm.

Yet Scratch knew this was no social call. Big Mackey didn't do social calls. If this were social, it would be Scratch visiting Big Mackey in his place.

Always a preamble, though, an exchange of pleasantries before business. Mackey tapped a finger on Scratch's hand, "You been lying low now since the end of May? That's, let's see, four months and more?"

"Like you say, Big Mackey. I haven't been with Chevy except now and again for a drink or a chat. Too much heat, you said, right?"

Big Mackey smiled his assurance, "Sure, sure, just right. Here's the thing, though. A certain fella won't, let alone what happened when you got our truck back. Everyone else has come to terms, so to speak. We're not to have any more fuss like that. Bad for business for everyone, right?"

Scratch nodded slowly, not sure where Mackey was headed.

"Now, you impressed me with what you did. Hell, you impressed everyone. Right, Lawless?"

Rory Lawless shifted the toothpick in his mouth and said, "Right."

"Now, you and me have talked about this. You're a college man. That's the plan. If you graduate in four years, you get a bonus. And I don't want any more odd jobs with Chevy or the other boys. We're saving you up, right?"

"Right, Big Mackey," agreed Scratch, still cautious.

The finger tapped on Scratch's wrist, "The thing is, though, we got this unfinished business with that fella I mentioned that won't let well enough alone." Big Mackey chuckles, "Actually, you know him already. Really tall and broad, you creased him that night. Gave him some migraines, I'll bet."

Rory Lawless added, "Out of action for six weeks, way I heard it."

"It seems he was an innocent bystander. He happened to be out walking when all this bother went down at the warehouse. Cops let him go. Lives not that far away," Mackey shrugged.

"On Pries, near the high school," added Lawless.

"Now, most times, I have Rory here take care of things. Trouble is Rory's just a little too well-known. Known to be my man, you see. Others might get offended, if I lift my hand."

Scratch nodded, now knowing where Mackey was going, worried about it, not liking it, but seeing it coming.

"So I was thinking, Scratch, that maybe you'd like to finish what you started." No smile as this is said, Mackey, being serious.

Not sure what to say, Scratch responded, "That night, it was a fluke, you know. I just kept shooting. Not like going after someone."

"See, it's a self-defense thing, Scratch," said Mackey. "He ain't gonna give up on this, he says, this guy, Eddie. He says we got the peace if he gets you. 'Course he knows there's no way we're gonna give him you. So he don't wants no peace. Others do, but they're not sure they want to run up against Eddie and his gang." Mackey shrugged, "So you'd be doin' a self-defense thing, taking him out."

Then Mackey shook Scratch's arm lightly, "Let me put it to ya this way. You put down five men in what? Six shots. Not running, walkin' straight at them, like a dozen guys firin' at ya. See, that kind of thing starts legends." He turned, "Am I right, Lawless?"

The driver nodded, "Yeah, a legend."

"No one up on the north side wants the Irish to have a livin' legend; he's so good with a gun." The finger tapped Scratch's shoulder again. "They'd just as soon see you put down, Scratch."

The boy felt no pride in what he was hearing. He was uneasy, picturing men in long coats hunting him, sawed-offs hidden by the skirts of their coats. "They don't know who I am?"

"Nah, they don't," admitted Mackey. "A good thing, too." He smiled, "You're gonna be our secret weapon, Scratch." Then, more serious again, "Let's get down to business. That Walther went into the lake like I told ya, right?"

Scratch nodded, "That same night."

"Okay, then." Mackey hands him a brown paper bag, heavily filled. "You're gonna need this."

Taking the bag, Scratch can feel the weight and outline of the pistol inside, "A revolver?"

Mackey shrugged, "It's clean, untraceable."

Lawless added, "You want to get close to him. Put one through his ear; that's always good."

"They don't know you're a kid," said Mackey. "That's not how the story goes. They think we imported a gunman out of Ireland. Can you believe it?" Mackey chuckled.

"This Eddie saw me," answered Scratch.

"Sure," Mackey shrugged. "What he saw was a man with a gun comin' out of the dark, unexpected, each shot he's firin' taking out a man. That's what Eddie saw until one of your bullets felt like it killed him, too."

"Eddie's from the Valley? He's Irish?" asked Scratch.

"Yeah, from the Valley but not Irish. Edward Stankiewicz, Polish fella. Some of his gang call him Stanko. Can you believe it?" Mackey laughed. "He wants the railroad yards and the warehouses roundabout. Well, he ain't gonna get them, Scratch. They've been ours for a mort of years."

So all this talk was Mackey setting it up for Scratch to kill a rival. If Mackey had gone at it directly, then it would have been a war that the Meatballs didn't want to happen. If Scratch does it, well, it's written off as self-defense. Mackey might even pick up the pieces of Stanko's gang.

Lawless cleared his throat, "There's a bar, a Polish bar, on Ridge in Lackawanna. Called the White Eagle. That's where Eddie hangs out. He's got a brand-new Lincoln towncar, light blue with silver trim. During the afternoons, he heads down to the bar from his place on Preis drives down South Park Avenue. You know that light on South Park just before you get to PS 29? Most days, he's got to stop there for a red light."

"Doesn't matter where you do it, Scratch," added Mackey. "But we figured if Lawless checked it out for you, you could take it from there."

Then Mackey smiled his broad Irish smile, "We gotta run, Scratch. It's been good seein' ya. Don't come by the club for a while, though. Oh, and I'll see that somethin' is put by for ya. Something to help out with school expenses or whatever." With that, he slapped Scratch's shoulder, a slight shove to the slap.

Three days later, Edward Stankiewicz, Eddie or Stanko to his friends, was shot two times while sitting in his car on South Park, waiting for the light to change. The second bullet went into his ear.

CHAPTER
SEVEN

SCRATCH SHAKES HIS HEAD, NOT WANTING ANY MORE MEMORIES FROM all those years ago. Instead, he thinks of Chloe and Penny, his dear young girls, and wonders what they're doing right now. He thinks he should call home and talk to Helena. Only he'd have to lie about where he is and what he's doing, and he's not comfortable lying to Helena.

He opens the car door and glances down at the FN P-90, his bulldog sub-machine gun. He pulls the newspaper off the passenger seat and tosses it over the weapon. Not that anyone's likely to peer into the car now that it's grown dark. The Beretta is nestled at the small of his back under his coat. The Taurus is at his ankle. He hopes he won't need any of this.

He steps out of the car into the snow bank on the curb. He waits by the car as a dirty white SUV slowly passes by. There are few vehicles out in the streets tonight. On up a couple of blocks, he can see a car, maybe a Ford Mustang, turning into an alley.

He peers around. No one is out. The lights of the corner

convenience store are on, filtered by the falling snow. Strings of colored lights, some twinkling, are on the snow-coated bushes and house sides along much of the street. Christmas is coming, so many places are decorated, some garish with Santas, reindeer, or Grinches, and here and there, a well-lit crèche with the baby Jesus being watched over by Mary and Joseph, whose statuettes lean crazily under the wind and ice.

He thinks again of Helena, how he hasn't gotten anything for her yet, how it's hard to give her things, that there's so little she wants. Books are okay, fiction, and maybe some clothes, though she can be precise in what clothes she likes. No jewelry, nothing too big or costly, maybe a family portrait, though not from a real professional photographer, instead a JC Penney or Moto Photo so that it's not too expensive. He'll have to give it more thought.

Scratch realizes he's hesitating, not wanting this possible confrontation.

He crosses the street quickly, goes up the front steps, and into the foyer. He looks at the mailboxes. The lower apartment isn't a name he recognizes. It looks to be French, Poincare, maybe a transplanted Canadian. Then he thinks maybe a Haitian. Thirty years back or so, Keith was renting the lower apartment to the Dempsey's.

The tag for the upper apartment says Angela Q.G. Jessup. Jessup? No recognition of that name, but Angela Q.G.? Could that be Angie? The Q.G. is right, though it gives Scratch a sinking feeling, the G. representing either death or divorce.

Abruptly, his gloved finger presses the doorbell button for Ms. Jessup.

In a moment, a tinny voice calls, "Who is it?' from the grill above the mailbox. The voice sounds old.

Without a thought, he says, "Scratch," though it wasn't a nickname ever used in the family.

There is no answer. He waits, uncertain. The seconds tick by, becoming a minute, a long minute.

The buzzer sounds, and he opens the inner door of the vestibule. He takes the stairs with a steady tread.

At the top, peering past the banister at him, housecoat tightly wrapped around her figure, is a much older version of the Angie Quaile he remembers. Her expression is stern, with a possible hint of fear.

Before he reaches her, she says, "Keith never believed you were dead."

He stops on the steps.

She stares at him, a hand now over her mouth as if to stop all the things she might say.

Scratch waits, feeling hollow, surprised by his own trepidation, "Keith?"

"Gone. Nine years ago, almost ten now. Crossing the street on a Saturday evening, and a drunk barrels into him doing sixty in a thirty-mile zone." Her hand is clutching the banister now as if to keep her standing. The words rote from long telling.

"You okay, Angie?"

No answer to that question; maybe she doesn't know the answer. "Why are you back?" Then she answers her own question, "Someone needs to die." The words bitter said with loathing.

"I don't know, Angie."

"I thought back then you were better off dead. The world a little safer."

"Angie, someone is playing me. I think I'm being summoned."

"Summoning the dead?" She laughs, an ugly, sour sound, "I'd

rather they summoned your brother. He was worth ten of you, Tommy."

"They are threatening my family."

For just a moment, she's puzzled, "Gloria?" Then she shakes her head, "No so you have a new family? Someone you care about this time?"

That one touches him, but he won't defend himself; there is no point. "Tell me, who runs the neighborhood now?"

"Those days are gone."

"Angie, Angie, someone sells drugs, someone runs the gambling, someone pimps the girls, someone runs the neighborhood. That hasn't changed; it never changes," now, his words are coldly bitter.

"I don't know," she pulls her wrap tighter about her, the gesture saying she doesn't want to know.

Then her chin goes up, "You'd better go. My man's shift ended at seven. He'll be home soon."

He nods slowly, "You okay then, Angie? How about Christine, Kevin, Rose Anne, Diana, Tammy and Stevie?"

She stares at him. He can't read her expression. Finally, she says, "We're okay. Everyone's married, and all of them are living honest lives. They've got nothing to do with anything."

"I didn't mean to imply otherwise," he answers.

Now, she nods.

"What about my kids, Jack, Ronnie, and Teddy? What about Gloria?"

She shrugs. Then adds, "Life happened to them. Gloria's been married four times. She's a lush. Well, maybe not now. She's trying again, and she's been off the sauce for a year. Married someone out of AA this time."

Then she sighs, "Your Jack is dead. Killed when a drug deal went bad. He was a young fool like you."

"Teddy's okay. He has been married twice and got his own family. Keith and Judith are your grandkids. He does something with computers, Teddy, that is."

"As for Ronnie, well, I'm not sure. She lives in New York, where she has a high lifestyle. We see her at Christmas most years, and that's it. She does something with magazines; she works at a publishing company. She never brings anyone home with her for Christmas. She's always chipper, smiling, laughing, just I don't quite believe it, you know."

He nods. The words hit him like stones, though he doesn't show it. They stare at each other in silence. Then he asks, "You need anything, Angie?"

Her softening turns brittle again, "You can't pay back thirty-six years. Nothing is ever that easy."

He gestures, indicating that wasn't what he was thinking. He tries again, "The neighborhood, Angie. Who runs it?"

Anger fills her face, but she tells him, "Go see Fionnuala, she's there 'til 3, go see the Donegals."

CHAPTER
EIGHT

O'CONNELL STREET IS QUIET IN THE FALLING SNOW AS HE DRIVES BY the house where Nuala MacGavan lives. He looks at it as he goes by; there is nothing remarkable about the building for this neighborhood except that even in the dark, he can tell it's well-maintained. Two-story, frame built like most of the houses hereabouts, though some are in brick or stone. It's not where you'd expect the head of a crime family to live, though, despite Angie's words, he can't believe Nuala heads the Donegals.

Though he owned the house where his nephew and niece lived, Big Mackey had lived in a couple of rooms over his restaurant, behind the banquet room, stage, and upstairs prep kitchen. Downstairs were the bar and the restaurant itself in two sections: the restrooms, business office, kitchen, and pantry. In the basement, besides storage and furnace room, was a lounge, the game room, and Mackey's office suite, with a waiting room. The basement was the gang's hangout.

Scratch wonders if Nuala has changed the layout. He hopes

she's updated the décor, which looked well-worn in '72. The food was good, Irish, of course, and the drink was good as well. He always thought the cook there, Gimp McElligott, made the best shepherd's pie in the world or, at least, in all of Western New York. Gimp was old back then, so he's likely long gone.

Angie said that Fionnuala would be at Mackey's until at least three in the morning. Still, he wants to get this over with. He needs to get home needs to see his Helena and the girls. He wants whatever is happening to get settled quickly. Besides, his stomach is growling, and his bladder needs a pit stop. Why not Mackey's Place?

He pulls up down the block. He can see the lights and several couples on the sidewalk ahead. There's now a parking lot next to the building. Shutting off his engine and cranking down the window, he can hear the laughter and loud talk as the two couples make their way to the cars in the lot.

Stepping out of the Camry, he adjusts his coat, where he's sewn in the leather straps and hooks. Then, leaning back into the car, he lifts the Belgian submachine gun off the passenger floor and sets it in his coat's harness. He also picks up the book he's been reading, *The Runagate Courage*, a novel written in maybe 1670 by a fellow who lived through Germany's Thirty Years War. He slips it into a wide coat pocket.

Straightening again, he smooths down the side of his coat, the bulldog resting comfortably underneath. Putting a gloved hand into his pocket, he reaches through the slit he's cut so that his hand holds the gun's grip and trigger. He takes a breath and walks toward Mackey's Place.

The windows along the front show a number of diners still at table. There are two front entrances. The side one opens on the stairs to the banquet room. The main entrance leads into a small foyer that protects those inside from the wet and cold of a Buffalo winter.

Scratch never liked that little glassed-in foyer. It always felt like a place where you could be trapped, guns blazing at you from several sides. In the old days, Scratch always went into Mackey's from the back, either from the kitchen entrance that led into the pantry first or the back hall entrance that customers could also use, the hall leading by the restaurant office, restrooms, and cloakroom.

Now, though, he steps into the little foyer and on into the bar. A young woman hurries over, dressed well but with a little too much cleavage showing. "Table for one, sir?" her gesture indicating the main room, separated from the bar by a half-wall topped by an etched glass screen, the etchings appearing to show the Irish countryside.

Scratch pauses, looking about. The subdued lighting makes the place look elegant, with the glint of silver and the rich dark colors of the walls and carpeting. Instead of the Irish fiddle tunes he expected, the music playing is classical, picked out by a piano and a few strings rather than an orchestra. Yes, elegant is likely the word to use, which isn't what Scratch expected for Mackey's Place and the whole First Ward.

He nods, "Yes."

She picks up a menu from the small podium by the inner door, "This way, sir. Or would you prefer the back dining room?"

The back room was where Mackey had his table. Scratch wonders if Nuala keeps a table back there for herself and those who need to talk with her. He's not ready to see Nuala. "The front room is fine, though I'd prefer a table away from the windows."

She smiles, "It is a cold night, with the wind throwing snow at us." Then, she leads him to table number ten, at least that's how it was numbered years ago, a four-person table near the archway to the back dining room.

Of the twelve tables in the main dining room, only three others are occupied: one party of five, one threesome, and an older couple. He glances at each as he follows the hostess. All seem honest diners.

There is a coat stand near his table. He slips out of the long coat and hangs it up, careful not to reveal anything odd about it. He retrieves his book. Then, as he sits, she hands him the menu.

"The specials tonight are here," the young hostess says, tapping a sheet attached to the inside cover of the menu. "I recommend the halibut with cumin-pepper curry." She leans forward to point out the rest of the menu, "Of course, we're famous for our steak Diane and our sesame-chili chicken." He can't help but glance at the swell of her cleavage. Realizing this, she straightens quickly, blushing, and gives him an automatic smile, and then leaves him to make his decision.

Mentally, he shrugs, wondering why so many women show off their bodies and then become embarrassed when they receive appraising stares from men. Perhaps it's not the young woman's idea to wear a revealing dress; perhaps it's what is expected of a hostess. He leafs through the several pages of the menu. The Irish food is relegated to its own half-page.

A young fellow is pouring water into a glass containing ice and a lemon. He smiles and nods at Scratch. The boy appears to be Hispanic, which gets Scratch thinking again about how the world changes.

Soon, the boy is back with a breadbasket. He nods at Scratch again and is replaced by a white-jacketed waitress wearing a black tie. The waitress, perhaps in her late forties, hair cut short and colored red, smiles, "I'm Elyse. I'll be your server this evening.

What can I get you to drink, sir?" Her tag spells her name with a Y instead of an I, which she pronounces as 'Ah-Lease.'

He's already picked out his drink, "I'd like a glass of the pinot noir. And I'm ready to order if you are?"

"Go ahead." Perhaps because she is tall, she goes down on one knee so she can look at him at eye level.

"I'd like to start with potato and leek soup. Then the roasted beet salad and the pork tenderloin."

"Would you prefer the garlic polenta, roasted new potatoes, or mushroom risotto with the pork, sir?"

"The risotto."

She smiles, standing again. "I'll put your order in and have the wine for you shortly."

She'd not written down any part of his order, but he is confident she's got it in mind correctly. Her competence contrasts with long ago when Bev Sullivan used to take an order here. She could never read her own handwriting. "Thank you."

As he waits, he opens *Runagate Courage* at the bookmark. Chapter 11 which opens with 'After Courage begins to lead an upright life she unexpectedly becomes a widow again.'

When on the road alone, it's his habit to have along at least three books as companions for meals and evenings. As he sits and reads, he finds himself anticipating a good supper.

After a bit, he decides it's time for the restroom he stands, careful that his sweater still covers the automatic tucked into his belt at the small of his back, and glances about as if uncertain. Then he steps down through the archway to the back dining room.

Quickly, he looks toward table 15, Mackey's old table, checking for Nuala or any fellow who looks like a tough. No one.

He passes through the back dining room to the rear hall and

the restrooms, his need suddenly feels desperate, as if his back teeth are floating. Afterwards, washing his hands and drying them on the cloth towel provided, he stares into the mirror over the sink. He looks old and tired yet resolute.

Back at his table, the soup is waiting.

As it proceeds, the meal is better than the First Ward has any right to receive. It's not so much the quality as the price such quality requires. Has the First Ward become prosperous in the past thirty-six years? Or are the diners coming from much further away?

For that matter, have the expectations of the locals for restaurant food become so much more cosmopolitan? If so, how do all the Red Lobsters, Olive Gardens, and Chili's stay in business, let alone the Denny's and MacDonald's?

"Would you care for coffee and dessert, sir? Or perhaps an after-dinner drink?" Elyse, the waitress, is smiling at him. It seems genuine as if she likes seeing a man who knows what he wants and enjoys eating it.

"Which is better, your ricotta cheesecake or the cornbread pudding with whiskey sauce?"

"I favor the bread pudding, personally. Although, I'd like to point out the baklava on the specials menu. It is our own, made with wildflower honey."

"Let's make it the bread pudding. And hot tea, please."

"I'll bring the box of teas, sir, so you can make your selection."

That's a good sign, he thinks, no coffee-flavored tea water that you get so often in restaurants. Why have so few restaurants mastered tea when they offer cappuccino or latte even at the cheap places?

The young Hispanic fellow brings the hot-water pot, cup, and saucer while the waitress comes back with a wooden box. As it seems to be her habit, she goes down on one knee and opens the box for his inspection. After debating between several green and black teas, he selects the Yunnan, thinking black tea is better than bread pudding. "This will do fine," he smiles.

She smiles back as if complicit in the thoughtful selection of a wedding ring or a single delicate rose for his beloved.

As the tea steeps and he awaits the dessert, he thinks about his next move. He realizes that all through this meal, he has been surprised. Mackey's Place has become so fine, so far from its origins, that he can't believe Fionnuala MacGavan leads a criminal gang that still calls itself the Donegals.

What would Rory Lawless or Twist Rafferty have made of a place like this? They would have laughed over their corn beef and pints of stout.

Twist went down over that Chinese restaurant thing. When was that? It must have been in '67, the year after Jack was born.

Too bad, too, because Twist was all right. It wasn't even one of the Donegals' gigs.

He remembers how it went at the Harbor View Gardens, a second-floor Chinese restaurant popular enough at the time. It was December, too, come to think of it.

Twist is there just having supper with the woman he was dating. About one in the morning, a small orchestra playing and a few people dancing, five men coming busting in with shotguns and pistols, quickly securing the place, saying something like, "All right, no trouble. We mean business."

Lining everyone up against the wall, some of the women customers weeping in fear.

Twist had separated himself somewhat from the line-up. While several of the robbers were forcing the cashier's cage and one of them was clubbing the manager, Twist pulled his pistol and began firing.

Though Twist hit one of the robbers, he'd had too much drink to do much good. He went down under successive shotgun blasts, as did several other patrons. Twist and some woman customer died, the woman on the way to the hospital. Peggy, something, if Scratch remembers right. Age 20.

In a way, Twist got his revenge. The fellow he hit sought medical treatment. That put the cops on the crew's trail right fast, though not as fast as Big Mackey.

That's where Scratch came into the fray.

Five men and, downstairs, two drivers, plus the guy that set it up and supplied the guns. Eight of them and a couple of girlfriends who knew what was going down. There were too many to keep a secret, even if one hadn't been winged.

Mackey wanted a clean sweep. He didn't want anyone left who touched a Donegal. Big Mackey could be damn fierce despite his genial exterior.

The fellow they called Blackie was the one Twist hit, Frank Franklin, all of nineteen. Why, with the fellow's Franklin surname, would his parents name him Frank? Just one of those common mysteries that occur.

Blackie's girl was Dorothy Moss. Lawless got to her before the cops and got all the names. He did better than the cops, even getting the second driver, the fourteen-year-old Tony 'the Kid' Messina, who was Ralph Gentile's cousin. Ralph being the guy that set the whole deal up.

The five in the restaurant were Blackie Franklin, Rocco Gentile, who was Ralph's younger brother, Herman Baumgartner, Jack Harlison, and Nickie Marino. The drivers were Frankie Riccio and Tony Messina. That left Ralph's old woman, Marcella King.

The cops were able to nab two, Blackie and his best friend, Jack Harlison. Those two went away to Attica. Both died in a prison riot a couple of years later, thanks to Big Mackey.

Dorothy Moss and Frankie Riccio went untouched for a number of years. After all, their testimony was key to sending up Blackie and Jack.

Scratch isn't sure who got the nod from Big Mackey to take those two out. He knows the girl died in a hit-and-run.

As for the rest of them, Lawless did two: Ralph and Marcella, in a rather too-obvious apartment fire. Scratch took out the others: Nickie, Herman, Rocco, and Tony the Kid—nothing fancy, just quick, almost painless hits.

Baumgartner he'd had to track to Albany, New York.

Big Mackey did warn him afterwards to start varying his method, "No matter what Lawless says, you don't want a signature with that bullet-in-the-ear thing. You understand, Scratch?"

"Sir, your dessert. I'm sorry it took more time than usual. Can I get you fresh hot water?" The waitress has broken his reverie.

She is not smiling at him now, which suddenly makes Scratch wary. Looking about, he sees that he's the only customer left in the dining room, although there are patrons at the bar. He nods, "No need. I still have tea."

The bread pudding looks perfect.

"Then I'll bring you your check, sir."

From the archway, a woman's voice, uncommonly deep, says, "There's no need, Elyse. This guest is on the house."

Nuala MacGavan steps to the table, her gait awkward but practiced, "You won't mind if I join you? Elyse, could you bring me a cup of coffee." Then Nuala sits down opposite Scratch.

CHAPTER
NINE

Fionnuala looks good, thinks Scratch with surprise. A touch of make-up, not something she ever used to do. Dressed simply but nicely, hands manicured, hair swept back, and pretty in a care-worn way, which is right for someone in their fifties. The hunchback still, of course, but it never bothered Scratch.

Nuala is studying him as well. She breaks the silence, "I heard you were coming this way."

He nods, thinking of the trail he's made, what with the guns and all. "Boyo?"

"Yes, Boyo's where it started, by way of Millicent. Do you remember Millicent?"

"Millie, his sister?"

She nods, "He tells her everything. Then she tells everyone else. It's why he had to go straight." She chuckles wryly.

"Gunny, in Cleveland?"

"Sure, Gunny, too. Only he tells one or maybe two, me included."

"Who else did he tell?"

"You're looking good, Scratch, all things considered. Healthy. If you wanted to stay that way, why'd you come back?"

"You didn't summon me?"

Her face is smooth, though her eyes widen ever so slightly, "Summon?"

"Someone gave me a call. Someone entered my home," saying it stirs a flame of anger.

She looks thoughtful, "Maybe Donovan."

"Donovan?"

"You don't know Donovan, his brothers, and their sister. They were born after you disappeared. The Taafe boys."

"Taafe? The Professor had a family?"

Nuala smiles that same broad MacGavan smile that Big Mackey used to have, "Surprised us all. He was fifty when he married. Four kids in six years, all on young Caitriona."

"Riona O'Lynch? That plain girl with glasses and braces? Why she couldn't have been eighteen in '72."

Nuala smiles again, "She became a beauty enough for a good dozen years, though she never expected it. Malachy Taafe saw it and scooped her up before she realized she'd become attractive. It was a love match despite their age difference. He passed away three years back, all of eighty-two. Died peacefully."

"He was a pimp."

"Yes, though better than most. Not like these Russians today. He only had a couple of girls at a time, and he treated them well. He only had the ones that wanted that life. Always protected them. Never used drugs to keep them, always gracious when they wanted to move on."

Scratch considers the idea of Malachy Taafe as a father, as having a wife, someone he loved. Malachy, who tended bar here at

Mackey's Place, rolled a printing press in the cellar of his Ma's house where he made moderate-quality twenty-dollar bills from an old set of plates he'd bought somewhere. Then, on to the current day, "Why would Donovan Taafe care about me?"

Nuala gets a distant look in her eye, "You remember back all those years ago? When the Italians were going after each other? Everything in turmoil, and no one knows who to trust. New deals being made and broken almost day by day?"

Scratch nods, "Sure, I was there. You were, what? Sixteen?"

"Ten years younger than you, almost to the day," she answers, smiling. "Did you know I was sweet on you then?"

"I was married."

"Gloria," she shakes her head. "A sorry story."

He stays silent and feels a stab of guilt.

Nuala's eyes search his face. Then she says softly, "You never knew, did you?"

"Knew what?"

She smiles at him, "Gloria was alive, exciting, wasn't she? Those unbelievable breasts and her ass that moved so smoothly when she walked near men. Always interested in what you had to say, not tall but perky, as if she were always on tiptoes looking into your eyes to melt you with hers." Nuala chortles.

The description is pretty fair, thinks Scratch. How that woman loved a party, dancing, talking, and catching your attention. Then it hits him what he never knew. What Nuala is telling him, "Who?"

Nuala shrugs, "Who knows. Gloria may not know them all herself."

"Who?" Why get angry now after all these years, and still he feels some heat. What is the point of this? And he realizes at least one answer, "Chevy?"

Nuala nods, "Sure, Chevy."

Still trying to connect the dots, Scratch asks, "The Professor?"

"Sure, Malachy."

He stops then. Takes a breath. "Why this ancient history, Nuala?"

"No history is really ancient, Scratch. It all keeps working in the present." Then she shrugs, "I'm guessing here. I named Donovan Taafe as your likely necromancer, summoning a ghost from the past." She laughs again briefly. Then she lowers her voice, "Donovan and his brothers know their Donegal history. At least, the MacGavan part of that history as it played out here in the First Ward. For that matter, in our circles, who hasn't heard the legend of Scratch, the Donegals' dark killer. You could be a comic book villain, Scratch."

"There were others, Lawless, Shiv Stolar."

"Sure. But only one unknown, who only Big Mackey or, after his heart attack, Chevy could conjure up. All the people in our trade knew Lawless would be by Mackey's side. And enough knew about Shiv. When was Shiv taken out? Must have been '71."

He nods, "Yeah, November 12."

"The three guys that killed Shiv? What happened to them?" She holds up a finger, "No, don't tell me. My uncle, Big Mackey, places a call. Now, the FBI can probably pull the transcript from their archives somewhere because they were definitely on top of Big Mackey by then. But you don't need to because I can tell you that the call was to one Chevy MacGavan, and it says only 'Put Scratch on it.'"

Scratch shrugs, his face wry, not wanting the memories.

"You have to understand, Scratch, that Chevy MacGavan was having what we'd call today a conflict of interest."

This catches him, Chevy?

Nuala continues, "It was the heart attack. Big Mackey was fighting retirement. He wanted to stay in the game, the only game he knew. Others wanted him out. Chevy wanted to take over. And everything's piling up: tax evasion charges, wiretaps, and the Feds about to tear Mackey apart. Which they did, and which that second heart attack the autumn of '72 finished."

"Now, try to imagine Chevy MacGavan running a gang of hoods successfully. Where's the restraint? Where's the patience? Where's the careful calculation and balance? Sure, he's got the energy, he's got the balls, he's got the cruelty, and, maybe, the street smarts to be a force. But he's missing what's needed. Right?"

Scratch nods. Then says softly, "All of us knew that, Nuala. That there'd come a time when Chevy would have to face reality."

"Right. Even I knew it, his kid sister, the cripple, all of sixteen. I figured he'd last a year, two at the outside, once Big Mackey was out of the game." She shakes her head sorrowfully, "He didn't even make it that far."

They sit silently for a moment. Then she rouses herself, "Even Chevy knew it. So he was seeking deals, allies—thus the conflict of interest. Those guys you took out were with the people Chevy was expecting to hook up with. The price went way up for Chevy. And you were part of the price."

CHAPTER
TEN

Nuala stretches, and Scratch can hear the creak of her neck. She notices, "It doesn't get any better. My back, I mean. Age just makes things worse. You'd think after fifty or so years, I'd be used to the pain. My doctor says I'll feel more discomfort as I age. I think discomfort is a word only doctors and nurses use with patients."

He nods, noncommittal. What can you say in the face of something so basically unfair?

"You want a drink, Scratch?"

He shakes his head no, knowing that the one glass of wine was enough, knowing to stay alert.

Nuala smiles, "Well, I'm having a drink." She turns and waves at Elyse. The waitress comes over quickly. "Would you ask Darren to pour me a Jack Daniels neat?"

"Yes, Nuala. Everything okay then?" The waitress's eyes Scratch carefully.

Nuala smiles, "Yes, yes. Old friends catching up on the years gone by." She does a shooing motion with her hands, then adds, "I think trade's pretty well done for today. Why don't you, Marie, and Txomin call it a night."

As the waitress walks away, Scratch asks, "Marie is your hostess?"

"Yes, why? She's new to this. Did she handle you all right?"

Scratch recognizes the businessperson in Fionnuala as she asks. "Sure, she just seemed a little uncertain about her cleavage."

Nuala laughs loudly, "Well, I think that's a little new to her, too. She's only seventeen. She's Kilbride's granddaughter."

"KK? That old thief? He's still around?"

"Well, sort of. He's alive. In prison, having burgled one hell of a vindictive attorney and got sent away for a good spell. 'Course, it was his third fall."

Then she adds, "Aren't all attorney's vindictive? Lawyers may or may not be, but it's pretty much a rule for those who call themselves attorneys."

"Kelan Kilbride was a pretty fair thief," he comments.

She shrugs, "Age. Drink. He grew sloppy over time."

"Well, he was good in his day."

"Yes, he was. He should have realized when it was time to change careers." She pauses, then adds, "You changed careers, right Scratch?"

He's saved from answering as Elyse comes back with Nuala's whiskey. The two women have a side conversation about scheduling hours for the coming week, then about the weather and what it might mean for the clientele.

Scratch takes the time to think. Why would Donovan Taafe be interested in him? The Professor and he got along well enough in the old days. The Professor was one of the few who knew how active a member of the gang Scratch was. Once he went to college, most of the others took it for granted that whatever he did for Big Mackey was on the white-collar side of the business.

On the street, they might nod at him. Tierney would say hello and ask about Gloria. KK's brother Pete came over to the house a few times. That was pretty much because of Scratch's niece, Christine. They were of an age. Most of the guys, though, didn't see much of a connection with that guy, Tommy, whom Chevy used to run with. Not many connected Tommy with the mysterious Scratch.

Only a few used the name Scratch—Big Mackey, Chevy, Lawless, the Professor. Nuala knew it but never used it back then. Now that he thinks of it, why would Angie know it, except maybe it surfaced once he disappeared.

Nuala turns back to him, "So, we were talking about careers. You changed yours, right? We would have heard otherwise. Would have known old Scratch was alive."

"I make toys. I have a family. And I'm not Scratch anymore, or Tommy for that matter." His words come out level, and even so, he wonders if it's true if he's sitting here with Nuala MacGavan.

"Family, huh? Boys, girls? What ages?" Her questions are almost wistful.

He doesn't answer at first, considering that in answering, he is placing his family in jeopardy. Decides not with Nuala, "Girls, eleven and thirteen. Grade school girls, sixth and seventh grades."

"I'll bet they do well in school," she's smiling, that wistfulness even stronger.

"What about you?" he asks. He doesn't want to say how proud he is of his girls and how much they mean to him.

"Me? No, I'm alone." Then she laughs, "Not that I haven't had offers. You'd be surprised at the number of men attracted to ugly."

Without thinking, he responds, "You aren't ugly, Nuala. You've never been ugly."

Now she's silent. Then, slowly, she says, "There's only one man I ever thought I loved. Only he was married, and then he disappeared." Then she laughs, "So a fat lot of good that did me."

He would like to touch her. To provide comfort, though there's no comfort he can offer. "If you are open to it, love comes in surprising ways," he thinks of his Helena, of meeting her in the rain as she tries to flag down a taxi.

Nuala changes the subject, "If it was Donovan, then I'm sure he knows you're here. One of his boys was at the bar earlier."

CHAPTER
ELEVEN

WHEN HE'D COME IN, WAS MET BY THE HOSTESS, MARIE; THERE MUST have been seven or eight people at the bar or the stools nearby, several of them women. He thinks back, picturing the room. Make that nine, there was a fellow at the far end, near where the wait staff pick up their drink orders.

None had done more than glance his way. Still, if they were regulars, they knew he wasn't from the neighborhood.

"So tell me more about Donovan Taafe and his brothers," he says to Nuala.

"Donovan's all right in his way. A bit like Big Mackey in his amiability, only more polite. Just as ruthless, too. Or he tries to be, seeing as he's not been tested much yet. He works out, carries himself well, and uses violence to intimidate but picks his spots carefully. Not reckless like Chevy was." She pushes back, considering, "On the whole, I could like him. Used to when he was younger."

"Cops or feds interested in him yet?"

She shrugs, smiling thinly, "They don't confide in me, Scratch." Then she pauses, "Probably not. He's a neighborhood menace, that and the rail yards, shipping, trucking, you know. The old game. I suppose if anyone were concerned about him, it would be the Coast Guard and Homeland Security and the same kind of fellows up in Canada."

"Why? He moves people, contraband?"

She nods, "Yeah, smuggling, that's part of the pie."

"Anyone gunning for him?"

"Sure, probably. He's pissed off the Senecas, that's for sure. Where he stands with all the others, I don't know. I guess they respect the muscle he can leverage, and as long as certain lines don't get crossed and certain payments are made, it's live and let live."

She throws back the last of her Jack Daniels, then looks him in the eye, "You got a place to stay tonight? If not, Mackey's old rooms are available upstairs. The last tenant was Marie until we ensured her ex-boyfriend wasn't stalking her anymore."

Briefly interested, Scratch asks, "How did you do that?"

"Well, he should be glad they invented aluminum softball bats. One of the old wooden sluggers might have hurt him. He hobbled out of the picture."

"Not you or Marie swinging that bat," he says, probing to see whom she could call on for that kind of thing.

The soft lighting touches her smiling lips, "I have a lot of friends, Scratch."

A thought crosses his mind. He gestures around him, "You've turned Mackey's into something fine, unusual for the First Ward."

Nuala looks about her as if trying to see how he sees her restaurant, "It took five years to clear up the legal mess after Big Mackey died, and another fourteen to move from boiled cabbage to what you see today. There were times when I didn't think the place would survive. Maybe there were times when I wished it wouldn't." She turns back to him, "This is a good place, Tommy. Not just the food, it's a place where people like Marie can be safe."

He nods, trying to understand what she's telling him. Then he leans forward toward her, "You were telling me about the Taafe brothers."

"Fergus is the one to watch out for, the middle brother. Fat Fergie. He hasn't any use for anyone who's not family. There's enough anger in him to be a nuclear bomb. The Professor never cared much for his second son; the boy never seemed bright enough, kind enough, just a resentful brute."

"The third brother is Young Malachy. Not physically tough like the older two, more cerebral. Handles the numbers side of the business. As for their sister, Gemma, she was like Catriona, blossoming late. In her twenties, she'd turn any man's head, even those not interested in females. She worked at modeling for a time in New York. Ronnie got her started down there. But she's been back here for a couple of years. She was married briefly to the son of a state representative. Now I hear she's home with her brothers. None of the boys are married. They have a house out in the country in one of the Southtowns, Hamburg, I think. They also have a place over on Macamley Street by Taylor Park." Her recitation is over, she folds her hands and looks at him.

"They have a gang?"

She doesn't answer for a time; she just stares at him as if searching his face for something. Finally, she asks, "What are you going to do, Scratch?"

"Go talk to them."

"Well, be careful. Yeah, they've got a gang, maybe a half-dozen guys, and they can probably call on some others. Altogether, counting themselves, maybe a dozen. About half of what Big Mackey had." She shakes her head, "It never really ends, does it?"

Looking at her steadily, studying the fine lines by her eyes, he says, "You never used to call me Scratch, Nuala." The childhood name said softly.

A flash of anger touches her face, "Well, Tommy is long dead. And whoever you are now when you're not in Buffalo, I don't want to know. As far as I can tell, Scratch is the only person sitting with me. A name that's faded into history here but which I fear is going to be heard again right quick."

He sits quietly, knowing they are almost done.

After a time, she pushes her chair back. "You want to find them, try Healey's bar on Abbott Road." Stands, considers, "Let me get you a key so you can use the apartment if you want to." She walks away.

He drinks a last sip of cold tea, down to its dregs, then stands himself, puts on the heavy coat, adjusting it carefully to make reaching the bulldog easy, then picks up his book, pocketing it opposite from the gun.

Nuala comes back and holds out a key, "It's the pantry entrance. If you don't use it, mail it back to me."

Now she looks tired, her twisted body making her witch-like in the soft lighting. Yet her trust in him surprises Scratch. He's not sure he'd bet on him coming back after seeing the Taafe brothers. "You said one of their gang was at the bar. Do you remember where he was sitting?"

"Kit? The big guy, loud, about halfway along, there with his wife, Lauralee." Nuala smiles, and the witchery is gone, "The wife's a lawyer."

As he takes the key, Scratch thinks back and places Kit. About thirty, give or take a year. Tall, thick-waisted, happy, jabbering away at the brown-haired woman at his side, she attractive enough, giving good-humored verbal jabs back. No recollection of either one paying any attention to him caught up with each other. "Kit short for Christopher?"

"Christian. Christian Cotter. Happy-go-lucky unless you anger him." Nuala shakes her head again, "I've had enough for this evening. You go on and do what you think you have to do."

Then, in that instant, Scratch realizes that until Fionnuala sat down with him, it was unlikely anyone in the bar had any idea who he was. By sitting with him, Nuala fingered him.

CHAPTER
TWELVE

CLOSE ON TO MIDNIGHT, SCRATCH SITS IN HIS STOLEN CAMRY ACROSS and down the street from Healey's. The bar is a neighborhood place, nondescript, neon beer signs in the small windows, a sorry single strand of Christmas lights framing the entrance, green-walled, two floors, too much heat escaping so that despite the snow, he can see a lot of gray roof.

Scratch has not seen anyone go in or out, though the lights are on, and he bets there's music playing. Well, he thinks, nothing ventured, nothing gained.

He opens the car door, steps out, adjusting his coat, and crosses the street to come up on the building from the side. The attached cowbell clanks as he enters the door, drawing the bartender's eyes. None of the other three at the bar stir; all neighborhood sots well into their drink by now. Scratch feels let down. Still, he doesn't hesitate. He goes to the bar and says, "Donovan in tonight?"

The fellow behind the bar is well-muscled, with hair long but caught up in a ponytail. He is in his late twenties, tats along his arm, and peeks out of his neckline. He doesn't look like he belongs in a place like this, even if it were busy this Friday night. The barkeep looks about him as if searching the place beyond the three sots, "Which Donovan is that?" he says sarcastically.

From up the lighted stairwell at the back of the room comes a thrum of voices, music, and a huge laugh. Though Scratch can't make out what's being said, the laugh is familiar. He shrugs, "Never mind, I hear Kit upstairs."

"Mister, that's a private party. You want to go up there, I've got to buzz you in." The bartender looks stubborn like buzzing Scratch in is going to take some convincing. "Strangers don't go up unless they say so."

Within Scratch, the heat is rising. The rage that flared when he saw that his house had been entered has been kept on simmer for some time. Still, he banks his anger back one more time, "If Donovan is upstairs, he'll see me. You can tell him it's Scratch."

"Scratch?"

"Yeah." The urge to put down this fellow and buzz himself up as a surprise runs strong in Scratch. But the Taafes have offered no violence yet, and Scratch is too uncertain about what's going on to torch the future.

"Dandy, who's this?" The woman's voice is pleasant with inquiry.

Scratch looks up and sees a young woman on the rear stairs, an empty glass in her hand.

"Says his name is Scratch, Gemma. Wants to see Donovan."

"Scratch," she repeats. Now, addressing him, "Well, Scratch, what can the Taafe family do for you?"

He can't see her well, the light of the stairwell behind her and the back of the bar room dim. Even so, the impression is one of striking beauty. "I believe your brother has summoned me, Miss. I'd like to confirm that."

"Summoned? What a fancy word. Scratch?" She laughs softly, "The Donegals, right? You know I never believed in you. All those stories they used to tell. What are you, eighty-something?" obviously thinking of her own aged dad.

One of the sots at the bar looks up suddenly, stares at Scratch in the bar mirror's reflection, and then slides away out of Scratch's reach, croaks, "A fuckin' ghost. This used to be a quiet place." The sot lurches up off the stool and, staggers away, out of reach, and goes around Scratch to get out the door.

This elicits a merry laugh from the girl, "Well, you livened up Old Joe. Guess he believes in ghosts." She addresses the bartender, "Dandy, I need another Vieve Cliquot. We're out upstairs. Then why don't you buzz me and the mysterious Scratch back up?"

Old Joe? Is there a hint of recognition in Scratch—not Jozsef Palka? What is this place, an old thieves' home?

Meanwhile, Dandy, the bartender, comes up with the bottle of champagne, its distinctive orange label, and hands it to Gemma, who has stepped to the far end of the bar. Scratch can see the blonde beauty in the light. She's a touch wasted tonight, but she looks better than all the others in any random collection of five thousand thirty or thereabouts females. Beautiful enough to seem unbelievable, plastic, a computer-generated creation, more freak than Nuala MacGavan. He looks away from her.

Gemma giggles, "My Ma always said don't worry about the ones who stare at you; worry about the ones who look away." Then she crooks a finger to have him follow her.

So he does. Up the stairs, the sway of her just ahead. Before she reaches the top step, the door is buzzed, and she swings it open and continues on in, calling out, "Fergie, would you believe who I found waiting downstairs?"

Scratch steps in and stares about. Pool tables, a dart board, an unused bar, tables and chairs, a jukebox pulsing with rock 'n roll Christmas songs, and ten people, not counting Gemma: six men and four other women, a private party. He recognizes Kit and Lauralee Cotter.

One of the men steps forward, the family resemblance to Gemma there, though broadened and layered, Fat Fergie. It's not really fat; it's heavy muscle sheathed in thickness. Beyond him, Kit Cotter, taller but not quite as broad, calls to his boss, "It's Fionnuala's Scratch."

Gemma laughs, sounding slurred even when laughing, "I always thought Fionnuala was a bull dyke. Fancy her having a man."

Another fellow moves to the side, a pistol held barrel down in his right hand. The bodyguard for Fergie thinks Scratch.

"I'm Fergus Taafe. You want a drink?" Fergie is standing out of Scratch's reach, not offering his hand but gesturing to the bottles on one of the tables.

Scratch nods toward the bodyguard, "Is this a friendly party?"

"Guess that depends on you. I'm willing to be friendly tonight. We're celebrating Christmas a little early or Thanksgiving a bit late," eyebrows raised, Fergus shrugs. Then he turns slightly, "You already know Gemma. Kit, here, recognizes you from Mackey's Place. His wife, Lauralee." Waving a hand, Fergie indicates the others, "Then we've got Mike and Patti, Enzo there, Adnan and Madiha, Gail, and over there with the gun, Gail's man, Doyle. Say hi folks."

A chorus of "Hi's" punctuate Fergus' introductions.

Fergus takes up where he left off, "So what about you, Scratch? You feeling friendly tonight?"

A fellow of Italian descent, an Arab couple, and the rest of Irish or mixed-breed Americans thinks Scratch an interesting combination. "Yeah, I can be friendly. A drink will do," gesturing to Gemma with his chin, "maybe some champagne. And yes, I'm called Scratch, and I do know Nuala from a long time back, as I knew the Professor, your father."

From across the room, Doyle says, "He's got a sawed-off shotgun under his coat, Fergie."

Scratch smiles, "Actually, no. It's a bit more than that." He opens the long skirt of his coat to reveal the submachine gun pointed roughly in the direction of Fergus Taafe and those near him. "Why don't I just set it on the table over here?"

Slowly, he unhooks the FN P90. The unusual design of the gun gets an inquiring look from Enzo and Adnan; its odd shape makes it distinctive. Seeing Scratch smiles, "Built so it doesn't snag on your clothes, yet it's capable of spraying 50 5.7 slugs fast enough to cover this room in seconds." He sets the gun down on the table and then slips out of his coat.

Suspicious, Doyle calls out, "What's in the coat's pocket?"

Pulling free the *Runagate Courage* book, Scratch waggles it before setting it and his coat next to the submachine gun.

Gemma laughs, handing a flute of champagne to Scratch, "A reader, an intellectual, right?"

"Better than television," answers Scratch with a smile.

"What, you get sports on that book, too?" inserts Fergie, chuckling at his own witticism. "Come on, come on, let's sit. Or if you'd rather, you can dance. Take Gemma; Enzo won't mind. He knows Gemma would rather dance than do anything else in the world. Right, Gemma?"

"Almost," answers Gemma, trying a frisky wink, only she does it so slowly that it looks like she's having trouble focusing. "We need to trash these Christmas tunes and get somethin' rippin' going." She sways over to the jukebox.

Scratch pulls out a chair and sits. The others look at one another and then do the same. Except watchful Doyle, who leans against the empty bar, his pistol holstered now, though he gives the impression it could be in his hand right quick.

"So, Scratch, you're back from the dead and doing social visits?" asks Fergie, sipping a Molson's ale from the bottle.

Gemma calls from across the room by the jukebox, "Says he was summoned. Hey, anyone want to hear…"

Before she can complete the question, Enzo yells with a laugh, "None of your Rap crap, Gemma. Get something classic on. You know, *Smooth* by Santana or something by Phil Collins."

"Summoned?" asks Fergie of Scratch more softly as the others take up their conversations, and Enzo joins Gemma.

"Fionnuala thought it might be your brother, Donovan."

"Fionnuala, that crazy bitch," snorts Fergie shaking his head. "What does she know about anything except the First Ward?" Fergie waves dismissively, "Hell, if my brother wanted to see you, he'd a called."

Fergie takes a big swallow from his green bottle, then "You go way back, right? What was it in the seventies? Ancient history. Though you knew Da, right?"

"The Professor, sure."

"What was he like back then, I mean, back in his prime? You know?"

"He was a cool hand, solid. Mackey relied on him to keep the home base. Not a violent man like Lawless. He'd listen to whoever sat at his bar. Still, a Donegal, a true malefactor," Scratch gives up trying to convey the Professor, with his odd humor, playing at words, being sympathetic but always thinking where was the advantage. In his way, the Professor was Mackey's intelligence officer.

"Well, he made the family fortune," laughs Fergie.

That triggers a memory; Scratch says, "I remember the time the Carbone brothers thought they'd break up the Professor's bar. It was a night when Chevy and his guys were out, and Mackey was laid up in the apartment with the flu. Joey Carbone comes in first and swings up a sawed-off to cover the patrons. Then Jimmy comes in with a sledgehammer, followed by Jules with another sawed-off. All sullen, doing payback for some slight that only those hair-brains knew about. That being the way they were."

Scratch eases back, sipping a swallow of champagne, letting it tease his tongue, "Anyway, the Professor calls out *Everyone here, stay calm. The brothers Carbone have a grievance, and it's best if we hear them out.*"

"So Jimmy, the youngest, says, *We got nothin' to say to you. Just step aside. We're goin' to smash everythin' in here.*"

"*Sure ya' can't say anythin' with a dry mouth*, answers the Professor. He sets up three glasses on the bar and pours out seven and seven's, that being the boys' drink of choice."

"Well, Joey figures a drink wouldn't hurt, so he lifts the shotgun on his shoulder. Joey was pretty reliable in thinking a drink never hurt. Jimmy shakes his head, makes a noise of disgust, and whines, *Joey, we're here on bizness.*"

"Joey shrugs, half his seven and seven already gone; *You want me to drink yours?*"

"Naturally not, so Jimmy sets the sledge on the bar, not gently either, and takes up his drink."

"That leaves Jules, shotgun at the ready. Now, Jules never said much. I suspect he had more brains than the other two put together, but he was big on family loyalty and was often led into disastrous adventures by the younger two. Jules says, *Don't touch mine,* meaning, I think, he intended to drink it when they were done."

"Joey answers, his drink already gone. Ya *can have a whole bottle later, right, Perfesser? And he winks at your Da."

"Your Da shakes his head sorrowfully. *Well, I'm afraid not, Joey."*

"*Why not?* Replies Jimmy, 'cause Joey's already drinking Jules' portion."

"*You said you were smashin' everything, right?"*

"*Yeah, so? That don't mean we can't save a bottle for Julio,* exclaims Jimmy with some heat."

"*Well, if you can save one bottle, then why are you smashing any bottles? After all, they're all full of drink, kind of like a national treasure."*

"Your Da says this very earnestly, very seriously, as if trying to understand the logic of an obscure point of philosophical argument. Jimmy stands there momentarily befuddled, then says obstinately, *We can do whatever we want."*

"But now Joey has picked up the thread of your Da's reasoning. *Not the good stuff. Jimmy, we should keep the good stuff aside."*

"*You boys have not thought this all through,* says your Da. He turns and pulls the best single malt whiskey in the house off the shelf. He sets it down reverently next to the sledgehammer. *Now this is like gold, no, much more than gold, like it's the whole family fortune. Even I only have a glass of it once in five years.* And he stares intently at the bottle as if expecting it to perform a miracle.

Smashin' that bottle, well, I mean, you don't go around the neighborhood smashin the bathtub madonnas, do you?"

"*No, I guess not*, breathes Joey, staring at the bottle, his hand reaching out to touch its shoulder gently, gentler than he'd touch a sleeping baby."

"Jimmy whines; *I still say we can do what we want. Joey, you can keep that one, and we'll get one for Julio."*

"*You don't want one, Jimmy?* Asks you, Da, his arm sweeping out in a gesture to encompass the whole bar. *If I remember right, you're also partial to a good rum served with coke. A Jamaica rum, right, one of the dark, flavorful rums."*

"Jimmy nods despite himself; *Yeah, whatcha recommend?"*

"It's then that Jules stomps over, picks up the bottle of single malt, and, in one swift motion, smashes it against the head of the sledgehammer. Then he shoulders his shotgun and stomps out of the bar."

"Joey looks like he's been shot; tears are spilling down his cheeks. *Look what you've done, look what you've done, you smashed the madonna."*

Fergie rumbles in laughter, "That happened?"

Scratch nods, "Oh, yeah. And your Da put it all on the tab of the Carbone boys' father, including repairing the dents in his bar."

Kit Cotter asks, "Where were you, Scratch?"

"At the far end of the bar."

"So you saw it all," chuckles Fergie.

Doyle calls over, "Why didn't you stop them yourself?" The implication being if Scratch is so tough.

"The Professor had it all in hand."

Doyle persists, "And if he hadn't?"

"If the Professor wanted help, he'd have gotten it."

Doyle looks like he would push it further, except Fergie stands up abruptly, "I got to take a leak. Stay here, Scratch. I want to hear more about Da." He calls, "Gemma, you ought to be hearing these stories of Da."

Gemma and Enzo are dancing slow and tight. She doesn't bother to acknowledge her brother.

As Fergus heads for the restroom, Adnan drops down in Fergie's chair. He nods toward the FN P90, "You get that in Cleveland from Gunny?"

Scratch nods assent.

Adnan smiles, "One of mine. We brought it in through Montreal."

"A good gun for its purpose," answers Scratch.

With that Adnan launches into a discussion of the finer points of guns and smuggling, his English accented pleasantly.

Two hours and one glass of champagne later, Scratch stands to say to them all, "Thanks for your hospitality. Time for me to go." He's learned a bit in the swirling conversations and thinks that if a Taafe is interested in him, it's the younger one, Malachy Junior. He's even had two dances, one with Gemma, who'd slipped a scrap of paper in his shirt pocket but is now snoring softly in a corner booth. His second partner was Lauralee Cotter, a pleasing woman who seems out of her depth in a room full of gangsters.

Doyle watches intently as Scratch picks up his submachine gun and re-hooks it to the harness in his coat. Fergus Taafe smiles, watching as well, "It's been a pleasure meeting you. All those tales from the past. They make you like a dark force, like the MacGavan secret weapon. It's like the reason they could thumb their noses at the Mafia and all the others. And you're just a guy." He struggles to his feet, "Let me walk you to the door."

Scratch turns at the top of the stairs and looks back past Fergie's shoulder. Doyle gives him a half-smile and cocks his hand in a pistol gesture, reminding Scratch of Rory Lawless years back. The rest look wasted. Lauralee Cotter, bored and absently rubbing at a spot on the table, her husband Kit, in a desultory conversation with Mike and his girl, Patti. Gemma is asleep in the booth, mouth agape, her fellow Enzo sprawled against the booth wall and nodding off. Adnan coming back from the men's room while his wife Madiha struggles to get to her feet as if to get her coat. Doyle's girl, Gail, is swaying, dancing alone, singing along to the jukebox song. "No girl for you, Fergus?"

Fergus Taafe grimaces, "I told them she was sick. The fact is, she broke up with me. Lori, this is." Then, as if surprised at answering Scratch's question honestly, Fergus goes on, "There's always another one around the corner. The fact is, they don't mean that much to me. Come and go. I don't know why that is. Before Lori it was Magda, before Magda, Pauline. Hard to keep track."

Taafe leans against the doorframe, sagging a bit. He runs a hand over his face, "Only two a.m., and I'm beat. Not getting any younger, am I?"

"Pack it in for the night. Get some sleep," answers Scratch.

"Nah, I got a guy comin' round about 3:30, messenger. Some stuff to do, to sign. The rest of 'em can go home, 'cept Doyle."

"Then you need coffee, Fergie," and Scratch pats him on the shoulder. "Thanks for the hospitality."

As Scratch descends the stairs, thinking that Fergie's ex-girlfriends would likely be a treasure trove for an enterprising federal agent, he sees Dandy behind the bar being buttonholed by a familiar-looking fellow. A half dozen other serious drinkers sit nodding over their bottles or glasses, some muttering to one another and at least one to himself. The fellow propositioning Dandy looks up suddenly, his eyes locked on Scratch. Scratch recognizes Old Joe, the guy who scuttled out when Scratch had come in. Again, Joe Palka turns and rushes out of the bar.

Thinking that Joe is going to give him a complex, Scratch nonetheless goes on alert. His hand reaches through the coat pocket to the submachine gun. He is thinking back Jozsef Palka? The man must be almost seventy. Joe was a thief. Way back, he'd been muscle, too. Sometimes, he was with Mackey and sometimes independent, though paying the tariff Mackey required of anyone operating in his territory.

Descending the last step, crossing the room, Scratch can't come up with any run-in he ever had with Jozsef Palka. Still, something sure makes Joe nervous about Scratch. There used to be a rumor the guy was a snitch. Is it enough that Scratch is supposed to be dead?

Dandy calls to him, "Be careful out there. I think Old Joe may have shopped you."

"What'd he want?"

"If you were still upstairs."

"Back door?"

"Yeah," answers Dandy, nodding toward the dark half of the room.

Somehow, that's too ready, too pat, from Dandy. Maybe Joe isn't the only one who made a sale, thinks Scratch. Instead, Scratch nods his acknowledgment to Dandy, then goes out the front door, stepping out of the framing light quickly and submachine gun up.

Nothing.

No Joe, no one else, just snow falling softly, the neon glittering off the icy flakes. Scratch waits, scans the street. Feeling the cold through the soles of his shoes. He thinks maybe he should simply go home. Home to Helena and the girls. But there it is again, that door of the house open. The house where his girls need to be safe.

He crosses the street warily. Walks down to his car. As he opens the car door and the interior light comes on, the first shot is fired at him.

He throws himself down, fumbling the submachine gun. A fusillade of shots shattering the Camry's windows, puncturing its door and fender, flattening one tire. He rolls away from the car and scrambles to his knees. The muzzle flashes were coming from between two buildings three houses up. It's gone quiet again.

Heart pounding, Scratch moves forward cautiously. Have the shooters fled, or are they waiting? Maybe they're shifting positions to get a better shot. He stays in the shadows, working his way along. Then he stops, the feeling coming over him that he's alone, they're gone.

From the neighborhood, nothing. Oh, a dog barking. No sirens, no one stirring from Healey's or anywhere else. Maybe they can't tell the difference between shots fired and firecrackers. Or maybe shots fired are too common to bother anyone.

Whatever, Scratch turns and walks back to the Camry to change the tire.

CHAPTER
THIRTEEN

SITTING ON THE SAGGING BEDSIDE, SCRATCH THINKS HOW OUT OF shape he is. Not just bodily but mentally. His reaction time is slow, his fingers not automatically grasping a butt and trigger like they should. Fumbling the P90 out there could have gotten him killed. He's certainly not twenty-six anymore.

He sighs, hating the necessity of all this, wanting to be sliding in bed beside his Helena. Hear her murmur his name, feel her warmth.

The idea flares in his mind: kill them all. The Taafe gang, Fionnuala, Joe Palka, everyone here from the past life. If he were to let his anger loose, maybe he could do it.

Only he's not Scratch anymore, not Tommy, not Kiddo. He's made a new life, a good life, a life where he matters to others, and they matter to him. Love, that poor misbegotten misunderstood word with its hopeless tangle of meanings. Yet, there it is; he loves and is loved, holding a trust for that love, fragile at times and at other times insurmountably strong.

He eases out the pistol from the belt at his back. Hefts it in his hand, the Beretta looking like a tool to him. He sets it down on the stand by the bed, close to hand.

He's tired—the long drive, the drinks, the sheer tension of not knowing which end is up, who to rely on for the truth. The bed is welcome, though sitting here in Mackey's old apartment over the restaurant kitchen seems strange.

He'd let himself in ten minutes earlier, using the key downstairs that Fionnuala had given him. Tracking several blocks through the snow in the alley to the pantry's backdoor, having left the Camry pulled out of sight off the street, tight against the side wall of a garage so that the damage to the car is not obvious.

Scratch isn't sure that sleeping here is wise. But it's better than leaving a trail at a motel. Fionnuala will know he's here. Who else? Was he tailed from Healey's, the ambushers wanting another try? If so, his senses didn't catch wind of it.

Not that those senses are honed all that bright anymore.

There was another ambush thirty-six years ago.

Summertime in Toronto is lovely if you're in the right part of town. Chevy and he were downtown. The hour late, like 4 a.m., so most of the revelers were gone, and they had the street to themselves. They'd had a few drinks that night. Not enough to get them tipsy and hardly enough to feel the effects over that many hours. They were there on business.

They were to meet some fellows Chevy knew. Chevy was all mysterious about its purpose. The whole thing a little odd because by then, Scratch was a hitter not used for other things, like muscle or thieving. And Chevy's regular guys, the ones who guarded his back in '72, Brawler and Timmie—that is, John Brawly and Timofeo Montefiore—weren't with them.

There they are on York Street when a car pulls onto the street ahead, a dark-blue Mercury Grand Marquis or whatever they were calling that model in Canada. Several men are in the car. Already, Scratch is pulling free his automatic when Chevy sprints inexplicably ahead.

The car swerves slightly toward the curb, slowing, and a submachine gun cuts on, then a shotgun blast. Even as Scratch goes prone, bracing his Canadian Browning, an Inglis, Chevy's body is doing its death dance. The car roars away, swerving toward Scratch to throw off his aim, then it's past, doing sixty, then seventy, then more. Still, Scratch fired four rounds into the speeding car as it came at him, then another two as it headed away.

The 9mm slugs must have torn into that vehicle. They must have hit something, maybe someone, at least three men in the car. The first two rounds punched through the windshield, the second two into the side doors, then one through the rear window, and the last through the trunk.

The hit on Chevy is like something out of the thirties. It felt like the Meatballs to Scratch or someone they hired, maybe French-Canadians.

That's what he thought all these years.

With Chevy down, what was there to do?

Scratch quickly picked up his cartridge cases and pocketed them. Then he walked away.

His first impulse was to rush back to Buffalo. Yet Big Mackey didn't have a lot longer to live. And if there was no Big Mackey and no Chevy, then what were the Donegals?

Scratch didn't much like some of the new guys, like Brawler.

Not that liking mattered so much, though a few held his respect, even a couple he cared about, the Professor, for one.

As he kept walking, Scratch turned over in his mind the hit.

Not a shot was fired at him. They might have taken down both of them. And why did Chevy run?

That they were set up was obvious.

There, on a street corner in Toronto, Scratch decided. It was time to go.

Now, unlacing his shoes, he thinks back to Gloria, the kids, Teddy, Ronnie, and Jack. How was it that he could walk away from them?

He doesn't know, yet he did it. Maybe it's a measure of how desperate he was to get out of that life. He'd planned enough ahead to have secured new identities and stashed enough cash to start over. Only there were no false IDs for Gloria and the kids.

From the time he was eighteen to twenty-six, he'd killed nineteen men and two women. He was sick of it all.

Yet, in his mind, he had less reason than he does now. Then it might have been money, or respect from Big Mackey, or even some form of affection from Chevy. Or it may simply be the satisfaction of being alive when your opponent is dead.

Now he's protecting Chloe and Pen, more important than any of those past reasons.

He stretches back against the pillow, still dressed, the little Taurus in his hand. He leans sideways and shuts off the lamp, then sits back and closes his eyes.

He holds the image of his beloved Helena in his mind for as long as possible.

CHAPTER
FOURTEEN

THE RUSHING STING OF THE HOT SHOWER MAKES THE THREE HOURS OF light sleep enough for now. He's already shaved and brushed his teeth, surprised to find the medicine cabinet stocked with new necessities. Shutting off the water, he turns the soap dish right side up, uncovering the little Taurus. He steps out of the stall and grabs the large white towel. Drying himself vigorously, he contemplates the day. Time to go calling on the other Brothers Taafe—Donovan and Malachy? Time to talk with Fionnuala again? And what about Jozsef Palka?

Time for breakfast first, he decides.

Time to call the office. Later, at lunch hour, it's time to call Helena, let her know he's doing fine, and check on her and the girls.

In the bedroom, he takes fresh underwear and socks from his carryall and replaces them with yesterday's clothes. Buttoning his shirt, slipping on his pants, lacing up the shoes, stepping to a mirror, and combing his hair, he feels good, better than last night.

Digging into the carryall, he locates his pill box and digs out a pair of pills for his blood pressure: vasotec and verapamil. Yeah, breakfast first so he can take the pills that keep him alive.

Scratch suits up, Taurus in the leg holster, Beretta at the small of his back, the FN P-90 re-harnessed in his overcoat. The rifle still sits under its protective blanket on the car's backseat. He's going to need a new car, the Camry being conspicuous now with its bullet holes.

He takes the crumpled scrap of paper from his shirt pocket and glances at it. Gemma's note is a scrawled phone number. He thought it might be. Call her today? Maybe.

Scratch swings on the coat picks up the zippered carryall, and heads through the sitting room for the door, ready to meet the day.

Only the day meets him. Before he reaches the apartment door, there is a solid rap of knuckles from the other side. Likely, Fionnuala thinks Scratch, but he swings out the submachine gun just in case.

He doesn't peer through the hotel-style spy hole drilled into the upper center of the door. He doesn't want any telltale motion there to cause slugs to come ripping through the wooden panel.

Instead, kneeling to one side, he reaches up to flick off the lock, then swings open the door quickly as he goes prone, the submachine gun poking out at the world.

"That's a little dramatic," says Fionnuala staring down at him. She's holding a tray with two cups and saucers, a steaming teapot, a small honey jar, another of marmalade, and a plate of warm blueberry scones.

"Good morning, Nuala," he says as he gets to his feet without embarrassment at his caution.

"Well, step aside. Time for some tasty carbohydrates."

Letting her in, he asks, "Are you always this cheerful in the morning?"

"Unless I'm sad." Then she adds, "Or if I've had too much to drink the night before."

"How common is that?"

"Too much to drink? About seven years back, on New Year's Day. Back before 9/11 when the world was young." She sets the tray on the coffee table before the couch.

"How about sad?"

"I don't get sad, Scratch." Then, gesturing, "Sit down and eat. I want to hear about your Healey's adventure."

Sitting, he lets her pour him tea and another cup for herself. Then she takes the chair, balancing the cup and saucer on her lap. "So, what happened?"

"Nothing much. A glass of champagne, some talk, mostly stories about the Professor." He breaks open a scone, the smell making his stomach growl. Pops a chunk in his mouth and chews.

She waits, obviously unimpressed with his level of detail.

"You're not eating?" he asks.

"I ate an hour ago."

"Five fifteen?"

"Early riser." She sips her tea.

"You like worms?"

She smiles at the weak witticism, "Referring to the Taafe brothers?"

"So why does Fergie call you a bitch?"

"Maybe he refers to all women that way," she sips again, obviously enjoying the bitter taste.

"Come clean, Nuala. What's going on between you and them?" He takes another bite, getting a lot of blueberry this time. He can also taste the cinnamon.

She grins, "They want the First Ward, and I won't let them have it."

"You and who else, or do you have a gang of your own?" He uses the little wooden honey dipper to place droppings on a large piece of scone before popping it in his mouth.

"I told you last night, Scratch, I have friends. Friends in the community, in politics, in law enforcement, on the street corners and around the block, and even in the criminal ranks. I cover all the bases." She gives a contented sigh, her legs curled under her on the plush chair, reminding Scratch of a cat.

Then she adds, "And I know too much about what they do and how they do it. Though I say nothing, they know I can say more than enough. And they'd all go away, except maybe Gemma." Then Fionnuala grins, "What did you think of Gemma?"

Scratch stops chewing, swallows, and sips tea, "You've given up using condensed milk in your tea?"

Nuala nods, "Yes. That was a childhood thing, too sweet for me now."

He nods, "Gemma is a little too sweet, at least to look at. Though I'm sure it's faded somewhat over the last decade, she still has another decade of mileage to get out of it. If she's not too rough on it, which I doubt, she might even go a decade more. Then where will she be? One of those elderly ladies trying too hard, too much make-up, too many plastic surgeries, all their glory in the past."

"So you're saying all she is is what you see?"

He sighs, "Based on last night, yes. 'Course, I may not have seen her at her best since she was pretty far gone when I met her."

"Is your wife a beauty, Scratch?"

"To me, yes."

"To the wider world?" asks Nuala, pushing the thought.

"For a woman of fifty, yes."

They're silent for a time. Fionnuala slowly sipping tea. Scratch finishing up the scone, then taking out his two pills and washing them down with his own tea. He screws the lid back on the honey. Looks up at her, "Shots were fired at me last night."

She shows no surprise, "I heard about it."

"Who from?"

"A friend." Then she goes on, "That neighborhood's a bit outside my reach, still I heard. A beat cop in this case. Said they got a call of shots fired near Healey's Tavern. There was nothing there when they sent a car. Found some broken car glass."

"Well, they didn't hurry. It took me fifteen minutes to change the car's tire." His voice has a hint of reproach.

She laughs, "No one wants to be out when it's snowing."

"Wasn't that much, maybe a couple of inches," he grumbles

"We got something more down here opposite the lake," she's still smiling.

"South Buffalo, that's not all that bad. Plows are keeping the roads clear." He nods thoughtfully, "The thing is, I should be dead, sloppy old man that I am. So either the shooter wasn't much good, or they didn't want to kill me."

"Which was it?"

"I'd say a scare, which doesn't square up with Old Joe." He stares at her, inquiry on his face, "All of a pattern, you see. A wake-up call in Arkansas. My home entered. Shots that are close but off-target. Someone is leading me on. The shooting to say pay attention, this is serious."

She sets her cup down on the tray, tea done, "What's this about Old Joe?"

"Jozsef Palka, from the old days. A drunk at Healey's 'til I walked in. Then he rushes out. Later, when I came downstairs, he's there again. Takes a look at me and flees." He remembers the look on Old Joe's face, one part fear, one part guilt, and one part avarice. Or is he just filling in the blanks and editing his memory? Well, the fear was there, and something more.

She nods, understanding, "Thought he fingered you. Not to the Taafes. They know you're there. Someone else."

"I don't figure it's the Taafe brothers got me into this. I could see you for it, Nuala, before them. Or it's someone else. Now, who else might it be?"

His voice is even toned, yet there is more than a hint of menace. She holds up a finger, "Only the Taafes and I are sparring over the First Ward. There are others out there who'd move in if they thought they had a shot at it, but none that would know or care about Scratch, the Irish nemesis from nearly forty years ago."

Up goes a second finger, "There could be relatives of your victims. Someone still carries a grudge and wants vengeance, but if they exist, I don't see them missing their shots last night."

A third finger, "I think we can rule out the various forms of cops. It's not their way to be subtle. And who's left on any force that knew of Scratch?"

She wags a fourth finger, "Someone else from the old days, someone from the Donegals or was a hanger-on or a son of one or someone else with an interest in the old days." Finally, her fifth finger goes up, "Or someone we just don't know about, who has some connection beyond our ken."

"Put that way, it still sounds like you, Nuala," he says mildly.

Nuala laughs, stretches, and settles back down, then answers agreeably, "It does, doesn't it." She smiles at him, "Much as I'm enjoying seeing you again, Scratch, I don't see me trudging in the snow after closing the restaurant to fire shots at you."

"No, I don't either. Though you seem to have plenty of friends." He gets to his feet, "I think I need to find Joe Palka. Any ideas?"

"I could make some calls. Palkie was never part of the gang after Big Mackey decided he couldn't trust him. If Palkie hadn't got sent away around then, likely Mackey would have had Lawless, or you solve the problem."

"Who's still alive from the old days?"

"Lawless is gone, Brawler, Red Frankie, Twist, the Professor, Tierney. KK is in prison. His brother Pete is around somewhere. Mitch, Touch, Shiv, Maxwell, Goods, 56, Shout, Rico, all are gone. I think Timmie Montefiore's in a nursing home. That leaves Palkie, I guess."

"You left out Dutch."

"Tomas Dudek?" She muses a moment, "I think he retired to Tennessee or Kentucky, somewhere south, warmer. I lost track of him."

"He's four years older than me. He'd be sixty-six now."

"Okay, so what have we got? Peader Kilbride, Tomas Dudek, and Jozsef Palka?" She smiles, "Plus me and the Taafes."

He shakes his head no, thinking, "You heard I was coming from Gunny in Cleveland. But you said Boyo called his sister, Millie, and she flapped about my resurrection. So, who all does Millie talk to?"

"Who knows? Peader, for sure. They go way back. And she's a shirt-tail relative to the Taafes since their mother, and she are close. She's like an aunt to the Taafe kids—I suppose it's Gemma she stays in touch with. Gemma even calls her Aunt Millie." Fionnuala nods to herself, "You may be on to something, Scratch. Millicent is connected all around."

"How so?"

"Her first husband was Martin O'Cannahan, whose younger sister Theresa was married to…"

"Dutch," fills in Scratch, nodding.

"Yes, and that's not all. Her second husband was Jimmy Maldonado, who was in the rackets connected in some way with the Italians in Niagara Falls. However, that marriage didn't last long. Then, for a dozen years or so, she was married to Eunan. Eunan Quinn, who was a gun for the MacCrossons when they made a play for the First Ward."

"Busy lady." Scratch smiles lightly, "What happened to the MacCrossons?"

"That was when the Professor was still alive, and I was friends with the Taafe brothers." She purses her lips, waving a hand, "Between us, we squeezed the MacCrossons out."

"Millie bear any grudges?"

"Maybe. She's pretty flighty. Still, she thought a lot of Eunan. He's been in the VA hospital for maybe six years now, pretty much a vegetable."

"Stroke?"

She considers, then says, "He suffered a fall. We were all surprised he lived. Not that he was in any shape to say anything about it."

Scratch stares at her, studying her, revising his thinking quickly. Angie had it right. Fionnuala and her friends are still the Donegals. Yet all he says is, "So who does Millie step out with now?"

"Peader Kilbride."

He considers all Millicent's connections, then says, "I think that still leaves you, the Taafes, Pete Kilbride, and Dutch Dudek, with Old Joe lined up with either you, Pete, or Dutch." Then he adds, "If you can get a line on Old Joe that may let me narrow it down."

"Sit back down. Let me make a call."

He sits as she digs into her pocket for a cell phone. "Thanks for doing this, Nuala."

She looks up, two cell phones in her hand, "It's self-preservation, Scratch. I know you. If you get too impatient or angry, you'll just want to take us all out."

Fionnuala slips the good phone back in her pocket and punches in numbers on the cheap throw-away, then says over the phone, "Donnie, check in with Number Five. We're looking for Jozsef Palka, called Old Joe. He'll make his way to a bar somewhere in the First Ward, the Valley, or Lackawanna. Yeah, that's a lot of bars. You can also have his place tossed over on Maurice, just off Elk. There's a buddy of his called Dusty. Yeah, suppose to be homeless. His crib is usually near the Bailey Avenue bridge. Dusty will likely know how to find Old Joe. Give me a call within the hour on this number. After that I'll call you and give you another number. Right, that's it for now."

Scratch smiles, "Donnie, a friend?"

Fionnuala chuckles, "Yeah, one of my friends."

"And Number Five is a cop?"

She shrugs, not answering, not denying.

"Why do you do it, Nuala? You must have enough money to get out of here. Why run the risks?"

Fionnuala looks at him oddly, "Because you did, Scratch? Got out, found a new life?"

He nods uncertainly.

Her face shows a mild derision, perhaps a form of contempt, "You got out and left wreckage behind. You could have run the

Donegals. That's what Big Mackey thought anyway. That's why he had Chevy gunned down."

That feels right suddenly. It's not the Italian mob who took out Chevy.

She goes on, "Chevy was going to give you up, have you killed. That's what he expected in Toronto. The price he was willing to pay to take over the Donegals and run the First Ward under the mob's wing. Only we switched the game on him."

"We?"

"Yeah, Uncle Patrick MacGavan and me." Her chin thrusts out, daring him to contradict her. "Why don't I leave?" she snorts, "This is my home. These are my people. I won't let anyone else in here, not that shit Artie MacCrosson, not the Taafe brothers, and certainly not all the other animals out there."

Then bitterly, she adds, "Scratch, I didn't summon you. Now that you're here I do want to use you. I'm like Harry Truman and the Japs. If I've got a nuclear bomb and it saves lives ultimately, I'm gonna use it. You're a nuclear bomb, you son-of-a-bitch. Being here, you change the balance of power."

"I won't be here that long."

She grimaces, "Long enough."

CHAPTER
FIFTEEN

Scratch pulls up in his newly borrowed Chevy Impala a block down from the bar called KC's. With its tinted windows and rumbling over-souped engine, the car is more conspicuous than Scratch would like. Still, they say beggars can't be choosers, and it's what Nuala could provide.

KC's on Ridge in Lackawanna is on the west end of the street toward Lake Erie and the industrial wasteland of the old steel mills and rail yards. It's outside Palkie's normal circle of dives. Yet it's where he was fingered, and if Scratch got here in time, it's where Old Joe will be found.

Scratch watches for a time from the car, engine at idle. He examines the street and watches the traffic. It's still early enough on a Saturday morning, yet the bar is open. Maybe, despite the law, it's always open.

Shutting down the engine, Scratch eases out of the Impala, adjusting his coat as he does so. Through the pocket slit, his fingers find the machine pistol's grip.

Walking towards KC's, he shivers a bit, though whether from the mid-20s temperature or nervousness, he couldn't say.

In the front door and stepping to one side, Scratch eyes the dim interior. A fat barman at the far end of the counter polishing glasses, two workmen looking like they came off a night shift talking sports at the bar, a fellow with the morning paper spread across a table, sipping a beer and scanning the want ads, and in a back booth, a codger, looking ill even from this distance, with a second man, his back to Scratch, but wearing the same hat Palkie had on at two in the morning.

Seeing Scratch, the barman nods, his chin pointing at the booth. So Nuala's influence extends this far out from the First Ward, thinks Scratch, as he walks toward the back.

The old man facing Scratch starts to scramble out of the booth as Scratch comes up. "Not me, Mister, you don't want me," he slurs, frantic to get away.

"You're Dusty?"

"Me, nah, I'm nobody. Nobody."

In the booth, Palkie stares up at Scratch, his lips trembling. "Why aren't you dead? I didn't believe Millie 'til last night."

Scratch doesn't respond, instead saying, "Goodbye, Nobody."

Nobody is on his feet, peddling backwards towards the rear door. When he reaches it, he calls to Scratch, "Don't hurt Old Joe, Mister. He ain't anybody, neither." Then Nobody ducks out the door.

Scratch slides in opposite Palkie, "Been a long time, Jozsef. How are you?"

"Good," Old Joe nods, "Still here." Survival itself is apparently an unexpected feat in Old Joe's mind.

"You look tired, Jozsef."

"Been up all night."

"You were busy. In and out of Healey's, then back again. Tell me why."

"I drink there sometimes. Them Taafe boys don't mind, long as I can pay my tab."

"Who else did you go see last night?"

"Saw the girls. You know, Millie, Riona, Mame, and Glory."

"Millie, Boyo's sister?"

"Sure, Millie and I go way back. I owed her a sawbuck. You bein' alive. I bet her Boyo got it wrong. He usually does."

"Ten dollars. That's a pretty fair bet," a tinge of sympathy to Scratch's words. "How are you making your money nowadays, Jozsef?"

"Oh, I get by. Got my Social Security. Do some begging come the end of the month."

Scratch nods, assuming Palkie is leaving out thieving and snitching, "So Millie was with Riona Taafe and two others."

"Sure, Friday night, they always get together, play cards, talk, drink a bit." Then Palkie adds, "Not Glory, not anymore. Drinking, I mean. Been on the wagon for most of a year."

"Gloria? My ex-wife?"

"Yeah, sure. She's one of the foursome."

Jozsef Palka sits there opposite Scratch, not touching the remains of his beer, trying to look earnest and failing. Scratch considers what Old Joe is not saying, then asks, "So Friday nights is the girls' night out. What do Pete Kilbride and the others do then?"

"Pete?" Palkie shrugs, "Bingo, I hear, at St. Stanislaw's."

"How about the others menfolk?"

"Riona don't have a man. The Professor was her one and only. Guess he was enough for her."

"She's not that old. About Fionnuala MacGavan's age, right?"

"A year or so more, I think," answers Palkie, considering. "She looks older, though. Put on quite a few pounds since the Professor died."

"Gloria and Mame?"

"Mame's husband, Roddy, he works second shift at the gas station on McKinley. So I guess he was there. Glory's husband, I don't know. He does as he pleases, be my guess."

"What's his name?"

Palkie looks surprised, "You don't know? Been out of touch. He's Cal Zawacki, though most people call him Trace."

"Trace? Why?"

"Don't know. Just what he's been called since high school."

"Cal short for Calvin?"

"Calder, I think." Palkie squints, thinking back. "There's a story there. Forget who told me. Big argument 'tween his dad and mom over naming him Czcibor or some Polish name. The mom saying his last name was Polish, so that was enough. He needed a given name from his Welsh side."

"Welsh, huh?"

"Sheila Kaint was his mother, pronounced Kent. Janos Zawacki was her second husband. He was a good enough guy, and he raised her two older boys, the Quinn brothers."

"So that's it. You ran out of Healey's to pay off your bet to Millie?"

Palkie shrugs, "Yeah, pretty much. Let them know I'd seen you in the flesh."

There is something unsaid. Scratch can feel it. He could press more get physical, only he's not sure it's worth it. He tries to picture the four neighborhood women with their Friday ritual: Gloria Zawacki, once upon time Gloria Wyeth, Mame, Riona Taafe, and Millie, once upon a time, Millicent Farry. Gloria is a year younger than Scratch, aged 61; Riona, at 53; Millie must be 58 or so; likely, Mame is of the same period, 50 to 60.

In his mind, Scratch repeats 'Gloria Zawicki,' feeling nothing for his ex-wife. Then he thinks about Zawicki and his older half-brothers, the Quinns. Scratch asks, "Eunan Quinn, over in the VA, is he Cal Zawicki's half-brother?"

"Yeah, sure," Palkie nods. "Look, I got to take a leak. Is that okay?"

"Eunan, the older or younger Quinn?"

Squirming, Palkie answers, "Older."

"The younger brother's name?"

"Everyone just calls him Quinn." Palkie screws up his face, thinking, "Llewellyn, that's it. Llewellyn Quinn."

"Was he with Artie McCrossan, too?"

Surprise in Palkie's voice, "McCrossan? Naw, Quinn was in New York back then. Working on Wall Street or somethin' like that. I disremember now." Squirming again, "Hey, I really got to go. Too many beers for an old man's bladder."

Scratch nods waves a hand.

Palkie manages to untangle himself from the booth to flee for the Gents.

Every part of this keeps going back to Millie, thinks Scratch. He sighs, hating the necessities of this old life. Kill Palkie now or not? He decides not yet and heaves himself free of the booth.

Scratch is driving back to the First Ward, thinking about who would want him back here and why. For vengeance, of course, but vengeance on who? Against Scratch, probably yes. Yet not directly. No one's really tried to kill him, though people know he's here. No, someone wants to use him.

Fionnuala does; she's declared it herself. Yet that's new, not something she put in motion. Of that much, Scratch is pretty sure.

The Taafes want the First Ward, but only Nuala stands in the way. Nuala wants the Taafes to keep hands off. Somehow, though, they balance each other, neither strong enough nor willing enough to force the issue.

Unless the Taafes are behind Scratch being here, only why would they think he'd attack Nuala? So that doesn't really play.

Millie and her old biddies? Well, in a way, at least. Millie, from Boyo, triggered the whole thing. She's got a motive for vengeance in Eunan Quinn, maybe. Couple her with Gloria, her husband, Trace Zawicki, and the other Quinn brother. Maybe they'd want Nuala and the Taafe boys out.

Only Riona Taafe is part of the Friday night quartet; surely she wouldn't want her boys harmed, though she too might want to see Nuala out.

Yet, why would anyone expect Scratch to take out Nuala?

CHAPTER
SIXTEEN

I<small>N THE BEAUTY PARLOR</small>, G<small>LORIA IS LAUGHING AT SOMETHING THE</small> hairdresser is saying. That much Scratch can see through the shop's picture window while sitting in the Impala. There are others in the storefront parlor, eight or more others, which is busy for Beauty Rose even on a Saturday afternoon.

As far as Scratch can tell, there must be a big high school dance tonight. Most of the customers appear to be teenage girls.

Still, it's nice to know some things don't change. Saturday at two o'clock, Gloria's standing appointment at the Beauty Rose.

Scratch must admit that Gloria looks surprisingly good for her age and being an alcoholic. You could take her for a handsome fifty and not the over sixty that she is. Course, he's not up close, and the car's windows are tinted, which probably helps her out.

It's been Scratch's observation that, in general, women keep themselves better than men. At least those who work in a profession; he's not so sure about the ones who sit at home.

A little after three now, she should be about done. Maybe

another ten minutes or so. He plans on meeting her as she comes out. He decides he'll leave the bulldog in the car; the two pistols should be enough for now.

Glancing in his rearview mirror he sees a police car trolling down the street, two uniformed officers inside. Looks routine, out on their patrol beat.

Then the patrol car rolls to a stop, idling half a dozen car lengths back.

On ahead, slowly approaching the Beauty Rose, is another dark blue car, followed by a nondescript gray van. Instantly, Scratch makes the car for an unmarked police vehicle with plainclothes cops inside. The van could be with them.

Scratch starts the Impala, the engine rumbling. He eases out of the parking space, flips his turn switch, and, without undue haste, turns into the alley next to the Beauty Rose, his eyes on his rearview mirror.

Sure enough, the unmarked car follows him into the alley.

Scratch pulls into the small lot behind the Beauty Rose and steps out of the Impala. Locking the car door, he watches the unmarked in the reflection of the Impala's tinted windows.

The unmarked stops in the alleyway, and the detectives inside are watching Scratch.

Ignoring the police, Scratch steps up to the back door of the Beauty Rose, one part of his mind wondering who fingered him to the cops and the other debating the wisdom of putting himself into this cul-de-sac.

Yet, as so often in the past, he is operating on instinct. There seem to be only two choices: act like a common citizen until treated otherwise or go into violent action, which is likely a losing proposition against the police.

Glancing sideways, he sees the unmarked start-up and

continues on its way. He pulls open the screen door and steps into the back hall, disquieted at his own disappointment in the lack of action.

The noise level is loud, mostly the chatter of high-pitched voices excited about the coming evening, but also some rap artist blaring from the CD player in an attempt at being provocative rather than musical, and, in Scratch's mind, failing at both.

Gloria is settling her bill with Lydia Prester, the shop owner. Lydia must be 75 now, with henna-colored hair denying her age. Has she been doing Gloria's hair since Gloria was like these teenage girls?

Lydia sees Scratch first and says something to Gloria.

His ex-wife turns, no surprise on her face.

The other hairdressers and the many girls realize something is amiss, and the chatter dies, leaving the lone rapper speaking his inane lines.

"You're looking dangerous, Thomas," says Gloria.

He shrugs, "You're looking pretty good to me."

She barks a laugh, "Going on thirty years dead, and that's what you have to say." She stands erect, back arched slightly, pushing her chest out just as she did all those years ago. "Angie said you'd come to see her. Millie had sworn Boyo knew what he was talking about, you being alive. But it was Angie who told us for sure."

"We need to talk, Gloria. Do you have time for a coffee?"

She stares at him for a moment as if deciding if he is worth the trouble, and then she nods, "Okay, I'm going to meet a friend at Caz Coffee Café. Mame's always late, so if you follow me over, we should have fifteen or twenty minutes."

Though much subdued, the others in the shop have returned to their chatter. Scratch is conscious of all the sideway glances he's receiving, thinking he's way too conspicuous, wishing he'd stuck with his plan of catching Gloria as she came out.

One young girl, bolder than the others, calls, "Glory, you were married to this guy? Uncle Quinn said your first husband disappeared years and years ago." She eyes the old fellow in front of her, apparently trying to reconcile stories she's heard with the man she's seeing.

"There you go, Thomas, they still talk about you to frighten the young ones. Right, Mandy?"

Scratch looks at the girl, uncertain where she fits in the Quinn family connections.

The gaze of his eyes causes Mandy to falter, the smile dropping from her face. She feels herself being weighed as if to determine how much she matters. She's sorry she spoke up under those searching eyes.

Seeing Mandy's reaction, Gloria laughs, "Yeah, you still have it, Thomas."

"Uncle Quinn?" asks Scratch. "That makes you Aunt Gloria to the young miss?"

"Yes, this is Amanda Quinn, Millie's youngest."

Throughout this exchange, every ear in the place listens even while all eyes and hands are busy elsewhere.

"Going out tonight, Miss Quinn?" asks Scratch.

The girl nods, "Holiday dance."

"Well, don't bother thinking about our generation. You just concentrate on having a good time." He turns back to Gloria, "Are you ready?"

"Sure. If you don't keep up, Caz is on Abbott just down from Potter Road."

He nods, already having made the connection from the café name to Cazenovia Creek and the Park.

Midway on the drive, the unmarked police car swings in behind Scratch, trailing him until he pulls up across from the cafe. The detectives continue on past, with the near side man eyeballing Scratch.

Not liking the attention, Scratch wonders if it has to do with the car and not him. Just where did Nuala get this car? Maybe he'd be less obvious in a bullet-pocked Toyota.

In the café, a pleasant enough place with a small buzz of customers, Scratch steps to the counter, just behind Gloria, who is ordering a steamer with a shot of hazelnut syrup. When it's Scratch's turn, he asks for a cappuccino for here.

As he joins Gloria at a small table, sitting carefully because of the mug of cappuccino in his hand and the bulldog hanging in his long coat, he notices a young woman, slight but pretty, Asian, staring at him. On his glance, she averts her eyes.

Gloria gets his attention with, "So, Thomas, in town for the holidays," on her face a faint smile. "Boyo saw you in Chicago, and now you're back. You couldn't stay dead?"

Up close, Gloria looks nearly as old as Scratch feels. Scratch knows he's no prize, either. Yet enough resemblance exists to their handsome youths to still catch the eye, especially here sitting together.

"Gloria, I can't make up for the past. I can't change what happened or why. Can't make it good." He shrugs, "I would have lived out my life like an everyday family man. Except Boyo did make me; Boyo did tell Millie; Millie told who knows how many, and someone came knocking their way into my ordinary life. So, yeah, I'm back, trying to piece the puzzle together."

"You carrying, Thomas?"

He stares at her a moment, then nods.

She nods, too, thoughtful now. "Yeah, if you're still who you were, then you'll use it, too."

"My patience is running thin, Gloria."

Her laugh is like a bark, "You were never patient." Then adds, "Except with the kids." Then, more wistfully, "And some of those long nights together in bed."

He waits, his eyes boring into hers.

She sighs, a hand gestures in surrender, "It's complicated here now. Nuala and the Taafes, Quinn and some other guys, then there's the gangbangers wanting in. Plus, there are the cops and the Feds, different groups of Feds, you know how it is, everyone eyeing everyone else. Nothing in the Ward worth all that much, really, yet no one wants anyone else to have it."

"So what are you, Millie, and Riona, the den mothers?"

"Maybe. It's Nuala's patch; she won't give an inch. Quinn hates her, of course, so my Cal sides with Quinn. The Taafe boys would love to pick up the pieces. Then, like I said, there are others out there. The Irish days are over even if Nuala refuses to see it." She nods and takes a sip of her cooling drink. "Yeah, I guess we're den mothers. None of us want to see this end in bloodshed."

"Who came calling on me, Gloria? Whoever it was wouldn't mind some bloodshed."

She sighs, looks away from him, then back, "You haven't even asked about your kids."

"Angie said Jack is dead."

"In 2000, he'd just turned 30. He was doing a buy-up in Niagara Falls. Got hijacked for his cash instead." Her voice is flat, but her eyes show hurt.

He nods, thinking that in 2000, his marriage to Helena was already past the diaper stage with Chloe 5 and Pen 3. "Teddy's doing well, though?"

Gloria visibly brightens, "Yeah, he's doing really well. Nice wife, Lailah, and the grandkids, Keith and Judith, they're wonderful."

"Ronnie?" asks Scratch.

His ex-wife shrugs, "Who knows? Don't see her that much; she being down in New York. Never married. Used to go from job to job, one magazine publisher or another, graphic design, photo design, fashion photography, one thing or another, and even some modeling. Now, she does her own thing, freelance photography. Not sure how she makes ends meet." All of it said in a kind of rush. Then, more slyly, looking at him, "I called her after Angie said you were here. She's flying up tomorrow."

That surprises him; what would it be like to see his Veronica again? What he remembers was a little girl of four, his sweetheart.

"You've got a new family, right?" Gloria asks.

He nods, cautious.

"Photos?" she asks.

Again, he nods, considers, and then pulls free his wallet. Although the two credit cards and the driver's license are false, the two small school pictures are real, his girls. He hands the photos to Gloria.

She studies them and looks back at him, "They look like you."

"No, they've got my wife's dark hair."

"But your eyes, nose, jawline. They could be Ronnie's sisters." She laughs, "I guess they are Ronnie's sisters."

Somehow, the way she says it, coupled with what Nuala had told him, gives him a sudden doubt, but before he can react, she asks, "And your wife? A photo?"

He shakes his head no, wondering for the first time why he doesn't carry a photo of Helena. All he says, though, is, "Teddy and Jack look like you."

Gloria looks at him evenly, catching the slight inquiry in his tone, "Yes, they do. Did in Jack's case."

He considers asking her about her past infidelities but doesn't see the point. How does that compare to the death of Jack?

She cocks her head to one side, that sly knowing look on her face again. He'd forgotten that habit of hers. "You hearing gossip, Thomas?" she asks.

"Gossip?"

Gloria nods, "Yeah, you have. Nuala no doubt, the bitch."

"What's the point now, Gloria?" he asks with a shrug.

"You were never unfaithful, Thomas?"

Truth be told, there were two incidents. One was a girl in college, Janine, who was so different from his world, so clean and innocent, and the wonder of the one night with her. Like a dream. Neither of them wanting more, just wanting that single experience of each other, that memory to hold.

Maybe he was Janine's bad boy.

The other time was with Chevy, up in Toronto, the day before it all came apart. Chevy hired a pair of girls. Had Scratch go with the older of the two, an Eastern European, maybe Rumanian. Scratch no longer remembers what name the woman was using. In his mind, he nicknamed her Thorough for all they did, all she put him through; he surprising himself with how eager he'd been, never expecting to make a connection with a prostitute, yet there it was. They had enjoyed each other.

Of course, there were women between Gloria and Helena, not many, and two were companions for some years, Leslie during his early 30s and Nina four years later, good friends but always the barrier of his secrets keeping them from being more than friends. Until Helena came along, and somehow, he's not sure how, nor what she saw in him, it was possible to be much more than friends.

And he has been faithful to Helena, going toward twenty years now. Though their marriage has not been as passionate these past five or six years, it never really was after the birth of Penelope, but it is still satisfying.

He sighs, "Let's get back on track."

Whatever else might have been said is ended, for Gloria exclaims, "Here's Mame, now." Gloria adds, before turning to her friend, "Tomorrow, you come see me. Ronnie will be with me."

"Where?" Then, before Gloria answers, Scratch says, "Let's make it here at the Caz."

Scratch excuses himself after a brief introduction to Mame, a heavy woman in her late fifties wearing too much make-up. Her cloying perfume, by itself, enough to put Scratch off.

At the door of the café, he pauses. The unmarked police car is idling right behind the car Scratch is using. Is it the car, or is it Scratch himself attracting attention? Why would Nuala set him up?

A voice at his elbow says softly, "You driving Hadley's car. He dead now. Shot last week over in Tonawanda."

Scratch looks down at the slim Asian girl standing next to him, the one who eyed him when he first arrived.

"Who's Hadley?"

"He a pimp." Then she chuckles. "Was a pimp. Did pushing, too. Probably took some of his own drugs."

"And you?"

"Call me Randy."

He looks at her, "Not your name, though."

She looks up at him, dark eyes catching the light, a look of good-natured mischief on her face, "You care?"

He looks back at Gloria and Mame, leaning over some of kind of brochure that Mame brought. He looks at the idling police car, the detectives inside, one on a mobile phone.

The girl says, "You can go out the side entrance or back in the bookstore." Then she adds, "If there's nothing in the car you need, you can ride with me."

"Who are you again?" He glances back down at her, seeing the short cropped red-tinted hair and black leather jacket—seeming lightweight for a Buffalo winter—and her chinos tucked into mid-calf leather boots—young twenty-something, maybe, her face dominated by the inquisitive eyes.

She stares up at him, "I think you need a friend. I know I need a friend. You come with me."

He looks out at the Impala. One of the detectives is opening his car door. There's nothing in the Impala of his. The rifle and carry-all are still at the apartment over the restaurant. Everything else is on him. Nothing in the car, not even fingerprints, given his winter gloves. "Okay, let's go."

CHAPTER
SEVENTEEN

LIFE IS A TEMPORARY LODGING, WHICH IS A COMMONPLACE IDEA, thinks Scratch. Many people shy away from the fact, he knows, and its corollary, that everything in life is transient, which, at least, makes room for new experiences, like clinging to the back of this unknown girl as she accelerates her Yamaha on the slick roadway.

Scratch has never ridden on a motorcycle before. He finds leaning on the curves similar to his singular experience on a dog sled one winter afternoon in the Upper Peninsula of Michigan or, more normally, riding a bicycle.

Wearing a helmet is strange to him as well. Still, it took them easily past the two detectives as the cops leaned over the Impala, trying to see through its tinted windows.

Yes, life is temporary; his early career making that reality more vivid to him than to most people. Rather than disheartening him, it had made each present moment, particularly the good times, all the more clear and, perhaps, affecting.

Whatever, he is enjoying this ride, enjoying wondering who

this girl really is and why he's with her, why this seems like a departure, a break, from all the pressures and concerns of these past weeks.

Randy goes by way of Abbott Rd. to Ridge, Ridge to South Park, then heads to Blasdell, a village in the township of Hamburg. At the point where Scratch is speculating on how far south they'll ride, Randy decelerates and pulls into the parking lot of an old apartment complex, its four-flat yellow-brick buildings looking sad in the winter light.

Dismounting, Randy points toward the third building, "Home, sweet home." Pulling off the helmet, Scratch only catches the "… home". He nods, then follows the girl.

Inside, Randy unzips her boots and steps out of them, her socks striped in red, black, gray, and white, contrasting with her black pants. Scratch pulls off his own shoes at her gesture, not used to the niceties of Asian practice.

The place isn't large, its living room stretching to a dining area and kitchenette, then a short corridor leading to bedrooms and a bathroom. Drapes are drawn across the picture window, dimming the room until Randy snaps on an overhead light. Furnishings are limited — a futon couch and a director's chair, a small flat-screen TV mounted on the wall, a bookcase with a mix of paperbacks and what appear to be photo albums.

The kitchenette and dining area runs to form, having metal and vinyl chairs tucked under a small matching glass-topped table.

Still, it's all neat and looks clean. Scratch says, "You're a tidy person, Randy."

She laughs, a pleasant sound, "I pick up this morning. My uncle brings my sister to live with me tomorrow."

Scratch manages an "Oh?" as a comment, only mildly curious.

"That why I need a friend today." Randy slips off her coat, hanging it over the back of a kitchen chair. "You can hang coat in the closet. It look heavy on you."

So she has noticed the weight despite the harness for the bulldog, an observant girl. He opens the small closet by the front door, seeing the vacuum cleaner, broom and mop, ironing board, a couple of medium-sized packing boxes, a wool pea jacket, a few other garments, and some empty wire hangers. He hangs his coat carefully, not certain he should leave the bulldog out of reach.

Turning back to her, he takes in how short and slight she is, though attractive in her tight chinos and white blouse, the darts helping to emphasize a bosom modest but well proportioned for her size and partially revealed by the two undone buttons.

Seeing his appraisal of her, Randy stares evenly at him with no flirtation about her, "My sister coming; I need earn cash. What you say to $250 for take me to bed?"

He feels a surge in his groin, despite his lack of interest, the body often betraying the mind. "I'll pass on the bedroom if it's all right with you. But I appreciate your help and will pay you for it."

She shrugs, "Okay, how much?"

He pulls free his wallet to check what's left. "Here's two bills. Will that do for now? Later, we can stop at an ATM if need be."

Randy smiles faintly at the proffered two hundred, "What am I getting into if you not want to make love?" She looks at him expectantly.

"I need a place for tonight. I don't want to go back to where I was staying until I sort out this car business."

She nods, "Hadley's car. Shock, see it pull up outside the Caz."

"You knew this, Hadley?"

"Sure, not well, not like my sister."

"Your sister who gets back tomorrow."

"Yeah, back from Rochester. She away there for seven months."

Hearing the significance she places on Rochester, he knows she's not just referring to the city. He thinks a moment, "Rochester as in?"

"RPC, actually RRFU, sister, call it Rochester Fucked."

For a moment more, he's unsure, and then what she's saying hits him, "You mean the Psych Center."

"Rochester Regional Forensic Unit in the Center, though she be in a halfway house for last three months. All the same, one misstep, and she back in Rochester Fucked."

"What'd she do?"

"Start a fire. Try to kill Hadley and couple his friends." She shrugs, "Sunny down for simple arson. Authorities not realize why she throw the flaming gasoline bottle."

"So, Hadley again."

"He her pimp. Had her on drugs, destroy she reality grip." She gestures at the apartment, "This for her. New place, I move here start of month. Away from Buffalo, away from Hadley and he friends."

"Where are you from originally?"

"Family from Viet Nam, come here after the war."

His turn to smile, he says gently, "No, you didn't grow up in America, not with that accent and speech pattern."

She shakes her head points toward the kitchen, "You want tea?"

"I want to use your bathroom first."

Joining Randy in the kitchen, he takes a seat at the table. She pours him tea in a small cup without handles. "Thanks."

They sip in silence, the tea being enough for now, an interlude, the light flavor of the green tea somehow calming.

Finally she asks, "You ever go to China?"

"Yes, a half-dozen times on business." He's tempted to say more but that would be getting into his life of today.

"Then you know I Chinese."

"Guessed you are."

"Most people here accept I Viet Namese. Sometime, I say Chinese from Viet Nam, if a question. I am small, like Viet Namese."

He studies her for a moment, trying to guess her age, knowing she's older than he first thought. "You came through Canada, illegal alien."

She nods assent. "With my *meimei*. Uncle paid way."

"Uncle as in brother of one of your parents or uncle as in your parents' generation?"

"Friend of my father's friend — an uncle."

"You had to re-pay him?"

She nods. "I work five years in company he own, pay back money. My *meimei* work three years but … " Randy sighs, "She have problem, not adjust, not do good work, like boys too much."

He nods.

"Not sure why I tell you all this," she says.

Scratch thinks, because who else are you going to tell.

She continues, "She pay back uncle from money earn on her back with boys— first gifts, like amateur. Later, Hadley get her. No independent in First Ward or roundabout. Then the drugs, so Hadley can keep her."

"If I drive Hadley's car, why didn't you think I was a friend of Hadley's?"

"You talk with Glory Glory, no friend of that crew. Glory run with Quinn crew."

"How do you know all this?"

"From Sunny. My sister crazy but not stupid."

He sips tea, thinking it through. Hadley obviously somehow connected to the Donegals, to Nuala. Big Mackey never liked drugs, left that to the wops. Maybe times have changed; maybe drugs are just too common.

"What I call you?" She asks.

He hesitates, wondering if she overheard Gloria call him Thomas; then there are his three other names: the one at home, the one on his fake ID, and his persona as Scratch. "Does it matter?" Then he shrugs, "Use Tom."

"Okay, you Tom, me Randy," she grins at the pseudonyms.

They sip tea some more, and neither feel a need to talk. Then she sighs. "We no fuck, want to watch a movie? Chinese kung fu, Chinese fight Japanese, Chinese gangsters, or Chinese romance? All I got."

The idea makes Scratch chuckle, "Sure, why not? No Chinese family drama?"

"Maybe. Got movie called *Shower*; it a good story. Make me cry the first time, has subtitles. Okay?"

"Okay."

So they pass the rest of the afternoon and early evening watching a movie about a father who owns a bathhouse in Beijing and his two adult sons, the younger retarded, who lives with him, and the older, a businessman, who comes from Shenzhen abruptly to visit, thinking a note from his brother meant his father was dying. And when it was over, Scratch was surprised at the dampness in his eyes, embarrassing himself in front of the girl.

Noticing his embarrassment, Randy says, "See, good movie, yes? I hungry. Now we go get something to eat."

"You don't cook?"

She laughs, "Sure, only good enough for me and sis, not for guest."

Guest? Thinks Scratch, bemused.

Over supper at a restaurant called The Poppyseed that caters mostly to middle-aged women, which seems to Scratch an odd choice for a Chinese girl, he tries again to learn more about Hadley. "You said Hadley ran with a group of friends. Are they all in the same trade, girls and drugs?"

Holding a leaf of lettuce on her fork and watching the soy sesame dressing drip from its end to her plate, Randy finally says, "Not sure. Some maybe. Some do other things, wild guys, you know. Maybe Sunny know."

"Tell me about Sunny, about your sister."

As if searching for words, Randy stares away from Scratch. "Sunny fifth child. Parents have our two brother and older sister. Sunny and me too many. Not really want us. Then Pa get sick, not work. We have to go. Uncle say go America. Pa get money. We pay back by working."

Scratch nods, not wanting the flow to stop.

"Sunmei, Sunny…" She makes a wry face, "Bamboo Shoot Beauty is how Sunmei translate. Pretty Bamboo Shoot."

"And your name?"

Another wry face, "Ruidan. Luck Be Born. Ma tough time giving me birth."

He thinks of common Chinese family names, "Li? Wang? Chen? Zhang? Liu?"

Randy shakes her head no, "We Zhuang. Villager."

Scratch puts it together, "Zhuang Ruidan; Zhuang Sunmei."

"Easier, Randy and Sunny."

Scratch nods in agreement but thinks about what it means inside yourself to change identities, "What about your ID?"

"Uncle get. Me Choi Meili and Sunny is Ip Lili cousins. Suppose to be girls whose parents are Chinese from Viet Nam. In Mandarin, be Cui Meili and Ye LiLi." Then she laughs. "So many names for same people."

"So Sunny couldn't adjust to the U.S.?"

"Ah, Sunny adjust in her way. Sunny always a little crazy." Randy pauses, considering, then adds, "Sunny always like sex, even as little girl. Not like you and me, we want, but it not push us always. Sunny, it always push, worse than needing to drink and eat. Makes Sunny scared of self, scared of what men and boys do she. Still need to have."

Scratch tries to understand, thinking about what it would be like for a girl being compulsive over sex. For a moment, he wonders what he would do as a father if it were Chloe or Penelope.

Randy continues, "Under control now, maybe. Sunny take drugs doctors prescribe. It make her tired a lot. She suppose to have job at store start Monday. Not sure if so tired, she can hold job." She shrugs, "We see."

"What about you? Do you have a job?"

"Sure. Office in Buffalo, mail room, sort and deliver, send packages—supplies for office. Work for office manager; she old woman, over 70, work there maybe 50 years. Can you believe?"

"Yet you said you needed money."

Randy waves a hand, "La, yes. New apartment, move, need clothes for Sunny, medicines for Sunny, food Sunny likes to eat. Savings gone. Another week 'til payday. Then Sunny want me buy other things, send me list. Couple books, cleaning stuff, tools, and things. I say, what for? She say, you see. I down to one twenty dollar bill, then you come along."

"You do whatever Sunny asks?"

A slight nod coupled with a grimace, "Not always, mostly. I take care of Sunmei; no one else do."

CHAPTER
EIGHTEEN

AFTER EIGHT IN THE EVENING, SCRATCH HAS RANDY DROP HIM OFF ON O'Connell. She says she'll shop for the items on Sunny's list now that she has Scratch's $200. They agree to meet at midnight on a street corner near Healey's, the Taafe bar. Scratch gives her the number of his throw-away cell phone, which he has used once so far to call Gemma.

With a spurt of slush and dirty water, Randy is off on her Yamaha Road Star.

Scratch watches her go, feeling puzzled by how much he likes this girl. Then, mentally shaking himself, he sets off for Mackey's to brace Nuala on the car she provided him.

As he expected, Scratch finds Nuala at Mackey's; only she's holding court in the rear dining area, so he waits at the crowded bar. Ignoring the hubbub around him, he watches the condensation on the side of the pint of Guinness that Darren, the barkeep, poured for him.

Scratch can feel how tired he is. His right leg aches at the hip and knee, and he has a slight headache.

Marie, the hostess and a waitress Scratch hasn't met, watch him warily as they handle other customers. Even Elyse, the waitress from last night, and Txomin, the busboy eye him once from the dining room entry.

He sighs, thinking how much he's messed this all up, his plan of sliding into town anonymously, dealing with the problem, and going home quietly to Helena and the girls. Not that he ever really thought it'd be that easy. Still, he knows how foolish he is in being notoriously conspicuous.

He sips the stout, savoring the flavor. At least something is good this evening.

The group in back seems to be breaking up. He hears deep-voiced laughter of several men over something Fionnuala has said.

The bar mirror gives Scratch the means to track everyone in the room, even as he keeps his back to the crowd. He watches as the three men come out of the rear room to the bar, all busy talking to each other. He recognizes one of the detectives who'd been in the car tailing him earlier.

With practiced ease he reaches through his coat pocket to grasp the bulldog machine pistol, just in case. The threesome go by without a glance in Scratch's direction, but then they wouldn't need to look if they'd already been alerted by Nuala's staff.

Relaxing slightly, Scratch takes another pull on his Guinness. Txomin comes up to him, "Ms. MacGavan will see you now, sir."

Nuala smiles at Scratch as he slides into the far side of her booth. "How are you holding up, Tommy?" she asks.

He hasn't been Tommy since he was ten years old. Somewhere a long time back, Scratch read that diminutives are used when a person wants to reassure themselves of their power relative to you.

"Why Hadley's car, Nuala?"

Nuala waves a dismissive hand, "Apologies. Donnie cleared the car at headquarters, but the message didn't get down to Detectives Ostrowski and Ramos until late in the day." Then she grins, "So you walked away from it after leaving Gloria? Must have been a long cold walk."

He feels like she's fishing for how and where he went, causing his distrust to flare. "Sounds like you're well connected with the police. Wasn't that Ostrowski I saw leaving here?"

"Saturday night, a lot of folks drop by. Yeah, cops, sometimes the pols, mostly though neighborhood people, some honest and some not, my world." The last said with pride in her voice.

Suddenly, it fills Scratch with disgust, Fionnuala being this big frog in a quite small pond. What is he doing here? Back in Buffalo when he should be home, wrapping presents after a day of Christmas shopping? Still, he feels he needs to finish what he's started, "The other day, you didn't mention Quinn and his friends when talking about your rivals for the First Ward."

"Sure I did, I told you about the McCrossons." She cocks her head to one side, "What's the matter, Scratch? You don't seem happy with me."

"How do you and Hadley connect?"

"Hadley? No connection, really. He ran his thing and paid the tariff. Was overdue when someone tapped him up in Tonawanda, which is how his car ended up in my sway." She shrugs, "A hood, like most of his friends." Then she adds, "If you want a different car, give me fifteen minutes, and I'll have one brought round. You mind a white van?"

"No concern to you, he was taken out?" asks Scratch.

"Maybe yes, maybe no. Ostrowski will keep me informed from their end. I've got it being worked from my end. The guy had pissed more than a few people off, so his ticket got punched. Someone got close to Hadley, two .25 caliber slugs, one through an eye and the other through the ear. Made me think of you."

"I didn't use that small a caliber."

She nods, "Yes, I know. More a lady's size pistol."

"Or a cheapie sold by a barkeep to a kid or a drunk."

She nods again, "Yeah, a kid, maybe. Doesn't matter much, someone's already taking his pitch. Says Hadley's best money earner's due back tomorrow from Rochester, where she's been staying some months. Guy's raring to get her back on the line."

Then, dismissing the topic of Hadley, Nuala asks, "So what are you doing next? Going to check out young Quinn?"

"That, and maybe the Taafe's again. I haven't met Donovan or Malachy Junior." Scratch adds, "Don't worry about my transport. I'll work that out myself."

Darren catches Nuala's eye from the rear room entry and holds up three fingers. She says, "Some people to see me, Scratch. Saturday night you know, always busy."

"I'll just get my things from upstairs."

"You're not staying here tonight?" a touch of surprise in her voice.

"I've made other arrangements."

"Busy afternoon, huh?" Then she nods toward the back hall, "There's a fellow in the back named Prentice. Tell him I said it was okay for you to go up, use the word spatula."

"Spatula?"

She chuckles, "Darren comes up with these. He's watched too many movies. Anyway, Prentice won't let you up without it."

Scratch has wondered about Nuala operating without a

bodyguard, but maybe Darren in front and Prentice in back are it, at least on a Saturday night. "Okay, spatula it is."

Trudging through the snow, the blanket-wrapped Finnish rifle in one hand and his carryall in the other, Scratch mulls over what he knows. His mind keeps taking him back to Millie, Gloria, and Riona, like the three witches in *Macbeth*, with their *double bubble, toil and trouble*. Maybe they didn't summon him, but they somehow put this all in motion.

The powers-that-be in Buffalo must like dealing with Fionnuala or, at least, prefer her to what they see as the alternatives.

Yet Quinn and his ilk and the Taafe boys want her out. Could they have teamed up? If so, it would be short-term, because once Nuala was out, they'd be maneuvering against each other.

Or would that be the case? Could the three witches have come to an agreement? Riona and her boys with Millie and Gloria for the Quinn gang? Somehow to divide the spoils after Nuala is put down, the question is how to put her down while leaving them with reasonably clean hands?

Is that where he comes in? Maybe the question was how to set him against Nuala.

Thinking back to high school, Scratch remembers how devious Gloria could be. Even the glamour girls of the jock clique didn't cross her.

He'd been angry with her for one episode, which left a girl who'd been friendly with him totally humiliated due to a laxative put in her lunchtime milk. Gloria claimed innocence, but Scratch knew she pulled the strings of the fellow who did it. As ever, Gloria turned it around, attacking him for not believing her and for being overprotective of Harmony, the girl.

Would she want vengeance for his leaving her all those years ago? Would she put a debit against him for every pound of trouble she had as a single parent? For her drinking, for Jack's death?

She was never a forgive-and-forget type. When they lived together, she could count every slight and grudge, every disappointment and irritation he'd caused her, dredging up instances from years earlier when she needed ammunition to win an argument with him.

Gloria wouldn't have changed. So the pleasantries of today were a mask.

He reaches the Toyota, still untouched since he parked it. A rim of snow and ice settled on its roof, and cowling. Using the key, he unlocks the trunk and sets the rifle and carryall inside. He stands there staring down at the wrapped rifle, thinking that maybe the simplest way would be to take out the three women, then find Boyo in Chicago and cross him off as well.

Boyo saw Scratch's current identity. Only Boyo could have given it to the caller to the Arkansas hotel or whoever entered his home, maybe not directly, maybe through Millie.

Scratch has been fooling himself, telling himself stories. Unless he takes them all out, all these Buffalo gangbangers, there's no going back to Helena and the girls.

At twenty-six, Scratch could have done just that. Now, at sixty-two he questions whether he still possesses the level of ruthlessness to eliminate all the threats to his home life.

And if he does do it, what manner of man is he to return to Helena?

CHAPTER
NINETEEN

S<small>ATURDAY IS LIVELIER AT</small> H<small>EALEY'S</small>, <small>WITH ELEVEN PEOPLE IN THE</small> place tonight, counting Dandy behind the bar. Maybe the Taafe boys should add a live band or offer door prizes. Obviously, this isn't where they make their money.

Scratch asks the bartender, "Gemma?"

"You're expected," answers Dandy grudgingly. "Go on up; I'll buzz you in."

At the top of the stairs, Scratch waits a moment before the buzzer sounds. He pushes open the door with one hand while the other holds the bulldog through the slit coat pocket.

Gemma is laughing. With her are Fergie and two fellows who are obviously their brothers, Donovan and Malachy. Nearby is Doyle, a Glock in his hand but not pointed at Scratch. For just a second, Scratch is tempted to spray the room with the bulldog, starting with Doyle. He thinks better of it. After all, the faces are friendly enough, not counting Doyle.

The middle fellow stands up, "So you're Scratch. Fergie and Gemma like you." Left hanging is whether anyone else will.

"You must be Donovan," answers Scratch.

Doyle says, "You want to pull that machine pistol out real slow and lay it on the table, seeing as we're all friendly." The Glock is now pointing at Scratch.

Scratch does as requested, even taking the coat off. He limps slightly to the chair proffered by Donovan.

"War wound?" asks the third brother, Malachy.

"No, old age, cold weather, and too much walking."

"You're not too old," puts in Gemma. Her grin seems genuine, "I know you've got a young heart."

"You can dance with him later, Gemma. Let's get down to business," Donovan orders with a smile.

Nodding, Scratch says, "Good. I'm a bear come out of hibernation to see what disturbed my rest. Seeing as it's winter, I'd as soon go back to hibernating."

"An analogy," pipes up Fergie. "Told you he was the literary type."

Donovan doesn't even glance at Fergie, "As I understand it, James Farry makes you at O'Hare in Chicago. Then, there are a couple of incidents that ruffle your hair. You conclude it's got to be your history in Buffalo. So you come back hunting, loaded for bear." He smiles slightly at the second bear reference, "Am I right so far?"

Scratch nods assent, waiting.

"Once here, you look up your old acquaintances, and," Donovan gestures around him, "you make new acquaintances. You stir things up, and make like a menace to our fragile state of affairs here in lower Buffalo, Lackawanna, and the south towns. Right?"

Scratch nods again, seeing Donovan's point of view.

"The easiest thing for me is to have Doyle here put a bullet through your ear, like your job in the old days. That was Malachy's vote." The younger brother sits up straighter with that admission. "Gemma here says no, just send him home. Fergie says he likes you but says it's my call." Donovan grimaces, like biting something sour, "Now, I'm not a violent man. I haven't even met you 'til now. But I don't see any way you being here can end up good for us. So here's my say, your daughter's coming from New York City to see you tomorrow. You have a brief reunion with her. Then you go home."

Before Scratch can reply, Donovan holds up one finger, "Hear me out. You go home and go back to sleep. You forget about Buffalo. 'Cause we won't forget about you and your nice family in Racine, Wisconsin. You don't go home quietly and live out your days; well, you and your family won't have many days left."

The cold inside Scratch is deeper than the winter cold outside. There is no rage. Instead, there is an absence of emotion.

Gemma laughs, "Oh, lighten up Donovan. Do I get my dance now? Is business done?"

Fergie adds, "You get to dance so long as Doyle and I don't have to dance with Scratch."

Scratch looks away from Donovan and smiles at Fergie and his analogy. Then looks to Gemma, "One dance, then I have to go."

A half-hour later, Scratch is walking toward his rendezvous with Randy, mulling over the words whispered by Gemma as they danced. *'What Donovan said … it was over the top. He wouldn't hurt your family. Just go home, Tommy. I can call you Tommy? I don't like the name Scratch. Just go home, and everything will be okay.'* Then she squeezed him tight and kissed his cheek.

What kind of kiss was it, just goodbye or more like Judas?

On ahead, under the streetlight, are two men and Randy. They're arguing. The bigger man is holding the motorcycle, and the other one is gripping Randy's arm. He's shouting at her.

As Scratch comes up, he catches the words, "... you fucking cunt, you tell your sister she's back on the job. Got it! Or do we put you on the job?"

The other fellow laughs, "Why not both?"

The guy with Randy snarls, "'Cause this bitch is a fucking puke. No fucker wants an unresponsive bitch." Then he backhands Randy, knocking her sideways with the blow.

Scratch calls out, "Get your hands off her."

The big fellow glares at Scratch, pulling an automatic from a shoulder holster, "Ain't none of your business, Pops. Get the hell out of here."

The fellow with Randy stares at Scratch, as Scratch keeps coming on, then as if daring the old man, without even looking at Randy, the guy backhands her again.

The big fellow's automatic is out but not up when Scratch lets loose with the bulldog, his finger tight against the trigger and the bullets stitching up the big guy's frame. Then Scratch swings the machine pistol onto the mean fellow, and the guy blows backward.

Scratch stops firing, the acrid smell breezing away.

Randy picks herself up from the slush along the curb.

"You okay?" calls Scratch.

"You could shoot before he hit me again."

"Let's go," Scratch responds, gesturing to the motorcycle.

As he steps past the smaller guy, whose body is twitching, Scratch adds another couple rounds into the man. Then he mounts behind Randy on the bike, and she hits the accelerator.

· · ·

Randy confides at the apartment, in bed together, their lovemaking having been urgent, "It was me, you know. In Tonawanda."

Scratch is lying there trying to understand what he feels about this sexual betrayal of Helena after all their years together when Randy's words penetrate. "Hadley, you mean?"

"Yes," she whispers.

"'Cause of Sunny?" he guesses.

"Yes."

"Those fellows would've forced Sunny back in the game."

"Yes," then she adds, "Sunny maybe go, too, not want it, but accept it."

They are silent, perhaps both remembering the spray of blood, tissue, and bone fragments as the men were jerked back and down.

She sighs. Then her barefoot runs along his leg, and her hand follows the length of his torso, "You not so old." She laughs softly.

CHAPTER
TWENTY

THE SUN IS UP. SCRATCH SHIFTS HIS HEAD TO TAKE IN THE SLEEPING Randy, her mouth slightly agape. The affection for her surprises him.

Her slight body is a contrast to his Helena. Pain at that thought, and he knows then that he's unlikely to go home again — maybe even unlikely to survive the next 24 hours.

He slides out of bed softly, trying not to wake her.

When he comes out of the bathroom, dressed after his shower, Randy is wearing a robe, watching TV news, and sipping tea. She looks across at him, "Those two you did make the news."

He glances at the TV, but the woman co-anchor is speaking about a fire.

She gestures at the TV and adds, "A few minutes ago, no leads, they said."

"My acquaintances here have already figured it out," he answers. "The P90 is a bit distinctive." He shrugs, "My guess is you're in danger now, too. Gloria saw us at the coffee shop, and those guys were after your sister."

Randy nods soberly, "Yeah, I think, too." Then she smiles, "What you want for breakfast?"

After 9:00, the doorbell rings. "Who is?" calls Randy through the door. The answer is in Guangdong wah, which Scratch doesn't understand. Randy says to him, "My sister," as she unlocks the door.

Scratch slips the Beretta back under his sweater.

There are effusive greetings from Randy as she hugs first the older man, the uncle, and then the girl, her sister.

Randy briefly introduces Scratch as her friend, Tom, without additional explanation. The uncle seems startled to find a man with Randy, a non-Chinese man at that. He sets Sunny's backpack down and quickly makes his excuses. With another hug from Randy, he's out the door and gone.

Sunny is less slender than Randy, though still a slight girl. She is also more even-featured, though her features are broader than her sister's, yet the resemblance between the two is striking.

There is a difference, though, in movement and gesture. More languid, more vulnerable, sexier than the energy and purpose Randy's body language suggests. Hard to define, yet Scratch is instantly attuned to the beddable sense that Sunny conveys, perhaps reinforced by the short skirt and leggings. Whereas in Gemma, it is art; in Sunny, it is natural, herself.

He can see how men want to have her, even to protect her, however crudely and momentarily.

All this he takes in as the two sisters continue to talk in a language he doesn't comprehend. There welcome in their voices, tenderness on Randy's part, and maybe relief on Sunny's.

There is also an effort to act casual as if the months in a mental institute were simply a trip away.

Soon, the three of them are sitting at the kitchen table, fresh tea in front of them, that Randy poured. Sunny asks, "You with my sister, Tom?"

Randy and he exchange glances, then he nods, "Yes, we're together," leaving unsaid *for now*.

Sunny chuckles, "Okay. Good, my sister needs it. You off-limits for me." She gestures at the apartment, "I like."

Randy shrugs, then says, "We won't be here long."

"Oh?" questions Sunny.

Randy states, "You explain, Tom."

"Some men were shoving your sister around last night. Something they won't do again. But others will put two and two together. In time, they'll find your sister." He doesn't say they'll also find him or, worse, his family.

"Hadley?" asks Sunny.

"No," says Randy. "Hadley dead, several weeks."

Silence for a few moments, then Sunny says, "Damnation. I want to do. How he die?"

"Shot, twice or maybe three times." Randy shrugs, "He is bad man. No surprise he come to bad end."

Sunny nods, accepting it. She digs into the pocket of her jean skirt and pulls out a crumpled slip of paper and a pencil stub. She smooths out the paper on the table and carefully crosses out a name on a list. As she does so, she looks up at Randy, "You do this?"

They stare briefly at each other, and some communication occurs between the sisters. "Okay," says Sunny. "These other two men, the ones who 'won't do that again,' what are their names?"

Randy folds her arms across her chest, remembering last night. "One was called Gif. I don't know the other."

"Gifford Clarkson," says Sunny. "Describe the other one."

Randy describes the big guy who held her motorcycle.

Sunny wrinkles her nose, "Not sure either. We just call him Fish." She looks at Scratch, "They dead?"

Scratch nods assent.

Sunny looks back down at her list and crosses off two more names.

Scratch takes a walk, letting the sisters have time alone together. The sidewalk hasn't been cleared, and he walks through crusted snow. The day is drear cold, with some flakes in the air, but he doesn't mind. It matches his mood.

There is an ache inside him. It is not just his habitual leg ache that he can handle. He is losing his family. He can feel it, see it happening. If he does as Donovan and Gemma say, if he just goes home, will that be enough?

Can he bury who he was again, who, after last night, he is? Will he still be a family man?

What does he owe Randy? Or Nuala? Or any of the others?

Then he thinks of Ronnie, his daughter, who he will see later today after an absence of so many years that it might as well have been death.

All he remembers of her is this surprisingly blonde, happy, laughing girl who always rushed to see him when Daddy got home. No different in her happiness than have been Penelope and Chloe.

Sunny's list had Fionnuala's name on it.

The list names the Donegals and those who receive their bribes or who pay their tribute so they can provide their evil services to the neighborhood.

If Sunny has her way, the Donegals will be gone, and it will be left to the Taafe brothers and the Quinn gang to fight it out or patch up an agreement.

If the Donegals are gone, someone stronger could come in, stronger than the Taafes or the Quinns.

Does Scratch care? He can't decide.

If the Donegals are gone, is the ghost of Scratch gone, too? Can he simply go home?

Most likely, though, Sunny will just get herself and her sister killed. Inexplicably, Scratch cares about that.

Scratch doubts it is enough to go home. Doubts the harpy card-playing women will let it be that easy, no matter what the Taafe boys say. Doubts Gloria is done having her revenge.

When Scratch returns to the apartment, Sunny is at the kitchen sink mixing the products she had Randy buy. "How volatile is all that?" he asks.

Sunny turns slightly, smiling at him over her shoulder, "Not worry. Needs one more ingredient." She points to a can of thinner paint with her chin, "Be trigger for enough heat. Make the rest go, whoosh."

Randy comes into the kitchen, "We let Sunny do." She sets a revolver on the kitchen table, some .25 caliber piece of junk, and then she reaches up and helps Scratch take off his coat; that done, she takes him by the hand and leads him toward the bedroom.

"Randy, I'm an old man," protests Scratch.

Randy tugs him harder, "Not so old. Long time I not be with a man. Maybe, soon, never again. You know?"

He nods, still not convinced he's up to the task. Not certain he wants to be her scratching post.

Then she smiles at him, "Besides, I like you a lot. If only, for now, we together."

In the darkened room, wondering at the time, Scratch is glad at the trust this young woman reposes in him, her warm form, dozing now, lying against his flank.

The memory of her from just after they entered the bedroom, how she stood there, wearing only the amulet on its red cord about her neck, her slim body with its modest yet handsome breasts, the relatively broad hips, looking so willing with her eager compelling eyes and hinted smile. He, lifting her to him, surprising himself, if not her, as her legs readily encircled his waist, and he carried her to the bed.

Like the memory from last night, her hair unbound, kneeling above him, caressing her own breasts as he stroked her.

He thinks now that it is the giving he likes as much as the sensations, the giving and taking of lovemaking, how it is only as good as your partner feels, how you heighten each other, how, maybe, this sharing is one of the great charities of life.

CHAPTER
TWENTY-ONE

Leaving Randy to sleep, Scratch returns to the kitchen where Sunny has six quart-sized glass bottles lined up on the newspaper-covered counter, each three-quarters filled with a viscous pale green liquid. As for Sunny, she is seated at the table with the last few pages of yesterday's paper, working the crossword puzzle and humming to herself.

She looks up as Scratch pulls out a chair and says, "The hardest part for Elder Sister was getting glass jars. Why all plastic nowadays? Everyone know plastic bad for environment. Had to buy old-fashioned milk. Sister, not even like milk." Then Sunny giggles.

For a moment, Scratch simply takes in the sight of this woman, trying to understand who she is beneath or within the craziness. On the surface, she is an amazingly attractive girl, though that is not a matter of mere features. Nor is it some exotic made-up look, like the archetypical dangerous oriental beauty. It is in every gesture, the arch of a brow, the way her eyes reach into yours, the artless purse and pout of her mouth, with its peeking tongue and flash of white teeth, even the casual wear of her clothes, but mostly it is the attentive focus saying only you matter to her.

Beyond her sexuality, who is she? Perhaps it's in the desperation hidden beneath, he thinks. Desperation transformed into rage, for fires are molten within her. Life has cornered her, and she is fighting back, he decides.

Or maybe it never was desperation; maybe it was always fire, which is the well-spring of the attraction she exudes.

Sunny laughs out loud under Scratch's stare. She raises a barefoot and strokes down the length of Scratch's leg, "You no start. You Sister's man."

Nodding in agreement, Scratch says, "Atonement."

"Atonement? What you mean?"

"For you, it's vengeance. For me, I think it is atonement for my past. More even than shielding my family."

Now Sunny stares at Scratch, then slowly nods. "Why we do this thing together?"

"Yes."

She leans forward, her look suddenly fierce, "I want to kill them all."

The heat of her wrath ignites his anger and thoughts about Donovan Taafe's threat to his family. "We will. Give me your list; I have names to add."

Randy is up again, showered and dressed. She has the TV on and is checking the news stations. Her sister is on the phone, arranging for a car. Scratch reads his book, *The Runagate Courage*. Before long, it will be noon.

When Sunny ends her call, she announces, "Harvey, bring his car, then we drop him off. We return it whenever."

"Harvey?" asks Scratch.

Sunny shrugs, "Old friend. He do what I ask."

"I need to be at the Caz coffee shop by 2."

Sunny nods, "Sister, tell me. Your daughter, right? You good father?"

The question gives Scratch pause, and then he answers, "Better now than the first time. Not so good for this daughter."

"My father no good, too," replies Sunny laughing. "He sell us."

Randy, hearing that part as she comes into the kitchen, protests, "No, he think he give us opportunity."

Flatly, accusingly, Sunny states, "He sell us for profit. He and Ma, too."

Mildly, Scratch says, "Maybe he did both."

The sisters stare at Scratch until Randy nods, and Sunny looks away.

Harvey doesn't look like he should be driving a car. In fact, he's so ancient that you'd expect him to be in a wheelchair. The car itself, though, is unexpected, a late model Mercedes, black with tinted glass, looking in perfect condition, scrubbed and polished, as if the day's street slush wouldn't dare touch it.

Sunny pulls Harvey to her, the man looking even shorter now that she has her heeled boots on. She kisses him on his balding pate with its wisps of hair, then hugs him to her bosom. She exclaims, "It winter, Harvey. I tell you, wear a hat. You get sick and die, I cry." Then she releases him.

He is smiling beatifically, "I missed you, Sunny. I really, really missed you."

Patting his cheek with a gloved hand, she says, "I know, Sweetie. Time away hard on all."

Turning to Randy and Scratch, Harvey says, "Hi, I'm Robert Crawford." He holds out his hand to Scratch, who takes it with some bemusement. Crawford continues in a whisper, "Harvey's just her name for me. Maybe I look like Harvey Keitel, the actor."

Scratch wonders if the name comes from the giant invisible pukka in Jimmy Stewart's movie, *Harvey*. "Should I call you Robert?"

"Better than Mr. Crawford," laughs Harvey.

"Harvey, a good name," says Sunny, smiling. "We go now.

Sunny is an aggressive driver, despite having only one hand on the wheel while the other caresses Harvey's crotch, Harvey having snuggled close to her. Scratch and Randy are in the back seat, sitting a hand's width apart. Randy leans to Scratch and whispers, "You not like be passenger?"

Scratch admits, "I'd rather be driving."

"You safe driver?"

Scratch winces as Sunny cuts off another driver without signaling her lane change, "Safer than Sunny."

"Me, too. Rather be on my motorcycle." Randy adds, "After we drop Harvey, then you drive."

Thinking that he might need to be a shooter, Scratch says, "No, you drive, Randy."

"Okay, whatever you say," she whispers. Her breath is soft against Scratch's neck, putting him in mind of Helena in bed at night. He still hasn't called his wife, not being sure what to say.

Randy rests a hand on his thigh, "You aren't Sunny. You no need do what she do."

"You know what she's planning?"

"Some little. She want to kill those who harm her."

He nods, "Yeah, she does."

"People, you know, right? Some were friends for you?"

"Maybe."

Her hand strokes his leg as she makes her point, "You go home. You have wife, family, wear wedding ring. You not need choose death like Sunny."

"What about you?"

"Sunmei, my sister, my *meimei*, little sister. I can't take care her, can only be with her."

He looks down into her eyes. Without thinking, he kisses her forehead, then says quietly, "After last night, it's too late for me to go home."

"Then you with me?"

He nods, "I'm with you." Though he knows it may be only for this day, these few moments of time.

Satisfied, she strokes his leg once and sits back to endure her sister's driving.

CHAPTER
TWENTY-TWO

PULLING UP TWO BLOCKS DOWN FROM THE COFFEE SHOP, RANDY SAYS, "We wait you."

Sunny leans over from back sit, "Could be trap, you know. All the bad men know you come see your daughter."

"You want, I go in first, check out shop," says Randy.

Scratch smiles, "I appreciate your concern. We're twenty minutes early. I can do the checking."

"Look," says Sunny, pointing up the street at a dark blue Ford Crown Vic taking a parking spot a block beyond the shop. Though it's too far away to really make out the cops, Sunny says with satisfaction, "Ostrowski."

There is a rustle and clink from the back seat as Sunny takes a bottle from the carrier, "I go on walk. You not worry about Ostrowski."

Thinking to himself that it's all now in motion, Scratch nods. He turns to Randy, "You might as well leave the motor running."

Instead of going directly, Scratch walks away from the coffee shop to the next intersection, then finds the alleyway and walks back toward the rear of the building that houses the shop and bookstore. He's left the machine pistol in the car with Randy. All he has is the Beretta and the little Taurus at his ankle. He's pretty sure that will be enough, though he is gripping the Beretta through the slit in his coat pocket.

On entering the side door and through to the coffee shop, he finds it busier than yesterday. Given that it's been snowing again, he finds that surprising.

Several tables are occupied with individuals hunched over laptops. Others have couples and threesomes in animated conversation. The smell and warmth of the shop is inviting. No one in the room seems threatening.

If it weren't for the police car down the block, he'd feel it was all natural. Stepping to the counter, he orders a small cappuccino — eyes alert to every reflective surface.

One small table for two near the passageway to the bookstore is open. He sits, stirring the foam to infuse it with coffee and raw sugar. He usually likes it with a sprinkling of cinnamon but didn't want to stand too long with his back to the room.

He watches everyone in the room and, through the window, the street outside. He also listens carefully for any opening of the side door beyond him.

Within five minutes, a red Mustang pulls up parallel to the parked cars across the street and then backs cautiously into the one open space. He watches through the window as Gloria steps out from behind the wheel and, on the passenger side, a tall woman in a stylish dark green cloth coat. He finds himself half-standing, taking in the young woman, eyes hidden behind her sunglasses, hair a cascade of honey blonde. This must be the adult Veronica, so beautiful.

For just a moment, he thinks to leave by the side door to avoid disappointing this young woman with his reality.

As Gloria and Ronnie cross the street to the shop entrance, Scratch sees that Randy has left the car and is standing across the street between parked cars, watching. She appears to have the machine pistol at her side.

Gloria comes in loudly, as always, wanting attention, "There you are. Ronnie, he's here for once, waiting for you."

Veronica stands at the entrance, looking across at him.

He steps out from behind the table and waits to see how Ronnie will come forward.

Gloria laughs, "Excuse the drama, folks." She exclaims to the other patrons, "Daughter meets father after the absence of thirty-five years or so."

A young fellow pipes up. "Was he sent away for bank robbery?" His two companions laugh.

Veronica takes off her sunglasses, eyes that same hazel green as her mother's, taller than her mom, though, despite the green coat, shapelier, and, if the thirty-something is like her four-year-old self, smarter than her mom.

Coolly, her eyes on Scratch, she says, "Mother, order the drinks. I'll have a green tea." Then she steps across the room, unbuttoning her coat, totally in command of herself and the room, as even the teenage wiseacre subsides.

She gestures for Scratch to be seated. He waits, though, until she takes a chair and then seats himself.

"This won't take long," she says. "Mostly, I wanted to see you for myself. All I've had is a high school photo of you when you were seventeen, looking solemn, with a mop of curly dark hair. Today, I brought my camera and want to photograph you."

For the first time, he realizes that she has a camera case, not a purse. "I've never much liked being photographed," he answers.

"No, in your line of work, it's a liability," she replies, opening the case and bringing out a large, expensive-looking film camera.

Cameras not being something he knows much about. He says, "My line of work is producing toys."

Gloria interrupts, bringing the drinks to the table, green tea for Ronnie, and a latte for herself. "Well, the famous outlaw finally gets his picture taken."

"We'll do a couple without flash and several with," says Ronnie as she glances about at the lighting. She's soon adjusting settings on the camera.

"Your mom said you're a freelance photographer. So how does that work?" A stupid question, given all the product shots he's arranged at work. Still, his impulse is to ask Ronnie all sorts of questions, like who does she live with or is she happy with her life, but doesn't feel he has the right.

"Do you want to smile for the picture?" asks Gloria, sipping at her latte. "Or just be your grim self?"

When he turns to stare at Gloria, Ronnie snaps the first shots, not two but closer to six in quick succession, as he turns back to her. "Mostly arranged over the internet. Quick contracts. Some months slower, some very busy," answers Ronnie while shooting.

Ronnie scoots her chair back, adjusts the camera, and comes up shooting, the flash going off like a strobe light.

Scratch feels foolish; other customers watching this scene maybe wondering if they should recognize him.

"You want him standing up? Maybe outside?" asks Gloria.

He wants to call a halt to this, just stop and hold a conversation with this young woman who used to be his little girl.

Maybe once this photography nonsense is over, except he's afraid she'll leave right afterwards.

"Sure," says Ronnie. "Can we step outside, Dad?"

Dad, she's said. He clutches at that word, nodding assent to more photos.

They pull on their winter coats and step outside while leaving their drinks back at the little table. As they make for the door, Gloria nods at an older fellow working on a laptop in the far corner. Scratch notices, but Ronnie is talking. "I know this is an imposition," she is saying. "I guess photography is how I deal with the world."

"You want to stand with mom?" asks Ronnie.

No, he thinks, but asks, "Is that what you want?"

He sees Randy still standing between the parked cars. He glimpses a silver van pull out, and proceed toward them from down the street. He notices Ramos and Ostrowski start to get out of the Crown Vic. He hears the coffee shop door opening behind him.

Without conscious thought, he dives to one side, pulling free the Beretta and calling out, "Get down, Ronnie."

The Crown Vic is suddenly aflame, and in an instant, an explosion rocks the car to one side. Someone is screaming, a human torch.

Scratch is staring up at the shop doorway, where the older laptop man is turning toward him to fire his Ruger automatic. Scratch has the safety off and manages a single trigger pull before the fellow completes his pivot. The bullet takes the man at the bridge of his nose and shoves his dying body back into the café.

Gloria is screaming, "Trace, Trace."

Scratch rolls to one side and scrambles to his feet.

The human torch collapsed to its knees when Sunny steps up

behind it and fires twice with her sister's little revolver. Only Sunny knows what happened to the other detective in the explosion.

The silver van's side door slides open, and two shooters are there already spraying bullets. Ronnie is on the ground on her side, shooting photos, but Gloria isn't so lucky, taking several hits in her back before folding like a rag doll.

Calmly, his head clear, Scratch is walking slowly toward the van, firing steadily at the shooters, one of whom collapses.

The driver-side window of the van shatters, and blood spatters the windshield as Randy fires bursts from the bulldog machine pistol.

The truck slews to one side and rams into the parked red Mustang, causing the other shooter to slip and fall out of the van's side door. Before the shooter can get to his feet, Scratch fires two rounds into him, drops the empty Beretta, and crouches to pull free the Taurus from his ankle strap.

As suddenly as it started, it's over — the near silence now as deafening as the explosion and gunfire of moments before.

Randy comes around from the back of the van. Sunny walks over from the charred body, no longer writhing. She is reloading cartridges into the revolver.

Scratch picks up the Beretta and stands.

He hears sobbing behind him and turns. Veronica is cradling her mother's broken body.

"We better go now," calls Sunny.

Already, patrons in the café are up from the floor and peering out the shattered windows.

Randy is jogging back to the Mercedes.

Scratch looks at his daughter. Gently, she is setting her mom's body down, her careful fashionable clothes in disarray, smeared with her mother's blood. He walks back to her and helps her up from the ground, saying, "I have to go, Ronnie."

His daughter stares at him, her eyes wide with shock. Softly, he kisses her forehead and then steps away.

In a moment, he's in the front passenger seat of the Mercedes, loading a fresh magazine into the Beretta as Randy pulls away from the scene.

CHAPTER
TWENTY-THREE

"Trace was with Quinn's gang," Scratch says to his companions while Randy drives to the First Ward. "And the detectives were owned by the Donegals. So the van was likely a set-up from the Taafe brothers, though it could have been more of the Quinns. Did either of you recognize the shooters?"

From the back seat, Sunny says, "No, not a good look at them."

Randy adds, "I see the driver before. He the bartender at that bar you went."

Scratch nods, "The Taafe's then, too." So much for Donovan's offer, he thinks. Maybe Gemma doesn't know her brother all that well.

If Nuala sent the detectives, then at least she wasn't out for his scalp directly, not like the Quinns and Taafes, who maybe are working together.

Sunny speaks up, "We go Mackey's. I bomb it, too."

"I'd rather take out the Taafe bar first," Scratch answers, wondering if he wants Nuala dead.

Stubbornly, Sunny says, "Mackey's. You can fight Taafe gang. I kill the Donegals."

Scratch wants to argue with her, perhaps persuade her to leave Nuala alone, but he looks at her expression and knows it's futile. He nods to her, accepting the harvest from the seeds sown.

Randy drops him off three blocks from Healey's, the Taafe boys' bar. Before pulling away, she rolls down the car window, "I come back after we done. I wait, you where?"

"Just down from the I190 on-ramp. We'll need to get away."

She nods her assent, then says, "I want us to get away."

For a bleak moment, he thinks of his Helena, then he attempts a smile for Randy, "Sure." He leans forward and kisses her lightly.

Walking along the alleyway that leads to Healey's back door, Scratch tries to decide how to do this. He's got the machine pistol now, having traded his Beretta with Randy. He still has the little Taurus. The Finnish rifle is in the trunk of the out-of-commission Camry unless the car was towed. It may be needed if the Taafe brothers aren't at Healey's and he needs to go hunting.

If he were the Taafes, would he be gathered and waiting to hear the result of the ambush they set up? Maybe.

By now, though, they probably know the ambush failed.

So they'll expect him to come after them.

So they'll likely set another ambush.

That's what he would do — at Healey's because that's where Scratch has met them. Likely on the approach, front and back, why let him in the building where there'd be more mess to clean up and more explaining to the authorities. Outside somewhere, there are a few good clean shots and no explaining to do.

He stops in the shadow of a garage overhang one city block back from the block with Healey's bar. Dandy is dead, along with the two unknown shooters. Doyle is likely leading the ambush, or maybe a Taafe or two themselves. Of the others he met the night of the party, he doubts Enzo and Adnan are involved. They had their own business dealings with the Taafes. Mike, though, may be part of it.

Nuala said the Taafe gang was smaller than the Donegals, so how many might that leave with three gone?

While these thoughts are running through his mind, Scratch is carefully scanning the way ahead, each parked vehicle and each window and doorway opening on the alley, looking for anything amiss. Quickly and alertly, he crosses the street to the last section of the alleyway leading to Healey's backdoor. Nothing seems to stir except what snowflakes and flotsam the wind swirls.

His usual detachment isn't in place. He feels a tautness within, nerves, maybe even fear; he's getting too old for this kind of shenanigans. Way too late now to just drive back to Wisconsin. He steels himself for what is to come and walks resolutely towards Healey's.

The blast of the shotgun comes from the landing of a stairwell overlooking the alley. Scratch is swung round by its force as the deer slug rips through the flap of his long winter coat. He slips in the slush and falls backward, rolling to his left to keep his gun arm free, as another slug tears over him.

Lying on his side, he fires a burst from the machine pistol, splintering and gouging the landing. Then he rolls and scrambles to his knees.

The back door of Healey's hurtles open as Doyle and young Malachy Taafe rush out, going to either side of the doorway. Doyle is already firing his automatic as he dives prone.

Scratch pivots spraying a long burst, cartridges ejecting hotly. Malachy is jerked aside, his blood jetting and melting snow.

The shooter fires his auto-feed shotgun again and again from the stairwell. Scratch ignores the shooter as he thrusts himself forward and down, bringing the machine pistol to bear on Doyle. Doyle fires three focused rounds where Scratch was, then clicks on empty.

Doyle's last shot is a hammer blow, making a bright sear of agony down along Scratch's shoulder and back before Scratch is fully prone. The line of slugs spraying from the machine pistol cuts across Doyle, exploding gouts of blood, tissue, and bone.

Scratch rolls and heaves himself up close to a backyard fence out of sight from the shotgun shooter's stairwell. Ducking low, he pushes quickly forward, hugging the fence and then the breadth of a garage door, before easing himself for a glance around the corner of the garage at the stairwell. No shooter.

Has the guy fled with Doyle and Malachy down?

Distantly a siren, growing in strength as it comes this way.

Healey's back door bangs open again. Scratch stares across the alley at Gemma, standing in the doorway, pale with shock at the sight of her brother and their henchman. She looks up at Scratch, and for a second, he thinks she'll say something; then she convulses and vomits down the side of the door.

He turns away to see Fergie, who is thirty paces up the alley, shotgun at the ready. Fergie steps forward, shooting as he comes.

Scratch collapses himself at the sight of Fergie, dropping to a squat, and fires the last several rounds from his magazine. Fergie is cut down, screaming as his shin bones shatter.

Laying the machine pistol down, Scratch grabs for his short Taurus while up the alley, Fergie writhes and sobs. As he brings the pistol up, Gemma is at his side, pointing a large automatic at him, maybe a Canadian Para-Ordnance, vomit on her blouse and tears on her face. Though she tries to pull the trigger, nothing happens.

Getting to his feet, pressing his revolver against her chest, he gently pushes her automatic away, knowing its safety is still on. "Where is Donovan?" he asks.

Fiercely, she spits at him, "He'll kill you."

"Where is he?"

She shakes her head, not knowing. Then she steps back from him, fumbling with her gun.

"Don't, Gemma," he says, knowing what the .45 caliber slug from the Taurus would do to her. Before she can bring the gun up, he lunges and clips her hard with the side of the Taurus. She staggers, and he hits her again, and she goes down.

He kicks the automatic away from her, burying it in the snow bank. He looks toward Fergie, who is sobbing but crawling with determination to the shotgun. He fires once, and the shotgun skitters away, its firing mechanism shattered.

The sirens are keening close now. He walks over to the FN-90, picks it up and slides it into the holster in his coat, then walks away.

CHAPTER
TWENTY-FOUR

Trudging toward the I190 exit ramp, each step bright with pain from the wound down his back, Scratch is numbing his feelings, tamping down the fear, self-disgust, and sheer bleak sorrow. Helena, Penelope, and Chloe are gone to him.

Less importantly, he doesn't have long to live — not with the kind of police manhunt that today's killings will cause.

There are plumes of smoke away toward Mackey's and a cacophony of sirens. People are clustered out in the streets, trying to make sense of the noise and events in their neighborhood. He's glad they're out, for it makes him less conspicuous.

Scratch glances back. He can see some blood splatters along his path, but the dirty slush obscures much of it. The cold helps; it should speed up the congealing of the wound.

He pauses and looks around, wondering if there's a place to discard the machine pistol now that its magazine is empty. If he can get to the Camry, there's one last full magazine.

Up ahead, no Mercedes is waiting at the ramp. Did the girls

not make it out alive? Or were they caught or wounded? For Sunny he doesn't care, but he puzzles at the anxiety he feels for Randy.

"Hey, mister," a teenage girl calls to him from a small crowd across the street and up a bit.

"Yeah?" he calls back, gripping the little Taurus tightly in his coat pocket.

Then, there is the shock of recognition in the girl's eyes, and he realizes who she is despite her winter coat and hat. Scratch calls again, "How was the dance last night, Mandy?"

The others in the crowd turn toward him. Scratch guesses the family members and neighbors of young Mandy Quinn. The older woman looks to be the girl's mother, Millicent Farry, when Scratch knew her.

"You're Aunt Gloria's Thomas," Mandy says loudly, focusing the attention of Millicent and the man next to her on him.

Scratch keeps walking, though the Taurus is ready in his coat pocket. He asks, "Were you out with a boyfriend or just with the girls?" but his eyes aren't on Mandy.

The man by Millicent, tall, ginger-colored hair shot with gray, has begun reaching into his coat; only Scratch is shaking his head no and pointing the Taurus at him now. "Don't do it; at six paces, I can't miss."

Slowly, the man turns empty palms to Scratch, and he says, "You think you can get out of this neighborhood alive?"

"You Quinn?" asks Scratch.

The fellow nods, "Yeah, and you're the legendary devil."

"Yes," says Scratch wearily, then he shoots Quinn three times.

The group scatters as Quinn staggers back and topples down. Scratch keeps going, heading toward the ramp.

Except Millicent doesn't scatter; she is on her knees now next to Quinn, and she's not cradling him or keening. She is reaching into the man's coat pocket for his pistol.

On ahead, down the street, Scratch sees the Mercedes barreling toward him, closer every second.

Millicent is up now, the pistol held in two hands, and she pulls the trigger.

Scratch turns back to her, "You have to take the safety off." With a surge of rage, he fires a single round, holing her in the forehead. She drops.

He stares down at the two bodies, now feeling empty. No, he realizes, not empty as anguish comes in a rush, the enormity of losing Helena and the girls. For an instant, Scratch wants to put the Taurus to his mouth and fire it.

Then the Mercedes horn is honking.

He stumbles to a run as the car door swings open, only Randy in the car, at the wheel, calling to him.

On the highway, he asks, "Your sister?"

Randy just shakes her head, tears running down her cheeks.

"Fionnuala?"

"Gone, too."

A pang in Scratch. Sighs, "We need to ditch this car. Make a switch."

"At my place. We take the Yamaha."

He nods assent, suddenly so weary it is too much to talk.

CHAPTER
TWENTY-FIVE

S<small>ITTING ON THE EDGE OF THE MOTEL BED</small>, S<small>CRATCH IS THINKING THEY</small> should split up. They're all over the news, the events in Buffalo. Their identities are known, and poor-quality photos appear endlessly in news reports and on the internet. Maybe Randy would have a chance if she could get to a city with a large Asian population.

Right now, they're heading south are already in Lexington, Kentucky. New York and Chicago are out of bounds. The West Coast is too far away. Atlanta is their target, and it's Midtown area where the Chinese live.

The alternatives would be the DC area, Boston, or Houston, but Atlanta seems the best bet for now. They can be there via Knoxville and Chattanooga by tomorrow morning if they can dump the Yamaha and pick up something else to drive.

Randy comes out of the bathroom, still twisting her hair. She's been in there a while. He could hear her crying earlier, even over the sound of running water. "You okay for now?" he asks.

CHAPTER TWENTY-FIVE

She nods and gestures at the bathroom, "Your turn."

Using the kit the motel provided, he shaves. He can only glimpse portions of his back in the mirror as he twists and turns. Then he tries showering, the wound down his back a torment. There's not a lot of damage, although it's likely the gouged flesh needs sewing, and maybe he needs antibiotics. He's running a fever.

Over the noise of the spraying shower, he can tell Randy has turned the television back on. It makes him think of Helena and the girls. They will have seen the news. Should he try calling Helena? What could he possibly say?

Scratch towels off gingerly. No bleeding for the moment, at least. He closes his eyes, and instantly, images from yesterday pop into his mind: Gloria, her body torn apart, with Ronnie bending over her; Fergie Taafe trying to crawl with his shattered legs; the surprise on Quinn's face as he went down. Scratch opens his eyes; enough of that. It had been a continuous reel in his dreams.

They'll need money, he thinks. He can give all he has to Randy. After she's safe, he will turn himself in.

Coming out, towel wrapped around his midriff, Randy says to him, "Your wife, she beautiful."

"Helena?"

"Was on TV

It's like taking a blow to his chest. "You saw her?"

"Yes, she say can't be you. You not this man."

He realizes he's nodding in agreement — Helena is correct. Her husband is not Scratch. Not this man. Her husband and Scratch simply occupy the same body.

Randy holds out her hand to him, "Her husband, not you. You my man now."

Hesitantly, he takes Randy's hand. He not really agreeing, but it's what she needs to believe he recognizes.

She draws him close, "It okay if you cry. I cry much. Then done with crying." She stands, kisses his cheek, then his lips, and hesitantly he responds.

Maybe he can just get this young woman to safety.

Another voice on the television draws his attention. It's Donovan Taafe. He's being interviewed but pulls away to address the camera, "Scratch, you're out there somewhere. Remember my promise."

And Scratch does, that Donovan would kill Helena and the girls. He pulls away from Randy's arms. "I've got to go back."

Randy reaches out to him, "What you mean?"

"He'll kill my girls, my daughters, my wife." He touches Randy's cheek, "You go on to Atlanta. It is safer if we split up anyway. I need to go back. I need to kill that man."

She shakes her head and does not turn away from him. She goes to the bed and picks up the bag from the pharmacy. "You lie down. I treat your back. Then I color my hair."

He submits to her ministrations. All the while, his mind is on the problem of getting back to Buffalo. What Randy is thinking he doesn't know, but she is humming a tune. The stinging pain of the antiseptic nearly causes him to slide off the bed.

"I must sew you," says Randy.

He bites the pillow against the pain as the needle goes in and out of the torn flesh. She pauses every so often to clear his bleeding with cotton gauze.

By the time she is done, Scratch is awash with sweat. "You rest. I rinse hair," says Randy, patting his buttocks.

He must have dozed. Bleary, he looks up as she clears her throat. He blinks. Randy no longer looks quite like herself. Her hair is long black, flowing over her shoulders. The wig she bought. Her own hair, underneath, black again. She has on rhinestone-studded glasses with magnifying lenses, which she bought at the pharmacy, making her eyes look huge. A set of three moles march from her lip up her cheekbone. The lipstick is dark red. Wearing the dress and shoes from the thrift shop, along with stockings. Her dress rests just above her knees, flower patterned, and looks nothing like her usual boots and chinos. She appears to be an exchange student, no a bit older, maybe a Chinese graduate student.

"You need a book bag and books."

She says, "Now you up. We change your look."

When she is done working on him, he looks ten years older. He wears a worn, oversized corduroy sports coat with leather elbow patches, a white shirt with a bow tie, ill-matching gray corduroy trousers, shiny at the seat and knees, and scuffed oxford shoes. Glasses perch on the end of his nose. Eyebrows, thinning hair, and a narrow mustache, all mostly gray. The crowning touch is his cane. They also have a walker for a more disabled appearance.

"Professor, I am your student. We on trip together." Randy laughs. "Next town, we buy books."

"Not going to Atlanta, then?"

She shrugs as if it doesn't matter, "We go back together. After you kill that man, we find place to live."

CHAPTER
TWENTY-SIX

THE OLD DODGE PICK-UP TRUCK TAKEN FROM THE SCRAP YARD DIED just as they reached Pittsburgh at dusk. After walking away from the heap, they cast about until finding an older model Mercury Zephyr in a parking garage. While the car itself was tucked far back and coated with dust, the attraction was its keys dangling from the ignition.

They could have gotten to Pittsburgh much earlier using the interstate through Ohio. Instead, they'd come by way of West Virginia, feeling safer on a less obvious route. An old pick-up truck seemed to fit better that way, although it was not a ride that seemed suitable for a professor and his graduate student.

A 1983 Zephyr seems a more appropriate ride, at least this one in near pristine condition. Scratch wonders if it's someone's pride and joy. More likely, it's owned by an elderly soul who doesn't get out anymore.

The car starts without hesitation. Dusty from sitting but well-maintained with a full tank of gas. In the glove box are the owner's manual, maps, insurance and registry documentation, a packet of Kleenex, a flare, and a Smith & Wesson revolver, the model 581, loaded. Besides the gun, there is a partial box of cartridges, another eight, with those in the revolver's cylinder, making fourteen .357 Magnum rounds.

Randy picks up a map and opens it wide, "How we go?"

Looking over her shoulder, Scratch says, "The fastest way is up the interstate to Erie, then northeast along Lake Erie to Buffalo."

"New York Thruway has toll booths," she says.

He nods, "Yeah, best to avoid them."

They stare at the map. Randy's finger traces an alternate route, "This way?"

"Longer, slower, but maybe safer." Scratch reads off some of the town names, "Kittanning, Brookville, scoot over to Dubois, then north, Ridgway, Bradford, Salamanca, Springville, Hamburg, Buffalo."

"Taafe brothers have house in Hamburg," comments Randy.

"Route 219," reads Scratch. "Okay, we'll go that way."

She smiles and pats his thigh, "They not expect us come back."

"We'll drive for an hour, get out of the area, then find supper and a place to bed down." He's glad she's with him and thinks it is selfish of him not to drop her off not to get her out of this mess, but still, he's thankful she's here. What she's feeling, he's not sure.

A set of cabins along the hillside make up the motel northeast of Kittanning. They arrive after dark, having stopped for supper at a roadside diner after crossing the Allegheny River. The sleepy clerk, too young to be anything but a relative of the owner, pays little heed to them, more intent on the movie playing on his TV.

The cabin is clean and functional, with minimal amenities, but it's enough. Somehow, it feels safe. Scratch can feel the tensions of these days easing from him. For Randy, it seems to be the same.

Soon, they are in bed, sleeping.

Sometime in the early morning, Scratch stirs. Finds Randy curled up against him, mouth agape, sound asleep. He finds his way to the bathroom in the half-light of pre-dawn.

When he returns to bed, she mutters, "Sunny?"

He kisses her forehead, "Sleep."

They rouse some hours later, the morning seeming preternaturally quiet. Drawing back the curtain slightly, Scratch sees new fallen snow. A couple of cabins over, a fellow is loading his car, then calls out to his wife and kids in their cabin to hurry along. All seems normal out there. The wife and two youngsters emerge, the kids asking about breakfast.

Randy comes to stand next to Scratch, a hand on his back. She leans her head against his shoulder. He puts an arm around her waist. "We need go?" she says.

Reluctantly, Scratch nods, not really wanting to end this respite. "Yeah, we go."

They stop late morning in Ridgway, a small town tucked between high hills along the Clarion River. A late breakfast or early lunch at Ling Ling's, a Chinese restaurant on Main Street, off Route 219. The staff seem attentive, maybe given the rarity of a new Chinese face in town. The food is decent, better than Scratch expected.

As camouflage, Scratch, and Randy discuss a pair of history books they'd brought to the table, one titled *Death and Rebirth of the Seneca* and a new book, *Iroquois Diplomacy on the Early American Frontier*. To Scratch, the topics seemed obscure enough to lend verisimilitude to their personas. As it turns out, they'll be driving through the Seneca reservation in New York State later today.

Still, he's a bit bothered by how much the waitress is staring at Randy. The sooner they leave, the better.

Then the waitress asks Randy something in Chinese. They chat. Scratch catches a few words, a reference to Carnegie Mellon, a university in Pittsburgh, and to Jamestown, Lake Chautauqua, the Chautauqua Institute, and the University of Buffalo, so he knows Randy is giving the woman the cover story they worked up. It all has to do with their supposed research on the Seneca and the talks he is to give at a conference.

The woman and Randy are laughing together. Randy is protesting something the woman asked. If Scratch were to guess, it would be whether they have a personal as well as professional relationship.

Something more is said in exchange, then another question to Randy. The answer refers to a Chinese university. Scratch isn't certain he's caught the name, but maybe Xiamen University since that's what he and Randy agreed on for her Chinese schooling. Then, the proprietor calls the woman away, much to Scratch's relief.

All this time, Scratch has been smiling, eating, nodding, trying to appear relaxed. Randy turns back to him and smiles, "Is okay."

After they depart, with waves to the waitress, Randy confides, "One mistake."

"Oh?"

"Chautauqua Institute not open in winter."

"Damn, I should have known that."

"No problem. I say special meeting."

Scratch nods, "A good rehearsal if we get asked again."

"I am, what word? Glib."

"Glib?" Scratch chuckles at the word and repeats, "Glib." He's not sure why this seems so funny.

They pass through Hamburg almost three hours later, turning off US 219 to enter the neighboring town of Orchard Park.

Stopping at a gas station, Scratch goes in to ask a few questions while Randy re-fuels the car. Coming back out, he tells her, "Yes, there's an internet café. It's somewhere along the town center, the guy couldn't say exactly. Says his son uses it."

They cruise the town's Buffalo Street until spotting the place in a nondescript shopping plaza. It's tucked to the far side, probably the cheapest rent in the row of six stores.

Randy goes in by herself. Scratch waits in the car, nervous again, ready to leave quickly if an alarm is raised over the Chinese girl.

Within twenty minutes, she's back out. She gets into the car and hands him a slip of paper with an address and a crude sketch of a map. "That his house. Not under his name. Company owns."

"On South Abbott. We practically were on top of it when we crossed Abbott on 219."

"Is so."

Scratch sighs, will Donovan be there? Or at the bar, Healey's? Or somewhere else? Please, lord, let him not be in Racine already. "If the Camry's still sitting in the alley, then we could retrieve the rifle."

"Go back to your neighborhood?" Apprehension in Randy's voice.

"After dark. It's not like anyone would expect us back there. We drive in check if the car's there and hasn't been towed. If the car can start, maybe we split up. You go find us a place to stay tonight. There are several motels along Southwestern not far from Abbott. Stadium View, Red Carpet Inn, others."

"We no split. We together."

Scratch can see she's adamant. He smiles, takes her hand, raises it, and kisses her knuckles, "Okay, we're together."

They eat supper at an Irish pub, Blackthorn's, in south Buffalo, maybe a mile or so from the First Ward neighborhood. The food is adequate, though clearly not to Randy's taste. They are mostly silent as they eat until Randy says, "When we make love, no protection."

Scratch looks up from his shepherd's pie, "Yes. No condoms."

"Worry you?"

"No, should it?"

"What if we make a baby?"

Scratch doesn't think they'll survive long enough for a baby. Still, the question surprises him. Would he want a child with Randy at his age? Then there is Helena and the girls; what of them? Yet, Scratch can't deny the idea of it a baby. Yes, he might like that. He says, "If we could raise the kid."

Dark falls early enough so they don't need to linger over supper.

The Camry sits just as Scratch had left it. Popping the trunk, he pulls out the Finnish rifle, wrapped in its blanket. In the car itself, he finds the last magazine for the machine pistol, fifty rounds. He's feeling lethal again. The Taurus at his ankle, the Smith & Wesson from the Mercury for Randy, the Belgian machine pistol, and the sniper rifle for himself. He closes up the Camry and gets back in the Merc with Randy, "Let's head for Hamburg."

"You want check Healey's bar first?"

Scratch shakes his head no, "South Abbott Road." He's operating on instinct, he knows, but it feels right.

Within the hour, they stop just past where the 219 overpass crosses South Abbott Road. They've driven past the Taafe house. From Abbott, they could only see one light on in an upstairs window. Unless the Taafes have one of those timers to fool burglars, someone is home.

"I'll go in from the back, across the field," says Scratch. "You stay with the car."

"Better if we pull car off the road. We go to house together."

Scratch gestures at the high embankments on either side of the road that can be seen in the headlights, "Nothing nearby. I'll back up under an overpass."

"Look for farm path, must take tractor into fields."

"If so, it'll be a long walk."

"Better if two of us go. I watch your back."

Scratch would argue but he sees the stubborn set of Randy's lips. "Okay," he says and pulls onto the road, looking for a break in the embankments. Less than a quarter mile further on, they find a field road and pull onto it, up over a culvert, up the wide gouge in the embankment, and then stop. Nothing is said as they check their weapons. Then, pulling open their car doors, they start their trek across the open fields toward the 219 highway, wind blowing in their faces and the night's cold settling on them. They descend to Abbott Road to walk under the 219 overpasses, then up the wooded embankment again, and across another field before coming up behind the targeted house.

The house has an addition in the back, almost the same size as the original place. Several windows are lit on the rear side. The flickering lights of a television against drawn curtains in what's probably a den. The kitchen windows shine with light, with no curtains to impede the view.

Scratch stretches out on a slight rise, Randy beside him. He uses the rifle's scope to bring a closer sighting, traversing the garage, back yard, and house. The yard is fenced, and there's a large kennel. A dog is roaming the yard, no, two dogs. He whispers to Randy, "I don't see security cameras. He's got Rottweilers in the yard."

There is movement in the kitchen, and Scratch swings the scope back, just catching a brief glimpse of Gemma Taafe. He stays on the kitchen windows, hoping for more.

A shift of the wind, not realized at first, but it sets the Rottweilers to barking. Randy says, "They smell our scent."

The back door light goes on, and then Gemma is there, barefoot and in a long T-shirt, not much else. She yells at the dogs. With the cold, she pulls back inside quickly; the light snaps off.

"Maybe only the girl is home," says Randy.

"Let's get closer and see if we can stir up the dogs again."

Swiftly, they cross to the next series of swales in the field, then ease up onto the rise toward the house. They are maybe twenty yards out from the fence line. One of the Rottweilers is up on his hind legs, forepaws braced on the fence, sniffing the air. Then he barks again, powerfully.

The second dog, a bit smaller, likely a bitch, comes to his side and adds her voice.

"Not bad dogs," says Randy. "Just protective."

Scratch stands for a moment, long enough for the dogs to see him, then he drops down. The dogs go wild with excitement.

He slides the bolt cartridge in place and sights on the back door.

The light goes on, and a head peers out cautiously, Donovan Taafe. Scratch fires.

The door slams open as Donovan's body jerks back and collapses against it.

"Let's go," says Scratch to Randy, sliding down into the damp swale, then up and running across the field, Randy at his heels.

CHAPTER
TWENTY-SEVEN

Out of breath by the time they reach the car but with adrenaline-fueled energy to haul open doors, Scratch places the rifle on the back seat while Randy gets behind the wheel. She pulls out slowly to avoid spinning wheels in the slush. They bump down through the embankment and over the culvert onto the road.

She heads south on Abbott, remembering the route from the map; they need to do a dogleg at Meadow Drive to cross to the Hamburg-Springville Road, then briefly north to hit the US 219 interchange. Then, they can leave the area, go down into New York's southern tier, or go into Pennsylvania.

Scratch says, "Let's try to get down to that town, Ridgway before we stop for the night."

Just as they turn onto Meadow Drive, a huge black Sierra Denali pickup roars by, going down Abbott. Glancing over his shoulder, Scratch spots Gemma in the crew cabin with others.

CHAPTER TWENTY-SEVEN

"Better punch it, Randy," he says. "We need to get to 219."

Randy puts the pedal down, and the old Merc surges forward, whizzing past the houses on Meadow Drive. She passes a Chevy doddering along at 35, the Merc doing over 30 mph faster. Coming toward the end of the street, she slows for the stop sign. "We sedate now, like normal folks," she says as they turn onto the Hamburg-Springville Road, the 219 interchanges in sight.

The Sierra Denali rockets up behind them, high on its lifted springs. It goes by them in a tear, then slowing at the interchange, perhaps indecision in the crew cab.

Randy has the presence of mind to put on her turn signal, entering the parking lot of a Tim Horton donut shop. Beside her, Scratch racks the machine pistol as he watches the big pickup down the road. She pulls up in front of the shop and parks.

"I get us donuts and tea for the road," announces Randy. "Act natural. You like glazed?" She slides out from behind the wheel and goes on into the shop.

Near the interchange, the Denali has pulled to the side of the road. A man steps out, then a second, a third, and then Gemma. They may be arguing. One of them is on a cell phone. *Calling the police?* Scratch wonders.

Gemma is looking around. She says something to the others, pointing toward the Tim Horton's, or is she pointing at the Mercury Zephyr?

Lousy timing, Randy comes out of the shop with a bag of donuts and two teas in a cardboard carrier. Even from the distance and the night, with Randy lit by the shop's lighting, Gemma must see she is Asian.

Without hesitating, Gemma runs toward them, two of the men with her, guns in hand, while the third hops back in the truck to pull it after them.

Calmly, Randy opens the car door and sets the bag and carrier on her car seat. "My pistol, please."

Scratch opens the glove box and hands her the Smith & Wesson. Then he's out of the car, too, running at an angle to the advancing foe, machine pistol up. One of the oncoming men fires at Scratch, but his handgun is no match for the FN-P90, as Scratch fires a burst in his direction. The fellow stumbles and goes down.

Gemma and the other one throw themselves to the ground, both firing at Scratch.

Using the roof of Merc to steady her arm, Randy squeezes off two shots at the prone man near Gemma. The fellow convulses as the bullets strike him.

The Sierra Denali has turned into the lot, barreling down on Scratch. Scratch fires bursts at the truck's cab, shattering glass and killing the driver, but the truck doesn't stop and clips Scratch hard as he tries to dive aside. The impact tosses Scratch into a sprawled heap while the pickup slams into a parked Nissan coupe, crumpling the little car like tinfoil before grinding to a halt.

Scratch is unmoving; blood smeared — more blood puddling.

Gemma stands and walks toward him, ignoring Randy and her gun. She kneels by the body and touches him. Then she stands, looks toward Randy, shakes her head, and shrugs.

Randy tries to pretend her eyes aren't wet. She watches as Gemma Taafe walks onto the road without looking back. There seems to be no point in shooting the woman.

The staff and patrons of the donut shop have spilled out. Someone is cursing about his destroyed car. They give Randy and her gun a wide berth.

Opening the car door, Randy shifts the donut bag and teas to the passenger seat. She climbs in and sets the pistol by the donut bag. She starts the ignition, backs away, turns the car, drives past

Scratch's body without a glance, and goes left onto the road. Southbound 219 is just ahead.

For just a moment, Randy wonders if Gemma Taafe will take Fionnuala MacGavan's place in the First Ward.

EPILOGUE

Helena and the girls are crossing Goold Street from the Zoological Gardens to Lake View Park, intending to walk on down to North Beach and maybe find lunch near the Marina. Chloe takes her arm. At 17, Chloe is taller than her mother. Penny is already across the street. At 15, she always seems to be in a hurry, and her exuberance propels her in everything she does.

"Dad would have liked this day," says Chloe.

It is a beautiful day, thinks Helena. Like Chloe, she never thinks of her husband as the man who died in Hamburg, New York. That terrible time, all those killings. No, her husband, Travis, was not that man Scratch. "Yes, a day for sailing on the lake."

"We see six schools on the coming trip and another five colleges in July, right?"

"Yes, that's the plan. Why are you thinking of more college possibilities?" Helena chuckles, thinking eleven schools already seems like too many.

"No, not really. Should I cut down the number we visit?"

"Talk it over with your sister. This is a preview for her, too."

"Do you think Gustavus Adolphus is too religious? We already see Carleton, St. Olaf, and Macalester in Minnesota."

Helena would prefer to leave off Grinnell in Iowa for the June trip, as it adds a lot of miles on the road. She says, "We included Beloit on the way to Grinnell but we could see Beloit any weekend. Are you sure you want to include Grinnell?"

"Penny does."

"Then it could wait until she's a Junior."

Penelope overhears that comment as Helena and Chloe catch up with her. "Are you changing our plans?"

They continue to discuss the hot topic of college visits as they stroll through Lake View Park.

Watching them, where she's walking with her son, the boy at just over two and a half, pushing the stroller himself, the woman, now called Cassie, admires how beautiful the daughters of Scratch are. During the first seven months, she lived in Racine; she worked at the InSinkErator factory on 21st St. until she was too pregnant to stay on her feet for eight hours.

Still, she saved enough to pay part of the hospital bill, and for her tiny apartment over the garage on Olive St. She did not go back to InSinkErator after the boy was born, even though it took another year to complete paying the hospital and doctor bills. She worked part-time for a while at Asiana Korean and at the chocolate shop. During that time, she began attending the Unitarian Church, just around the corner from Asiana.

She barely eked out a living, even with the two jobs. But it was at the church that she met her boss, Frances. Maybe it was pity for her, Frances taking her on at the toy design studio. No, think of it as compassion. That is who Frances is: a compassionate person. And Frances knew Scratch, employed and worked with him for many years. Not as Scratch, of course, but as Travis. Not that Frances knows that Cassie is the infamous Randy, who ran with Scratch for those few days over three years ago.

She leans down to her son, "Tommy, we go to Kids Cove Playground. If you get tired, you ride, and I push."

ABOUT THE AUTHOR

Thomas Sundell is the author of A Viennese Waltz and A Bloodline of Kings (published by Crow Woods Publishing and, in Greek, as Philip of Macedon by Minoas SA), along with twenty-six other novels and novellas, including Massachusetts in Rebellion and Casework. He has also published two anthologies of short stories and flash fiction, titled Views of Imagined Lives. You can explore more of his work at sundellwritings.wordpress.com.